The Evil Angel

B.D. Weddell

This is for Braeden,
Who always had a rebellious streak of his own,
But always looked to the future,
Love you, bro.

Table of Contents

Zachariah

In the tank, he slept. As he slept, he dreamed. He was hardly awake, but when he was, it was always as if he were in a nightmare he could never truly wake up from.

He had always had nightmares. He never had what would be considered a 'good' dream. However, the nightmares were not like many, fragments of memory or fears combined and twisted in a halo of images and a sense of terror which just shakes you awake the moment you see it. No, his nightmares consist of recollections twisted in a false reality that he would make up to try to numb the pain. What he actually *remembers* is vague. All is only pain. And since he never truly wakes up from such nightmares, he is now stuck *in* the land of nightmares, haunted by both fantasy and reality, and the cruelty of The Queen.

But still, pieces come together eventually. At some point in time the answers become clear, and everything can be pieced together like a puzzle. If you were to ask him long ago where he had come from, his only answer would be, 'The void.'

Today, he could tell you with just a little bit of clarity.

He was seven when it had happened. It was a typical day in the village. What was it called though? That he could not remember. But he knew it was on the outskirts of the Wasteland north of the Dark Forest. They were loggers and traders, not huntsmen nor warriors. They could have been attacked by raiders or pirates at any time, but instead people from all over came to trade, even those less desirable.

Was there ever a name? He often wondered this during the most miserable of sessions.

His earliest memory as a small child was looking up at the sky and watching hovercraft pass by. Sometimes they were merchant ships, sometimes they were something else. He couldn't tell how they were different, but every single time, it would frighten him to see it. To him, they always felt like a bad omen, a danger on the horizon just as a rabbit would feel upon seeing the shadow of a bird blocking out the sun. But as a child he could not grasp the concept of how or why.

He remembered one day seeing trained soldiers wielding guns for the first time. Men in black armor wielding guns with blades along the barrel and coming in to shatter the illusion of what he thought was the real world, and converted it into the horror of what reality really was. As a child, such innocence can be easily shattered because the world was full of evil people with evil intentions. They came to pillage, rape, an destroy.

But how it all fell apart he could not tell. They were gathering, yes, but pieces were still pieces. Like pictures, fragments of a memory long torn away and yet waiting to be put back together. Because there are other parts too, other dreams, other memories. But what was real, and what was in the never-ending cycle of his current life? After all, he was never truly *awake*.

What made it worse was little by little, piece by piece, more would dissipate into nothingness into The Void. He never knew if he actually welcomed the forgetting of such fragments of memory, or if he hated it. Because in the end, does one truly belong in a cycle of unknown pain without reason? To live without truly living?

Because what truly happened the day of the descending of ships? The chirps of photon lasers blasting, burning shrapnel blasting everywhere, some fragments landing in the dry, sandy ground, or worse into the flesh of a nearby villager. The men in black, wielding those terrible rifles, which tore through… shadows? People?

Someone else is there, their face crystal clear. Older, wiser, taking him by the hand and telling him and someone else taking him to what he could only imagine was a home. He felt heartache whenever he remembered this place, this shack of wood and sheet metal held together by mud and clay. Who was the little girl running alongside him? Just another fragment of his memory, or another lie? A fragmentation that could be his very brain deceiving him with the nightmares. He only knew that he trusted the woman leading them to the house. The way she looked at him, a look of desperation and sadness and terror. Such a look was rare among commoners and strangers. But what did she look like? What was her hair color? How was her cheek structure?

Who was she?

He remembers the trapdoor in the wooden floor where the storage room sat beneath the planks of wood. He remembered being inside, and above their heads the two heard more gunfire-

(but was it gunfire?)

-and the clashing of metal. He heard the screams of men and women outside the house, amidst the fighting outside. The screams always joined him in his sleep. The souls of the damned and forgotten, crying out to him it seemed. And with such screams, he saw shadows between the planks of wood above him.

Worse, he remembered feeling as if rain was pouring on him. Coming through the floorboards among the shadows above, droplets of crimson rained down on him. Splashing across his hands, arms and head, was blood like a pagan baptism. The horror at the blood on his hands, the feeling of absolute dread, made him scream in reality-

(but what is *reality?)*

-and he would scream in the real world within the murky waters of the tank.

He would sometimes be kicking, biting and clawing in his dreams. The ghosts of special forces in white Tech-Armor reacting as if they were in the tank with him. But then they would fall upon him, and everything would fade to black.

The dreams would always come back, sometimes with another piece added, sometimes another missing. Whenever he would be awake (if he was actually awake at all), he would be somewhere distant as he felt stuff dig inside of him. While unconscious, he would feel something sharp sliding into his chest, moving around his organs and more sharp pricks on different areas of his body. But the dream would continue as he felt himself being mutilated by shadows standing above him with a blinding light behind their heads. What was happening? What were they doing?

But then he would find himself back inside the tank. He felt the water-

(was it water?)

-pour around him, rising up past his chest and eventually submerging his head. He felt his hair wave around inside the water like kelp, and he'd occasionally feel the bubbles passing through his oxygen mask they would plug over his mouth and nose. Another sharp prick in the small of his back, and slowly, little by little, piece by piece, his vision would fade in and out and the dream was fading completely.

He wasn't asleep anymore.

He was waking up.

His vision was cloudy, both from years of sleep, and the fact that he was in murky water. He was naked with only the oxygen mask on his face. His head foggy, he felt somewhat exposed as he began to recognize voices and see shadows of the many people standing outside his tank. He felt the rush of warm water and the recognition that he had relieved himself washed over him, only to feel the pressure change as the water was filtered and became clear. His vision became more clear with the water, and he looked down at his hands, which were scarred and muscular, as were his forearms which were covered in more scars. He checked his palms, expecting the lines in them to be filled with blood, but they were clear. No blood. He wasn't being baptized again.

On his right bicep was the serial number they gave him when they first brought him to the facility. The tattoo had never faded.

464. His new name. His new identity.

He peered through the thick glass, trying to see the figures outside the tank. The only one he was able to clearly see, was a man. His face was covered by a shield-mask of black, little digits and coordinate sensors flashing within. He was checking 464's vitals, probably. As he did so, 464 looked him up and down, observing the black Power-Armor he wore, which was lean and slick as a carapace. He noticed two machine-pistols at his hips, the holsters in a utility belt around his waist. Across his back were two swords, their scabbards angled so they looked like two featherless wings had jutted out of his shoulders. He held up a hand to the glass, as if the one within the tank was an ape who would respond to his gesture with a hint of kindness, innocence.

But 464 felt no kindness of any sort to the man. Only hatred. Unsure and unreasoned hatred for he did not know this man, but still he screamed into his oxygen mask at the man, a cloud of bubbles erupting in front of him. He punched at the glass, feeling some small cracks beneath his knuckles, the crystal in his chest right where his heart would be glowing brightly as if reacting to his anger. The purple glow illuminated the tank like a lava lamp, the angry boy within like a vengeful genie wishing to escape and wreak havoc on those who deserved divine punishment.

"You will do," he heard the man say outside the tank. His voice was disoriented, robotic through the Power-Helmet on his head. But the trace of content was there, almost mockingly. "This one will do. I want him fully-functional within a week."

Another voice, this one belonging to Dr. Gray. Dr. Gray... whom he also knew. At the sound of him 464 growled into his mask, a reaction, really. "He has responded well to the procedure. Better than the others I might add. Will he be going with you to Nineveh?"

"No. There is no need. He will be useful for our next mission. Until then, I want him wiped clean, and hard-lined for battle. Then we will see if Project Eleven will be a success."

"I imagine so. Look, it is responding to him, giving him strength."

"And knowledge I sense..." the man in the armor sounded anxious as he trailed a finger across the cracked glass 464 had created on the tank. He was hiding it from the doctor, but 464 knew he was anxious. He couldn't hide it from him. "Prepare him for the Virtual Room. I will be letting The Queen know, and then I will be off to claim Nineveh for the mines."

"And then, sir?"

"Wait for my call, and *my* call only, Doctor."

A surge of energy in the water, and 464 felt something *slam* onto his head, a helmet of some sort by the way it felt snug. What made him panic were the many pricks he felt in his head, drilling into his brain. He screamed out as the pain in his head intensified and his vison went red. He thrashed for a moment, and then became docile, limp in the water.

"He will be ready," Dr. Gray said greedily but 464 no longer cared. He was no longer scared of the dreams. He was nothing more than a shell of a man; a machine awakening. "It will finally work..."

"Oh, it will doctor," the man in black said with a chuckle and then added, "For your sake."

"R-right," Gray said, the fear in his voice obvious even to one who was not psychic.

"Soon the Lower Division will be ours, as well as the entire North. And then from there, my friend, the rest of the country. Let us see if that witch's black magic will save her now."

"Think she will be more responsive this time?" Gray asked, the voices now fading away as they departed from 464 in his tank.

"Oh, she will," the man in black said. "No one can withstand the power within The Dreaming, not even those strong in magic. Soon, everyone will realize that."

464, who was fading away, couldn't agree more.

Zachariah... My name... is...

He was gone.

<u>Markus</u>

Markus sat in the center of the courtyard within the castle of Levitika, a staff of wood and metal endings in his left hand, for his right was still in a sling. He had been practicing with his left hand when it came to combat, so ideally by the time his right arm completely healed, he would be talented with both hands rather than one. This had proved to be difficult at first, but as time went on, it became as natural as breathing.

His hair was blowing in the light breeze of the early morning, and the sun was shining bright above the partly-clouded skies. The snow that had covered the city was beginning to melt, and water spilled from the rooftops only to flow down the many cisterns and then through the massive walls like great ravines and rolling waterfalls. Miles beneath the floating city, the Wastelands were thawing as well. Rivers began to flow again, and here and there patches of dirt and grass were breaking through as well as the dormant animals beneath. Snow still covered the land, but it became thick and moist. It had been a long, cold winter, and now finally, spring was beginning to thaw the planet out of its cold slumber.

Earlier that morning Markus had taken his Eagles Wings for a flight around the city. He had joined those who were on patrol who had all been impressed with his flying, although they wouldn't shut up about the role he had played during the battle against the Ninevite Fleet. As a result he had wandered further than the patrol usually went so he could fly in some relative peace. He had noticed that the Dark Forest was miles behind them, and still miles ahead of them appearing as a splotch in the distance, was the city of Nineveh. Only six weeks ago, he had escaped that horrible place with his sister, Ruth, and his new friend, Ashlyn. They had made it to the city in search of refuge and ended up in a colossal aerial battle, immediately after the devastating loss of Ruth who had died on their way to find the ancient floating city of Levitika. Her sickness had finally caught up to her, and took her away just before The Levitikans brought them to the city. A devastating blow indeed, for still so-young Markus.

There were still many casualties during the battle with Baron Ovid, including Damion Black, the Hunter who had saved them from the monstrous bounty hunters that the Baron of Nineveh sent after them during their escape. During these past few weeks, there had been plenty of mourning in the lost City of Angels. Markus, who was still dealing with the reality that his sister was gone, kept himself busy with practice and meditation. It was the only thing to do that actually worked, since reading in the Grand Library only depressed him now it seemed. His broken arm hadn't helped either in that regard, as his training was heavily restricted. Thankfully Shadow was as decent a teacher as one could be in terms of combat.

During this time as well, Markus had learned so much more about the city, as well as the whole region's history. How there was another realm among their world known as The Dreaming, which influences not only dreams, but the real world as well. There was still so much more from him to learn, and after this mission concerning

Nineveh, he would go to The Kaiknen Isles, and find the man known as Abram, Damion Black's own mentor.

Damion…

He had not told Ashlyn or the queen of Levitika's daughter, Princess Esmerelda, another friend he and Ashlyn had made when they arrived in the city. He did not know what to say to them. How could he explain it to them? Whenever the thought crossed his mind the two Dream Crystals containing the souls of ancient spirits would glow as if the trapped Abner and Fethawit within were trying to communicate to him. But he had heard nothing from them since they had visited after the battle with Baron Ovid. It was like they had decided to go to sleep, and just simply hadn't woken up yet. They were there though, they were conscious enough to have a reaction to his thoughts and his feelings, but other than that, nothing.

For now, the only thing clear was Levitika's current destination; the floating island was heading for Nineveh. They were going back home, where they would take the city, and prepare to go to war with the other districts in the country. With the Baron being dead, only General Veegar was in charge the city and the Ninevite Guard. The spirits willing, Nineveh would fall and will be under the rule of a new leadership with the aid of Levitika. It made Markus sick to his stomach at the thought of going back to that horrible place. But maybe after the mission was complete, it would become better under the rule of someone else under Queen Elizabetha. She was a good leader, with strong supporters besides the Elders, who appeared more interested in their political agendas rather than the conquering of the Dark Empire and bringing prosperity to the Northern Wastelands.

As someone who has a bond with the Dreaming Crystals including The Eldest in some way shape or form, Markus was a powerful piece in this game of chess being played out.

But such thoughts were far from the boy who was quickly becoming something more. Now in the courtyard as he meditated among the many barrels and props, such as scarecrows and boxes stacked into crude barriers for target practice. When he wasn't meditating, he was being trained by General Grim, Black's replacement when it came to swordplay. His methods of teaching were very different than Black's, for Grim was a native from The Wastelands, where swords and axes and other makeshift weapons were used rather than Laser-Rifles or Photon-Cannons. Black's methods were more graceful, more controlled, and the fact that he too was a Carrier of the Dream Crystals made him stronger, faster, a true mentor to train Markus, who easily overpowered Grim but still managed to learn finesse and techniques necessary to turn the tide in any battle.

During his time of meditation, Markus was to empty his brain into a sort of jar, a way to unleash negative feelings and thoughts so that his mind could be clear, for a clear mind as necessary to perform the magical miracles the Dream Crystals offered to those who shared a bond with them. Black emphasized this before his untimely death at the hand of the witch bounty hunter, and considered it the most important lesson in magic and in life. For the most part, this was easy, but other times there were painful memories that Markus simply had to let hurt in order to move forward with a mind as clear as glass.

He had found, however, another method that made the pain a little easier to bear and actually downright ignore. Sometimes during meditation, he would imagine a more peaceful world in a more peaceful time. In his mind, he would picture his fantasy into reality, and the illusion that he was home, in his old shack in a Nineveh that was far away. The home would sit in a sea of grass and wildflowers, and a looming birch tree would stand beside the shack. He would be there, working on some contraption, with his sister, alive and living with him free from any ailments. Whenever he entered this sort of world, something else would be added to it, creating the perfect fantasy that Markus sometimes wished was real. He would see his father there, working on a project with him with tools and parts scattered across the grass, the robot or vehicle they were working on between them as they were covered in grease and oil. Sometimes Ashlyn was there, and she would often come by and offer the two food or drink that she and Ruth would make, or even be talking to them about something as they worked. They were all clean, healthy, and had no trouble at all in a world that actually didn't exist.

Sometimes, occasionally, Damion Black was there. But he was never conjured up by Markus' conscious or subconscious mind. He was never thought about in a clean, bright light, only a necessity of life that was somehow far away in this world. But sometimes he came, and he always appeared disappointed, as if Markus was doing something wrong. Try as he might, Markus could never seem to alter this personification, and had even once tried to blot this memory of Black out of this world, but the Hunter even dead seemed to haunt him, making him feel almost... almost...

Guilty?

Yes, perhaps that was it. Because the Hunter would never say anything, but hang back like a shadow, appearing as a constant reminder that this world wasn't real no matter how bad Markus wished it could be. It was something that Markus simply conjured up for some temporary comfort, to escape the reality that his life had changed, his family was gone, and he and Ashlyn were really at war rather than at peace. Deep in his heart, Markus knew that he was wrong, why else would his conjuration of Black cause him such distress whenever he felt himself growing lost in this false reality?

Still, he welcomed that distraction, because sometimes he would find himself in that world for hours and wake up hungry or cold with Ashlyn and Esmerelda wondering where he had been all day. He'd come back to reality, which could never be escaped for better or for worse. And he did so right now willingly, without the need for Black's constant gaze like an angel watching over him. He bade his world farewell, and returned as easily as a bee would return to the hive with their payload of sweet nectar. He was still cross-legged on the grassy ground when he finally awoke from his meditative state, and Markus began to stretch. His body felt stiff from however long he had been sitting there. His mind was wide awake though, alert, and present.

Subconsciously, as this was becoming a more natural thing for him to do, Markus' mind stretched out as his body did, reaching out enough to detect the life essence of all nearby. The plants, the bugs that had lied dormant among the roots, the few human and mutant beings that wandered the borders of the courtyard, all like flickering flames of a candle, beckoning for attention. Likewise, he could detect a form of life moving towards him like a predator stalking their prey. For his sense of awareness alerted him to unseen movement to his left. His eyes were closed still as he stretched, but he knew he was being watched, and approached.

And with that, Markus stood up fast, spinning and deflected the incoming blow with his walking stick, catching the staff of Grim the Reaver, who grimaced as the boy caught his attack. He smiled at the old man as he had the many times the soldier tried to sneak up on him.

"You saw me," the mutant said, his gray face stern and a little disappointed that he didn't catch Markus while he was awakening.

"Nope," Markus said still grinning. "Morning, old man."

Grim grinned as well, pleased still that Markus was weary enough to stay alert at all times like a true soldier. Over the course of his taking over Markus' training, the two had gotten to know each other well enough so that the whole 'old man' thing didn't bother the mutant as it would if any of his subordinates dared to say the same.

As a Wastelander, the nuclear storms that plagued the lands left a powerful but thankfully undeadly impact on the man's body and mental capacity. The Great War thousands of years ago caused many birth defects due to radiation poisoning over the millennia, but little by little the effects slowly drifted away as the world purged itself like a human body cleansing itself of a virus. The result of today's radiation defects were still very clear on Grim like many from the Wastelands, with his leathery skin that appeared to be always burnt or dry. He also had a third nostril in the middle of his large nose which was broken multiple times in fights. He also had six fingers on each hand, as well as six toes on each foot (or so the stories go by the soldiers of Levitika). He was a short man, only five foot, but was as wide as an ox. Muscle, strong and thick were webbed beneath his leathery skin, making him the strongest man in Levitika today (or so the soldiers say once again). His black eyes peered at Markus, who held his ground as if he too were as strong as Grim himself.

"Nice catch," Grim admitted with a thick and, well, grim accent. "But you forgot something." He said this confidently, and releasing one hand and reaching for his belt, Grim pulled his knife and sliced at Markus- who in turn spun his staff and caught the blade in the wood, knocking Grim's own aside which laid as if forgotten in the grass between them.

Markus smiled. "Not yet," and using the energy coursing from the crystals resting in his pockets to his body, Markus spun his staff, and at the same time somersaulted to the side, the swift speed alone knocking Grim back as if he was a speck of dust being blasted away by a harsh wind. Grim skidded back as he caught his balance, and then squared up again, his knife at his side.

"Impressive. You have gotten cocky however."

"Have I?" Markus said with a small smile as he retrieved Grim's staff and tossed it to the mutant who caught it effortlessly. It was always fun to have someone willing to keep going despite being outmatched whether Markus liked it or not.

"Yes," Grim said and then he charged at Markus. "Keep it up."

He swung to the side, but Markus caught the attack with the staff, and angling it, he deflected it away before smacking Grim in the side. Grim however, was by no means done, and spinning around, swung his own staff back around towards Markus' chest, and got him right in the arm. The wood did not cut his skin, however a sharp pain shot up Markus' arm, only to be distinguished as both crystals surged energy into his arm, not only numbing the pain, but also healing the broken vessels beneath the flesh to avoid bruising. Markus swung upwards, but Grim caught the attack, only to strike again. The two sparred again and again, catching each other's attacks only to be lucky every once in a while and score a hit on one another. They sparred until sweat dripped from their brows and their arms grew heavy from use. Markus felt no fatigue however despite the strain on his body. He felt like he could go for a four-mile run after this, that he could fight another Grim. That was how good he felt. However, he had to restrain himself as if he were a normal human being, and it soon came time to end the lesson.

It was a strange concept still, being one blessed with the power of some magical stones and having to remind oneself that they are still human. But Markus, who was humble in knowing about his own limitations, accepted such facts and allowed himself to still remain the student and *never* the teacher.

"Enough," Grim finally gasped while sticking his staff into the ground and rubbing his palms as if they were irritated. "You did good today, Markus."

"Thank you, Grim," Markus said now sitting on his heels. "Whatever I hadn't learned yet I've learned from you."

"Ain't never gonna find someone better than a Wastelander to teach you," Grim said with a touch of pride in his strained voice. "I mean, look at Black. Damn fine swordsman."

"Right," Markus said, sad at the memory but reluctant to let it show.

Black was in his mind in the past, a monster who killed his father. Even if in the end, he did save Markus and Ashlyn, there was still a little weight of hatred still in the young man's heart. According to Queen Elizabetha, all the evil that Black did was a necessary evil, but in the end, Markus was still out a father and also a sister. Despite all Black had showed him since their arrival to Levitika, that grudge was still there. Not that he would ever tell Ashlyn or anyone else. That grudge was against a dead man, and Markus had to accept what had happened, happened, and Black had tried to redeem himself for it, even if it meant his own life. How could Markus hold something against someone who tried so hard to the bitter end?

Such questions were not to be on the mind right now. "So, what now?" Markus asked dismissing any trace of such thoughts.

"Well *I* need to rest," Grim said. "Ain't easy admitting you have spunk, y'know. Even if it's with that magic stuff. You held your own, not a lot can. Those crystals are definitely helpful."

"Aren't they though?" Markus said uneasy. They *were* helpful, but at the same time dangerous. They made him feel, unlike himself. As if he was just one of many pilots in a massive vessel, but not at the wheel at times. He had thoughts unlike his own, old, ancient, and sometimes sinister. He had been able to suppress them after that fateful night, when he last saw the spirits. But every now and again, both when he was most stressed or angry, and even when he was asleep, swimming in the land of dreams and nightmares.

"Well, I guess I'll go to the library then."

"Are you ready for the meeting tonight?" Grim asked.

"Yeah, I'm gonna get this arm out of the sling before then." Markus assured his teacher. Provided it all works out, he reminded himself. It would be nice to actually scratch the itch under his cast again. "Thanks again, Grim."

"Anytime." With that he turned and left.

Markus stayed behind to enjoy the sun that for once in a long, *long* time, warmed up the entire planet. Winter was departing, and spring was turning her beautiful face towards the world. A time for a new beginning, and new life. But all things must one day die.

<u>Ashlyn</u>

Ashlyn was in the castle's Grand Library reading an old scroll on the history of criminology. The ladder she used to get it off the three-hundredth-or-so shelf still stood where she left it, a couple of tables away from her. Her auburn hair was in a braid thanks to Esmerelda, and her fresh tunic glowed bright white beneath the chandeliers of gold. Her old clothes were in the wash, and more of her new clothes which she had purchased with the princess back in the city were still in her room.

But this afternoon she wanted to be comfortable, take her time to read, a trait she had learned over the last few weeks with her friend. The princess was a wonderful teacher, and Ashlyn was ecstatic with how many great stories were here. And when she stumbled upon the old scrolls of ancient stories and nonfiction, it made her as giddy as a child with a toy. Seeing history unfold before her, a gateway releasing mere words and letters to any passerby, but to her, it was a path of both knowledge and incredible opportunities. She enjoyed reading the old fairy tales and storybooks of old, but she could not help but fall in love with history books, books that taught her how to knit or learn new languages. And even the old book copied onto scrolls on criminals of old she now had opened before her, opened her to the vast knowledge of evil both old and new. All of this knowledge and all of these stories, and she had lived most of her adolescent life illiterate and unschooled, even with all the resources her father had at his disposal back when he could be considered as such. She often wondered during the times she studied under Esmerelda or just got lost in a book or scroll, how Kira would have thought of all of this.

It was fascinating, all the voices in every book and scroll, especially this particular author's way of putting the criminal mind onto a piece of paper so that one could understand the methods of mental illness before the effects of radiation and other unfortunate events that today's everyday life consisted of. Some of the crimes committed and recorded here made Ashlyn's stomach do barrel-rolls but she persevered as she tried to understand the background of what could dismantle a person in such a way.

Having finished this scroll, she put it away and came across a book about a history of magic and witchcraft. Feeling something of a connection between her and the book concerning her mother, she took the book off the shelf and returned to her spot at the table where a muffin and a cup of water sat waiting, half-eaten and half-drunk.

Ashlyn pushed a bang away from her face so she could peer at the words before her. Numerous words she remembered her mother once muttering whenever she used to cast healing spells. It appeared that her mother was by no means a witch. A witch received her power through deals with sprits, or through the concoction of potions and herbs presented by Nature which concealed the elements of life on earth. Or the ancient words used with the combination of the four elements of Nature. Earth, water, fire, and air.

The words she spoke were mostly to help brew the concoctions of healing remedies and potions. It was incredible, really! How had her mother learned such things? Ashlyn remembered asking, once, but she never got an answer. Not too long later, the betrayal of her father left her mother and sister dead and completely bastardized any knowledge involving them.

Was it hereditary? This question came to mind as Ashlyn read on. There was no information regarding whether this was true or not, only that some spirits passed on attributes down the generations like a stray dominant gene, but such cases were rare. Rare, unfortunately, but *still* intriguing.

"Hey."

The voice made her jump, but Ashlyn was relieved to see Markus, out of his workout gear and into a set of fresh pants and a clean white shirt. His dirty-blonde hair was damp and he smiled at her as he sat down, being careful with his bad arm.

She sat her book down and smiled back. "Hey, how was it?"

"It was good. Grim says I'm getting better."

"That's good."

"Yeah." He looked down at her book. "Whatcha reading now?"

"Just some spells I found."

"Spells?"

Ashlyn shrugged. "It's interesting to me."

She never told him the reason *why* her own mother was accused of aiding Xerxes and why she and her younger sister, Kira, was killed. She had told Markus almost off-handedly, as it was still a delicate subject. Besides, no excuse from General Veegar could be satisfactory enough for what he had done. Her mother had known how to brew healing potions, and so, her father, used that as a reason to be rid of his family so he wouldn't have any ties as he climbed the ranks for Baron Ovid. She didn't feel it necessary to tell Markus, but she felt the sudden desire to do so now. It was as if the history of magic had been a key all along that seemed to have unlocked something inside of her that was ready to spring out the door.

But now wasn't a good time. It never truly felt like a good time.

Markus asked what spells interested her, and Ashlyn showed him. She tried not to sound apprehensive but also not too eager, as it was probably impossible that she would ever carry the power her mother once had. As she did so, the nagging question still scratched against the inside of her skull like a trapped gerbil. *Could* she tell him? He did after all knew her mother was a touchy subject considering that her entire family was dead.

Well, *almost* her entire family. If the resources she had back when she lived in Nineveh were up to date, there was no true heir to the throne, and since Baron Ovid was now declared dead, Veegar should have been next in line to rule over the city, unless something else had happened. Soon, that wouldn't matter anymore, especially if Levitika still planned on moving on to claim Nineveh and overthrow the old guard.

All of this was a tough subject for Ashlyn herself to bring up. She didn't know for absolute certain whether or not her mother was a witch, it was always so secretive just like the pain of seeing her husband change from the man he used to be to the right-hand of a tyrant. So much secrecy, and whether she meant for it to be or not, Ashlyn felt herself cursed to remain as silent as her mother. It was the least she could do, to preserve her mother's honor, as well as her sister's whose only crime was being alive. Just like her mother, Kira died and yet Ashlyn alone was given a chance to stay alive.

Why was that? Another question Ashlyn figured she would never have an answer to, nor would she discuss this with Markus just yet. It just never seemed appropriate to ever bring up in light of all that had happened both prior and during the battle against the Ninevite Fleet. Ever since then with Markus' training and his healing, she just didn't feel like she could burden him with any of her own baggage.

Best to wait until things calmed down, whenever that may be. By then, perhaps she could tell him all of this and then some. She could probably tell him everything, as she trusted him with her life, so why not her secrets too which kept her up late at night?

Ashlyn cleared her throat before changing the subject off of the book which she realized she was getting a little *too* invested in to talk to Markus about. "Are you ready for the meeting tonight?"

"In all honesty? Not really. I don't feel mature enough for such a discussion. Only thing I *can* understand why Elizabetha wants Nineveh, not just for support but for the mine. It's a *massive* mining kingdom, useful for developing more weapons and droids. It could help us in the upcoming war with Xerxes and so forth."

"This whole thing just keeps getting bigger and bigger, huh?" she said with some dread building up in her chest.

"Got that right." Markus nodded in thought.

They had discussed their part in this whole thing, something neither of them particularly planned on being part of. But because of his bond with the crystals, Markus didn't seem to have much of a choice in the beginning. When they had seen The Levitikan Crystal, the one crystal that defied the laws of gravity for this island and made Levitika the City in the Sky, he seemed to have a change of heart on the matter and Ashlyn agreed to stick by him until the end. He never talked much about it, but what sort of spirit was in that crystal? The child of the Mad King? What sort of experience had that been? Markus himself was holding back a lot, and in turn, both he and Ashlyn both seemed so close and yet so distant. It was as Ashlyn had thought, there never seemed to be an appropriate time for her to discuss her thoughts with him, as he was constantly busy and occupied with something going on for Levitika.

She understood it, and hated it at the same time. Still, she was determined to stick by his side no matter what.

He then turned back to Ashlyn. "Hey, there is something else I need to discuss with The Queen- after the meeting."

"Oh?"

"Yeah. But the Elders and the other members of the court cannot get wind of it. And I want you and Esmerelda there when I talk to her."

Ashlyn felt a prick of worry touch the back of her mind. A woman's intuition, she might have called it, but not right now, not when it felt important. Also, was it just her, or did Markus look like he had a sort of *haunted* look in those blue eyes of his?

"What's it about?"

Markus looked away, confirming her suspicion. For a moment he looked… scared.

"Mark?"

He looked at her again. "Just something I need you all to know."

"You can't tell me now?"

"No. Not now. Not here. What if a camera is watching us? Or a droid is overhearing us?"

"We're alone."

"As far as *you* know. Listen, I *promise* I will explain tonight. *After* the meeting. Okay?"

Ashlyn gave him a look, but nodded nonetheless. "Alright. I trust you," and she thought to herself, *What are you hiding?*

Markus looked somewhat relieved and that in it of itself made Ashlyn relax, just a little. "Alright. Thank you."

"Alright." She looked at his eyes again. "How are you? With everything?"

"I'm alright," he said, obviously lying partially. She could tell when he was unsure or lying now. Another reason they had gotten so close since they first met.

"Are you?" she pressed.

He sighed, finally giving in. Another trait. "To be honest, Ashlyn? I miss her."

Ashlyn nodded and leaned over to hug her friend. She knew who he was referring to, and he didn't need to tell her. He rested his head on her shoulder as she hugged him tight. This was necessary. This was needed. And it felt right.

"It'll be okay. She's in a better place."

"I know," he whispered. He wasn't crying this time. A sign of healing, or maturity. Acceptance, nonetheless.

She nodded and patted his head, where his mass of blonde hair cushioned her hand. With a smile, she commented, "You need a haircut."

He laughed and pulled away from her. "Maybe. I'll ask the doc when we get this cast off."

"When are you going for that?"

"An hour."

"Want some company?"

"I don't wanna pull you away from your reading."

She smiled at him and closed her book. "Well *I* need to go to the range and practice my shooting soon. Might as well do it now while we have time. Do you want to do that before your appointment?"

"I can't shoot a rifle," Markus shrugged his bad arm.

"Doesn't mean you can't shoot a pistol," she countered with a wink. "C'mon, you chicken?"

Markus smiled at her, a daring smile that clearly said without words, 'You're on.'

Vic's shooting range was a level beneath his workshop and consisted of a concrete room filled with mounds of dirt to catch shots with rows of moving practice dummies before a wall where one could leave different kinds of weapons to practice with them. Markus was getting really good at shooting one-handed as he got used to it just like how he was getting better with staff's and swords. Every time a pop-up target came up down the range, Markus would fire three shots each, all in a constant area in the center of the chest. The range was far enough from prying eyes, and the facility was sound-proof to quiet the shots. The local arms-dealer and mechanic, Vic, who owned a small bar in town would let the two practice here when the Royal Range was being used by the soldiers. Recently, Ashlyn had been coming here a lot more recently even though she received plenty of time to train with the soldiers, and Markus didn't quite understand why as he didn't like Vic, not entirely anyway.

Ashlyn, who stayed braced as she held the rifle against her shoulder was by far more accurate, firing either heart-shots or head-shots in the same consecutive spaces. The wooden men would combust into flames wherever her laser hit. She was getting better and better with a gun, and it was just a *little* hard for her not to make fun of Markus every time he *did* miss.

"You be quiet," Markus said after a comment she had made. He was smiling though as he removed another empty photon cylinder from the pistol and insert another. "Besides, it's easier to aim with two hands."

"Sounds like you're just jealous."

Markus smiled. "Maybe," he admitted.

"Well least you're good with a sword."

"Staff mostly."

"You also got magic on your side," Ashlyn added firing a final shot and blowing another head off a dummy. Splintered wood and straw flew everywhere and burned like paper in a fireplace. "You just need to keep at it with a sword. Can't be too careful or rely on one thing for everything."

"I know, I just…" Markus sat down his pistol on the table. Ashlyn waited patiently, taking her time as she fired down the range. At last he said, "That's *Black's* sword. It doesn't feel right to use it. Also… whether he was supposed to or not, he killed my dad with it."

Ashlyn nodded. "No one is forcing you to use it, you know."

"I know," said Markus. "But he also gave it to me when he died, and… I dunno, it doesn't feel right but at the same time it does. Does that make sense?"

"I get you. But like I said, no one is forcing you to use it. If you don't want to, don't. Find another weapon. At the end of the day, it isn't the sword's fault who it hurts or even kills. It's just a tool."

"I know." A clear message from Markus, meaning: Change the subject. Please.

"Let's get these back to Vic," Ashlyn said folding her rifle and placing it in her bag. "Then we can get you to your appointment."

"You're done?"

"Been done." She smiled at him and said, "Got nothing else to really prove to you here."

"Har-de-har," Markus retorted with a smile in return and together they walked back and up a flight of stairs up to the surface. They opened the metal door, letting in the bright sun and the sounds of the bustling streets of Downtown Levitika. The two stepped out and closed the door behind them. They then turned the corner to Vic's Vendor, where he stood hunched over his counter talking to a cyborg who was missing most of his limbs as well as half of his head. She appeared uninterested in the big man so the two stepped in and slammed their bags onto the counter, making Vic jump. His brow furrowed like a hairy caterpillar over his three eyes.

"Was that necessary?" he demanded.

"Nope," Markus said, and by the sound of his voice he didn't care too much. "Thanks for letting us use the range, Vic."

Vic turned to see the woman walking away. He turned back with a cruel grin, displaying how unpleased he was for their interruption with those stony teeth of his. "No problem, *kiddies*." He grabbed the bag and tucked it under the bar. "Want anything to drink?"

"Water," Ashlyn said.

Vic disappeared under the bar only to return with two bottles of purified water which he handed to the teens. "How did they treat ya? The guns, I mean."

"They feel no different than the army's weapons," Ashlyn said while taking a sip of water.

"Yeah, but I take 'em apart and put 'em back together, sometimes with different parts. The queen doesn't like makeshift weapons, too many variables, ya get my meanin'?"

"In all honesty, Vic," Markus said after taking a sip of his water. "A gun is a gun in my opinion."

"Yes, but there is a big difference between a pea-shooter and a Vulcan Canon, eh."

"Maybe," Markus admitted. "How is everything treating you anyway?" he asked trying to be polite.

"Not bad, mate, same ol' crap. Those scoundrel Elders and that bastard Slagar's still doing anything to keep everyone under their thumb, and the queen ain't much help in that regard. They don't like the thought of non-soldiers having guns. Me being the patriot that I am, would rather be prepared than a slave. There are many more like me out here in the city, brave men and women who construct their own weapons in case the government fails. Which may, or may not. The war is still early, but we already lost a lot in the process eh?"

"Right," Ashlyn said. Having their own history with Nineveh's government, both she and Markus understood his caution. But at the same time, his reasons felt unwarranted and given how conflicted Esmerelda's story sounded concerning the mutant, it was hard to tell for certain. Also, Slagar and the council didn't make it any easier, given how they treated Markus when they had first arrived.

"Vic," a voice said behind them making Markus and Ashlyn turn to see someone walking towards the vendor.

A large man with skin like ebony wearing a black leather hoodie came over. He had a large belt with energy cartridges strapped in the loops, and across his back was a large Photon Rifle. He rubbed his balding head as he stopped before the vendor. "Got a minute?"

Vic took a sideways glance at the kids, but returned his attention. "Yeah, what is it?"

"Dere's a tribe a'couple miles from Nineveh, where we goin' right?" The man sounded like a foreigner, far from the Northern Wastelands the way his English was slightly choppy. Ashlyn wondered if he was from the Southern Sands.

"As far as I know, yes. What do I care about a couple savages?"

"Well, dis tribe worship spirits, use Pluton-Oil in sacrifices."

"Pluton-Oil you say?" Vic said sounding oddly interested, all skepticism gone from his face.

The man looked at Markus and Ashlyn. "Dey okay?"

Vic looked at the kids. "Right as rain," he assured him. But he looked back at the Wastelander seriously. "But we *should* discuss this later, at Viper's Kitchen, eh?"

"Yeah. Sure," the Wastelander nodded.

"Meet me there in an hour, Brick," Vic said to his buddy.

"Got it," the man named 'Brick' said bobbing his head to the man and then turning away.

When he was gone, Vic turned to Markus and Ashlyn. "Sorry about that."

"What was that about?" Ashlyn asked. "Why did he look nervous to talk around us?"

"And what's with the Pluton-Oil?" Markus added.

"I got a project going down," Vic explained. "This is on a need-to-know-basis if you's know what I mean."

"What is Pluton-Oil?" asked Ashlyn.

Markus answered in his own mechanic-way which always made him sound like he knew everything. "Pluton-Oil is a mixture of radioactive oil that rose to the surface a couple years after fallout. The condensed air forms some kinda rust on the surface, and if there is say, a well of the oil, it mixes around. Mixing, channeling beneath the crust. It's a useful fuel for vehicles, takes forever to burn. Some of the Ninevite guards had some stockpiled for the Hellhounds."

Vic clapped his hands. "Spoken true. But the reason why *I* need some is to make a new kind of weapon."

"A weapon?" Markus asked.

"Aye, a, shall we say, fail-save in case the city is doomed. Believe it or not, it's actually a project for the queen, and the queen *alone* without the nosy Council."

"You won't tell us?" Markus asked with a small smile that looked honestly genuine to Ashlyn.

Vic smiled in return, although with no such kindness. "Nope. Not yet. As soon as I get the 'okay' from the queen, I will. But don't go asking her about it, aright?"

"All right," Ashlyn said. "We got the meeting and everything tonight," she reminded Markus but in reality wanted to just go. "We gotta go now. Thanks again, Vic."

"Wait," Markus said looking at Vic. "Can I ask you a question, Vic?"

"Go ahead," he said as he lit a rolled piece of parchment with a match and the stench of Buckweed greeted the teens when he smoked it.

"How well did you know my father?" Markus asked, surprising Ashlyn. When Vic was talking about Johnathon when the two of them were taking a tour with Esmerelda, the princess warned him about the mutant when it came to his father. Markus, it seemed, wanted to know why. She kept quiet though, curious as well.

Vic shrugged. "Pretty good. Like I said, we used to fly a lot back in the day. Was always interested in ways to test those crystal-thingy's out."

"Was my father a good person?" Markus asked.

This time, Vic chuckled as if he was reminiscing fond memories. "My friend, 'good' is merely a matter of perspective."

"So, was he?" Ashlyn asked.

Once again, Vic shrugged. "He was always good to me. Only bothered me once when he came over looking for a fight. Apparently, something to do with some lady."

"Some lady?" Markus asked immediately looking intrigued.

"Yup. Came in, got all up in my face, and a small scuffle broke out. He apologized afterward, but he used his crystal on me. Scared the bejesus out of me."

"What did he do?" Markus asked. "What did he show you?"

Vic shook his head. "Don't remember. Part of his apology was wiping that part out of my head. He kept the argument and the fight in so I could remember it happened, but what he showed me is long gone now. As far as I was concerned, he and I didn't have any problems again up until he left. Then I never saw him again. Obviously."

Markus nodded. "Did he think you were talking to someone like... flirtatiously?"

"Ha!" Vic cackled. "I like that word. Good pick, kid. But, no. That's another thing, it's vague. I don't quite remember clearly, but I *do* remember him asking what I gave someone."

"Do you know who the lady was?"

"Not a clue."

Markus looked disappointed at that. Ashlyn wondered if he was thinking that the lady was possibly his mother. "I see..."

Vic looked at Markus and said, "You look so much like yer dad, y'know that?"

"I've been told..."

"Yeah... other than the hair, you look like a carbon copy."

"Thanks."

Ashlyn cleared her throat. "We should really get going." Markus didn't argue this time, and agreed that they should.

"Stop by again sometime, 'kay?" Vic said. "I'd like to finish another small project, maybe you can help me out when you get yer arm back, Marky-boy?"

Markus gave Vic a huge PR smile, a clear indication that he either did not like the nickname, or had no intention of coming to help with a project. Ashlyn figured it was the first, because Markus had loved working in Vic's workshop for Esmerelda's miniature Dragonfly Drone. "Will do."

The two thanked the mutant vendor again, and they hurried off towards the castle to get Markus out of his sling and ready for the meeting.

Esmerelda

Princess Esmerelda stood beside Markus' bedside while the droid known as 'Doc' worked on her friends arm, doing a series of tests and stretches onto Markus' shoulder and elbow. Ashlyn stood next to her, also watching the operation. As they talked, she played with her long black hair which was curly and loose over her shoulders. She wore a simple dress under a black jacket. On her shoulder, the dragonfly-shaped robot she named Q-Pid sat curled, her wings folded along her sleek and bronze body. After the attack from Baron Ovid, Markus had fixed the robot up best he could with his single arm. Thankfully, the gift he had given Esmerelda was up and running, and watching Markus with intelligent sensors.

One of the discussions during Markus' final operation was around Vic's supposed 'failsafe' weapon, which she did know about but only a little.

"It's not really something he is building, more so he is trying to refurbish. This castle had a secret weapon in one of the towers, an ancient cannon used during the separation from The Capitol. The Owl was the one who helped designed it, and they used it to blow up the Mad King.

"The Shi Ray?" Markus asked and the droid asked him to stretch his arm over his shoulder.

"That's right," Esmerelda said. "Thing is, when they used it, the island crashed down. It took up a lot of energy from the Levitikan Crystal, and so they never used it again. Never had to once the island began to levitate again."

"Was the spirit inside okay?" Markus asked sounding concerned.

"As far as those who had the Dream Crystals could understand," Esmerelda said. "But then again, he hardly spoke to anyone. Didn't trust anyone other than The Owl, who unfortunately died along with The Eldest."

"Until he met you, right?" Ashlyn asked Markus.

"Guess so." Markus then asked Esmerelda, "Do you think we'll ever have to use the Shi Ray?"

"Even if we wanted to now, it isn't ready. It isn't stable, especially with how big the city has gotten. In the meantime, no, I don't think so anytime soon. My mother wasn't planning to use it anytime soon anyway, especially not against Nineveh since we are trying to, y'know, save it."

"That's right," Ashlyn said uneasily. "Nineveh, tomorrow."

"Yeah, we're going home," Markus said. He said the word 'home' as if he was actually saying 'hell.'

"Done," the droid beeped once it was satisfied that Markus' arm was completely healed.

Markus said, "Thanks, Doc. For everything."

"You're welcome, Markus." The droid gave a salute using one of its thin appendages before hovering away and leaving the teens alone.

"No, Markus," Ashlyn said after the robot was gone. "*This* is our home. Not that horrible place."

Markus said nothing.

"Maybe when we take over, it can be again," Esmerelda said coming over to Markus. "My mother will make sure that we start a new kind of rule. More kind, and with more justice than what your city received from that monster of a man."

"Hard to imagine Nineveh being a place like that," Markus said.

"Indeed," Ashlyn said appearing distracted by the way she was looking out the nearby window.

Markus looked at her and said, "You think your father will surrender?"

"I don't know."

"What are you thinking?" Esmerelda asked, concerned. She knew about General Veegar and his connection to Ashlyn, and knew that it might be hard for her to see her father again, especially considering their last true encounter. But Ashlyn wasn't really giving much of an opinion, let alone an actual response.

"I don't know," was her friend's only reply.

"Hey," Markus said standing up and approaching her. Using his healed arm, he reached out and placed a hand on Ashlyn's shoulder. "It'll be okay. I'm sure everything will be okay."

"How do you know that?" Ashlyn asked him while looking at Esmerelda who tried her best to look comforting or somewhat supportive of her friend. "I just don't know for certain."

Markus replied, "I don't know either. But I do know that you got us until the bitter end. He might have been your father, but he was no true parent for you or Kira."

Ashlyn sniffed. "It's strange, really. Ever since that night, I always wished he would die. I told you I resented him back in the wilds, but that doesn't even touch the tip of the iceberg. He was and is a selfish man, who chose pleasing the Baron over his own family. In the end, it didn't take much for him to throw us all away."

"He left you alive though," Markus pointed out.

Ashlyn nodded. "That's the other thing. I remembered wishing he would die. But I honestly just want to know why. I want to hear it from his own mouth."

"Then we'll make sure to bring him in alive," Markus said while offering that cute smile of his. He would always give that whenever he was trying to be sincere or nice. This time, it was a smile of support. Esmerelda knew that much in the weeks she had gotten to know him and Ashlyn.

Ashlyn looked at him, and then to Esmerelda with a small but sad smile. "It's just... I don't know if I could handle seeing him again."

"You don't have to, you know," Esmerelda said.

"I want to. I want him to see my pain, my anger, I want him to actually know just what he did to me and my family," Ashlyn clenched her fist at the thought. "I want him to understand my pain."

Markus nodded. "We'll get him to. I promise. Hopefully no one else in Nineveh has to suffer because of that."

"That's right," said Esmerelda.

"If anything," Markus said. "We might not even have to fight at all. Hopefully we don't have to."

Esmerelda agreed.

Ashlyn smiled, and looked over at the clock on the wall. "Thanks, guys."

Esmerelda nodded. "We better get going. The meeting is about to start."

Markus nodded removing his hand from Ashlyn's shoulder. "Agreed. Let's go."

For some odd reason, Esmerelda felt her body loosen up when she saw Markus' hand leave Ashlyn's shoulder. She didn't even realize that she had been uptight. She felt silly for it, of course. Markus was not an ordinary kid. He was a Keeper, one who had a bond with the Dream Crystals. He was to play a major part in this war for the North. Her mother had emphasized this drastically for many, many years. All this time, The Keeper was grown in her mind as a powerful warrior capable of twisting the laws of fantasy and reality and help bring order to the land.

But, in the end, he was still just a kid. A kid close to Esmerelda's age.

A kid, a *boy*, she had started to become very fond of, she realized. But such an idea was never going to work. Not if the two of them were technically related considering who Johnathon was when he was alive here.

Best to let that dream die out. Best to leave it alone.

Markus

Markus stood between his friends in the back of the throne room amongst the many counselors and elders who appeared to hear Queen Elizabetha speak. She was accompanied by Grim and Slagar, who helped her set up the plan for the upcoming battle against the Ninevites. As Elizabetha spoke, the two men would pull up holograms, depicting various maps and locations as well as enemy infantry and AA-Guns. How they planned to attack the city without putting Levitika in harm's way, and most importantly avoid civilian casualties.

"The city's AA-Guns are stationed here, here, here, here, and here." Elizabetha would point at various sides of the massive walls around the city, and each spot lit up in a bright blue color. "The range of those guns are about ten miles with their scopes. So, we will tether the island here."

She pointed to a mass of land to the southeast of the city limits. "Our Angels will distract the gunners, while ground troops will take the Caterpillars across the plains and to the wall, where they will attempt to scale the walls and come up from the other side. Once our Angels are inside, we will begin the attack on the various outposts of the yard. Markus, you did deliveries to most of these men, so I assume you know where the central control is that leads to the AA guns yes?"

"Yes, ma'am." Markus remembered how big the place was too. Whenever he had made a delivery back then, it was always big with either parts, or food with drink. He was never allowed past the checkpoint desk, but he had seen inside the tactical control room whenever the pressure doors would open.

"You will take a few soldiers with you and destroy it. Once the main antennae are destroyed, it will scatter the radar systems, and the guns won't be able to get a lock on the island. We will then send out aerial troops in to storm the castle."

"What about the mine fields?" someone blurted out. "Shouldn't we avoid them?"

"I believe Slagar has a plan involving that." Elizabetha stepped aside to let the old magician take a place at the stand.

"I would like you, Markus to sneak into the city, and head for Field Development. That's where they launch the mines and upkeep them. At least, that is what Black told us."

"Black was the closest to The Baron," Markus said. "His word is as good as an actual Guard."

"A guard can lie though," Slagar pointed out. "But besides that, if you can get in, you can blow the mines and give our Caterpillars safe passage. From there, move on to Central Control, and shut down all radar."

"How will I be doing that?" Markus inquired.

"You and two others will be using a special tunneling pod that will go underground and get you to the walls. From there, it's up to you to find the Control Center and the Field Development. That way you don't have to worry about the mines they laid out around the border."

"There's one more problem," Markus said receiving many uneasy glances.

"Yes?" Grim asked.

"The Behemoths," said Ashlyn.

"That's right," Markus continued. "The Baron uses Behemoth Robots as a fail-save in case the city was about to be breached. Not your usual ones wither, *big* ones. They were used in the last attack from Xerxes. If we don't take care of them first, then there is no way we'll make it."

"Veegar will sic the robots on the city if he has to," Ashlyn said her voice stiff and angry.

Eventually, someone finally spoke up. "We should, probably- you know- get rid of those things then."

"Agreed," Slagar said. "Markus, think you'll be able to get in past the walls? You know the city better than anyone- besides you Miss Ashlyn."

"I can get in, through one of the sewers. But I need to know where the nearest pipeline is."

"I can show him," Ashlyn said.

"Huh?" Markus asked looking at her.

Elizabetha seemed to ponder this. "You two, and an Angel, do you think that should be fine?"

"Not at all!" Markus exclaimed. "Ashlyn, you can't go."

"Why not?" Ashlyn demanded. "I can do it."

"It'll be dangerous."

"So was crossing the Wastelands."

"Ashlyn..."

Ashlyn looked Markus dead in the eye. Those hazel spheres were darker than usual, as well as determined. "I'm going." She looked at the queen and said, "With your permission of course, Elizabetha."

"I think that is a good idea," she said. "Two pairs of eyes that know the city better than any of us. Plus, you both have some experience now with your personal trainings. I see no trouble. Does anyone have any objections or suggestions?"

"Should we *really* risk that?" Slagar asked. "Sending those two? They don't have the hardened training that our Angels have."

"No," Grim agreed. "But Markus has become decent in swordplay, and obviously, he has an advantage that few humans have. Besides, I've seen Ashlyn at the shooting ranges. She'll be fine to watch his back."

"You can count on that," Ashlyn assured him and everyone else in the room.

"Then it is settled," Elizabetha said. "Unless you have anything else to say, Markus?"

Markus had *plenty* to say. He didn't want to risk Ashlyn going and getting hurt. This wasn't like crossing the Wastelands to find Levitika. This was crossing into enemy lines in an actual war. Looking at her, he saw her watching him, waiting patiently. She had made up her mind, and he felt that he wouldn't be able to change it. He didn't like it, but he thought that he wouldn't have anyone else with him other than her, especially in Nineveh. Plus, she did know the sewer system better than he. He didn't want to risk her life, but he would rather her close by than two Angels with him in Nineveh.

"You sure?" Markus asked her, ready to accept whatever response she had.

"Of course," she said with a gleam in her eye. "I'll get you in, no sweat. Between the two of us, we can also cover more ground and get everything set for everyone."

"So, we splitting up?"

"It'll be faster," she pointed out.

"And more dangerous." Markus thought about it and said, "We'll see when we get there. We don't even know if anything has changed since then. If Veegar knows that Baron Ovid is gone, he might have taken even more precautions than AA-Guns and mines."

"Okay," Ashlyn said. "Deal."

"Alright, I'll take her," Markus told the court.

"Excellent," Elizabetha said running a hand through her black hair. She appeared pleased. "Then we will wait for you two to remove the robots before making an entry. We will have to keep in touch via two-way."

"You can count on us," Markus said. "Who will be coming with us?"

"Me, of course," Grim said with a proud smile.

"I feel safer already," Markus said and there was minor chuckles among the court.

Slager cleared his throat for attention and said, "After the robots are down, we move on with the plan. Storm the castle, no causalities. Everyone got it?"

"Your majesty," an Elder said to Elizabetha standing up. "What about division? What will happen once we set up shop in Nineveh? Who will take over while Levitika continues its rounds?"

"Levitika will stay with Nineveh until we decide our next move," Elizabetha answered. "We cannot attack other districts until we get more information which we will find in the castle. Until then, I will remain in charge and The Elders will continue their authority as such until a leader is selected. As for Nineveh, that will be for the Ninevites to decide with our help. They should be the ones to choose their new leader."

"With all due respect my lady, we need to make sure we are prepared for the future. Besides, can we really trust the Ninevites to make good decisions since they have been under a tyrant all their lives?"

"Prisoners will realize they are free when they open their eyes to see that they no longer are in chains," Slager said. "Your queen has spoken."

The Elder wasn't convinced. "But-"

"The siege first," Elizabetha said. "Then we will consult with the Ninevites and plan everything then. Until then, everything else in the future is a distant bridge that we will cross when we get to it."

The Elder seemed to be trying hard to hold something in. He wanted to say something, *badly*. But he held his tongue. He bowed. "Your majesty," and sat back down.

"Any more questions?" Slagar asked. "Concerns, comments?" When no hands were raised, he waved. "Dismissed. See you all set to go tomorrow at dawn." With that, everyone stood to leave.

All, except for Markus and his two friends, leaving them, and Queen Elizabetha, Slagar and Grim. When Elizabetha saw that the teens had not departed she left her two men and strolled over to them, hoisting her elegant purple dress up as she walked. When she reached them, she looked at them with a funny expression.

"What is it?" she asked. "You two have a big day tomorrow, and I need you ready to assist me in the morning, Esmerelda."

"Your majesty," Markus spoke up standing up. "I need to talk you." He looked behind him to look at the girls who were standing back up as well. "To all of you."

"Can it not wait?" Elizabetha asked taking a glance at Grim and Slagar who were staring at the group with such interest.

"Ma'am," Markus insisted. "This cannot wait, and cannot be discussed in front of anyone else. It's seriously important. It's about Abram."

She eyes Markus for a moment, and then eyes the two girls who looked just as mystified as she was. Finally Elizabetha sighed. "Alright, let us go to my quarters." She then turned to Slagar and Grim. "I must speak to the Keeper privately. Will you two follow us to my room and wait outside? We will discuss the rest of the plans after I talk to them."

Slagar sniffed. "As you wish milady. Grim and I have to make some preparations for the Caterpillars. We shall join you presently."

"Thank you." And with that, Elizabetha blew past the teens, and began to exit the throne room. Markus and the girls followed close behind, as they ascended the castle to Elizabetha's quarters.

<u>Markus</u>

The queen's bedroom was far more elegant than any Markus had seen since his arrival here in Levitika. It was an enlarged version of his and Ashlyn's room, with far brighter drapes and sheets upon the bed that seemed to stretch as long as a Dragon. An oak dresser sat beside a desk of similar wood and elegant red leather. Many notes and books were stacked upon it, revealing that the queen was always at work inside this room.

Elizabetha had removed her a gold necklace with a purple gem on the end and sat it at the foot of her bed. She offered the children to sit upon it while she pulled her desk chair over to join them. When they were all seated, The queen turned to Markus.

"So, Abram."

"Who is Abram?" Ashlyn asked, now looking at Markus worriedly.

Markus pursed his lips in thought of how exactly he was going to say it. He ran it through his head millions of times, but now that it was time, his mind was blank as empty piece of paper an author struggles with putting words on it. After a moment of silence, he finally spoke out. "I have to leave after Nineveh."

Elizabetha looked at Markus for a long time. She did not appear surprised or concerned, unlike Ashlyn and Esmerelda, who was now staring at him with complete shock.

"What?" Ashlyn asked, her voice barely above a whisper. Esmerelda said nothing.

"Go ahead," Elizabetha said. "Tell them."

Markus did so, slowly, carefully actually. "The spirits inside my crystals said something about Black's old teacher, a hermit named Abram in the Kaiken Isles. Said he taught Black how to harness and better control the magic that emit from the crystals without the influence of The Dreaming. This could be valuable information, if and when we find The Eldest. Black said to go, in order to better understand The Dreaming, and learn to control the power that I feel with these crystals."

"Why didn't you tell me?" Ashlyn demanded, now furious. "Why are you just telling us now?"

"Mark," Esmerelda spoke up. "It sounds risky. The Kaiken Isles and the waters around it are controlled by pirates and the king who controls the villages and tribes within. It's too dangerous."

Ashlyn looked to Elizabetha who had remained silent during this discussion. "You are seriously thinking of letting this happen?"

"Also, Mother," Esmerelda added. "Shouldn't we find the Eldest first, after Nineveh?"

"Where would we begin?" Markus asked with his hands raised. "The Wastelands is a large place, with many tribes. Who knows where that Hunter took it? Your men lost his tracks, he could be anywhere."

"Besides," Elizabetha added not answering Ashlyn's question as of yet. "It would be easier to scour the entire Wastelands when Markus has better control of his power."

"And, I have to go alone," Markus said albeit hesitantly under the harsh gazes of the girls. "I have thought about this for a long time, and consulted with how the spirits reacted such thoughts. I need to be undistracted, and untied in order to understand the Dreaming. I need to find myself, and I think the spirits agree with me."

"Oh, so we are a *distraction*!?" Ashlyn demanded. "You're insane if you think of going alone!"

"You speak just like Damion," Elizabetha commented. "I believe you, Markus."

"Mother!" Esmerelda cried out. "It's-"

"Look," Markus said trying to calm the girls down. "Black talked to me before he died. The Crystals? They need to be destroyed. Both to free the spirits trapped inside The Dreaming, but to basically cripple the bridge The Eldest needs to escape The Dreaming. Even without the Eldest Crystal, we can trap him entirely. If we're gonna do that, I need to learn what Abram taught Black, and I also need to get his crystal. According to Black, Abram has a crystal on his person. It was his last dying wish. Not to collect The Crystals, because they are too dangerous to be in the hands of anyone alive or dead. To be honest, I feel the influence of The Dreaming as we speak. Whispers, nightmares, good memories and dreams all flooding my head. After The Leviathan blew up, it was because I let the power and the spirits energy take over. I was powerful enough to destroy the ship and save Black, but I wasn't *myself*. I felt like I was invaded, not by the spirits of the Crystals, but The Eldest who haunts The Dreaming. I may need that power again, and I need to know how to better control myself. Both to keep myself safe, to harness better power to find The Crystals, and how to better destroy them and maybe one day, The Eldest, and the crystal that keeps this island afloat."

Silence submerged the room like a flood of dark water. No one said anything, not even the queen, who Markus addressed after a moment.

"That is my destiny isn't it? To destroy the new bridge between our world and The Dreaming, and reconstruct how it was meant to be. So that fantasy and reality can remain untouched. Then we will have a better chance to save The Region from The Dark Queen and anyone else who wishes to abuse that power."

Elizabetha smiled softly, sadly even. "Spoken just as Black did, when he left to find Abram long ago."

Her words hung in the air for the longest of time. Elizabetha stood up with a tight expression and walked over to the window above her desk. She stood looking through it for a long time.

During this time, Ashlyn said to Markus, "This is *insane*, Markus. How do you even know this Abram guy is legit- Or even *alive*?"

"Black recommended Abram. So I must heed his words."

"This coming from someone who still holds a grudge against a dead man!"

"Ashlyn," Esmerelda said. "We-"

"And if this is a *trick*? What then?"

Markus looked at Ashlyn calmly. "Then I come back."

"And how exactly do you know that you need to do this? Something about a bridge you said earlier, what does *that* mean?"

"I can't explain."

"Try!"

Markus threw up his hands in exasperation. Still, he tried. "It seems like, the longer I am in contact with these crystals, the more I am understanding. Only bits and pieces, fragments that buzz through my head. I can't get them out of my head. I can't stop the voices, I can't stop the images from coming to me, even in meditation. If I can understand more, and learn more about what exactly I have in my pockets, I may be able to know how to better defend myself. I have had some time to go over the prophecy Elizabetha has told me. And I need to at least slow down The Eldest so we can stop the war. If we can keep him from coming sooner, we can have more time to know how to make sure he never escapes. I need to know more about magic, I need to know more about The Dreaming. This is the only way. No book holds the answers to my questions. If Abram is even the smallest chance of understanding, then I need to take it. Once The Eldest is trapped, then our only enemies, are real people without the use of twisting reality."

"You're this determined, aren't you?" the queen asked approaching the teens again.

Markus nodded. "Yes, your majesty."

"Mark," Ashlyn said grabbing her friend's shoulder. There was no anger in her voice anymore. Only desperation it seemed. Her hand squeezed the muscle in his shoulder, as if trying to make him physically understand her fear. "This is *crazy*."

"I agree, but what else can I do?" Markus asked this honestly. "The more I have these things with me, the more I *see*. I hate it. I can't explain it, but I can feel as if someone is on my back right now. Not the spirits, they never made me feel so heavy before. It's like The Eldest is always watching, crouched at the door that may or may not open, and then I'll be overcome. Even with two crystals seeming to block out the terror, it's still there. It's still a threat."

"What if you get hurt? What if you get caught?"

"I won't," Markus said. "I *can't*. We can't afford to pass this up, Ashlyn. I don't know anyone else who can help me prepare myself more. Besides, you know it's the right thing to do. You saw the devastation I caused with Baron Ovid. That sort of power, no man should have control of."

"Mother," Esmerelda spoke up. "I must protest. This is dangerous, you can't honestly think Markus should go, do you? We should wait until we can get closer. We need to get to The Kaiken Isles anyway at some point down the road. Why not wait until then?"

"I believe that this cannot wait, my daughter," Elizabetha said. She looked as if all hope and spirit was drained from her face. "Black knew more about The Crystals than I do. If destroying them is that important, then we need to do what he would have wanted. He deserves to rest in peace, knowing that we did what we could to prevent The Eldest from rising again. Markus, are you sure you are up for this?

"I have to," he answered. "After Nineveh is taken, I will go. I already made my decision to stay with you guys when I saw the Eldest's son holding this island up. I need to go through with it. I need to make sure no one feels the dread I feel now."

"Everyone feels dread at some point, Markus," Elizabetha pointed out.

"Not like this," Markus said shaking his head. "Not like this."

Elizabetha nodded, understanding despite not. "We will make the necessary preparations when the time comes."

"Thank, you your majesty."

Ashlyn stood, appearing bitter and frustrated. She bowed to the queen, not saying anything, as she stormed out of the room. Esmerelda looked at Markus reproachfully, but he didn't react. He only stared at the open door sadly.

"You best go," Elizabetha suggested.

Markus thanked her, and he and Esmerelda left the queen's presence. They stepped outside to pass Slagar and Grim who started to say something, but Markus hurried past them, eager to catch up with Ashlyn who was heading in the direction of her room.

"Mark!" Esmerelda hissed grabbing his hand. She was holding him back, but he wasn't letting her. He was too strong, and the crystals in his pockets were fueling his determination to move forward. It appeared they too agreed with Elizabetha. Now if only they could take a break of hiding and actually talk to him.

Up ahead, Ashlyn turned the corner, and by the time Markus did the same, her door slammed shut. He was about to reach it, when Esmerelda stepped in front of him. "Wait!"

"What?" Markus said annoyed and angry.

"Just, wait for a second, okay?" Esmerelda took a deep breath and said, "Look, we are only concerned about your wellbeing. We get it, it's a big deal. It's huge, especially since we lost The Eldest. But that doesn't mean you have to get yourself into danger."

"I won't."

"How can you be so sure?" Esmerelda demanded.

"I can't expect you to understand," Markus said. "I feel it right here." He pointed at his head. "If you could see what I see, feel what I feel, you'd be scared too. Desperate even to find answers. I need to find Abram. This whole thing, it depends on me finding him."

Esmeralda looked like she was about to cry. "I know you're the Keeper. I know this kind of stuff is something beyond my understanding. But... you're just a kid!"

"We are all kids," Markus argued. "But I don't have a choice. I need to do this. I'm going to do it. And I'm promising you personally that I will be back."

Esmerelda looked down at her feet. "I just don't want anything to happen to you, Markus. You're too important. To all of us."

"No more important than you, Ashlyn, and everyone here. This is bigger than you or me. Ashlyn once said this whole war is bigger than *me*. Whether I like it or not I have been chosen, and I need to do my part. It's important for everyone."

"Can you really afford to bear that sort of weight right now on your shoulders?"

Markus answered, "We all have a part to play. And my part is finding the one person who can help her."

Esmerelda finally looked up, appearing to think over his words for a moment. Then she stepped aside, and said, "I trust you." For a brief moment, Markus heard a voice. It sounded like hers. It said, *For better or for worst.*

He felt the crystals emit some sort of pulsation in his pockets, giving him a surge of power. They were letting him hear her. He needed to. Because she cared, and was afraid, but she trusted him. Hearing her thoughts, reminded Markus of what happened during his rampage against the Hunter Lee.

He hated it feeling this again. He felt as if he had invaded Esmerelda's privacy and trust by doing that. He felt disgusted, like he had violated her. Thankfully, the crystals didn't surrender any more thoughts that were meant to be secret and known only to Esmerelda of Levitika.

"You okay?" she asked seeing his face had gone pale and he looked like he might throw up.

"I'm fine," he said. He thanked her for what she had said, and pushed the thought of hearing her thoughts again far into the back corner of his mind. He did not want to do that again. It felt too close to what he felt like back on the Leviathan.

The feeling of having some nightmarish demon resting on his shoulder, whispering evil intentions into his ear. *This is you, and more.*

Suppressing a shudder, Markus pushed that thought away too, and stepped forward. He knocked on Ashlyn's door, and he and Esmerelda waited.

Reproach

<u>Markus</u>

After she *finally* opened the door, Markus and Esmerelda stepped inside Ashlyn's room. She had immediately turned and sat on the bed crossing her arms as Markus approached her. For a long time, no one spoke, and Esmerelda looked uncomfortable just standing there.

So, Markus tried to speak. "Ash-"

"I'm mad at you," she said which to Markus felt like the understatement of the whole evening. "Actually, I'm freaking *pissed*, Markus. How could you not tell us this? You've kept this hidden from us for this long!? Then all of a sudden, you are gonna ditch to find some guy on an island who may or may not help us!?"

Markus held his hands up in surrender. "Hey, calm down-"

"Don't you *dare* tell me to calm down!" She shoved a finger into Markus' face nearly poking him in the nose. "You can't just leave Markus, you just can't!"

"I don't have a choice!" He didn't mean to yell, but it happened. It happened, and it was like dumping gas onto a fire.

"*Wrong*. You *do* have a choice, Markus. Just like your choice to hide this from me!

"Ashlyn-"

"We were supposed to stick together, you *dick*!"

"Guys..." Esmerelda tried to speak.

"What if we don't make it Ashlyn? Huh?" Markus held his arms up like he was ready to be crucified. Which, given the amount of anger coming from Ashlyn, was a pretty close comparison. "What if The Eldest comes back? What if we run into something more dangerous than Ovid and The Leviathan? I need to learn more about magic, and how to control the influence of The Dreaming. And I can't do it here. Abram may be our last hope to figure out just what exactly we are up against. What do we actually know about this whole thing? Nothing. Absolutely *nothing*. We hear The Dreaming, and know nothing. I get clips, bits and shards of what it *could* be. And guess what: What I feel sucks! It scares the living hell out of me!"

"That doesn't mean-"

"Wouldn't it be good to know what exactly The Dreaming is? What exactly it has to do with these crystals? Why The Eldest is so keen on escaping the place and making what I feel a reality?"

Ashlyn tried to say something, but Markus wasn't done yet.

"I know you don't understand," he said. "I know you're mad I didn't tell you, and I am sorry. I also know it sounds crazy, but Black's advice feels more real because of what I feel the more I have contact with these crystals. I even left them in my room one day and I *still* felt something! It wasn't far from the courtyard but even when I was on the other side of the city, I felt as if something was stalking me. I am *scared*, Ashlyn. If you felt what I felt, you would be too."

Ashlyn was silent. She stared at Markus for the longest time. She looked at Esmerelda with a look that clearly said 'help me out here!'

Esmerelda sighed. "The one thing I'll say I don't agree with is you going alone, Markus. I get it, you want to give this Abram your undivided attention. I still think you should have someone travel with you to Kaiken. An Angel, someone."

"That someone should be *me*," Ashlyn said. "After all, it was me who went with him and Ruth out into the Wastelands and we made it here." She then shot an accusatory glare at Markus. "Or did you forget?"

"Come on," Markus said feeling his temples throbbing. "Ashlyn, why can't you understand that this has only become more dangerous since we came here. With these crystals and me being called the 'Keeper,' this has become even bigger than you and I had bargained for. I need to go so that I can expand my knowledge."

Ashlyn crossed her arms and turned her face away, her jaw set and her shoulders trembling.

Still, he persisted. "You're right, I should never have kept it from you. I'm very sorry about that. I just didn't know what to tell you. I've made up my mind, and I am going. I'll take an Angel with me if I must like Esmerelda said, but this is something I need to do alone. You can't come with me, Ashlyn. I don't like it any more than you do, but it is what I have to do. I feel it with these spirits. Ever since I felt that terrible presence, I wanted to take back what I said, about being the Keeper and helping Levitika. I now sometimes wish it could have been *anyone* but me. But I don't have a choice, it's branded me somehow. It's something I need to do. I'm sorry, but this is something I can't have anyone else brought into. Least of all you. I don't want anything to happen to you, either because of me or because of things beyond our control. In the Wastelands, you helped me keep my chin up when I felt hopeless. This is something I need to do myself, and learn to stand myself."

With his monologue finished, Ashlyn lowered her eyes. She was crying. Markus looked at Esmerelda, who shrugged sadly. She walked over to Ashlyn, and sat beside her rubbing her back. Markus, eventually joined on the opposite side.

"I'm sorry," he said placing his own hand on her back. Thankfully, she didn't turn him away. His fingers touched Esmerelda's, which were cold but he welcomed the support. "I'm sorry, Ashlyn. You too Esmerelda. I didn't know what to say. I didn't know how to explain, or if you guys would understand. I *still* don't completely understand it. This feeling, this fear, I wish you could feel it. Just a small touch of it, and maybe you would see how scared I really am."

Ashlyn

She didn't know how or why, but when Markus said that, Ashlyn *did* feel something.

Her tears stopped immediately. The fear she had felt before seemed to disappear in an instant, like a thundercloud passing overhead. What took it's place, was a sense of dread unlike anything she had ever felt before.

No, she did feel this before. She felt it, when she saw her mother and Kira shot by Veegar's men, and her father screaming at her to run. "Run away and never let me catch you!" he had bellowed. The adrenaline surging through her body as she fled, as the Ninevite Guard gave chase, was the worst feeling she had ever experienced in her life. The grief of losing her family, the betrayal of her father, it was like a heavy weight crushing down on her even when she sought refuge behind some dumpsters that served as her hiding place for the night. The cold, bitter sensation of being all alone and abandoned, nearly broke her.

This feeling she experienced right now, was similar to that. It was as if something else was in the room with them, laughing at her misery and saying to her, 'I got something else in store for you.' It was terrible feeling, and she felt her skin erupt in gooseflesh. She heard Esmerelda give a shudder at the very moment. It only happened when Markus had touched her, and said he wished they could feel his fear.

But now Ashlyn did. It was terrible, a sort of foreshadowing dread that only one reading a horror novel might feel when something very wrong was happening. The turning of a corner expecting some monster to greet you with opened arms.

Without meaning too, Ashlyn shrugged Markus off. Immediately, upon his hand leaving her back, she felt fine. She still felt the fear of him going away, but it was nothing next to the experience she had felt.

Was it the crystals? Something Markus was now capable of? By the look on his face, the pain in it when she shrugged him off, it became clear to Ashlyn in that moment that he had no idea what had happened. He didn't know that she felt what he felt. Minor, maybe, but the threat was still there.

"No," Ashlyn aid shaking her head. "No, Mark, *I* should be sorry. I flipped out on you. I understand, you didn't know how to explain it. You're right, I don't understand." *Not entirely, anyway.* "And instead of being supportive I flipped out. I'm sorry. I believe you. I..." It hurt to say much of anything else. What else *could* she say?

A look, as if seeing if she was just saying that. Markus, probably still thinking she was shrugging him off because of him, was probably overthinking the gesture. Yes, she was mad at him still, but she now understood. She hoped that he could somehow read into that.

He did, and he scooted closer. He opened his arms to offer a hug. For a moment, Ashlyn was afraid that if she touched him again, that horrible feeling would wash over her like an evil baptism. In the end, she gave in to his embrace.

No bad feelings. Only warmth, comfort.

Pulling her into the hug, Markus also reached out and pulled Esmerelda into it as well. Esmerelda was a little cautious as well, but eventually wrapped her arms around Ashlyn as well. He held all three of them together, hoping his reassurance and act of serenity would calm Ashlyn down, and ease Esmerelda's thoughts. This was the real Markus, not whatever entity Ashlyn was feeling.

She knew how dire it was. And she trusted him to make that decision.

Markus

Glad that Ashlyn wasn't completely angry anymore, Markus still felt worried when he felt the girls relax in his arms. This had been a difficult decision, but in the end it seemed that they were slowly accepting it. He wished he could take it all away, give this whole thing to someone else. But he made himself a promise when he first saw the Eldest's Son underneath the city of angels. Now that he was feeling the consequences of such a decision, he knew how deep he was in and believed the spirits when they gave him the sensation of dread whenever he thought of leaving it all behind. He really didn't have much of a choice, and Ashlyn and Esmerelda were both being as supportive as they could now.

But, they needed his support as well, and by God he was going to make sure they understand as best as he could.

"Hey, hey," he told them. "I promise I will be here when we go to Nineveh, and I will come back after I find Abram. I'll bring him *here* if I have to. But I *will* come back to both of you. I promise." He reached down, holding his hand out with his palm up. A simple, yet meaningful gesture. He did the same with the other across Ashlyn's back. He hoped the two girls would see.

Thankfully they did, as he felt their fingers intertwine with his. He squeezed them, and felt them squeeze back. Together they sat there, their arms wrapped around one another, and their hands holding tight to the very things they cared about more than anything else in the world like an team of ancient missionaries praying for safe travels and to come home together before vanishing into the untamed jungles of some third world country.

"I promise," Markus said once again, making sure that he himself understood this promise as he made it.

Zachariah

Zachariah opened his eyes with a gasp. Another nightmare had awakened him from his slumber, not the electric pulse he had endured from scientists observing him from within his tank.

Zachariah. His name was Zachariah.

Zachariah. Zach… Son of… son of…

He could not remember. His mind was a void of darkness and nightmares. He was merely a shell of a man. Empty, hollow. Dark. He was just a child when they took him. He was no longer a child. But he was also not a man. He was… alien. Unknown. He had no complete memory like a computer that needed files manually installed. He could not remember his tribe. He couldn't remember the name of his own village. He could not remember the faces of his family. He could not remember playing as a child. All that he could remember was the horrors he witnessed that day. It was as if his brain was trying to make sure he never forgot the one thing that changed his world forever.

That this wasn't some fantasy dream, that he was trapped in a twisted reality he never asked for.

His worst fears continued to gnaw at him, his anger for The Capitol, and his hatred for the men and women standing before him fuming like adrenaline in his being. All of them were here now, gawking at him. Studying him as if he was some pickled rat in a jar. He slammed his fists against the glass and screamed at them. His cries were muffled by his oxygen mask and the only sound being released was a ripple of bubbles. He looked down at his skin, which had faded to a pale gray color, his fingernails the color of coal.

"He's finished," said the man walking closer to the glass. Dr. Gray placed his own wrinkled hand against the glass, as if trying to communicate some form of kindness towards his prisoner, like how one might consider how the first contact with an alien lifeform would transpire.

But his smile proved otherwise. It was malicious, like a viper promising a rabbit that he wouldn't bite. "We did it. It is a success. It *can* be done without the ritual!"

"Download is still only ninety-eight percent," someone pointed out, but it was beyond Zachariah's perception of sight.

"That's still an 'A.' Look at him! He's completely coherent and the energy levels are off the charts!" Gray was now pointing at a nearby monitor. The screen was bright and hazy, and Zachariah couldn't understand it. "EMF levels are in the red, higher than the crystal by itself! There is no doubt in my mind, he's ready!"

"Should we tell Ghost?" another voice of the assistants asked the scientist.

"No. He is occupied with the siege. We will tell him when we receive word of his victory. Until then, I want to run some simulation tests. I want to make sure he is functioning properly. Give him one more physical; make sure he is indeed healthy and ready for the field."

"Yes, sir."

A thin wave of a dark liquid was then pumped into the water Zachariah now floated in, and as the 'mist' went through the oxygen mask to be filtered, he felt faint and soon knew nothing but black as the people before him faded away. And from the blackness that surrounded him, Zachariah witnessed only the horrors of his dreams.

Within the shadows, of those who destroyed what few memories he had left, Zachariah saw a terrible face burning with glee. Dark red eyes, burning like fiery coals in the depths of a great cave. Was it smiling? There was nothing else to be seen. It only stared, and laughed at his painful and yet few memories.

Lost… lost, and automatic. A machine, really. I feel that pain…

And in that darkness that was almost eternal, Zachariah, 464, screamed.

The Cyborg

Lee

Lee was screwed and he knew it.

After being dragged off the Leviathan and losing his auto-mail foot above the ankle in the process, the injuries he sustained were far from treatable out in the Wastelands. But that did not stop him from trying to trudge it back north for the past four weeks.

His black power-armor was useful only for protecting his mortal body and keeping it warm, for the boosters were destroyed in the fall, and his weapons were sliced off when he was captured. Now he was terribly hurt and was now bound by the wrists between two poles in some pirates' camp. He sat on his knees with his head low, with more of his robotic parts having been stripped away with his weapons for parts. His eyes were closed for he did not want to see all who walked among him, who constantly mocked their cybernetic prisoner. They would gawk, and often kick him like a dog as they did with the other prisoners in the camp.

But he listened, and he learned. He heard the unsettling animals that trudged throughout the camp the Metal Heads used for travel. Ahools, Dragons, and other creatures used for either hunting, fighting, or food. There were times Lee would watch the other prisoners be tossed into what was known as 'the pit', where the biggest Dragon was kept. The only thing you could hear other than the screaming prisoner was the roar, followed by the tearing of flesh and crushing of bone. Lee was sure that soon he would be next if the leader of the Metal Heads, Kizuato, got tired of his interrogation of the Hunter and decide to just be rid of him. After all, he had taken a majority of the parts of Lee's body, the Hunter was pretty much a cripple at this point.

Despite the aroma of meat over a smoky fire and the sound of his rumbling stomach, Lee did not show his hunger to the pirates. Despite the feeling of rocks striking his armor followed by the laughter of children, he did not stir. All he did, was sit tight, ignore his discomfort, and listen. The more he could learn, the more prepared he can be to make his move and escape. He just needs to reattach some Auto-Limbs he can get from the storage tent. After that, he had to find the Eldest and continue his journey to Mt. Nudushi.

At some point, a familiar repetition of footsteps came closer, only to stop what sounded within a yard of Lee. He heard the children scatter like hyenas would at the arrival of a lion. He did not look up however, ignoring his visitor as if he did not notice. The visitor didn't leave though. He was here, and he was waiting. When he realized he wasn't going to get one, he cleared his throat.

"You seem to be enjoying yourself." The voice was male, young and rich in a mocking tone. "You getting hungry yet, boy?"

Lee opened his eyes, seeing the ground before the man's feet. He wouldn't look up yet though. He knew who the visitor was without having to.

"What do you want?"

The Metal Head Second, Raki, chuckled softly. "Oh, come now, is that any way to speak to someone who saved you from the blizzard?"

"What do you want?" Lee asked again. Ever since Raki had brought him to this terrible place, he had been the worst out of all the pirates combined. Whatever the man wanted, he wanted Lee to get it out and over with.

"Hmph. You're no fun. The Captain wants to see you, again."

"Am I gonna get my legs back?"

"Maybe." Another chuckle escaped.

"Then, tell him to go-"

One of the feet swung back and the toes came back with a sharp kick to his head. His right temple flared, and his vision was all starry from the blow. He snarled up at Raki, seeing the man laughing in his leather boots and waving his rifle to and fro in front of the Hunter's face. He was clean-shaven including his head, which was emblazoned in tattoos. He bent down to Lee's face, his breath smelling like rotten meat, his metallic teeth flashing with his nasty grin. "You ain't got a choice, robo-boy. Let's go."

It was then when Lee felt the bonds on his wrists loosen, but immediately were shackled again as two more pirates lifted him up like he weighed nothing and carried him away from the poles, following Raki. They passed the many campfires and tents, as well as the tethered Dragons and Ahools that screeched as children in rags tried to take their food. Small Dragonfly choppers made of rusted parts sat idle past the camp, their vibrating wings down and dormant as if they had never moved at all. In the distance, Xerxes was far south, a mere speck in the distance compared to the mountains to the north and far east.

They passed by some more prisoners, they either tried to poles in a similar matter to Lee, or locked in cages like animals. They were being fed scraps of meat from the bones of whatever the animals ate, and they all appeared scrawny and malnourished. All of them, men, women, and children, all doomed to become slaves as part of the trade, or mere entertainment to these savages.

Soon, they came up the captain's tent, which consisted of black tarps sewn together and held up by steel poles. Over the fold of the entrance rested a human skull painted in red and green colors around the eyes to make the sockets appear like flowers. Lee was thrown inside, and he collapsed at the captain's feet. The interior of the tent was crowded with many boxes which contained many treasures and trinkets found both out in the Wasteland and off of unwary travelers. The skulls of many different kinds of beasts lined the top of a chest in the corner, and many weapons from guns to swords were stacked on a shelf near a makeshift cot. Captain Kizuato sat on the bed studying something in his hands.

He was a thin scarecrow of a man, but his image dared not fool anyone. Captain Kizuato, Great Leader of the Metal Heads, and terror of the Wastelands have killed many men and monsters. Soldiers, women, children, Leaper Dragons, waterbeasts, it didn't matter. Kizuato was born a Wastelander, and grew up to be a dangerous man. He was by no means as popular as the pirates near the Kaiken Isles, however his reputation in the land between the sea and the Razor-Back mountains filled the lands with a sense of terror. No man or woman was safe should they travel in the Northern Wastelands without an army.

Today, he looked haggard. His eyes were sunken, and his skin was unnaturally pale. Something was wrong. Lee could sense it, the thin blood of his father resonating a likeliness of his lost sister. A part of him, he despised because of his inferiority compared to Lameika.

But now she is dead, Lee remembered.

Dead and gone, something said to him like the echo of a whisper. Lee felt a shudder pass over him, and he began to realize what the captain of this band of Metal Heads was inspecting.

When the man acknowledged the paraplegic at his feet, he immediately stood, his black trench coat swaying as he circled his favorite prisoner like a shark. His makeshift rapier gleamed at his side, his revolver in it's holster across his chest. He came fill circle around Lee, and then crouched down. His scowling face was only a few inches from Lee's who remained lying down like a dog would to his master. Kizuato then he held up his hand, revealing a large crystal the size of a small orange, and glowing blood-red and black.

The Captain had been playing with the Eldest. That wasn't good.

"I recognize this," the man said in a cold and eerie voice. "It looks like the same crystal the one known as The Hunter Black carried with him. So pretty, so dark, so... interesting. It is no wonder the man was a deadly adversary when he decided to come to the North."

Lee said nothing, only stared up at Kizuato, who was clicking his own metallic teeth in thought. "It's been getting worse, my friend. I hear voices as I touch it. Whispers almost. It tells me things, not a lot, but quite a bit. My men, think me crazy, except for dear Raki. You failed to tell me who you are when we took this gem off you. It has power, and I want to know what it is. Where did you get this? And how do I learn more from it, young Hunter?"

"I ain't telling you shit," Lee said the only thing moving being his lips.

The Great Leader grinned as he reached underneath his coat and whipped out a small baton. With a flick of his wrist it telescoped out to three times its size. With one press of a button, the baton began to crackle and glow bright blue. Lee stared at it with a familiar sense of dread.

"That exoskeleton may be difficult to cut compared to your legs," Kitzuato said. "But we can still fry you in there." And with that he jabbed at Lee, who tensed up as his muscles clenched and tightened as the electric current flowed through his body. He dared not cry out though. He would not give his captors the satisfaction of hearing his pain.

Kizuato said as he shocked Lee, "I cannot sleep anymore. I hear him! My men think I am going crazy, but I know I am not! There's something special about this gem, what is it? Tell me, so I can unlock the power that Hunter Black had!" He removed the baton from Lee's side, and allowed the Hunter to catch his breath. To rethink his secrecy.

Even in death, that bastard haunts me, Lee thought to himself and said to Kitzuato, "You don't want to know."

Kizuato narrowed his pig-like eyes. Raki stepped in, standing above Lee and stepping on the Hunter as if he were a prized animal that had been hunted and brought down.

"Captain, I hear them too. No one thinks you crazy. The crew, they just don't know what to think. You know how they feel about magical items."

"Nevertheless," Kizuato said with a dismissive wave of his hand. "I want to know. What is this?" He shoved the crystal into Lee's face this time. The crystal barely brushed his cheek, but it felt like a cold hand was caressing him. The Eldest had done this. And now he was taunting Lee.

It is because without Lameika, you are weak.

Lee gritted his teeth. Those thoughts, those words, they had been told to him numerous times as a child and even into his young adult life. But that wasn't true. He was here. Lameika, was dead. Dead, and *buried*.

"I will never tell you," Lee said in a low voice. He would not give in to this man. The Eldest was his, whether the dark spirit wanted him or not. *He* was the one taking Akuta to the Well of Souls, not this lowlife Wastelander. He could feel the Eldest's displeasure, and through the energy in the room, felt Kizuato's rage spark like the fuse of dynamite.

Kizuato responded to Lee's words by shocking the Hunter a second time, and then a third. The desperation in his eyes strained his skull. He wanted answers, to stop whatever was going on in that head of his.

When he finally stopped, he stood straight up and said, "I grow tired of you."

"Captain?" Raki asked somewhere behind Lee.

"Take him back to the post. No food or water. He will feed *my* Leaper Dragon should he not break soon."

The sounds of the screaming prisoners being tossed into the pit came to mind. Lee didn't show his fear though. He couldn't. He had to escape. He had to get the Eldest back.

Patience.

Lee felt his breath get caught in his chest. The Eldest...

If you truly have what it takes, patience.

"But-"

Kizuato kicked Lee again, and told Raki to have him taken away now. "When I'm done with you," he warned Lee. "You will rue the times you have been spiteful." In the shadow of his tent, his strained face looked like one of his human trophies. Skeletal, hungry.

A dead man walking.

Patience, Hunter. A low rumble, before the thunder of a great storm roared. It seemed, that there was a chance.

He wasn't done yet.

<u>Markus</u>

Markus awoke with a start. Cold sweat covered his body like a second layer of skin, and his arms were riddled in gooseflesh. He had a nightmare, that shot through his dream like an arrow tearing through a balloon.

He sat up and rubbed his eyes. He looked over to the window where light shined through the glass. The sun was beginning to rise, making the morning skies turn purple and orange like a streak of mango and berries on a canvas. The clouds looked dense and mountainous, like a magnificent beast coming for them.

The invasion would be taking place in a few hours.

He could have gone back to bed. He could have slept for another hour or two. The clock on the wall said it was just a little past seven. No one would be rallied in the castle for another hour or so, with those in the barracks already preparing for the war. Cannons would be checked and Eagles Wings oiled and fueled. Those in the kitchen downstairs would probably be preparing a good breakfast for everyone, not just those in the castle. There would be a good chance not many of the soldiers would come back alive. Those who were at their homes now getting ready, were probably kissing their family goodbye. The silence that enveloped the castle, sounded like the calm before the storm of war.

With that wonderful thought in mind, Markus got dressed and left his room.

He walked rubbing his head until he made it to the throne room. It was empty and felt eerie standing alone in it. The sun shined through the stained glass windows, letting loose a rainbow of colors arching across the room and shining off of the polished floor and thrones. Markus lingered before the gold and silver throne, and then turned to look out the nearest window. Condensation was on the windows from the rain, and the sun shone brilliantly through them like miniature bulbs of light. Beneath the clouds, Markus saw the faint smudge of Nineveh's walls along with the massive citadel that stood above the walls like a single mountain. Seeing it made Markus anxious and his palms became sweaty. It was almost time.

Once the city was liberated from The Guard and General Veegar, the city would be not only a base for Levitika, but a new hope for the people of Nineveh. A new government would take place, a new order for the kingdom. Maybe when all of this was over, Markus thought he would have a chance to come back. Build robots and other inventions like his father once did. When he was finished with what his father was a part of, maybe, just maybe, he could go home.

But then again, what was home anymore?

"Good morning."

Markus whirled around. He had been so focused that he had not heard or even sensed someone else in the throne room. It was Slagar. Instead of wearing his usual robes, he was wearing a suit of leather, with an ancient Kevlar vest resting over his shoulders. His features usually being hidden, Markus was surprised to see that the man was bald and the little bit of hair on his chin was a full-black goatee. His eyes were blue, unlike the faint flash of red that Markus had seen when they first arrived in Levitika. He nodded another 'hello' and joined Markus by the window.

"Did you sleep well, Markus?"

"Yes, sir," he lied. The nightmares he had tried to rear their ugly heads in his own, but he pushed them away. "You?"

"I've been up all night."

Does he ever sleep? Markus wondered.

After looking out the window for a moment, Slagar returned his attention back to the boy. "I have made you something."

"You did?" Markus asked giving Slagar a peculiar look.

The Court Mage nodded, his black goatee bouncing along with his head. "Something to ease the carry of your … burden." He said the last word almost too carefully. He pulled his hands out from behind and revealed a small backpack of gray color, and straps of iron-rope.

"What's that?"

"It's your Eagle Wings."

Markus' curiosity immediately turned into repulsion. He stared at Slagar angrily, feeling gooseflesh erupt on his skin in borderline disgust. "You've been in my room."

"Only to grab this," Slagar answered without breaking face. "You can check if anything is missing if you wish. But you weren't there for me to ask permission."

Markus felt heat rising to his cheeks but held his tongue. He was glad he wasn't in the room with Slagar alone, but at the same time it felt like an invasion of privacy; even though *he* was the one as a guest in this castle and Slagar was just as much a member of this castle as the royal family.

"Go on, try it on," Slagar handed the bag to Markus, who took it and slung it over his shoulders. He bounced the bag as if unsure about something.

"It's lighter," Markus said.

Slagar nodded. "Yes, I've swapped your original wings- a good duplication with the combination of Bronze-Alloy and steel I might add. This is made of Everglade, a special mineral we make here in Levitika for our own wings. When mixed with Bronze-Alloy and copper, the minerals dissolve away leaving only the reinforced skeleton within. It is what we used to make our Guardians and our own Eagles Wings. Yours is now not only lighter, but faster, and more maneuverable. And, easier to deploy. Go ahead and flick that little switch on your left strap. Yes, that one."

Markus did so and the wings extended, both being longer than his own height, and as Slagar had said *far* more lighter. What surprised Markus was a small extendable nerve-connector that popped out between the joints of the wings and stuck to the base of Markus' skull. His first thought was panic and the wings stretched out. Wanting them to move back, they did so. They moved without lag and without a second to process. This pair was far more advanced than his pair before. Markus flicked the switch again and the wings and nerve-connector retracted and folded until they were once again back in the backpack. The boosters remained as they were for a moment but soon they too slid into the slots on either side of the pack.

"That's pretty cool," Markus admitted satisfyingly. He was a little sad still that his father's Wings were altered in a way he hadn't made them, but there was no denying that this pair had potential.

"I'm glad you like them," Slagar said his face still stiff and showing anything but gladness. "There is one more feature I would like to let you know." He then handed Markus a small slip of paper with some writing on it.

"What's this?"

"It's a list of keywords for an extra measure in aerial combat. If you say, 'Fire,' the joints in the wings will open up a small nine-millimeter turret for a sweeping attack. Now this will only work when the neurological clamp is connected to your brain so that it can adjust and avoid shooting you in the back of the head."

Markus didn't want to know what caused them to add such a precaution. He took the sheet of paper and read over it. "And the others here?"

"Emergency is self-explanatory."

Markus nodded. There were three more words on the sheet. 'Return,' which had to mean the Wings can find him due to Slagar calibrating it to listen to only his specific vocal pattern. The blood sample the nerve-connector takes helps to track him as well. There was also a 'Self-Destruct' option, but Markus didn't feel the need for that. Finally, there was 'Reserve' which releases a small canister of reserve fuel should the boosters run dry.

"This is pretty cool," Markus said again while pocketing the sheet of paper. He was sure he could remember all of that but wanted to hold onto it nonetheless.

"I do have one more thing for you," Slagar said.

"Oh?"

Slagar motioned with his head, communicating to Markus to follow. They passed Queen Elizabetha's throne and took a left down another hall, where a steel door sat. Slagar placed his palm over the lock panel, and the door opened, revealing a small laboratory. Creatures and body parts sat in jars of goop like pickled rats, tables were full of machinery parts, and many vials of numerous liquids lined the shelves more than the books. Markus marveled at the room as he followed Slagar deeper within until they came across a workbench. Slagar removed the item from it, and presented them to Markus.

It was a pair of leather gauntlets with an electric-band interior and a couple of slots that appeared to have a locking clamp around each. The fingertips were cut off to let the tips of Markus' fingers slip through once he tried them on. They felt nice, flexible and sturdy and he noticed that on the knuckles were iron plates like a pair of brass knuckles. The bracers went down to almost his elbow. This here is where the slots were located.

"I figured it must be difficult having to reach into your pockets to use the crystals," Slagar said while Markus marveled.

Markus said it wasn't too much of a hassle.

"Well, these gauntlets will not only hold and keep your crystals under lock and key, but the electric currents produced in the straps are like currents that can transfer energy between you and the crystals. It's the same principle that we use for the First

Crystal to power the kingdom. That way you can have contact with them, without necessarily having to touch them."

"How did you get them to work?" Markus asked.

"It was a small project while The Eldest was here. Since The Eldest used a robotic suit to use the crystals power, why not make a small piece of armor a *carrier* could wear? It makes carrying them easier, and you are still able to use magic without necessarily thinking about it."

"That's incredible."

"May I?" Slagar asked holding out his hand.

Markus reached into his pockets to hand the mage the crystals, but all of a sudden, the crystals felt much heavier. He looked at his red and blue gems questionably as he doubled his efforts. It was as if his hands were reluctant to let them go, but eventually he managed to release them into the wizard's hand. Upon dropping them into Slagar's palms, Markus got a sense of dread coming from the crystals and he immediately wanted them back but decided to not say anything.

He must have worn his thoughts on his sleeve for Slagar was smiling at him now.

"I see you have grown accustomed to them," he said almost shamefully. He pressed the crystals into the gauntlets empty slots on Markus' bracers, and by pinching two pressure points on the grips the crystals were soon locked in place. Markus marveled at the blue crystal in his left gauntlet, and the red on the right. Markus immediately felt reassurance wash over him like a bath of warm water. He felt like he was back in contact with Abner and Fethawit even though he wasn't holding them in his hands.

"I have to admit, I felt the influence as well," Slagar said crossing his arms and watching Markus marvel at the gauntlets again. "They are by no means as dangerous as The Eldest, but they have grown to become a part of you, and in a way, tried to force me to drop them. The crystals are indeed dangerous artifacts."

"It's the spirits within," Markus found himself answering as if he were possessed and his words weren't his own. But then again, he felt a little truth come out of his mouth as well. "They... they don't seem to like you."

"Or anyone else I gather," Slagar said without the slightest hint of offence. "I mean, they chose *you* after all. The Keeper and all that. Who am I to think otherwise?"

He did in the beginning. Whether that was Abner or Fethawit, Markus couldn't tell for certain. It was the first time he heard them spoke in a while.

He realized he might have looked a little too surprised, for Slagar was watching him with those keen red eyes. Red eyes, like a hungry viper. He cleared his throat and said, "Thank you, sir. Seriously."

"Of course," Slagar said with equal amount of caution. "I only hope that it will help you with your mission today."

Feeling the need to say something else, Markus asked, "Do you think we are ready? To let the world know we are here, I mean."

Slagar thought about this for a moment while staring at a glass jar where a human hand rested and looked to be being feasted on by little fishes. It was gross, but Markus focused on the mage himself so he wouldn't have to look.

When Slagar finally answered, he sounded genuinely optimistic, but careful nonetheless. "I know not what the outcome will be. Only that the people of Levitika are ready for war, our warriors ready to fight. And the people of Nineveh deserve purification from the vile creatures who have it by the neck. And I believe you *might* be ready, despite all that you have personally been through."

"Thank you. I think..." It sure didn't sound like a compliment but Markus wasn't going to question it.

Slagar then gave Markus what he thought was the stink eye. With Slagar it was hard to tell what kind of mood exactly the old man was in. "Make no mistake, boy, I still believe you are dangerous. Maybe more-so than Black ever was. You know that, don't you? My feelings betray me whenever you use those blasted things. I'm sure they whisper tantalizing thoughts in your head about me. But I will not deny that I still think it was a *mistake* to have you brought here. But if the queen is convinced of your valor, then I shall carry through my orders and assist the people of this city, and this country to the best of my ability. For the future."

"Any way I can prove you wrong?" Markus said only half-meaning what he said. For he too still had his doubts and questioned the prophecy and his destiny himself. But he did not dare let Slagar know. All the mage needed to know, was his own distaste for the man.

Slagar didn't seem to care either way for the rest of this conversation. "Let us capture Nineveh first, and *then* we will talk."

The Beginning

<u>Markus</u>

Markus strapped on some leather armor underneath a light jacket and cargo pants. His boots, which he had received from the armory as well were black and military-style. As he got dressed in the Throne Room, across the pews Ashlyn and Esmerelda were speaking to Slagar and The Queen, who finally woke up.

As she spoke, The Queen was helping Ashlyn into her own leather armor, this one of a black color. "When you get inside, tell us the situation and we will guide you to where the stations are."

"Got it," Ashlyn said tying her hair into a pony-tail.

Markus joined the group, placing his new staff into the scabbard across his back above his backpack. "We will get there faster with the new Eagles Wings Slagar made."

"Indeed," Slagar said. "Remember, the AA guns will shoot you down once you pop up on their radar, so stay low and land as soon as you reach the wall."

"Will do," Markus said looking to Ashlyn who was all set for war. "Ready?"

"Ready."

That was when Grim entered the throne room, in one hand a photon-rifle and pistol, the other carried Blacks longsword. When he came up to the group he handed the guns and holsters to Ashlyn, who strapped them onto her waist and back. To Markus, he handed him the sword.

"I don't think I should." Markus said taking one step back. "I can use my staff."

"Markus," Grim insisted. "That staff ain't gonna save you in a fight against a gunsword."

"Then I'll avoid the swords," Markus retorted. "That blade belongs to Black, I... I don't think I should carry it."

"Well at least keep it on you?" Grim asked his eyes almost pleading. "You don't have to use it but keep it just in case?"

"It might slow me down."

"You're supposed to take it slow anyway."

"Markus," The Queen said stepping in. Since no one in the castle was up she was now wearing simple clothing as opposed to her normal dresses as well as her crown. She looked almost like a mother who rolled out of bed. "Grim means well. And I'm sure Black would insist that you take that as well."

Markus looked at her, then to Grim, and then finally the sword. He then reached over his back and removed his staff which he retracted until it was only a foot long. He then exchanged with Grim for the sword, which he then sheathed across his back.

"Fine," he said when the scabbard was finished adjusting itself to fit the blade.

"Thank you," his teacher said relieved. "Maybe your buddy Abram can teach you more about how to use it with your magic eh?" He winked.

Markus looked to Elizabetha who shrugged. "He deserved to know," she explained.

"Come," Slagar said walking past the group towards the outer balcony. "It is time the two made their way to the city."

The others immediately followed. Ashlyn and Esmerelda walked along side Markus who kept his distance between Slagar and The Queen. He did not want to talk, he did not want to think. He only wanted to get this over with.

When they reached the upper balcony, a soldier was standing guard near the edge. When he saw them he ran over to them. "Milady," he said bowing to The Queen. "Scopes have found a small problem."

"What is it?"

"Come," he led the group over to the Communications Station by the railing of the balcony. It looked like a simple computer with a radio antennae shooting out of the main generator block. "Control, send the image to Station Two-seventeen."

"Roger. Coming up on screen now."

Upon the screen an image showed up. Markus recognized the scarred surface of the northern wall of the city, but what was *in* the wall was what surprised him. It looked like a tank, but it looked like if it was standing straight up it could easily be taller than the walls. Over a mile of unknown black steel with many treads along the bottom. Clamp-like anchors secured it into the ground, and at the front was a large drill. And the drill itself appeared to have pierced through the thick walls. Something attacked the city already.

"Take a look at that," Grim said pointing to the top of the machine. It was hard to see at first, but as Markus peered at it, it soon became clear that there was a symbol painted on top of the machine. A black bat with its wings fully extended, screeching into the air and in its claws it was carrying a sword and a pistol.

Grim declared, "That's the emblem of Xerxes."

"They finally made it," Markus said. "They must have found out The Baron had left the city and decided to attack."

"There appears to be no movement," the soldier explained mostly to The Queen than anyone else. "Not from the drill itself nor around it. Not even along the walls. There seems to be movement in the castle, and in the guard towers so the defenses are still up."

"So what do we do?" Slagar asked The Queen.

"We stick to the plan," she turned to Markus and Ashlyn. "You two continue as plan, survey the city so we can assess the situation. We will move forward with the plan once we figure out what that drill is doing there."

"Alright," Ashlyn said while Markus nodded.

"Make sure they get their earpieces in." She then said to Slagar. "I want to hear what they hear, and see what they see."

Slagar responded by holding out his hand where two distinctive looking ear plugs resided. "Got them right here, your worship."

"Perfect." She then turned back to the youths. "Are you two ready?"

"Yes ma'am," Markus nodded.

"Good. Report to the port wall for deportation."

"Will do."

"Slagar, Grim, move to your positions." Elizabetha said walking away from the youths including her daughter. "I want you both ready to launch the attack when the children are ready."

When they became out of earshot, Esmerelda turned to her friends. She hugged Ashlyn, and told her to be careful. Ashlyn said she would and then turned to Markus who nodded. "Markus?" Esmerelda said.

"Yeah?"

"Can I talk to you, before you go?"

"Sure."

Esmerelda looked at Ashlyn, almost pleadingly, who seemed to have gotten the message and excused herself from the two. She waited by the main doors to the hallways as Esmerelda turned back to Markus. "Are you still thinking of leaving, after all of this I mean?"

"I have to," Markus said. He had hoped this discussion was over, at least until the battle for Nineveh was over. "Who else is better to teach me how to use these things?" He held up his arms for Esmerelda to see the crystals. "I need to be at my best if I'm going to be of any help here."

"You are a big help Markus," Esmerelda said folding her hands together. "Just by being here, that's helpful enough. But I understand. I just want you to be safe and careful."

"Hey come on," Markus offered a small smile. "We'll see each other after all of this. I ain't leaving until I am ready."

"Okay good, you need to say goodbye to me." She said smiling back.

"I promise."

"Okay," She shuffled her feet and then stepped in for a hug. Markus hugged her back, letting her rest her head against his chest. "Be careful. Both of you. I..."

"I will." Markus said pulling away. "I promise. We will make it back."

"You better." She said with a fox-grin.

With that Markus turned and walked away, leaving Esmerelda alone in the throne room. When he met Ashlyn at the door Markus and she waved at Esmerelda as they closed the door behind them, shutting both her and the glamorous room out of sight. And while they descended down the dark hall lit with the eerie flames of the torches that spewed green fire, Esmerelda was left alone with her thoughts, and her prayers.

<u>Ashlyn</u>

Ashlyn was quiet as she and Markus made another turn and went through another set of doors which led to a small bridge that crossed over to one of the city walls. As they walked along the wall to the port side, Ashlyn would steal quick glances at Markus who appeared nervous, but at the same time stern. As if he had something on his mind.

It was incredible, how much he held in when he was out of his room. He acted more confident, braver than he truly was. He was always there for his friends, in fact when Ashlyn had her own nightmares Mark was there to comfort her, to let her know it was going to be okay. In turn she did her best for him when the doors were shut and the lights were out. Because in the solitude, away from everyone out here in Levitika, he would become broken, sad, and vulnerable. The wounds he had sustained within Nineveh were just as horrible as her own, but Ashlyn had him, and he had her. She had always wanted a brother, and another sister. And here with Markus and Esmerelda, they were all the family she needed.

But was she enough for them? For Markus? He was like a brother to her... Maybe... No that can't be. Not that. She didn't want to yet somehow...

"What is on your mind?" she said breaking the spell her own mind was under.

Markus remained silent, his stern demeanor softened however as he thought of what to say to her. She noticed that the scratch he received on the side of his chin was healing up into a scab. That would soon become a nice scar. Where he got it, he didn't know, nor did Ashlyn ask him. That battle against The Leviathan, Ovid and that horrible witch was enough to give anyone bad recall.

He had said something then, and Ashlyn mentally kicked herself for not listening. "I'm sorry, what was that?" She asked.

"I don't know," he said. "It seems sad, going back to that place."

She nodded. "I hope everyone is okay."

"Me too. I don't like it that Xerxes attacked again."

"Me neither. Guess we'll see what happened once we get inside."

"Guess so."

They walked the rest of the way in silence. They then came to another soldier, who stood beside two small pods that looked like giant black bullets. They were at least six feet in length, and about a yard wide. He nodded when he saw the two coming forward as he placed his hand upon a console between the two pods. "Glad you two made it. Appreciate what you are doing for this cause."

"Thank you, sir," Ashlyn said.

"What's your name?" Markus asked.

"Jacob," the man said. Markus saw that Ashlyn was admiring the rifle at the man's hip so he picked up the conversation.

"Pleasure to meet you, Jacob."

"Likewise. I was one of the men in the battle last week. Anyways, I'm the one who's gonna drop you."

"Come again?" Markus said not sure if he heard the man correctly.

"I'm the one who is supposed to drop you down to the surface using the Bullet-Pods."

"I keep hearing that word, drop."

"Yes." The soldier acted like that was completely normal and did not understand Markus' concern.

"Like *drop* drop? As in you let go, and gravity pulls us to the ground at break-neck speeds."

"Yes. Is that a problem?"

"I'm a little concerned about flattening into a pancake once we hit the ground."

Jacob started to laugh, leaving Markus and Ashlyn stunned at this. When the man calmed down he wiped a tear away. "You've never used one of these? I thought they were popular in Nineveh?"

"Yeah, apparently we don't like jumping off of buildings," Markus said sarcastically.

The soldier didn't seem to catch onto that. "Well what these do is compress the impact once you land, your pod will shoot through the ground and using pressurized plating as well as air propulsion I will guide you back up and angle you so that you stop above ground right at the foot of the wall."

"Oh," Markus said still seeming unconvinced. "Great."

"Don't worry it is perfectly safe. We've used them before."

"Okay."

"C'mon," Ashlyn said stepping towards one of the pods and placing her hand on the smooth surface. "It could be fun."

"Yeah, what's more fun than falling to possible death?" Markus said taking the other pod opposite of her.

The side of the pod slid open, revealing a leather seat with many seat belts and straps. She stepped inside and sat down, buckling the ten buckles around her body and shoulders. She looked around the opening to look at Markus who was all strapped in himself. He smiled at her, that cute smile of his and gave her a thumbs up. She did likewise as Jacob placed both hands on the pods.

"Okay listen up: Once you get there the pods will be useless, just hit the red button above you to get out. Don't hit it until you are sure the pods stopped moving."

"Got it."

"Turn on your headsets, make sure they work."

They did so and then Markus spoke. "Check, check?"

"Received," Slagar's voice said into their ears.

"Check," Ashlyn said.

"Gotcha."

"You got eyes Slagar?" Jacob said into his earpiece.

"I see you."

"Alright we are all set." Jacob looked at the youths again. "Good luck, guys."

"You too."

Jacob nodded as he hit something, closing both doors and leaving them in darkness except for the red button that blinked red above them.

"Man it's dark," Ashlyn said to herself. She then felt the pod moving, as if they were being shoved off the side of the wall.

And then she felt as if she was floating, and know they were freefalling head-first towards the ground. The feeling was unnatural and scary, and made Ashlyn screamed. She hated the dark more than anything, but being in the dark while falling head-first to the ground? And she sounded *so* confident before.

Not anymore.

She then felt the impact of the pod hitting the dirt and she bounced around in her seat but the straps kept her secure. She felt a change of pitch and then a minute later of constant movement they slowed to a stop. Ashlyn panted, catching her breath to recover from her violent screams. She cleared her throat, and convinced it was safe, hit the red button, releasing the entrance panel and letting in light. Beautiful, wonderful light.

When her eyes adjusted, she was able to see where she was. The pod was indeed right next to the wall, for it now towered directly over her. To her right was The Wastelands, where not even a week or two ago she had crossed Mark and his sister Ruth. The memory made her sad. The sun was now over the Razor Back Mountains to the East, and was shining over the once-frozen plains which were now covered in melting snow. It was still cold, but not nearly as bad as their last trip.

She looked behind her to see the other pod, empty. She peeked over the pod to see Markus with his hand against the wall, his back was arched and he was making choking sounds. When he turned around, his eyes were blood-shot red. "Not natural. Never, *ever* doing that again."

"Agreed," Ashlyn said stepping out and rotating her shoulders. "Looks like we made it."

"Yeah," Markus was looking up the walls towards one of the towers. "Think they noticed?"

"I don't think so."

"Good," he then turned to Ashlyn. "Brings back memories don't it?"

"Yeah,"

"Let's go find that tunnel."

Ashlyn reached to her left and grabbed her pistol. She tossed it to Markus who caught it with one hand. "Just in case," she said.

He didn't argue.

<u>Markus</u>

After walking for a bit, they had finally found one of the release tunnels. The grate was rusted and covered in sludge that oozed out in thick ropey moss that looked like snot.

"This is nasty," Markus decided as he lifted up the grate for Ashlyn to climb in first.

"Indeed," Ashlyn said wiping her hands on her pants. She pulled her rifle up as Markus climbed in and gently closed the grate behind him. He too pulled out the pistol he was given, and in the other hand he flicked on a flashlight. The beam of light shined down what seemed like a never-ending tunnel of darkness and slime. It was if looking down the throat of some bio-mechanical monster.

"Ready?" Ashlyn asked him.

"Let's do it."

And together they began to trudge down the pipe.

It indeed felt like the tunnels were never ending. For what felt like miles they trudged through the sludge, the only sound they made between one another was the squishes beneath their feet. Other than that neither of them breathed a word to one another, but both thinking of the same two things. One, that hopefully nothing was going to be flushed through here anytime soon. And two, their mission after escaping this drainpipe. Ashlyn would keep her rifle close and ready in case something came tearing down the tunnel, while Markus tried to read for any life essence in the tunnel as well as the streets above. All he got was the presence of rats which scurried among the scum long before the teens ever got near them.

After an hour of silence Markus finally spoke. "Ground must be thicker than I thought."

"What makes you say that?" Ashlyn said pointing at a nearby man-hole ladder up ahead.

"We've been walking for a long time and the only thing I've seen that's life is you, the rats, and the occasional footstep up top. It's quiet, I mean."

"Incredible that you can see *that* much."

After some time they finally came across a maintenance ladder which was bolted to the side of the pipe and went up through a circular hole similar to that of the pipe itself. Shining his flashlight up it, Markus could see the hatch high above their heads. He allowed Ashlyn to go first who shouldered her rifle and climbed up the rusted runes. He followed close behind.

Ashlyn pushed up on the manhole and peeked out. She gasped and came back down. "What?" Markus asked.

"Mark, look."

She scooted aside so Markus could pass her, the two of them crammed together at the top of the ladder. He pushed up on the cover and peeked outside. And what he saw, was the worst he had ever seen Nineveh.

Shacks were burning of left vacant with the doors hanging off of hinges and windows smashed. The smell of smoke and gunpowder was strong in Markus' nose, as well as the taste of sulfur and copper on his tongue. The wires that were strewn around the city would always have a body or two hanging by it, but it looked like the whole district hung from those now. Men, women and children hung by the neck staring down the streets with bulging dead eyes. Markus in his state of blissful shock, came out of the manhole despite Ashlyn hissing at him to come back and he stood out in the street staring up at the many dead above him. He thought he smelled meat cooking, and realized that some bodies were burning in the houses that were alit. His lips trembling in both rage and horror, Markus finally doubled over and vomited there in the street. Ashlyn, who was just coming out of the manhole saw the act, reacted in a similar fashion.

"Good God…" Markus said after catching his breath and wiping his mouth with the back of his hand. "How could they do this?"

"Markus, look." Ashlyn was looking between one of the buildings and when Markus joined her, he saw.

"Xerxan soldier," Markus said. The corpse in question looked to have been shot multiple times, splotches of burnt marks had turned the black beetle-like armor into ash, the side of the helmet in particular having been sheared away and exposing a blackened skull.

"Where are the rest? Where are The Guards?"

"I hear no gun shots," Markus answered deeply troubled. "They might have barricaded themselves in the castle, it's the most defended building within the walls."

"Do you think they took some of the others in? Protected them?"

Markus frowned. "I wouldn't bet on it. The Guard didn't care much for the safety of their citizens." He was looking at the bodies hanging on the power lines, all hung together shoulder to shoulder like pigs ready to be butchered.

"What do we do now?" asked Ashlyn, doing everything in her power not to look up.

Markus pressed a finger against his earpiece. "Elizabetha, are you seeing this?" He knew the earpiece had to have some sort of camera on it, he didn't believe Levitika wouldn't have one in order to truly see what was going on.

"Yes…" the Queen responded the static unable to hinder the pain in her voice. "This is horrible."

"The guns are still operational, it is safe to assume the city is still heavily armed. Me and Ashlyn are going to have a look around on our way to the main control station."

"Do what you must, and please hurry. If there are any survivors, we need to know. When the guns are down we'll storm in and take the place back."

"Roger," Markus then terminated the connection.

Ashlyn had been watching him. "So we still going with the plan?"

"Yes, but we need to be careful. If we see any survivors, we free them, any Guard? We stop them."

"And the Xerxan soldiers?"

"The same."

They moved on, eventually making their way to the center of the city in search for Central Control, using the buildings and garbage dumpsters for cover. Every once in a while they would pass by a patrol of soldiers wearing pure black power armor, all bearing the emblem of Xerxes on their chest in a brilliant shade of blood-red. Small drones and tanks would travel down the streets, searching for anything still alive in the city. Once Markus and Ashlyn saw a wild dog running across the street, and was soon torn to a thousand pieces as the tank mini-guns blew it away in a flash of red. Markus had to pull Ashlyn away from the horrible sight. As they got closer they soon saw the tip of the drill that had pierced the wall. The massive thing was easily fifty feet in diameter, and a large slot-like door was in the front. The drill bit in question had penetrated much further, destroying everything in it's way as easily as it did the wall.

"It's like a syringe," Markus realized. "The drill passes below the radar of the AA guns, and once it breaks through the wall it lets in all the soldiers and drones." He shook his head in bewilderment. "That's incredible."

"One way to put it," Ashlyn pointed out her back against the wall of the building as she peeked around the corner. "Another patrol coming by. No Guard still, ju- Wait!" she hissed, her eyes wide. "Markus look!"

Markus peeked and saw what she meant. Between two Xerxan soldiers was a group of civilians, all wearing their normal rags that were now blackened with soot. They were chained together and were being led towards the drill. Their faces were down and sullen, and the Xerxan soldiers constantly barked at them to keep walking.

"They're taking prisoners," Markus said with a look of anger. "They are taking the survivors into the drill."

"What do we do? Stop them?"

"No, there is way too much activity near the drill. Look at all those photon-cannons, we'll be blown apart. Let's get to that building and let the others in, we need to get more help before we try anything. A drill that big can't make a quick getaway anyway." He clicked on his earpiece again. "Elizabetha."

"Go ahead."

"Some men are taking some prisoners on the giant drill, they are taking whatever survivors they can and killing those who won't go. As soon as the guns are down, we need to send some men to the drill, we cannot let that thing get away."

"Of course. Is there any news on The Guard?"

"No."

Slagar's voice then spoke into Markus' ear. "As soon as you shut down the guns head towards the castle and tell me what you see."

"Yes sir,"

"Be careful."

Markus turned his piece off. "Oh we will."

"Alright," Ashlyn nodded. "Let's go."

She took lead across the street, her gun on a swivel as they crossed. They continued down passing through numerous buildings and shattered alleyways. What made Markus upset was the debris scattered throughout the homes. Broken toys, shattered frames, books that have been burned, and many more. This place, this city, it was never really a good place to live. But seeing it now, seeing what Xerxes was capable of, it made the scene much more grim.

It soon came to pass when they passed by The Drunken Badrat. There were some people tied up and loaded in trucks in front of the now smoldering bar, the picture of the large rat a splintered mess with only the mug still intact. Amongst the group was a pair Markus knew all too well. Jim the bartender and his daughter Kaltrina, who were bound and gagged with chains and leather. Their clothes were covered in dirt and blood, and Jim's nose was bleeding over his mustache. Kaltrina's shirt was torn and ragged, and even as she sat hunched close to her father, one Xerxe soldier was laughing and pulling back at her black hair.

"We need to save them," Markus said starting forward until Ashlyn stopped him.

"Wait, look."

Someone was making a run for it. Two people, actually. The guy head-butted one of the soldiers so that his girlfriend could run. She had brown hair that billowed behind her as she tried to sprint away. A slightly robotic voice cried out "Fire!"

The woman was soon blown forward as photon lasers burned into her back, killing her instantly. She smacked onto the road with a sickening *crack*.

"You bastards!" the man cried out punching at the man, only to be shoved down and shot in the head with a nine-banger. The shooter was obviously the leader by the looks of his power armor which was black as well as the face-plate which flickered blue and red. Markus figured it was a helmet that can you can see functions and hydraulics against the glass without sacrificing vision. Markus could almost see the lights form a face that was human, probably more like an android. Two sword scabbards stuck up from behind his back, and at his hips he carried pairs of Uzis and laser pistols. He shoved the nine-banger into its holster and turned to the guard who shot the girl.

"What have I said about losing the prisoners?" the leader was demanding.

"To shoot them on sight if they escape. Sir."

"Right, and before that?"

The soldier appeared to gulp in hesitation. "Don't give them the opportunity."

"Exactly. You followed the second order well so I will forgive your first mistake. But I will not be so lenient next time." The warrior then turned to the rest of his forces. "Don't let the prisoners escape, I want as many alive as possible. The Guard are still putting up a fight at the palace, so once we get the trucks loaded up, move out. Chances are we will have to blow them out."

A chorus of 'yes sirs' then followed and the warrior hopped into a Hellhound cruiser which hovered up into the air just above the rooftops of nearby buildings and then took off towards the direction of the palace.

"That's the station," Ashlyn said pointing to a small gray building a block away from where the prisoner truck sat. "If we can get passed them, we can shut down the AA guns."

"Let's do it," Markus said looking up and around. He knew they could not make it across the street without being seen, and going back was not an option. They had to find a different route.

"I have an idea." He grabbed the nearest drainage pipe against one of the buildings and planting his feet against the wall, began to climb. "Follow me."

He leapt across another gap between the buildings and froze after rolling to muffle the fall. He peeked over the ledge to see the men still occupied with corralling prisoners into the trucks. More drones and tanks were heading towards the palace where muffled booms and cracks could be heard.

Markus signaled Ashlyn to jump, and when she did so, she crawled over beside him. "Not a bad idea. But what if a drone or Hellhound comes by?"

"Play dead," Markus said simply.

Ashlyn looked at him like he was crazy.

"No, really," he insisted. "There are plenty of bodies hanging or laying in the street, if we see one we stay still, maybe they won't notice."

"We don't particularly dress like a civilian."

"I doubt they're gonna care"

"Such a wonderful plan," Ashlyn muttered sarcastically as Markus began to move on to the edge at the end. The next building was the gray building, Central Control. He contacted The Queen and Slagar. "Guys,"

"Go ahead," said Slagar's voice.

"We're at Central Control, ready to shut it down. Get everyone into position. After we get this done, Ashlyn and I are going to save the prisoners."

"Negative, stay out of sight, our Angels will swoop in and get them while the Caterpillars scale the walls. We need you two safe."

"Can't do that, they'll kill the hostages if they have to respond to another call."

"Can't be done, Markus. This is an order: You need to-"

"Sorry, another call coming in." And Markus terminated the call and for good measure, he turned off the headpiece altogether.

"You're not serious?" asked Ashlyn.

"I'm dead serious." And without waiting for a retort, Markus leapt and landed upon the roof of the Control station.

There was a roof hatch to which he pulled open as Ashlyn appeared next to him.

"Gimme a hand," he said.

She grabbed his hand and he leaned into the hatch, taking a peek inside. Two soldiers- not guards- were at the control panel, checking the AA cameras as well as the security cameras around the palace. There was no sound but Markus saw the flashes of machine and photon gun fire. Explosions appeared around the building and many Xerxan soldiers fell. The Guard were indeed in the palace, making a final stand. But not for long.

With Ashlyn's help, he was then lowered feet-first into the station, directly behind the men who turned dials and clicked different switches as they studied upon the cameras.

"Looks like we got a bunch of birds coming," one said.

"Birds?" said the second. "Those don't look like birds, too big."

"Or Ahools, I can't tell. Wait, they are all like golden or something, big things."

"Least we get a better show here than out there."

"True," Markus said before striking one of the soldiers at the base of the skull with the hilt of his sword- Black's sword which he had managed to unsheathe as easily and soundlessly as an ancient samurai.

When the other soldier spun around to intercept him Markus punched him in the center of the forehead. A normal person would have either broken his hand or merely surprised their victim. However, with the energy from the crystals flowing through him Markus' punch was enough to not only knock the man out cold, but send him flying across the consoles only to crash into the generator in a shower of sparks. Ashlyn flew past Markus and he watched the main doors as she got to work on the consoles.

"Alright," she took out a small flash drive-like object and plugged it into the computer. She then stepped back with her rifle ready as the downloading process began. It took a little under five minutes of anxious waiting.

During that time Markus' eyes never left the main door, if anyone was going to come in he would be ready. Until then, the silence was nearly killing him until a sharp *ding* sound came from the console. "Done," he heard Ashlyn said as she fired her rifle at the console, destroying it completely. "AA guns are down," She called into her earpiece.

"Beginning decent now," said Jacob's voice.

"Caterpillars launched… look at em' go- Scaling the walls now," another voice that sounded like Grim spoke. "Some foot soldier fire's coming down but we got this."

"Good work you two," Elizabetha said to Ashlyn and Markus who had turned his earpiece back on to hear all this.

"Yes, grand," said Slagar, "Now, stay hidden until The Angels can alleviate the amount of-"

"Negative we're going after the prisoners," Markus spoke out.

"Oh, look who's back. The Angles *will take care* of it, Markus, it is too dangerous for just you two."

"Doesn't matter, if that truck looks like it's leaving, I'm attacking."

"Dammit," Slagar hissed. Nevertheless he added just as suddenly, "Jacob, send half the team to the drill and disable it, take care of the occupied soldiers around it, just get their attention. You and the remaining, home in on Markus' location and help with the prisoners."

"Roger that," Jacob answered.

"Let's go," Markus said to Ashlyn.

She nodded, but before she could say anything there was a hollow banging against the main doors of the building. "Hey!" a voice called in. "You okay in there? We heard an explosion?"

"Uh, yeah just fine," Markus said in a deep but turned falsetto voice.

"You okay Tor?"

"Fine, we're fine in here."

A pause, and then, "Jess?"

Ashlyn immediately took initiative and said in a deeper voice, "What?"

Another pause, and Markus could hear his heartrate racing now. Then, "Alright, quit screwing around I know when you are lying. Open the door."

"Um…" Markus pointed up to the ceiling towards the hatch. "Just a minute." He sheathed his sword and crouched, cupping his hands for Ashlyn to jump in. She placed one foot in, using his head for support, and then stepping on his shoulder with the other hoisted herself up to reach the hatch. When she got there, she pulled herself up.

"What the- Tor, I'm not kidding. Jess! Open the door!"

"One second!" Markus said jumping up to reach Ashlyn's hand and using his feet to help her, he was soon pulled up just as the main doors were busted down. He closed the hatch just before anyone could get in and together he and Ashlyn ran off the roof and jumped into the alleyway between the two buildings and began to make their way back around.

It was not long before the city's Central Control alarm sounded, wailing in and out in a shrieking bray.

Ghost

Ghost stood among his army of soldiers and tanks as they fired upon the main doors of the palace. General Veegar and his dogs had gone into hiding, abandoning most of the artillery being used along the walls save for a few brave fools. Bad enough most of the Ninevite Guard had abandoned their people to their enemies, worse still that they dared to still defy the Xerxan Army while hiding inside like the rats they were.

"Keep firing men, we'll drive the rats out of their nest!" His hand immediately went to his chest, where the city emblem sat over his heart. He pushed against it, as if to make sure it was still closed and secure. He could not afford to lose it, he was confident in himself about everything he did, especially for the good of Xerxes, but what he kept against his heart he could never afford to lose. His power suit was the most powerful ever created, with a few mild modifications of his own, he had no doubt that the suit would not only protect and strengthen the man inside, but the precious cargo *with* him.

Turning his attention away from his chest, he called through the main radio. "Quick-shot, you got eyes on him?"

"Justa coupla cowards behind the glass. Can't seem to find the one we's lookin' for."

Ghost sighed. The sniper would have taken the shot if he saw Veegar. The fact that he had not spotted the failure of a leader concerned him. "Keep an eye out."

Through his visor but also through his own eyes Ghost could see the life essence of all who were in the building. Men, women and androids all cowering behind support beams and walls trying to fire back at the unrelenting force of his army. Amongst the flickering figures of white, he could not identify which one was Veegar, if Veegar was still alive anyway. If that was the case The Guard were no longer fighting for their district, but only to survive. But survival was no longer an option for them.

Before Ghost could say anything, the city's alarm suddenly began to blare. He turned towards the wall where the drill had entered, and through his telescopic visors he saw what was coming before his men even did. Men with giant golden wings descending upon those at the walls and entering the city, attacking his men and drones.

"Sir!" one of his soldiers called to him. "What are those? Ahools?"

"Impossible..." Ghost said to himself. *This* wasn't supposed to happen, not yet. He then called out to his soldiers. "Scramble all Hellhounds and drones skyward! We got company, and a hell of a lot of them!"

"Sir!" the soldier cried again. "What is going on! Reinforcements? Ahools?"

Their leader looked down upon them. "Trouble. Keep this palace locked down! No one is getting in or out until my say!"

"Yes sir!" they all chorused.

Ghost then took his two machine pistols out, and then pushing them together and twisting some knobs and cranks, he had combined the two into a single machine gun. With that he clicked his boots and the rockets within them propelled him skyward.

He changed his pitch and soon he was flying for the upcoming battle. The legends were still true, The Angels have come back.

The Angels of Levitika…

Ghost pitched his body forward and rocketed towards the incoming enemies. They were *not* going to interfere with his job here in Nineveh, nor any job he had planned, for the sake of Xerxes *and* otherwise.

They were not going to interfere again.

<u>Markus</u>

Markus turned the corner with Ashlyn right behind him just as The Angels entered the city. Some had gone to attack the drill, but Jacob and the remainder were moving in on the prisoner trucks. They watched as men fired into the sky as their tanks and drones exploded around them.

Jacob landed and using his wings folded before himself as a shield, he moved in firing back with his own rifle. Markus and Ashlyn who hung back, fired upon the soldiers as well. Many fired back but were soon overcome as more Angels appeared around them. Some dropped their weapons and raised their hands, while others fought until their last dying breath. Markus tore across the street to one of the trucks, he called upon the prisoners to come out and that they were being rescued. He then moved on to the next, and as all the women and children came crawling out, a few older people followed.

One of them was a familiar face.

"Jim!" Markus cried hugging the old man and knocking his glasses off as well as the wind right out of him.

"Holy- wha- Markus!?" Jim began to laugh despite himself and hugged Markus tight, but then held him at arm's length his face red with anger. "You stupid son of a-"

"Kaltrina!" Markus interrupted tackling Jim's daughter in a hug. "You guys are okay!"

"You too!" Kaltrina said cupping Markus' cheeks. "My god, we've been so worried. Where have you been?"

"Indeed, boy!" Jim said but his attempt at anger was overshadowed by overwhelming joy as he hugged Markus once again. "We thought you were dead after you escaped!"

"No, I'm here," Markus said. He looked at them more seriously after he was able to escape Jims clutches. "Guys, it *is* real. Levitika, The City of Angels, everything. We've come back to help you."

"I noticed," Jim said looking up at the men flying upon Eagles Wings. He even peeked at the men holding the surrendering soldiers down. "It's incredible."

"Markus," Ashlyn called running up to him and the others. "Hello Jim, Kaltrina."

Jim eyes Ashlyn. "Hey, you're the-"

"No time for that," Markus cut in. "What?" he asked his friend.

"I just talked to Slagar. The Caterpillars are coming over the wall now."

"Wait- what!?" Jim said looking back towards the wall. Sure enough machines that looked like giant caterpillars were crawling down the wall on many leg-like treads, leaving great craters where they grasped the concrete and steel. "*Now* I have seen everything."

"You're gonna hear and see a lot more soon when the city gets here," Markus said. "Jim, you and the others need to head back towards that wall near the Caterpillars until this is over… Wait…" Markus was now looking around studying all the faces of the prisoners who were gawking at him. "Where's Aventis?"

Jim's expression suddenly went dark and brooding. He bowed his head sadly. Kaltrina patted his back and said, "He didn't make it Mark. The soldiers killed him."

"What?" Markus muttered. "A is dead?"

"I'm sorry," Jim shook his head. "Xerxes don't like mutants that much… I doubt any are still alive in Nineveh."

Markus shook his own head. "Don't be… Oh man…" He felt as if the rug had really been pulled out from under him. The state of his old home was nothing compared to know that Aventis who never hurt a fly and like Jim was like a beacon of light in such darkness, killed for nothing more than what he was.

He looked back up towards Jim and Kaltrina. "Get to the Caterpillars. We are going to stop these monsters and take back the city."

"Give the men guns," a citizen came between him and Jim. "We can help."

Jacob suddenly appeared beside Markus. "It would be a good idea, but you all would be in danger and we cannot protect you all out here in the open."

"We don't care." Jim said. "This is our city, and we will take it back. We will fight. The women and children? Please take them but us men we are going to take our home back."

Markus looked to Ashlyn who shrugged. And then looked back to Jacob. "Let's do it."

Jacob nodded. "Grab the soldiers guns, all the women and children back on the trucks. I want you all by the wall ASAP." As the men grabbed whatever guns and cannons they could use, the remaining civilians piled back into the trucks and were soon driven back to the walls, where a deafening explosion shook the city. "Sounds like the drills down." He said to Markus. He then called out, "Alright men, let's go! The foot soldiers are in, onward to the palace!"

This was met with many cheers including from Markus and Ashlyn. The revolution to purge Nineveh has now officially begun.

Ghost

Ghost hovered over the city area of The Bodegalane, scanning everyone and everything within. He assessed the situation as a responding general would have, if not better.

The Levitikans have entered the city, and more troops have come in over the wall. Heck of a time to do so. He looked back and saw a few Hellhounds on their way to intercept the troops, while the rest remained near the palace shooting through windows and whatever opening they could fine. They have tried landing troops inside but they would be immediately blown away and sent spiraling down to the ground below. He heard gunfire and felt something strike the suit. It moved him slightly but the photon laser did not penetrate the armor. He looked up at a surprised Levitika soldier diving at him, rifle ahead and wings dipped. Ghost then took aim of his own rifle, and fired. The soldier fell in a shower of metallic feathers and blood.

He spoke into his piece. "East side, what's going on over there!?"

"It's a buncha men with wings sir!" a frightened soldier responded over the screams of static as many others tried to speak over each other. "They just blew the tank on the drill and I thi- HOLY SH-"

Boom!

Ghost looked across the horizon to see a giant fireball climb up the walls. He groaned. The drill was gone and before his eyes he saw Caterpillar tanks crawling down the walls as well. More troops were coming in by the second. Sooner or later there would be two armies to face. He could not lose Veegar and the palace now.

He called out, "Any news on the palace itself?"

"Sir!" it was Quickshot. "Blast doors to the hangar are opening... Standby."

"Keep me posted. Men, whoever is not on the palace get your asses over to East Side. We got company, and a lot of them."

"Sir!" Quickshot exclaimed. "It's a Behemoth!"

"*Great,*" Ghost said shaking his head. "Take it down, we'll hold off the intruders, but I want Veegar alive. He is mine!" He then blasted off to assist the nearest Hellhound who was laying ground fire against a cluster of buildings.

Markus

Markus extended his wings and used them as a shield in front of him as a swarm of bullets began to slam against the metallic wings. Ashlyn stuck close behind him, getting off a shot or two back at the firing soldiers who hid behind the corners of buildings.

As the entire militia moved up while Jacob led on, more Angels flew overhead taking down Hellhounds that were returning fire at more prisoners who were escaping. All around them photon cannons exploded as well as buildings that imploded into balls of fire. Drones fell from the sky or exploded in the streets due to constant fire. Every once in a while, the two kids would pass a dead body, either riddled with bullet wounds, or burned with photon lasers. One even looked to have been crushed by a drone.

"Keep going!" Jacob said who took to the skies to uppercut a soldier who was on top of one of the roofs. The man was sent flailing through the air before he could get a shot of one of the prisoners.

"The Caterpillars are in the city and are coming by, get between the buildings!"

Markus and Ashlyn did as they were told and sure enough fast as freight trains the Caterpillars scurried by carrying more soldiers and weaponry. "Keep going!" Jacob said overhead. "To the palace!"

"Come on," Markus said to Ashlyn as they resumed their progress towards the center of the city.

It occurred to Markus that he and Ashlyn were doing just fine on their own for the most part. Whenever a drone or soldier came running Ashlyn would shoot them and then take cover with Markus behind the wings. If a soldier happened to get close enough Markus would take him out. He tried to avoid using Black's blade, using the hilt or his fists. The crystals were powerful enough to make him stronger and faster, catching the gun before the fire, the punch before the throw. His staff was all but useless weight on his back, and he quickly discarded it after some time in their advance.

Still, it was impossible to do it forever, and at last as a soldier lunged for him, he thrust forward and the soldier fell upon it at the chest, gasping and gurgling as Markus finally shoved him off. He had stared down at the dying man for a brief moment before Ashlyn got him to keep moving.

He fought on, the man he had just killed left behind but not completely. He fought, he protected Ashlyn. He would then send the men flying back with a sharp punch in the chest leaving them laying down in fetal position clutching their chest. When a drone came by he reacted so suddenly he made Ashlyn cry out in shock. He grabbed her and leapt up ten feet into the air, and used the wings to propel even higher until they were onto the nearest rooftop away from harm.

"Don't ever do that to me again," Ashlyn said clutching her stomach.

"Sorry," Markus said not really sorry as he tried to hide his grin. Especially when the drone that had come in to shoot them was shot down as easily as a sitting duck.

He looked over to the palace, which seemed to be standing much taller now that they were closer. The Angels flew around it like a swarm, firing down upon the soldiers who were on the ground and The Guard who were hiding behind the walls. Hellhounds fell from the sky in a fury of fire, and drones exploded like mines, incinerating all who stood too close. He crouched beside his friend as they watched the carnage together. Was this really what war looked like? This was different than being in the air fighting against Ovid and his forces. Up there in the sky you watched aircraft and bodies fall, you did not have to watch anyone for too long.

Here? This was face to face. And it was nowhere even *close* to a fair match.

These are human beings I am killing. This time, I can see their faces.

He watched as a soldier jerked from side to side as bullets tore through his armor and body while another got blown back by the shot of a photon rifle. A drone exploded nearby incinerating a group of soldiers who jerked around and flailed as they were cooked inside their own armor. They watched both the Xerxan soldiers as well as prisoners fall in battle whether by gun or sword, it mattered not. Each death was horrible to witness. Did Markus even wondered how the men he took out were doing? Did he consider the fact that they were slowly dying from their internal injuries? He watched as an Angel dive-bombed towards a group of soldiers swords out, lopping off their heads as he passed right over them. That same Angel was then shot by a photon cannon, and was soon among the dead on the ground where man was meant to rest.

"This is madness," Ashlyn spoke his thoughts. Before Markus could say anything in response, she immediately pointed. "Look!"

Markus looked to where she was gesturing to, which was the palace, and saw immediately what she meant.

It was a Behemoth Battle-Bot, similar to the ones that the Baron sent outside the walls what felt like years ago but this one was different. It was a whole lot bigger.

Standing half as tall as the palace itself, it crushed a nearby building beneath its heel and swatted an enemy Hellhound out of the sky with a swipe of its massive hand. Its humanoid face peered down at the soldiers still around the palace, and from the eyes shot out concentrated lasers that disintegrated everything in their path. People reduced to bones and ashes, drones and machines an inferno of molten metal. Some Angels attempted to shoot at the head area but ended up either swatted away like flies or burned to a crisp. One got swatted and was hurled straight for Markus and Ashlyn, who dove out of the way before the body could crush them. Markus looked back up and took a deep breath, and began to look *into* the massive machine that had joined the battle.

Beyond the shadows of all the men and women on the ground and in the air stood the Behemoth, and within the robot was something Markus had not expected. When he last saw a robot he saw only mere flickering of life essence, which he figured was really just the artificial intelligence within the machines. However, the Behemoth was lit up as if it was a live person. Behemoths were not like droids, who had artificial intelligence, they were mostly like drones, controlled by either a remote or a pilot to make it run. But looking into the Behemoth made Markus feel like he was looking at a person rather than a machine. Until he looked up at the head of the giant. Lighting up like a beacon was a man, and at the controls in front of him, a massive source of energy he had only felt a few times before.

"It's your father," Markus deducted speaking his mind so that Ashlyn could hear. "He has a crystal."

Ashlyn looked at the Behemoth with renewed emotion. Markus thought she looked angry at first, but her face seemed to twist or better yet dissolve into a look of fear more so than anger. She was afraid. Markus crouched in front of her, shielding them both with his wings.

"I need to get that crystal," he told her. "If I can take it out it may stop that thing from killing any more people."

"And my father? What about him?" Ashlyn said to him with such ferocity it startled Markus however he did not show it. "I'm going with you. If you can get me in, I will take care of him."

"It's too dangerous, I can't let you get hurt."

"Just get me up there, besides they need you out here. You can't let the Xerxans win, and you need to distract Veegar until I can get in."

Markus bit his lip. "Okay, hold on." He then turned Ashlyn around and embraced her from behind in a strong hug, and before she could protest they took to the skies where Angels and Hellhounds both fell.

<u>Markus</u>

As they took to the skies, Markus would barrel-roll away from gunfire and falling machinery while Ashlyn fired at their attackers. Some soldiers in exo-skeletons leapt at the two teens swinging empty gunswords and other melee weapons from swords to even clubs, only to be cut down by a swift slice of Markus' sword or Ashlyn's gun.

Ashlyn took a shot at the eye of the Behemoth, not causing any damage but definitely catching the giant's attention. The two eyes began to glow blood red and Markus' eyes went wide.

"Hold on!" he cried as he dove downwards just as two laser beams shot towards them. He picked up height and barrel-rolled as the giant turned his head to try and catch the teens in the streams of energy. However as they got closer, the robot could not move fast enough to catch the evading teens, and before long they had landed upon the shoulder where the neck met the collar.

"Good job," Ashlyn said panting never letting go of Markus as they crouched to keep their balance as the Behemoth turned to and fro in search of its prey. "But don't *ever* do that to me again..."

"Sorry," Markus said understanding that this wasn't the time or place for a joke.

Both looked around the head trying to find some point of access. The crystal within the machine made it so much easier to see the many gears, hydraulics and parts within the giant. Within a few minutes Markus was able to eye an air vent from a slot above the ear-like piece of the head.

"Up there," he said pointing in that direction. "I'm going to-"

He cut himself short for what he saw made the will in his heart falter. Across the main courtyard over a cluster of untouched buildings, the soldier Jacob was locked in combat with the same leader of the Xerxe army that they had seen earlier. He was not doing so well.

He could not gain an advantage on the warrior, who seemed to bend the will of the air around him as he deflected each blow only to counterattack Jacob who would catch some of the blows with his sword or wings, but would sometimes earn a nick by the two blades the man wielded. He appeared more focused on keeping the man occupied on him rather than the guns at his waist.

"I gotta help him," Markus said leaping up and carrying Ashlyn with him. He grasped the ear part with one hand and with the other hoisted Ashlyn onto it so that she could pull off the ventilation cover and place her legs in.

She looked back at Markus before dropping in. "Be careful," she said.

"You too." And he opened up his wings, letting the current of air pull him from the Behemoth and as he curved his body he turned and began to descend towards the two fighters sword-ready.

<u>Ghost</u>

Ghost was expecting resistance, but he was not at all prepared for the Angel that flew past him, slicing his rifle in half.

That was sloppy, and now Ghost was stuck to sword-combat. He was a good swordsman, especially with his two katanas which he had unsheathed so fast that even the Angel appeared impressed, however with all the gunfire as well as the Behemoth destroying his forces along with the city, it made it difficult to focus. But as time went by he could see the energy drain from the warrior's face, and as more sweat and blood dripped from his body, Ghost knew that his time was short. Then all that would be needed would be for one of his blades to pierce something vital.

Crossing his blades together he caught another blow from the Angel, and with a sharp kick in the belly he sent the man flying back. The Angel man almost immediately regained his balance with those blasted wings and dove back after Ghost. He tried to reach for his sidearm but the man was too quick; with one good swing of his blade it struck the side of his helmet. It did not damage the suit or any of the electronics within but it still gave Ghost a headache. He lunged for the Angel again, who tried to block the attack but Ghost was too strong, and manage to land a blow to the man's arm. The two then sparred in midair as bullets and lasers zoomed around them. One Angel tried to assist his brother, but Ghost changed altitude, ducking beneath the diving Angel and then raising his blade so that he caught the belly of the man with edge. The man gasped and was soon tumbling down to the streets below holding his bleeding belly in his hands.

"Bastard!" the previous Angel screamed as he attacked yet again. Ghost was just about to block the attack when he felt something. A disturbance in the essence around him. At first he thought it was coming from the Behemoth like before, this too was also powerful- and it was getting closer.

He turned just in time to see a blade swinging towards him.

<u>Markus</u>

His sword would have cleaved the warrior in two, but Markus was stunned to see that his blade had never touched the man. In fact, he had caught it with his own blade and managed to hold his own against Markus' blow.

Hellfire, he's strong!

But Markus could see why. Beneath his vision he could see a glowing blue aura around the man, centered particularly on the chest area.

"Now *this* is interesting," the man spoke his helmet sparkling with electricity. It was then when Jacob's blade met the leader's other blade. This warrior was much faster than they had anticipated, but maybe together…

"Get him!" Jacob cried swinging again. Markus did so, and together the two attacked the leader of the Xerxes army while the two armies fought each other as well as the Behemoth that was now striking down yet another Hellhound.

The man was just too fast. For every flick of Markus' blade the warrior caught and deflected the attack before blocking Jacob's as well. Markus could see that the man was using something to make him faster, that power armor of his was fast, difficult to crack, and made of advanced technology. But something else was powering it up as well as whoever was inside.

The man had a Crystal within the armor.

Markus could feel the influence of the two crystals locked on his wrists as they too sensed the presence of their brother, the urge to let go and have them take control was coming over Markus once again, a feeling he had not felt since the battle of the Leviathan. But Markus held it back, he could not allow them to take over again. He would beat this man, without letting himself be carried away.

He swung at the warrior once more, remembering his training from Black what felt like ages ago-

"A sword used nowadays is always fit with a cross guard to allow a last effort to protect yourself. However when fighting with a staff of blade without it, you must angle it in such a way that your opponents will not trail down the blade, or have you ending up wielding the blade horizontally and gaining no further advantage."

-he angled the blade a few degrees up in case the warrior caught the blade. He in fact did, but the two held each other at arms-length, pressing against each other's swords in an effort to break the other's hold. Markus smiled, and flicked the switch on the hilt of Black's blade, immediately the blade snapped to the color of blue, and the smell of ozone was strong as an electric current flew from the blade to the enemy, delivering a powerful shock through the suit. The warrior jerked back grunting at the pain, but recovered fast enough to catch Jacob's downward strike bringing his own blades into a cross again and catching Jacob's sword right between them. He boosted upward, not only breaking free of the attack but blowing a blast of heat from the rocket boots into Jacob's face. Jacob fell back in pain, but Markus realized too late what was going on, and before he could even gasp a word, the warrior turned his body and dove downwards towards Jacob, blades pointed directly for his chest.

"No!" Markus cried out as the blades pierced Jacob's chest, and he was then shoved downwards by the blades only to crash into the streets below with the warrior crouched on top of him, the katanas running deeper and into the ground beneath him. Markus cried out feeling the anger take over, and turn his aggression into pure rage as he dove for the warrior, his sword ready to behead the man.

But the warrior stood up, prying the katanas from Jacob's broken body, and he hopped into a balanced stance, his swords ready to meet battle yet again as Markus' sword met his own.

It was all rage that drove energy from the crystals to Markus' body and mind, and from there his sword to which he unleashed his fury upon the warrior. He was unable to withstand the deflecting blows of his opponent's attacks, but every hit he scored would slow his opponent down, damaging the suit but not enough to seriously do damage. He kicked at the man, who countered and tried to slice Markus' leg off- but was unable to prevail.

Markus saw bright blue as he pushed himself harder against his attacker. He was more aware of everything that was happening around them as the battle raged on. The fear in both the Angels and Xerxan soldiers' hearts, the power of his opponent crystal, crying out to both him and its master, the dread of the Guard who remained hidden in the palace while some ran in fear for their lives, and even the sense of bravery of the prisoners as victory seemed within their grasp.

And within the Behemoth who continued its razing fury upon all who opposed it, Markus could sense Veegar in his state of panic while he operated the machine, and Ashlyn, who had just made it to the main control room.

The warrior who defied him danced about him like an acrobat and struck at Markus again, this time taking the offensive and saying through his helmet, "You're gonna pay for using that sword on me."

<u>Ashlyn</u>

After minutes of crawling through the ventilation system that seemed to twist and bounce as the Behemoth moved, Ashlyn finally slipped through the grate that exited into the main control room. She got up from her belly and squatted into a crouch behind some power stations. She peeked around the corner to see what and who was within the head of the giant.

Two large eyes were positioned in front of the giant mech connected to two cannons that were powered by generators on opposite sides of the head. In the middle of the eyes two wires met into a wide screen, where the images of men being blasted, crushed and shot were being shown. Before the monitor was a large console, curved into a crescent shape all covered in many buttons and switches. It reminded Ashlyn of a Hellhound console, but much, much bigger.

What caught her eye the most however were two things: One the small glowing crystal that shined a shade of violet in the center of the console, and the man who stood before it working the multitude of controls as he moved the Behemoth in for another attack.

Her father stood motionless even as the Behemoth rocked as it walked across the buildings and streets and fired its lasers. He could have been a statue for all Ashlyn knew, but she knew better. That man was her father, and Veegar was making a final effort to destroy the two opposing armies.

She came out of hiding, her rifle aimed at her fathers back. "Hey!" she called out.

Veegar turned on his heel in shock, his face a spread of stress and shock. His goatee had not been trimmed lately and he had grown stubble. He gave off a more rugged look of a commoner rather than a commanding general. He was so deathly pale and thin that if he had never done the things he had done to his family, Ashlyn would have felt sorry for him.

Almost.

"Remember me?" she said taking a few steps into the light. Veegar's left hand twitched and Ashlyn could see the pistol that sat on the console a yard away from him. "Be my guest, it will give me a reason to put you down once and for all."

"A-Ashlyn?" Veegar's voice cracked.

"Oh, you *do* remember?" Ashlyn said her voice dangerously low; a combination of both gladness, anger, and rage. The better of the three evils were slowly soaking into her heart, but she held back if just for a little she was trembling so much. She had to know.

"Honey, I-"

"Don't you *dare* call me that!" she said taking another step forward her hands gripping her rifle so tight her hands began to whiten.

"How can you be here? How did you *get* up here?" He stammered his hands outstretched and palms up. "I thought you were dead..."

"I would have been. And you would have liked that wouldn't you, so I could end up like Mom and Kira? Huh!?"

"I *spared* you didn't I..." Veegar stammered again, sweat was pouring from his pores at now. "You were supposed to be brought to me, did you know that? I spared you, and you were supposed to come. They told me you were found dead."

"You goddamned liar," Ashlyn said through clenched teeth, her rage erupting inside her head like a nuclear bomb. "You *liar*. You left me to die in the streets. You didn't even double-check, unless I had to steal to live. My name was on the wanted lists! You didn't care about me. You killed my mother and my sister and left me for dead, your word is *useless*."

"Come on honey, don't be like-"

Ashlyn pulled the trigger almost unconsciously, and a bolt of energy shot out and connected with Veegar's leg. The pants and flesh were burnt off, cauterized by the intense heat but was still enough to knock the old bastard to the ground clutching his leg in violent screams.

"Don't, call, me that," Ashlyn said walking towards her father. This time she aimed at his head, she felt resistance in her heart, whether it was pity or some other force she did not know, but the urge to both pull the trigger again or keep her hands steady was a constant battle on her conscious. "You've lost, *father*." She spat the last word out as if it was acid. The Behemoth shook as something struck the side but Ashlyn kept her balance surprisingly "Surrender, it is over."

Now Veegar was looking up at his daughter down the barrel of the laser rifle with such fury that it was almost monstrous. "You little bitch... Do you not understand what I've done to get this far! My lord-"

"Baron Ovid is dead." Ashlyn said feeling glee as she watched the hope drain from her father's face. "My friend Markus killed him when he attacked The City of Angels, and now the city is here to take back this one back. Nineveh is lost, it always *has* been because of selfish, ignorant, power-hungry monsters like Ovid. Like *you*."

"I had no choice!" Veegar shouted, the rage back and turning his face purple and veiny.

Ashlyn was now close enough to shove the barrel of her rifle against her father's forehead. The man's face went pale as the blood drained from it and his mouth trembled like a whimpering infant. Mask on, mask off.

Like always.

"Be quiet," said Ashlyn. "You're going to crawl to that control module, and when you do…"

She faltered then. She felt as if something was tugging at the back of her head and she nearly turned around to see what it was. She caught the sudden smell of lilacs which had not been present when she first entered the control station of the Behemoth, and she became aware of the second presence in the room. Her eyes darted around but she could see no one.

Veegar began to chuckle. "You feel it too," he whispered. "She's trying to speak, to both of us. She's telling you to spare me…" He leaned his head back and was appearing to be staring intently at the crystal in the console. "She wants me to live." He looked back to his daughter. "You won't kill me anyway. I've done a lot of wrong to you, honey, I know that. I'm a terrible father, but you wouldn't kill me, would you? Not your own father?"

Ashlyn's strength began to falter. It would be so easy just to pull the trigger, and make the monster that destroyed her family pay for everything he has ever done. But still, in the back of her mind she remembered a simpler time.

No, that wasn't quite right. It was if those memories were being injected into her mind like a syringe, foggy like a good drag of Buckweed.

Father was just a Guard back then, working all day but coming home at night for supper with his family. Mother would make soup usually, for she enjoyed giving away the rations The Baron would give them for her father's service. It was against the law for members of The Guard to have families, but Veegar had joined after being married, because he wanted to have a better life for him and his daughters. Kira had not been born yet, but Ashlyn who was only four years old remembered when he had first joined. For awhile, things went pretty well especially after her sister Kira was born. Her father hated his job, but he liked seeing the smiles of happy children and a wife who adored him.

Then one day, when Kira had just turned four as her sister once had, he came home disturbed. He was talking to mom about a new position, she did not like it, yet she comforted her husband telling him it was going to be okay.

Oh, how she was wrong.

Ashlyn remembers being thrown out of her house with her sister and mother who was already in the streets held at gunpoint by two guards while the rest burned their home behind them. Father was standing amongst the Guard looking very grim. Ashlyn remembered calling to her father, as well as her mother who cried for help.

And then, out in the cold Veegar cleared his throat. "By order of his majesty Baron Ovid, and confirmation from the new brigadier commander yours truly-" Ashlyn could see the horror in her mother's eyes when he said this. "-you are to be stoned for your crimes of the use of witchcraft, as your children watches." Ashlyn then felt strong hands pick her up, dragging both her and her sister way from her mother. They cried and screamed for her as they watched their mother hold up her arms in attempt to protect herself from the stones being thrown by both Guard and civilian.

When she was confirmed dead, Ashlyn was horrified to see her sister being taken to the pile of stones. "No! Not her too, please!" she screamed reaching out for Kira who was crying uncontrollably. "Kira!"

"Shut up." She felt a hard smack against her head, and all faded to black.

When Ashlyn woke up, she was covered in a thin layer of fresh snow. She groaned as she sat up wiping her eyes. When her vision cleared the streets were cleared, save for two broken figures amongst a pile of rocks and blood. She screamed her mother and sister's name as she crawled over to them, feeling the frost bite her bare hands and feet. She reached them and began to cry over them, feeling the stickiness of chilled blood on her hands and arms as she laid on top of them crying their names as tears fell from her face. The silence of falling snow feeling more like an insult than comfort, as did the silence that always shrouded Nineveh in times of grief and despair.

How long she stayed out there, she had no idea. She was not even aware of the hands that pulled her away, and took her away from the horrible sight that would never ever leave her memory for as long as she lived.

Ashlyn stood motionless as she now stood before the monster who caused all of that to happen. Veegar had been attempting to stand up during Ashlyn's minor revelry but her anger at the memory had snapped her right back and she shoved the barrel harder against Veegar's forehead.

"I have no father," she said, and the old man's eyes widened.

Before she could do anything else the front of the room exploded in a flash of flames. The heat blew her back into the rear generators, her father right next to her. Immediately the pitch of the machine changed and through the giant hole in the face Ashlyn saw the streets of Nineveh far below. Her gun and multiple other parts of the robot fell into the streets below, and then she too began to fall screaming past the main console that was sparking and falling apart, down to the streets below.

Markus

Markus smashed through the face of the robot with the force of a meteor. He had missed his repost and had earned a sharp slash of the warrior's sword across his face, followed by a sharp kick to the belly that sent him flying through the air and into the face of the Behemoth, having only just enough time to flatted his Eagles Wings against his back in an attempt to cushion his fall.

It did not work as well as he had hoped.

He had not broken through but a large dent had appeared in the face and he could feel explosions inside the robot as he began to peel himself off of the metal. He took flight as the robot staggered behind him, using the palace itself for balance. He met the warrior's height who hovered waiting near the palace's thirtieth line of windows. He was spinning his katanas in hand, mocking Markus.

"You are good child," he spoke. "But not *that* good."

Markus bared and gritted his teeth, taking hold of his blade in both hands once more.

"I do not care for the city," the warrior spoke and began to circle Markus, who did likewise in the opposite direction until they both were going in a complete circle around one another. "I don't even care about you. All I want are the citizens, and the crystal Ovid had kept hidden. Considering the fabled City of Angels is here can only mean Ovid is either lost, or dead. So the crystal is here, and I intend to get it."

"What do you want with it?" Markus demanded.

"Does it matter?"

"It does, because I ain't leaving until I get it either."

"Seems we are at an impasse. Should have figured. Well, that is a pretty big Behemoth don't you agree?"

Markus said nothing for he was curious as to where this was heading.

"You must have figured that it would require a lot of power to get that to work even with modern-day generators and power sources- save for what keeps Levitika floating of course."

"I've noticed."

"Well then," the warrior said reaching into his belt and pulling out a small flat disk. "Let's crack that tin can open then."

And with a click of his boots he rocketed towards the head of the Behemoth and as he passed it, he tossed the disk against it, immediately the front of the head exploded in a flash of blue light and fire. The robot stumbled and blindly attempted to swat away at whatever struck it. It then doubled over and was now standing hunched like it was about to throw up. He saw parts and wreckage fall from the face towards the streets below, but his eye caught something else amongst the rubbish.

Ashlyn was screaming and flailing as she fell towards the streets, just barely managing to snag a frayed wire which held her weight and left her suspended over a deadly fall.

"No!" he screamed and using the full power of his Eagles Wings, he flew towards her as fast as he could.

He spun past debris and sliced away chunks of metal as he flew towards the hunched over machine, and his friend who dangled and spun about like a fish on a hook. She cried out, and her screams were almost as terrifying as Ruth's coughs when she was dying.

No, not her too!

That was when Ashlyn lost her grip and began to plumet downwards arms and hair flailing in the wind as she fell to the streets below. But she did not make it so far, for Markus had caught her, the propulsion from his wings sent the two of them past the robot and into the palace in a puff of dusty rock.

Markus groaned as the two of them peeled off the wall and fell to the lower platform of the palace. His wings were badly smashed, having used them to cushion their crash against the building. Even while he laid on his side his wings crumpled and sparking he held Ashlyn close, and began to tremble. Ashlyn turned to face him, her face deathly pale and her breathing was at the point of hyperventilation. Eventually, she calmed down when Markus opened his eyes.

"You alright?" he whispered.

"I'm fine…" Ashlyn said as Markus released her. He got onto his hands and knees and shook his head free of the stars that had flashed in and out while Ashlyn curled over to her side, her back facing the palace walls. Markus was then alarmed at the sight of her eyes growing wide. "Markus!"

Markus turned to see another figure dangling from the husk of the destroyed Behemoth. A man garbed in black and red, screaming as the Behemoth began to falter, its shoulder rubbing against the side of the palace.

"I got him," he said and leapt off the building. His wings were in no shape to take flight, but they were in good enough condition to help him glide across the streets towards the head of the Behemoth. He felt the wind rush past his face, and he held his sword-arm back and his other out. He began to call for the man, realizing that it was indeed Veegar when the man turned to the sound of his voice. This was the man who abandoned his citizens and left them at the mercy of that fiend and his army of Xerxans.

He swooped in reaching out to Veegar's extended hand. He almost grabbed it too.

But then a force of a body slamming into his back shoved him away, carrying him across the street and into one of the buildings of the palace. Before they had crashed through, and the debris blocked his vision, Markus watched as Veegar's fingers finally lost their strength, and he began to fall screaming to the carnage far, far below.

They had smashed through two walls, the second causing them to separate, causing Mark to tumble across the floor and smash into a third wall, his sword skittering beside him. He groaned as he felt the nervous-system mechanism smash, depleting all power to his wings and rendering them useless. He managed to slip them off his shoulders, but the pain in his head was so much he collapsed onto his side. He reached out for his sword, only to have his hand crushed by the heel of a steel boot. He cried out as was kicked onto his back, being pressed down by the barrel of a pistol that was shoved against his forehead.

He glowered up at the warrior above him, his helmet flickering with data and other things unseen by Markus, only by the wearer of the power armor. He seemed to look down at the hand he was not stepping on, and reached out for the crystal on the gauntlet. A sharp flash of light came between the man's hand and the crystal, causing him to retrieve his hand and shake it free from the jolts.

"I see," he said more to himself than to Markus. He faced the boy again, whether from curiosity or amusement, Markus could not tell. He merely scowled at the face of his defeat. "I never figured the new Keeper of the crystals would be a mere child, let alone one like *you*. But then again, I suppose we've all seen our share of firsts, right?"

"You could say that," Markus said through clenched teeth. He tried to suppress the feeling of defeat that was now shrouding his mind like a plague, the shame of such a failure already seeping in.

"Like I said, I only want the crystals now. The city is lost to Levitika and the citizens anyway. You crushed a well-formed army. Impressive. But now I need to go, and I would like to take with me what I came for. Including yours."

"No," said Markus trying his best to harness the power of the crystals to knock this man off and send him sailing across the room. But the strength of this warrior was too strong, and his mindset too fixated on this failure.

There was a thundering crash outside the building, shaking the floor beneath Markus. "And there it goes," the man muttered as if bored. "You don't have a choice. I see that the Crystals have chosen you. Both of them. I cannot blame them, you *are* the Keeper after all. I can sense it in you. However, there is *always* a way to undo a bind."

Markus reached out with his hand and grabbed the man's leg. "You kill me, and I will cook you inside that suit of yours," he hissed, using his very anger as fuel to push forward and do *something*. "I will make sure you don't make it out, you murderous piece of filth."

The man chuckled as he pressed the barrel harder against Markus' head before drawing it back. "You *are* full of surprises. Full of fire too. I can see where you get it from. I should kill you, kid."

Markus braced himself, ready. But the warrior did nothing, and instead shook his head almost deliberately.

"No, that won't do. I need the crystals, not you. So I will take them from the one place where they are vulnerable."

The man seemed to stoop lower towards Markus. "Tell me boy, what do you fear the most?"

With that he reached out with his free hand and grabbed Markus' head. Immediately he felt intense heat pouring into his head, and as Markus screamed he was pulled away.

At first, he was nowhere. It was all pitch-black darkness. The floor felt soft however Markus could not see it. He waved his hand as if trying to see it, but was shocked to feel no air pass through his fingers or brush his arm. It was as if he was in The Nothing, where the lost were sent to wander for eternity.

But he soon felt something brush his leg. He looked down and was surprised to see a small cat brushing against him. It was a scrawny stray, with matted fur of black and eyes of emerald green.

"Delilah?" he asked crouching and reaching for the feline with delicate fingers. He felt the fur along her back, and caressed upward, receiving a loving purr from the cat that should have been dead long ago. She *was* there.

"What is this?" he asked as the floor began to harden and take form, and as if light was coming from the floor, the streets of Nineveh was suddenly visible, glowing bright white with snow.

However, he felt no chill in the air, which made him uneasy. Buildings began to grow from the ground up, shacks, towers, this was the street he grew up on. The stray he and Ruth used to pet was there, and soon the smell of cooked meat was in his nose. He was home, but something made him uneasy.

That was when he heard the sound of swords clashing. He spun around, causing Delilah to turn and run in indignation. His eyes went wide when he saw his father once again fighting The Hunter Black. The two battled just like they had years ago. In beautiful rhythm their two weapons clashed and sliced flesh. There was no one else besides them which was unlike what had happened before. In fact, it appeared to be a different reality altogether. Like a memory that was missing pieces. But before Markus could even understand what was happening, he cried out as Black lunged forward, stabbing his father in the heart.

"No!" he screamed as Black kicked the body off of his blade, and then turned to eye Markus. He leapt up in the air, and swung downward towards Markus' head.

He had covered his face with his arms awaiting for the blade to slice him in half, but when nothing happened, he peeked to see Black standing before him, his blade not in him, but a little girl who was crouched between them. The girl was facing Markus, and looking down at the blade that now stuck through her chest, she began to cough.

"Ruth!" Markus cried pulling her towards him, holding her tight. In an instant flash of shadow Black disappeared, leaving the two alone as Markus tried to calm his sister like he tried to before, but to no avail.

"Why..." Ruth whispered. "Why didn't you save me..."

"Ruth!" Markus cried as his sister went limp in his arms once again. He began to cry, screaming towards the heavens as two separate hands touched his shoulders.

"Why did you let me die!?" Ruth suddenly screamed out at Markus, her young and innocent face suddenly aging and wrinkling, turning gray as heads of maggots and worms burst from her cheeks and wriggled about. Her eyes melted like ice in their sockets and spilt gelatin tears down her ruined cheeks which the worms lapped up and she lunged for Markus, her small hands turning witch-like and coiling around his neck and beginning to strangle him.

"YOU LET ME DIE!!!" Ruth screamed fetid breath into the screaming and crying face of Markus.

The two hands that held Markus' shoulders from behind firmly squeezed. A third hand dropped upon the top of his head, and this hand seemed to calm Markus somehow as he heard a familiar voice say, "It isn't real, Markus."

But that was impossible. He was dead too.

"Awaken," the two voices of Abner and Fethawit said in unison.

That was when pain exploded in Markus' shoulder, and all faded to black.

Zachariah

It was time for another test.

Zachariah watched as his own body moved without his consent; it was being controlled by the helmet he was wearing which suppressed his bodily control. As the scientists went through procedures, they made him do various tests and physicals. After the hours of constant bio-exams and experimentation, they were now ready to begin their trials, and make sure that their project worked. From sprint lines to high jumps, from tests of strength to tests of finesse, over and over again.

He watched helplessly as his own body ran across the frozen courtyard wearing nothing but the shorts he was given; the snow and ice burned his bare feet and the cold air chilled his body to the bone, however he did not slow down. He had no choice in the matter, only to endure the pain. He leapt over obstacles and ran across walls, punched through walls of wood and brick, and did some basic maneuvers when the security lasers opened fire on him.

Now it was time for the final test, and without his consent, his head looked up towards the large window built in the wall of the lab, all cameras around the four-sided walls trained on him. He listened to the voices in the headset, and his body kept at attention despite his desire to run and hide.

"Begin the battle-simulator," Dr. Lucas' voice spoke, which made Zachariah growl in anger of the man who tortured for him for so long.

Why were they doing this, what had he done to deserve this? He could not remember what he did so wrong, and as usual, there was not enough of his memory to remember who exactly he was. Only bits and pieces of the horrors he had witnesses.

His body then crouched as a lower set of doors opened up below the window, letting out a multitude of droids armed with shock-batons and shields. They surrounded him in a tight circle, awaiting the order. And despite Zachariah's will to flee, his body stayed put. Hunched, tense like a Werecat about to spring.

"Begin," Lucas spoke, and the robots advanced.

Zachariah watched as his body leapt into action, where his heart should be surging with energy and releasing a pulsating purple light. For every robot that tried to jab at his body, it reacted quickly and effectively; if it did not dodge the attack, it dismantled the droid by either smashing the head in with it's bare hands, or making sure it could not get up again by tearing off the arms and legs. It spun with two in hand like a deadly tornado, smashing all who got within range of the spinning droids. His body then threw them both at a cluster of them, destroying them all instantly in a flash of parts and controlled explosions.

That was when it finally made a mistake, for one droid stabbed Zachariah in the back with a broken baton, the jagged piece piercing his body and exiting out the front.

But he felt no weakness. Pain, but no weakening sense. And his body turned and grasped the droids head, and it tightened his fist, crushing the robot's head. He then reached down and ripped the broken shard from his body, and where it had pierced him Zachariah saw no blood, only the hole where he had been speared, however he watched in amazement as before his very eyes the wound closed up, as if he was never stabbed at all or if his flesh was really manipulated clay. As soon as it was completely closed, Zachariah felt no more pain nor had any memory of it. His body then resumed to battle, smashing and destroying every droid that got in its way. Eventually, every droid was destroyed, and his body turned to face the window yet again, awaiting new orders from it's new masters.

"Magnificent," Lucas' voice spoke, almost greedily. "He's simply magnificent."

"It's complete, it works!" another voice spoke. "We did it!"

"We did it," Lucas whispered. "Deactivate him, and send him back to the tank. We need more notes. If we can recover some of the energy in him, we might be able to-"

"We've already taken out samples of his blood sir."

But what blood was there? Zachariah was bloodless, and he knew it.

"Excellent! Then it is official! It's a success!"

"Yes sir, a new weapon of mass destruction. Ghost will be pleased."

"Such energy spikes... So much power..." Lucas said even more greedily, and behind the glass Zachariah could see his face pressed against it, and his essence was tinted with green, the color of greed. "Like a newborn droid, living on instinct rather than emotion."

"Not... A weapon..." Zachariah said through clenched teeth, and like his teeth, his fists began to clench and Zachariah's body began to tremble. He felt the crystal in his chest surging again, seeming to defy the helmet and the neurons that kept him as a puppet for these madmen.

"Sir, something's wrong..."

"What is it?"

"The headset it-"

Zachariah cried out and lifted both hands onto his helmet, and delivering as much energy as he could into the set, the device despite it's desperate stride to regain and keep control, exploded. His hair was singed, but he felt no pain as he felt his own body come back under his control and he was finally allow to fall to his knees panting heavily from the exhaustion that overcame him with the pulsation from the crystal.

He was free, Zachariah was free, and even as he was now on his knees in the snow, the relief made him begin to shed tears that had not been able to break free for so long. A flood of memories came rushing in, momentarily immobilizing him until he calmed himself down.

He then controlled his breathing, and looked up at the window with a fire in his eyes, and his chest right over his heart began to glow dark purple. He felt energy go into his legs, and he pushed off of the ground propelling himself towards the window where Lucas stood wide-eyed and throwing his hands up for protection.

As he smashed through the glass Zachariah plowed into Lucas, tackling him right into a console and smashing it into a heap of sparking debris. He snarled at Lucas with a vengeance as he grasped the doctor's throat. Ignoring everyone else in the room who was staring in both amazement and fear, Zachariah snarled at Lucas.

"You did this to me."

"Look wait a min-"

Zachariah cut the man off with a sharp punch in the jaw, knocking a tooth free from its owner's mouth. Oh, how good it felt to finally be able to hit what you wanted, to hurt *whom* you wanted. "You *hurt* me."

"Guards!" Before Zachariah could react he heard many gunshots followed by many bullets tearing into his side. He cried out as he fell onto his side. As he closed his eyes he heard Lucas crawling away. He heard more footsteps coming towards him, and he then felt the barrel of a gun against his temple.

"We got 'em," a voice said above him. "He ain't going anywhere."

"What's up with his-"

Zachariah smacked the gun away with enough force to send it flying across the room, and with one sharp punch to the soldier's chest, sent him flying into another soldier as they smashed against the wall. The one crushed was still alive and groaning, but the one that had been punched wasn't breathing anymore as his sternum had crushed his heart.

Zachariah then lunged towards another two, smashing both of their heads together and knocking them out. He then grabbed one of their weapons and fired upon the scientist going for his own weapon. The man fell in a flash of red as the laser struck him in the chest. Zachariah then turned to see Lucas escaping through an elevator along with another doctor. He lunged for the doors and using both arms he attempted to pull the doors open. He eventually was able to trip them open, and using his arms and legs for support he slid down the elevator shaft as the laboratory alarm started to sound throughout the building. He smashed through the escape hatch and landed inside the empty elevator and stepped out just before the doors closed.

He saw that he was in a big circular room with a deep, deep pit in the middle surrounded by a small fence. Around the flooring there were many shocked guards and scientists staring at him while many more made for any of the doors that circled the railing. Zachariah's eye caught Lucas heading through a door which was marked with a large '4' in red above it. He began to make his way around it, ignoring the calls and orders from the guards who began to advance upon him with shock-swords and more rifles.

One came upon him but Zachariah threw him over the railing just as another tried to slice him with his sword. He wrestled the blade out of the attacker's hand and struck him in the center of the forehead with the hilt fast as lightning. The man crumpled like a sack of laundry as did anyone who attempted to apprehend him. All he knew was fury, and his hands struck and grabbed, threw and smashed, his vision red with rage and he felt no remorse, only the deep desire to catch up to Lucas and end him.

He finally reached the doors the doctor had escaped through and he barreled right in, shutting the door behind him just as he ones with the rifles began to fire at him. He ran inside and tossed aside a scientist who attempted to run past him, sending him flying through the air and into a glass container which shattered and spilled out some liquid and glass onto the floor along with the poor sod. He ran further in ignoring the great many containers full of different colors of liquid and even the few the contained something or someone floating inside a pea green liquid. He tossed aside documents as he ran past consoles and desks until he caught Lucas in his sight, the scientist he was with was holding a pistol and aiming it at Zachariah while Lucas looked to be trying to find something in his desk.

"Lucas!" Zachariah snarled marching towards him and ignoring an intercepting scientist who was demanding him to stop. He seized her coat and tossed her aside so he could get to Lucas who looked like he was trying to disappear into the wall behind him.

"Wait- wait a bloody minute!" he cried out as Zachariah seized the man by the coat and slammed his head through his computer monitor and then slammed him down onto the floor with a mighty *crack!* His chest began to glow but Zachariah thought nothing of it, even as Lucas was staring dumbfounded at his experiment's breast. Zachariah then seized the gun the other scientist tried to press against his head, he back handed her with the weapon and then pressed it against Lucas' leg and fired.

"Gah!" he cried out in anguish.

"How does it feel?" Zachariah demanded in a low voice as he tossed the gun away. He heard the door open followed by a few incomprehensible orders from the soldiers coming into the room but he ignored them, keeping his full attention on Lucas.

"Who am I?"

"What are you talking about you crazy son of-"

Lucas was cut off as Zachariah slammed him against the wall, knocking the wind right out of him and squeezing him tighter.

"You took me apart- you took my life!" Zachariah screamed in the man's face.

Lucas was wheezing from the pressure against his chest but he managed to say with bulging eyes, "I... I was only doing my job."

"Who am I?" Zachariah demanded again, ignoring that last remark.

"You, are the only successful experiment- ahhh!" He cried out as Zachariah pressed harder against the man's chest. Somewhere behind them now, the soldiers finally arrived and one was shouting at him to put the scientist down and get on the ground, emphasized by the cocking of weaponry.

"Tell them to back off," Zachariah said ignoring the soldier who pressed the barrel of his rifle against his head.

"Guys, back off, he won't do it," Lucas said desperately. "For godssakes, back off!"

Zachariah felt the pressure of the weapon release from his head but the tension of the four rifles aimed at him was still too much for comfort, however he came this far and he was not going to stop. Not when he had this bastard in his hands.

Lucas said hoarsely, "In all honesty I never gave a crap *who* you were- I was just told to erase part of your memory while you slept, while you were in The Dreaming. You are now controlled by your fears, and if that's not a powerful weapon I don't know what is." He said all of this with a pained smile as if the whole situation amused him. "You were the only successful subject, but who you were is gone, four-six-four. Who you are is *better* now." He said this while looking at Zachariah's numeral tattoo on his right bicep.

"Who you were is dead," Lucas repeated. "The life you once lived is no longer possible. But you are better, I *made* you better."

"But why?" Zachariah snarled, repeating his question again in a low whisper. His lips were trembling, his anger momentarily mixed with a sense of loss and frustration.

"A weapon," Lucas said softly. "A weapon to make the world a better place. Let me go, let us perfect you, and I promise when it is all over, you'll-"

"I don't think so," Zachariah said seething. No words honeyed enough could make him feel otherwise. He was angry, his very identity and life taken from him. "And the name, is Zachariah," he told Lucas.

Energy surged from the crystal, passed through Zachariah's clenched hands holding the scientist up, and then through Lucas himself.

"Wha-" Lucas started but his words were caught in his throat as liquid began to drip from his very pores like sweat. So much of it so fast that Lucas' skin began to shrivel like a squeezed sponge releasing water. His mouth was open in a dry and empty scream, and his very tongue turned to dust in his mouth. As Zachariah finally let the scientist go, all the water in his body had been flushed out of him and Lucas dropped to the floor crumbling into dust as the mummified corpse he now was.

The soldiers reacted by firing back but Zachariah dived forward tackling one to the ground and using him as a shield he commandeered the weapon being used and fired back at the remaining guards. When they all fell, he forced the man to his knees and smacked him in the temple with the gun, knocking him unconscious. He tossed the gun aside and leaving the dead men and terrified scientist with their sleeping guards.

He stepped outside and more men seemed to be flowing out of two of the many doors. From the space in the middle of the vast room a Hellhound floated up and leveled out so that it was just above the main floors. A Gatling laser slipped out from beneath the ship and aimed at Zachariah, who dove to the side and took cover back behind the steel doors as the barre of concentrated energy shot into the steel. Zachariah knew he could not be too badly injured, but he did not want to test his limit, so he stayed behind the steel door taking quick peeks around to see the many soldiers taking up positions around the guard-railing. He saw some setting up temporary barriers and taking cover behind them, their rifles set on top and fire-ready. Through the walls Zachariah saw the whispering essence of a line of soldiers on either sides of the doors, awaiting for the Hellhound to cease fire and storm into the room. Zachariah bent down, crouching like a cat with glowing purple eyes, and waited.

Eventually the firing ceased, followed by an eerie silence that seemed to hang in the air like a dense fog. The Hellhound being the only thing making noise, which was just a silent hum as opposed to the usual engines that were loud like a jet fighter from the old times. Zachariah heard shuffling outside as well as someone clearing their throat. Other than that the overwhelming silence accompanied by the Hellhound's monotonous hum kept its hold on the facility. Through the walls Zachariah kept watch on the whispering shades of light of the soldier's life essence, many having an orange-like hue as they awaited to storm the room. Eventually, he saw the two in the front of the lines moved their arms and as one, they all started to converge onto the doors.

Zachariah stayed back, his legs tensing as they got closer and he saw the two muzzles of the leaders weapons. When he saw their hands pass the doorway, he pounced.

He slammed the gun of one into its owner's throat and kicked the other in the chest sending him plowing through his men like a line of dominos. He then summersaulted across the back of the one he struck in the throat and brought his heel down on the head of the next soldier in line. The Hellhound then open-fired upon the cluster of confused and frightened soldiers in an attempt to put Zachariah down, however the boy was much faster. He spun one man around, using him as a shield as the shots came swarming in. Zachariah felt the body go limp and hot as the concentrated heat burned throughout it. He threw it over his head, striking the windshield of the Hellhound with enough force to crack it. It ceased firing and wobbled in the air as the pilots were startled by the sudden force of strength in the throw. Zachariah then struck two more of the men down, and then ran towards the guard railing as more lasers zipped around him. He jumped onto the railing and leapt across the chasm towards the Hellhound, grabbing hold of the Gatling and hanging from the ball and socket joint that made it turn. He pulled himself up and hooked one arm around the wiring, and using the other hand, he aimed the Gatling, letting a current of energy flow through his body and into the weapon, allowing it to fire upon all of the soldiers around the room. Bodies, guns, and shields blew apart and scattered across the floor or fell over the edge to the darkness below. A section of the floor collapsed, sending chunks of concrete after the falling men.

When all of the soldiers of the floor had fallen, Zachariah released the Gatling, and kicked it off of its hinge. He then began to cross beneath the ship and swing himself up so that he was on the nose of the Hellhound. He crawled up, digging his very fingers into the metal. When he got to the Hellhound's cockpit, he punched in the glass, letting loose a rainfall of glass onto the two pilots of the ship. He grabbed ahold of one by the collar and tossed him out, sending him screaming down the chasm to disappear into the darkness. The other, had his head slammed down, smashing the control consoles in the process. Zachariah then kicked back, leaping backwards and turning his body so that he could catch the side of the wall beneath the railing. The Hellhound pitched and slammed into one of the walls mere feet from Zachariah, only to spin and crash down the chasm in a ball of fire.

Zachariah then climbed up the wall, and pulled himself back onto the floor. He then took off sprinting towards the elevator he used to get down to the massive room. When he was inside, he looked up the emergency hatch, seeing the doors of the upper floor. He tensed his legs, and then leapt, passing the hatch and soaring nearly halfway up the shaft. He grabbed ahold of the wall and kicked back, gaining more height with each kick from wall to wall. Soon he was finally out of the shaft. He panted for a bit but the strain on his lungs soon subsided and he took off running yet again out of the broken window he had smashed through to get to Lucas. He landed back into the courtyard in a *poof* of snow. He jumped again, scaling the wall and crawling over the barbed wire ignoring the few snags he received as his skin closed right back up. The emergency guns went off and began to fire at him as he dropped down to the other side of the wall.

He took off running, never looking back even as a shot nearly knocked him off balance. He was tired, and he felt more energy depleting from his very being with every stride and every breath he took. But still Zachariah ran. With no memory of who he was, and only the sensation of pain and suffering, he ran. He ran until he was completely out of range of the emergency guns and the sirens of the facility slowly faded into obscurity and he ran some more.

And so, his journey began.

How far he ran he could not tell. The snow soon gave away to a slush and from there to wet ground. He figured he was going south, so he pressed on ignoring the blisters that were beginning to officially form on his thawing feet.

Gunfire erupted behind him, startling him but he pushed on. He took cover behind some rotten trees panting heavily as Hellhounds rushed overhead, their spotlights lighting up the landscape like a submarine beneath the crests of the sea. When the lights faded from view and the roaring engines a distant memory, Zachariah finally began to relax. He collapsed on his side splashing up mud, and just laid there. His heart, or at least the area it should have been hurt so much it was beginning to make his chest itch. He went to scratch it but he felt no skin beneath his fingernails-but something harder, kind of like rock. He opened his eyes to see that a faint purple glow was coming from him. He looked down at his chest for the first time, and gasped. For in his chest just where his heart should be, was a glowing crystal or dark purple, the edges gleaming bright and a hint of power sparked within the stone. He touched again, and felt an odd heat coming from it. He looked at his palms next, and then struck it against a nearby rock. His knuckle busted open, but before his eyes the bloodless wound closed up like it never had happened.

"What happened to me..." he asked himself. He touched the crystal in his chest again, and felt a sudden urge to leave it alone, like a wound meant to scab up and heal.

A flash went through his mind and he saw a glimpse of a young boy sitting beside him, staring at him with a look of pity. And in an instant, he was gone. Zachariah reached out in vain in hope to somehow resurrect the image but it was no use. Who was he?

A thunderclap sounded overhead, and Zachariah looked up just in time to have a raindrop hit him directly in the eye. He swore and rubbed his eye with an angry fist. He looked back where he came from, and then brought his attention to the spot of dirt between his feet. The ground appeared to grow darker as the rain began to pour with a new vengeance. He could not stay here, it was unsafe and the rain would not make the situation any better. He needed somewhere else, somewhere warm and dry.

But he was so tired, so weak...

He sighed and Zachariah pulled himself to his feet using the tree for balance. He then began to continue where he was going; this time at a leisurely pace, his back to the horrible laboratory, and towards the moon that shown bright and white before it was soon consumed by the darkness of the storm clouds moving overhead. Like a ship to the light of a lighthouse, he pushed forward.

Zachariah

He walked for what felt like days, feeling his feet's blisters rip open only to close and reopen again and again. Zachariah was so tired yet he did not sleep. All he wanted was to get as far away from the laboratory as possible.

On a few occasions he caught the sound of Hellhounds coming near, and he was forced to hide amidst the grass that had sprouted up when Winter's final breath finally let out.

Seagrass... That's what they called it back home. Home. It felt like a memory-no. More like a dream. Was it real?

His mind went back to those gruesome images, of his mother being killed and he being dragged off to become a lab rat for those monsters. But what of the rest of the memories? Was there more to his family? His village? Did he once act like a normal kid? Zachariah did not know, and in his heart that was no longer there, he felt sick.

Why so glum?

"Why do you think?" Zachariah muttered irritably. A bug had just bitten him but the insect paid as the bite healed over completely, and next to it the stain of where the little annoyance used to be.

Well, time heals all wounds. Obviously not your outer body anymore, but your brain is just like any other important organ in your body. It takes time to heal, and something as special as a lost memory must be in there somewhere, trying to break free of the darkness.

"That is all I see," he spoke again.

Give it time, you might just surprise yourself.

"Heh, right."

You must be getting hungry, right?

"I haven't felt hunger since we left. I don't think I've eaten ever." His hand instinctively went to his chest, where his crystal began to glow just a little bit brighter, as if the sun that shone above was casting his brilliant rays against diamond. However, Zachariah knew it wasn't the sun lighting up the crystal. How he knew, he did not understand.

Nevertheless, you need to take care of yourself. Look at you, you're breaking up.

Zachariah's eyes immediately turned to his right, where he saw a whisper of smoke squirming into the sky, and below it a lump of what looked like many tents jumbled together. He then turned towards it. *Are you sure that is a good idea?*

"You got a better one?"

I suppose not, but there could be pirates, and they could be worse than those Ahools flying overhead.

As if on cue a shadow passed over Zachariah but he thought nothing of it. "As long as I don't look like I'm dying they'll leave me alone."

How do you know that?

Zachariah eyed the tents, trying to get a closer look despite the brightness of the sun above him. He saw more and even more as he saw the whispers of life essence swirling about the camp.

"I just do," he said without another word and without knowledge of *how* he knew.

As Zachariah neared the camp which he saw was full of people, he felt a strange sensation in his heart. As if something was pulling him with a string towards the campsite. The sensation made him both curious and uneasy. That did not however hinder his advance on the campsite, and when he was within the camp line he took cover behind one of them and began to make his way around it to get a closer look at the locals.

There were mostly men around the camp, however a few women and children were among them. They all wore leather or tattered garments, as well as the few who appeared to be wearing power armor. Some were healthy-looking while others looked deformed due to radiation poisoning, there were even some with auto-limb arms and legs. Animals were stored in cages, from as small as a Bogfrog, to the size of a Leaper Dragon. Those who were merely tethered to stakes were mostly Ahools and Lizards who hissed and clawed at one another when the other got too close to their scrapes of meat and bones. He watched as some men played roulette with a pistol, while others played cards or worked on weapons. Judging by the many crates from Nineveh and Xerxes, Zachariah knew that these must be pirates. What also gave it away were the few men and women tied to stakes around the campfires. They were beaten and dirty, and their clothes were merely shreds as they hung by their ankles and wrists against the wood.

His vision was then caught by the Dragonfly-chopper parked outside one of the biggest- and he supposed in pirate terms 'fanciest'- tents. He watched as some men took another wearing power armor by the arms towards the rear of the camp. Following the men looked to be the captain, and in his hands was a large red crystal. When his eyes caught the stone he felt his heart burn with an even stronger force. He trailed the stones path with his eyes, never taking them off of it. As he felt drawn to the stone, Zachariah followed close behind using the tents, crates and whatever else he could use for cover.

Stay away from that...

He didn't listen.

He soon came across where the men were taking the man and the stone, which he saw was a large pit, and within the pit was a dragon. It clawed at the sides of the pit hissing furiously but its claws could not help it escape its prison. The wings had been cut off and as it wasn't a literal fire-breathing dragon, it was no more harmful than a giant salamander as long as no one fell into the pit with it. The pirates held the man in the suit at the edge of the pit on his knees, laughing at his discomfort as they bent his arms at the shoulders. The captain, who still carried the stone came up to the man's side beneath his arms and appeared to be whispering something in his ear. Zachariah's eyes peered in a flash of purple as he listened in from afar.

"I will give you one last chance," the captain snarled in the man's face which remained hidden beneath his helmet. "Where did you get the crystal?"

"Go ahead and throw me in," the man said defiantly. "I hope The Eldest brings you nothing but misery, you bastard."

The captain then chuckled as he backed away from the three men, caressing the stone beneath his fingers as he nodded. "Toss him in."

That was when Zachariah lunged for the captain at the speed of a leopard, arms stretched wide ready for the attack.

He grabbed ahold of the captain, who squealed as he was hurled over Zachariah's head and into a tent which collapsed on impact. The two pirates holding the man turned in shock, which turned to an even greater surprise when the man pulled all of his weight down, smacking the twos heads together. He seized one by the throat and then tossed him over the side, where the dragon waited below. A vicious roar and a tearing sound, the screams of the man suddenly ending as quickly as they began. The other he struck with an uppercut below the chin, sending the man into the air, only to be slammed back down by both of Zachariah's fists. He stood up staring at the man who nodded and then turned his attention to the captain who was crawling from the tent. He strode over and grabbed ahold of the captain by the throat.

"Gotcha," he snarled in the man's face.

The captain took hold of a little remote he had in his pocket and flicked a switch; immediately a siren sounded throughout the camp, alerting the rest of the camp. "There's no escape for you," the captain wheezed.

"Neither for you," the man said and with a mighty swing of his arm sent the captain flying through the air and skidding across the dirt until he was mere inches from the edge of the pit. He gasped as he tried to back up, but was immediately shoved back down with the mighty boot of the warrior.

"What was that you said?" the man asked in a sinister tone. "That I would be screaming for death to take me? Well, let's see what that's really like." And with a hard kick to the back of the head he casted the captain into the pit. Zachariah watched the man watch as the captain screamed and cry for mercy followed by the roaring of the dragon and tearing of flesh.

"No! Please! Please, please, please help me! Help-" *Shriip!* and the screams stopped, followed by the sound of something crunching and cracking.

The man turned to Zachariah, obviously eyeing him. He strode over and without saying anything his helmet retracted, revealing a scarred man no older than eighteen within with a little hair of black on his head, and eyes that burned bright with anger and tiredness. "Who are you?"

"I might ask you the same thing," Zachariah said walking over to the tent where the captain had landed and reached within, pulling out the large crystal and holding it gingerly in his hands. He did not know if it was the voice in his head that spoke, or some voice in the Nothing, but it seemed like the stone was whispering to him. He felt a hand on his shoulder, and he turned his head to see the man standing beside him looking somewhat protective of the crystal. "I appreciate the help my friend," he spoke in a dangerous tone. "But that there is mine."

"Is it now?" Zachariah challenged but before he could say any more he realized that the two of them were being surrounded by many pirates wielding laser rifles as well as assault rifles, all aimed at the two men in their little circle. One pirate broke through the crowd, chuckling grimly. By the look on Zachariah's new friend's face, he hated this man.

"Lee, Lee, Lee," the man said shaking his head with arms wide open as if welcoming a long lost friend. "How much trouble are you going to cause before we put an end to your miserable life?"

"Lee huh?" Zachariah spoke from the corner of his mouth.

The warrior called Lee, ignored him. He hobbled over towards pirate, and Zachariah then noticed that he was missing one of his feet. How did he miss that? "Like Kizuato?" he asked in a low voice.

"What are you talking about?"

"Your captain is dead Raki."

The pirate called Raki gasped, his eyes two large disks of white. "You lie."

"I don't. He screamed like a little girl as your pet ripped him to shreds."

Raki turned red he was seething with anger. "Kill them!"

Zachariah cried out and held his hands out as the lasers and bullets flew, and was astonished in his own rights when some invisible force changed the direction of all the shots, sending them skywards. Not letting the act distract him like it left the pirates, Zachariah charged one side dropping the crystal to the ground in the process while Lee took the other side towards Raki, who drew his sword.

Lee

Lee sidestepped Raki's downward strike and kicked him in the side, sending him flying into the crowd as if they were pins. He spun and clocked a pirate who attempted to shoot him, breaking his nose as he took the gun and fired at the man before firing at all of the others. He spun again and caught Raki's blade with the gun, and spun the gun away yanking the sword out of his enemy's hands before striking the man in the throat followed by another punch in the chest sending him into the same crowd again. He was trying to get up when Lee saw his rescuer spin two men over; twisting their arms and knocking them back down again before striking more down and knocking them out with sharp punches and kicks to the head. Soon all who stood before them were down and either out cold or crawling away to nurse their injuries. He nodded to the stranger who walked towards him.

"Impressive," he said to the kid when he reached him. "Most impressive. Tell me sir, who are you?"

The kid who was not quite a man just yet but sure was built like one, bit his lip in thought. While he took his time to answer Lee noticed with surprise the glowing crystal in the chest of his rescuer.

"Zachariah," he finally said.

Lee nodded looking back at the man's face studying him closely. "Where did you get that?" He said pointing towards his chest.

"I don't know," Zachariah replied, but Lee could see the man was hesitant to reveal any information. Zachariah then jerked his head towards The Eldest which sat in the ground pulsing with dim light. "I might ask you the same thing."

"It is not a matter that concerns you," Lee said stiffly. "I thank you for helping me, but I must be on my way and return this to its rightful owner." He strode ahead and scooped up the crystal, curling it into his arm like a precious child.

Zachariah smirked at Lee. "But you do know of these things, yes?" he said this while pointing at his chest.

"Yes I do, however you are a completely different circumstance that I have never seen before. I have seen robotics and ships powered by such objects as well as many phenomenal miracles, however having a human host is a different matter altogether."

"Host?" Zachariah asked.

"Where did you come from anyway?" Lee asked.

"I don't know. I escaped a laboratory in the north and fled south. That's when I got here."

Lee nodded deeply disturbed at the news. "Xerxes…"

"What?"

Lee shook his head. "Nothing. I am sorry I cannot help you, sir, I must return to my duties."

Zachariah took a few steps towards him, which made Lee back up defensively. "You know about this thing in my chest."

"Take a big step back sir," Lee demanded dangerously. "I've had a rough day as it is." In the back of Lee's mind he thought he heard a voice, mere whispers by the sounds, but by the look on Zachariah's own face, he was definitely hearing something. And his eyes were planted on The Eldest.

He looked back up to Lee. "That thing is alive…"

Not knowing what to do precisely, Lee whispered a command into his suit to send all pressure towards his right arm. He stepped forward casually. "In a way yes, but no. Not yet anyway. Do you know how you got that crystal in your chest?"

"No, but you have an idea." It was not a question.

"Some. Might not be right but I will admit I have some theories." He took another tentative step towards Zachariah. "But I am not sure."

Zachariah marched over to Lee and placed a hand on his shoulder where the neck met the collarbone; the suits automatic head-protection kicked on and his helmet closed up hiding his expression which was dark and daring. "What is that thing? What is in my chest?"

"Wouldn't you like to know?"

Lee then swung at Zachariah's temple, releasing all hydraulic pressure into his swing, and when his fist met Zachariah's head the man flew backwards and crumpled into the ground cold. Lee strode over and stood over the man. He pressed his fingers against the neck and felt no pulse, yet he felt air escaping his nostrils. He was alive but his body had no pulse. Interesting.

"Still, can't sense the heat building up in my arm can you? Sucks when half of you is robotic." He reached down to touch the crystal in the man's chest. However when his finger touched it he saw a flash of something go through his mind. Something big and on fire; it was roaring with double rows of teeth and eyes glowing like a cat's. Lee jerked his hand back as if he touched something hot, his eyes full of terror as he looked down at the guy.

"Bastard..." he whispered to Zachariah or so it seemed. He got back to his feet, thinking of what to do with the man. Unsure of his options he quickly turned his attention over to one of the Dragonfly choppers. He looked back to Zachariah, and then he scanned the many tents. All of the pirates were either dead or out cold, but their women hid behind the tent flaps, their children behind their skirts.

He sighed decidedly and hobbled over to the chopper and climbed in. With a flick of a switch the vibrating wings began to pick up speed. He flicked another and saw that the front had duel flame-throwers on it. He looked back to Zachariah's body and then back to the tents.

And beneath his visor, Lee grinned wickedly as the seductive words of The Eldest whispered in his ear. He was told to leave the boy alone and the crystal. They didn't matter.

Take me home...

Zachariah

Zachariah awoke to the sun in his eyes. He shielded himself with his forearm and slowly removed it as his eyes slowly got used to the light around him.

He turned onto his belly and got onto his hands and knees, shaking his head from the massive hit he took. His attention then turned to what he felt between his fingers. He wiggled his fingers to realize he was feeling grass. He looked down to see the bright greenness rippling beneath him, and when he looked up he saw that he was no longer in the pirates camp, but somewhere home or so it seemed.

He stood up to see that he was a field of grass rippling in the high winds, and far at the edge of the fencing were many shacks and tents made of steel and animal pelts. Wooden houses were scattered among them, and smoke rose from every chimney and fire pit. But there was not a soul to be seen, even with his enhanced vision. He immediately went alert and began to turn to and fro looking for the bastard who knocked him out, which led to the other problem: where were the pirates and the other camp?

"There is no need for that," said a voice behind him, making him spin around ready to fight.

Before him sitting on his haunches was a weasel, its fur was of golden orange and its eyes like little black beetles. It stared at him curiously, almost amused that he had started like that.

Zachariah merely peered at the creature. "What are you?"

"Isn't it obvious?" the weasel asked, and before Zachariah's eyes the weasel shimmered in golden light, and where it once sat now laid a thin scarecrow of a man wearing an orange cape over a suit of power armor. His hair was red and his face was dotted in freckles; his eyes were as green as the grass and he also had a small necklace of a blue opal around his neck.

"And never too surprised it seems." He smiled at Zachariah with perfectly white teeth.

"Who are you?" Zachariah said still in stance.

"Oh, relax will you? I'm not gonna hurt you." The man laid back again with his arms behind his head, he appeared to be watching the clouds floating overhead. "Shame really, all I get are memories of others here."

"Who are you?" Zachariah asked again this time his arms lowered. "I'm not in the mood for-"

"Did you know, that when people dream, their minds can connect somehow? That has of course never been *scientifically* proven of course, but hey- you're in a completely different realm, not like the laws of physics and science matters much here, eh?" He acted like he had never heard Zachariah.

Zachariah took a step forward, satisfied to see the man finally dart an eye in his direction. He had the man's attention now. "I'm not going to ask you again, who are you?"

"Gosh, straight to the point, eh Zachariah?" The man smiled when he saw the look of surprise on Zachariah's face. "*There's* the surprise look about you. As for my name, I was once called Akuta, when I was alive of course."

A feeling of dread began to put weight on Zachariah's heart. "I am dead?"

"Dead? Heavens no, far from it. Just taking a little nap due to a slight bump on the head. You'll wake up soon. I envy you people, you are able to wake up."

"Who are you?" Zachariah demanded. "Where am I?"

"I thought we covered who I am and where we were."

"No," Zachariah feeling irritated as his crystal began to glow.

"Ahh there I go, giving you energy through your anger. I would love to take you for a spin one day."

"What are you talking about?" Zachariah asked more angry than ever now.

"Please sit, and I will explain."

Zachariah was hesitant, but eventually he took a seat beside the man eyeing him every second of the way.

"There, now isn't that better? I do like the feeling of grass I really do- at least how I remembered it." He smiled at Zachariah. "Yes, yes, you want answers, and I got *some*. But not all." He cleared his throat before continuing. "You see, you aren't dead, but you are not necessarily alive. What I mean is, you are banished from death as long as I am with you. And friend of mine..." He tapped the crystal on Zachariah's chest, sending a current of coldness throughout his body. "You and I are stuck together in the same body."

"I don't get you," Zachariah said scooting away from the Akuta. He did not want to be touched by him again.

Akuta held his hands up as if in surrender. "Didn't mean to make you uncomfortable." He dropped his hands. "Anyways, like I said, you ain't dead, but you are not alive. You see, that crystal in your chest, that is my life source, that is what keeps me both trapped in this place, and tethered to the world. However, *you* are now my tether, being the host in both body and mind. I tell you, those men put a lot of work into you. You were definitely special, the way you tried to save your family after your mother was killed-" He was cut short by Zachariah who took ahold of the man's throat, his face red with rage.

"My goodness you are *just* like they predicted..." Akuta choked.

"Who the hell am I?!" Zachariah demanded. "You know who I am- do you!?"

"Don't you remember? No? Well see, that is the whole point. Your life has been erased! That's right!" He wheezed as his throat was squeezed tighter, still he spoke with a smile. "However, not entirely. You see, your anger is because you only know so much, and all that you do know is the horrors you have experienced when they took you away."

"That's right..." Zachariah said easing his fingers just a little bit.

"Yeah, exactly," Akuta said not even attempting to rub at his raw throat. "You having been killed only to be brought back to life, via that crystal. I am the one keeping you alive, and as a result, not only are you stronger, faster, and you may have noticed- able to see the unseen as well as walk among your dream as I do, my crystal has given you extraordinary power."

Zachariah released the man and sat back on his haunches. It was a lot to take in, that he was killed and then brought back to life in such a matter. "But what of my memories?" he asked. "Why can I only remember the horrors of that day?"

Akuta sighed while rubbing his sore neck. "I'm afraid I do not know the answer to that one. However, I *can* say this, when I was trapped in The Dreaming, I lost all memory of who I was as well. But little by little, it *does* come back. Maybe in time the same will be done for you."

"This is The Dreaming?"

Akuta nodded. "Yes, and that crystal- the one your new friend had –is the most powerful, and most dangerous one of all. In fact, you could say it is nothing like my brethren. Wish you could have met one of them today, they could help me explain. Anyways, that one that your new friend had, that one is the father of all crystals in existence, The Eldest. And within, like me, is another person. But that person is..."

Akuta hesitated then, only now his expression turning with sudden anger. "He is a liar, a deceiver. Twisted by evil, and if he were to get out, could bring the destruction of the entire world."

"What?" Zachariah said clearly shocked. "Such a thing exists?"

"Yes. There is much more to tell you in order for you to understand- and believe me, it is a lot. But you must awaken. I feel your arm burning."

Zachariah looked to his left to see that his left arm was on fire, and he awoke with a start.

He sat straight up crying out as he saw his arm ablaze. He slammed it against the ground, sending out sparks every time he struck his arm down. Eventually the flames died out, leaving horrible burns all over his flesh; the smell of cooked meat was strong in Zachariah's nostrils, but before his very eyes he watched as the dead skin fell off and new skin replaced the areas that got badly burned. In less than a few seconds his arm was completely healed; not even a scratch was to be seen upon his arm.

Zachariah then looked around however, and like his arm was the entire camp was up in flames. Tents were now mere structures of fire, their rods and poles snapping in the intense heat; the animals were still in their cages but they were long dead, and as for the pirates both buccaneer and female: there was none to be seen besides a few fiery skeletons blackened out by the flames. It made Zachariah sick just looking at the dead so he turned his head and began to crawl away from the scene. When he made it at a safe distance away from the flames he turned and laid on his back panting heavily.

Lee must have done this, he burned the whole village in revenge for keeping him here. Where the little bastard was now, Zachariah didn't have a clue. But that was all and well for him, because Lee had taken that crystal with him; and as far as Zachriah was concerned the further away he was from it the better. The evil thing gave him thoughts unlike his own; temptations whispering in his ears. Akuta was similar, for even now he could feel the man watching the sky as they were while he was dreaming, probably thinking of the same things. Why was it made, and what did it have to do with Akuta?

He looked to his left and a glimmer in the dirt caught his eye, turning his body he peered to have a closer look. It was another crystal of the same color and hue as his own, and much smaller than The Eldest.

That there, is another one my brothers, the voice said. *Another gateway into the land of dreams and nightmares.* Zachariah crawled over and placed a hand on top of the crystal, tenderly as if he might be burned by it. When nothing came over him he picked it up, studying it with nimble fingers and keen eyes.

Come on champ, he heard the unmistakable voice of Akuta speak in his head. *It is best we leave. You've been through a lot, and I fear that if we stay here soldiers or some other worse creature is bound to find us. Worry not about The Eldest, it shall be reckoned with one day.*

"You have plans concerning it?" Zachariah said sitting back up and rubbing his sore head.

Oh yes, but first I believe we should focus more on you, wouldn't want my new body to get eaten, would we?

"I'm not giving up until I have answers, and The Eldest has them."

You sound so certain.

"It is because he *did* speak to me," Zachariah explained standing up and looking towards the south where a flock of Ahools were flying towards. "He said he would help me remember who I was, and who authorized my experimentation."

Did you not listen when I said 'powerfully dangerous?' Akuta demanded as Zachariah began to move south. *This is The Eldest who is offering you such a thing, but he is not to be trusted. He is a deceitful, and evil person, The Mad King himself, grandfather of the Dark Queen!*

"He wronged you, hasn't he?"

More than you can imagine. What I am now, that is just the tip of the iceberg. Trust me when I say you cannot trust The Eldest, Zachariah. Your time will come when you will have to deal with The Eldest, until then I plan to make sure you are alive and strong enough to do so. You are not originally part of the plan, but due to measurements Xerxes had taken, you and I have little choice. We are both stuck in your own dead body, and of course, you want your memories back.

"Yes..." Zachariah admitted keeping his eyes straight ahead.

Then let us go, there is a certain someone I would like you to meet, maybe he can help us both get what we want.

And as Zachariah took some clothes that were left unscathed by the flames and continued his way southbound. As he began his journey, he handled the crystal Lee had obviously dropped in his hand as Akuta explained what this plan of his was.

You familiar with the Great War? asked Akuta.

"No."

Impatience radiated from the crystal, sequestered then by understanding. *No matter. We have plenty of time. Let me tell you- It's a long story, and recent events had only made it longer.*

So Akuta told Zachariah, and Zachariah walked, and listened.

Markus

Markus was now walking in the streets of Nineveh. He had a bundle of firewood wrapped in blankets in his arms, and was now heading home with his load.

When he finally arrived home, he saw Ruth playing with a doll in front of the shack; her jacket obscured her face as she played. Markus smiled and walked over to join her. Hearing his footsteps, she turned to him and he stopped dead in his tracks for Ruth's face was covered in blood.

She grinned at him with teeth stained red, and her lips dripped with crimson spittle. "Hey Mark," She smiled.

"Hi," Markus said stiffly.

"Do you think Dad will be home for dinner?" As she said this, the shack seemed to melt into a state of deterioration, complete with the whole thing going up in flames which illuminated the whole area and shrouded Ruth's crimson mask in shadows.

"I don't know," he replied in a voice that was dry as a bone.

"I hope he stays safe," she said returning to her doll.

"Me too…" Markus and before his eyes Ruth faded away in a whisper of crimson smoke. She didn't scream out at him or anything like before, but simply faded away, as did the shack and the buildings around it as if the world itself was being erased.

"You were a good brother to her."

Markus looked beside him to see a man with long black hair; his golden armor glistening in the sunlight. He smiled down at Markus in a way that almost looked sad.

"Hello Markus."

"Abner," Markus said dropping his arms realizing they were now empty, the bundle of firewood was gone. "What are you doing here?"

"You are asleep, so I have come to see you," he said simply. He began to look around the empty city of Nineveh. "Your mind tells you lies. You are not responsible for Ruth's death. She doesn't blame you."

Markus looked away, embarrassed, and a little upset that the spirit would say such a thing. All he could remember was Ruth's decomposing face just screaming at him, her hands choking him as if she wanted retribution for what he couldn't prevent.

"No one can prevent everything, Markus," said Abner behind him. "One of mankind's biggest flaws is the idea of complete and utter control. There is no such thing. Man has tried and tried again to keep control, keep everything safe and close to their chests. One of the greatest examples of this was the nuclear fallout that decimated the planet in the first place. But you do not need me to tell you this. You know Ruth doesn't blame you."

Markus sniffed. He didn't realize that he was crying. "I know… but…"

"You blame yourself."

Markus nodded. Realizing he had tears running down his face, he wiped them away briskly and said quickly, "Where is Fethawit?"

"He is gone," Abner said in a grim tone. However, he refused to say more, and before Markus could ask where he was Abner spoke again. "I felt that you were touched by the influence of the other fighter."

"Yes, he just…" Markus sighed at the memory of the horrible image influenced by the warrior's touch. "It felt like I was being put to sleep, and then everything came crashing down at once." As he spoke the image of Nineveh faded into black, leaving only him and Abner visible to his eyes. The two of them, the only real beings in a void of nothingness.

"That is one of the many powers of the crystal gateways," Abner explained. He began to pace in the nothingness with Markus at his side. Where they were and where they were going he did not know, but Markus kept up to listen to what the spirit had to say. "Not only are the spirits within able to influence you, make you stronger; they can also be used for you to influence anyone of your choosing through The Dreaming. What that warrior did was enter the realm through a bridge between both of your minds. And with that, drew out your darkest fears. I know, for I saw the energy passing between him and you as he entered The Dreaming. However, his method is alien to me, for his crystal and my brother within was not with the warrior, but in the *suit* which was controlled by the warrior."

"How does that work?" asked Markus. "A machine can't access the Dreaming, can it?"

Abner shook his head. "I don't know. I can only assume this means that the man has ways to create powerful weapons such as the Behemoth you faced. And that was one of the many steps The Eldest took to create his new body. *That* is what will begin the world's spiral into chaos. For if there is no bond, and force is used to extract power from The Dreaming, that is where evil thoughts begin to rise from the pits of the most degenerate of man."

Markus nodded both ashamed and angry. The warrior had knowledge enough to use the power of the crystal against him, and he was not able to defend himself. The thought of the spirit trapped within the crystal having being forced to submit power into the suit was just horrible. What torture could the spirit be facing when forced to have its energy sucked out of him, could such machinery be created? In a way Markus was not at all surprised. The Behemoth was proof enough, and that alone was all that was needed to see what horrible outcomes attempting such experiments could bring.

"You still have not told me about Fethawit," he said.

"As I have said," Abner said sadly. "He is no longer with us, but I hear him faintly, he calls to you."

"You're ignoring my question," Markus said stopping in front of Abner.

The old man twitched his nose slightly. "It is best that you find out for yourself."

"What is it with you?" Markus demanded. "Is that all you are here for? To tell me what the guy *did* to me?"

"No," Abner said patiently. "I came to comfort you, on behalf of a friend of ours as well as the bond you and I share ourselves."

"What friend?"

Abner shook his head. "I cannot say. I promised I wouldn't."

Markus threw up his hands, not realizing he had only thrown up one. "Fine. Well, I know Ruth doesn't blame me for her death. It's just hard... that's all. I'll... I'll be fine."

Abner nodded. "I believe you." The way he said it however made Markus feel like the spirit did not.

"But what about Fethawit?" Markus asked again. "You sure you can't tell me anything?"

"There is not much time. The more I linger, the more I put you in danger. The Eldest is still listening, Markus. He does not know where Fethawit is, I don't believe, and I would prefer to keep it that way."

Unsatisfied but understanding, Markus nodded. "All right."

"Abram will explain further what you are up against. Abram will help you find him again, for soon you will find out where he has gone whether you like it or not."

Markus nodded again. "I am still to go find Abram then." It was not a question.

"That is best," Abner nodded. "He will help you develop the skills you need to control your power, for you were almost consumed by your anger, influenced by Fethawit's despair in battle. The poor man only lived in agony, even during his death."

"What good is he then?" Markus asked feeling himself wake up. He had never truly liked Fethawit in comparison to Abner, but his connection with the Hunter Black had made it easier to carry the spirit. "Why did I need him?"

And before everything faded away, Abner spoke in the darkness. "Light cannot exist without darkness, and good cannot exist without evil. You will know when Abram shows you the way. Say hi to Ashlyn for me."

And then Markus was awake, but for minutes that turned to hours his eyes refused to open; leaving him alone in the darkness behind his lids with the sound of a constant beeping beside him.

Eventually however he was able to peel his eyes open slowly, letting in as little light as possible that was shining upon him. His eyes opened to a room lit by the sun that shone through the window, illuminating the vase of daises in front of it. He turned his head groaning at the pain welling up within it. He saw Ashlyn sleeping in a chair in the corner of the room, her hair loose and her pajamas rumpled and messy. He turned his head to his left where he saw a massive machine that bleeped every second, a monitor with a line bounced with each beep. He trailed the wire going through the machine and found it stuck within his left arm. Figuring it was important he left it alone. He felt the fresh flow of oxygen being pumped through his nostrils through a pair of tubes that were connected to a canister just beside the machine.

He looked down at his most and saw that he was shirtless, and his lower torso was covered with a clean white sheet. *How long had I been out?* he wondered.

He then saw a small table across the room where his clothes were as well as the sword and gauntlets, but something was wrong. He saw only one, and that was his left one where his father's crystal still rested, the glow coming from it fading in and out like a heartbeat. Where was the other one? Markus soon became aware of an itch building up in his right forearm, and carefully reaching with his left hand he went to scratch it.

But his fingers scratched the cot instead.

Curious he turned his head a little more to the right and gasped. Where his arm should have been was empty, and he stared dumbfounded at a stump covered in bloody bandages and gauze on his shoulder.

Not believing what he was seeing he reached out with his hand to touch the stump. Sure enough his stump was hot to the touch and blood seeped through the wrappings and kissed his fingertips. His arm was *gone*.

This revelation caused Markus to sob miserably. No sound passed his lips as the silent tears rolled down his cheeks and he tried to cover his eyes with his right and feeling nothing cover him he gritted his teeth and covered his mouth with his left to keep from screaming.

His arm was *taken*. That was what Abner meant. Fethawit wasn't with him anymore because his right arm had been taken from him while he was out. That damned warrior sliced his arm off like a hunk of meat! He really did want the crystal bad enough to severe one of his limbs. Did he keep the arm as well as the crystal, or did the man throw it away like a piece of trash? The thought of a part of him lost in the world-taken from him by force made Markus sick to his stomach enough to make him feel like he might puke. He turned his head to the wall where the monitor sat by, and sobbed softly as the machine beeped away.

After having letting his tears dry Markus simply laid there in the cot like the dead. With his arm gone how was he supposed to go on now? How could he do it? He couldn't even *work* single-handedly let alone fight.

His thoughts were interrupted when a soft knocking sounded upon the door. He did not move however, pretending to still be asleep.

He heard Ashlyn yawn and something crack. "Come in," she said softly.

The door creaked open and closed just as fast. He then heard the voice of Esmerelda speak out. "Has he stirred yet?"

"Looks like it, but I was asleep. He looks asleep still."

"Yeah…" There was a pause. And then, "You haven't left his side since the incident."

"I couldn't," she said. "He's saved me many times before, I'm not leaving his side. Because Mark will never admit this; but he really is afraid. Seeing that his arm is gone will only trouble him more."

Markus squeezed his eyes shut tighter. The truth being just as painful as the loss.

"You're a good friend to do such a thing for him," Esmerelda continued. "I can see why you two get along so well. You know, I never asked, what do you think of all of this anyway? The prophecy, the crystals, Markus' plan, everything."

There was a pause. And then, "I think it is stupid and reckless to be honest. I think it is too dangerous, and I can't stand the thought of him running off like that. But knowing Mark, when he sets his mind to something he pushes for it regardless, so it doesn't matter what I think."

"I doubt he thinks the same way."

"… Maybe. I feel like a horrible person, but I kind of hope that this will make him not leave. That it will make him stay here."

Markus heard the shuffling of feet on the floor and Esmerelda said, "The others aren't going to like that…"

"Tough shit," Ashlyn said bitterly. "We've already been through two battles, and Markus has finally lost his arm. Isn't that bad enough?"

"Ashlyn, don't raise your voice," Esmerelda was saying sternly. "You're gonna wake him up."

"Sorry… I just don't want him to go. I don't want him to put his life in danger, especially now. I almost lost him, and I can't stand the thought of him getting hurt worse than he already is."

"Then… then we have to let him decide, right?"

A pause, perhaps Ashlyn was nodding. "But he's my friend, and I will by his side until the end."

"I appreciate that," Markus said rolling around to see a look of shock on both of the girl's faces. Esmerelda was wearing a nightgown similar to Ashlyn, and her black hair was brushed down. Tears welled in both of their eyes as they dove to him, hugging him tightly against the cot and he tried to hug them back best he could with his one and now only arm.

He couldn't hold back anymore, and began to sob with them.

For long minutes they held each other, the girls' tears dripping on his shoulders and his side aching from the extra pressure on him. But the pain was nothing compared to what was lost, and Ashlyn and Esmerelda grieved with Markus for the loss of his arm, as well as the spirit who had been connected to it.

"That was so sweet of you," he said to Ashlyn when the three of them finally let each other go.

His comment earned him a soft slug on the cheek. "Shut up," Ashlyn said as heat rose in her cheeks.

He chuckled, faking a smile as best as he could. "Just good to know you care."

"How are you feeling?" Esmerelda asked her eyes more serious now.

"Like I got hit by a Hellhound," Markus said his smile disappearing. He looked down at his stump, not saying anything while the girls stared at him. It still didn't seem believable.

After this moment of uncomfortable silence he looked up at Ashlyn, "What happened to me?"

Ashlyn bit her lip, tears threatening to spill once more. "The soldier you were fighting, I could not see clearly but he did *something* to you. You looked like you were asleep, or even dead. He just stood over you like an executioner, until finally he swung down with his blade and…" She shook her head. "I took a shot at him before he could cut the other arm off. He flew off with your arm. It was…" She fell to her knees beside Markus so that she could speak to him at eye level. "He just *took it away.*"

Markus nodded, his mind flashing back to that moment he went after Veegar. "Took it like a thief would a tool. And what about your father? What about him?"

"Dead," Ashlyn said stiffly. "Hit the ground."

"I'm sorry," Markus said laying back into his pillow. "I couldn't save him."

"It's not your fault," Ashlyn said though her tone was coarse like salt.

"Yeah," Esmerelda said at the foot of Markus' bed. "I was watching as we pulled Levitika over the city, there was nothing you could have done."

"Still," he said the regret of not being fast enough being a major burden upon his heart. "Would have been nice to get some more information out of him at least. And what of Nineveh and the Xerxans?"

"We ran Xerxes off," Esmerelda said. "As soon as Levitika crossed over the walls they took off, all of the Ninevite Guards surrendered. The city is ours now."

"Where are we now?"

"The palace," Ashlyn said. "Levitika has landed beside the city, and everyone is working hard outside to rebuild the city, and Esmerelda's mother is speaking to the Elders about their next plan of attack."

Markus couldn't help himself but laugh at that. It distracted him from the loss of his arm at the very least for a moment anyway. "'Landed,' heh, almost like parking a hovercraft."

Ashlyn smiled at this. "Kinda, yeah."

"I believe the plan is to stay here near the southern border and better prepare ourselves," Esmerelda said her hand on her chin. "The mine will be useful in producing more of our weapons, and with the citizens help we will rebuild the city and our army will be able to grow again. From there on I don't know what exactly my mother and Slagar are planning when it comes to Xerxes."

Markus nodded. "Makes sense."

Esmerelda then eyed Markus. "And what about *your* plan?"

"What do you mean?"

"You know what I mean."

He did know, and he shrugged which felt completely alien without the weight of his right arm. "I still believe I *need* to go," he said as he laid back down staring up at the ceiling. "I dunno..."

"I don't think you are in any shape to do anything right now," Ashlyn said a still at his side. "Don't you think-"

"The reason why I ask," Esmerelda said almost coolly. "Is 'cause my mother has asked Vic to come in later today."

"For what?" asked Markus.

"She said something about auto-limb."

Markus raised his head to look at the princess who nodded and he thought about what it would be like to have a robotic arm and looking down at the spot where his right arm should be, he tried to picture it. "Sounds cool," he said at last. "Besides being poked and pronged by that creep."

Ashlyn laughed though it sounded forced. "I mean, it'll be good for you to have your arm back."

"It won't be my arm though," Markus pointed out. "Just gears and clockwork, but it's better than being stuck with just my left hand forever."

"I'm going to go get my mother," Esmerelda said making her way to the door. "Don't move."

"Can't even if I wanted to," Markus said earning him a smile from her as she disappeared.

When she was gone he looked at Ashlyn who was eyeing the door Esmerelda had disappeared through. "Hey, thank you for saving me."

She smiled. "It's nothing, really."

"No it wasn't. You saved me. Thank you."

"Of course."

"What's on your mind?"

Ashlyn shook her head. "Dunno yet."

"You sure?"

"Yes."

Markus nodded, not satisfied with her answer but not wanting to push the matter. He knew what was on her mind, but if she didn't want to talk about it who was he to continue asking?

He asked her then, "How long have I been asleep?"

"Four."

His eyes snapped open. "Four *days*!?" he said shocked.

"Yeah, four since this afternoon," Ashlyn said with a smile.

He shook his head. "Unbelievable."

Ashlyn started to laugh. "You should have seen your face."

"You're a jerk."

She reached down and placed her hand upon his which he had rested on his chest. "I'm glad you're okay." she said softly.

"Yeah, me too," he said letting her joke pass. "By the way, Abner says hi."

Before Ashlyn could say anything, the door swung open and Esmerelda walked in followed by Elizabetha who cried out as she strode across the room, her face bent in anger.

"So you're awake now huh?"

Markus gulped. "Yes?"

"Do you have *any* idea how dangerous that was, attacking the Behemoth and going on without orders!?" Her face calmed down a bit and she sighed. The Queen gave Markus a small smile. "I'm glad you're okay, Markus."

"What's left of me, anyway," Markus said still shaken about the sudden outburst.

"How do you feel?"

"As good as I look, I guess."

"Good. Vic will be here soon to operate on you. When you're up to it you can join Grim, Slagar and I for briefing on future plans- most of which you will *not* be participating in until you are fully healed."

"That sounds wonderful," Markus said his stomach piercing the silence with a rumbling growl. He tried to cover his belly forgetting that his right hand no longer existed.

"Good thing I ordered the chefs to make some food for you," Elizabetha laughed. Ashlyn covered her mouth to hide her smile which made Markus turn redder. "I tell you, The Baron had a good stock of fresh food, enough for the entire city. There was feasting since the liberation."

"You don't say," Markus said smiling. "That is good."

"Did Ashlyn not tell you the good news?"

"That you liberated the city?"

"No."

"You captured The Guard?"

"Not that."

"I give up."

"Markus," Ashlyn spoke up. "When I fell out of the Behemoth I managed to snag the crystal operating it. It was falling, and I just reached out for it. I grabbed it just as I fell out of the face. When you dropped me off on the palace roof I tucked it into my pocket."

"And here it is," Elizabetha said holding up a small sack with an odd light seeping through the fabric. With the light, Markus felt a thrilling urge of escape which had to be the spirit sensing his presence.

"Wow," Markus said looking at Ashlyn with even greater respect. "That *is* good news," She smiled at that. He turned back to Elizabetha who placed the bag on the cot next to him. He looked at her curiously.

"You're the Keeper," Elizabetha said. "You deserve to handle them more than everyone else here. I cannot let Slagar or even the elders handle it, and there is no one here that can be trusted enough to use it. I'd rather it be in your hands."

"Thank you," Markus said looking down at the crystal. "I needed a dark crystal anyway."

"Yeah, Black's crystal ..." Elizabetha started.

"Just a setback, I guess," Markus tried for a smile.

"This is serious Markus," Elizabetha said. "You could have died."

"Maybe, if it wasn't for Ashlyn." He smiled at her.

"Even so, you are in no shape to leave."

"Well not anytime soon at least."

"No, you're not going *at all*."

"What?" Markus asked not sure if he had heard correctly.

"You're not going to the Kaiken Isles. Before you argue with me, listen. You are hurt, and you're missing an arm- you're in no shape to travel, and I need all the manpower here in the city in case Xerxes tries to attack again. There is work to be done here in Nineveh to prepare Levitika's departure and advancement north. I will not allow you to head out on a wild goose chase."

"Your majesty," Markus said trying hard to keep his voice level despite the absurdity of all of this. "If we move into Xerxes sooner or later I may run into that man again. Now he had a crystal, and he was able to use it. He used some of the magic on me, and sent me to sleep. I need to learn how to better defend myself."

"You still be safe here," Elizabetha said sternly. "But you are not going anymore. I will not allow it. Do you hear me Markus, you are *forbidden* to leave the city in pursuit of this Abram guy. You will stay here and help us here until you are fully healed. Do you understand?"

Markus clutched his fist tightly. He wanted to point out that it was Black himself who told him to go, and though he really was in no shape to go anytime soon, he would have to eventually. "Yes ma'am."

"Good," she sighed. "Thank you, Markus, I know the need is great, but I cannot let our only hope get killed when he is not at his best. Be patient, help us. When you are ready, when the *city* is ready, we will talk about what to do. Okay?"

"Okay," he said silently.

"All right." She turned to her daughter. "I must continue with my paperwork, food will be brought up soon. Markus when you are ready, Slagar and Grim will visit soon. Until then, just relax alright?"

"Okay," he said.

She smiled and then turned to leave. As soon as the door closed Markus cursed under his breath.

"She's right you know," Esmerelda said turning to him. "You're in no shape for travel Markus."

"Doesn't matter even if I don't want to go," he argued. I have no intention of leaving anytime soon, but as soon as I'm healed and have another arm, I'll need to."

"Mother's not going to like that," said Esmerelda nervously.

"She's not gonna like a lot more if Xerxes now has more than one crystal in their possession." Markus shook his head. "I need to learn how to defend myself better before I lose another arm or worse."

"Don't even joke about that," Ashlyn said sharply.

"I'm not joking."

"Markus," said Esmerelda. "My mother understands the importance of the crystals and your training, but she is right, you can't go anywhere yet. She didn't say you are never allowed to go to the Kaiken Isles."

"Sure didn't sound like it to me."

"Well, what can you do about it right now?" Esmerelda demanded. "No offence, but you don't look like you can even leave that bed anytime soon."

Markus opened his mouth to argue but stopped himself. Esmerelda was right, whether he liked it or not. Still, he said, "All right, I get it."

"Good," said Esmerelda satisfied.

Markus looked to Ashlyn who appeared more relaxed. He smiled at her. "Lemme guess, you're happy that I ain't leaving anytime soon?"

Ashlyn shrugged nonchalantly. "Maybe a little."

He laughed at that. They all did.

Markus

Food was soon brought up and while they ate pheasant breasts with wild rice, Esmerelda got Markus and Ashlyn caught up about the recent events, primarily concerning Slagar and The Elders.

"He was pretty upset when my mother refused to have him study the crystal from Veegar's Behemoth," she explained between bites of rice. "It got worse once he found out that you lost the last one, had a real cow which made the council question my mother's decisions to let you keep the crystals."

"That guy, I swear…" Markus shook his head. It was moments like these where he wished Black was still alive; the Hunter would have no trouble putting the hypnotist in his place. "Why does he even want it when he knows it's dangerous?"

"Well, he *did* study The Eldest the most and realized the danger behind it. Even the notes left behind by The Owl's council were not enough for him to understand the very gravity of it. Maybe he thinks a lesser crystal would be easier to study, to understand. As you can imagine, Black never let go of his even when he came to Levitika in the first place."

"I don't blame him," Ashlyn commented her meal already finished. She had been kind enough to cut Markus' meat so that he only had to use his fork, his own meal propped between his legs on the cot.

"Well there's nothing *to* understand," Markus said. "Nothing for Slagar anyway. We need to destroy them."

"Thankfully," Esmerelda pointed out. "Some of the Elders agree with that statement and argued on my mother's behalf. But that isn't all Slagar was giving my mother a headache about. He's spoken up about how it is pointless trying to rebuild Nineveh, and he's got The Elders backing him up on this."

"Talk about making a mess and leaving someone else to clean it," Markus said bitterly. "What the hell are they thinking that for?"

"They're saying we are wasting time here in the city," said Esmerelda. "They want to just focus on Levitika and then move on, perhaps with someone other than The Keeper."

"It was their Owl's prophecy to begin with," Markus argued. "I can't believe that all of them think that now, especially given how far we've come so far."

"That's just it," Esmerelda said cautiously. "Their leading argument is that you are still a kid."

"So is half of the Angels," Ashlyn pointed out. "Some of them are barely older than Mark and I."

"Doesn't matter. When it comes to power, they think an adult would be better suited, and we obviously know which adult they are referring to. Also, it doesn't help when we are told we are wasting the crystals on a- Ahem, 'crippled child,' as were their own words, especially Slagar."

"Oh, how sweet of them," Markus said taking a swig of water. He wiped his mouth and continued. "They had just captured the first of many cities to liberate and they are already arguing about what actions to take concerning the crystals? Shouldn't that be what *I'm* worried about?"

"What did your mother say?" Ashlyn asked Esmerelda.

"That's the hard part," said Esmerelda. "The council is needed to make sure my mother makes the right decisions by the people. However, with Slagar being the sleaze that he is, he's managed to turn some of them against her. I think that is why so many are collaborating and wanting to rebel against her. They want to take Xerxes now and leave this place defenseless, and they want to use the crystals to make super-weapons. And although that is not a *horrible* idea, we need the support of the people in the country, without them we won't be able to hold against The Capitol."

"That's what your mother said?" asked Markus.

"That was the basis of her argument in terms of moving on, anyway. As for you and the crystals in particular, the little support she does have backed her up and say to trust in The Owl's judgement as it was proclaimed. That got most of them to back down, so for the time being, yes, you are still The Keeper, Markus."

"And here I was thinking I could retire early," Markus said with good humor. Though he doubt he would be of much help until he got another arm in, as well as find Abram.

Moving on, Esmerelda added, "She wants to try and make a deal with the queen of Xerxes. The queen there is an honest person, if she will not bargain with us she will let us know. However, if she were to join us, the entire southern region could possibly hold against the Capitol. And seeing as Xerxes is trying to break free of The Capitol already, I can't think of a better ally and the Elders can't argue with that either."

"I can," said Markus confidently as he pointed at his stump. "This aside, that warrior I fought said he was here for slaves, and the crystal Veegar had on him," He cringed at the look Ashlyn gave him at the mention of her father's name. He would need to remind himself to check on her about that later. "No offence, but the leadership of Xerxes doesn't fill me with much confidence."

"Just like our own council," Esmerelda pointed out. "You can't judge the queen based on her subordinates."

"Even so, it doesn't sit right with me. Why would the queen make such an order?"

"Hold on," Esmerelda said holding up a hand towards Markus. "I understand you're sceptic about it, but trust me when I saw Queen Psyren isn't that kind of woman. She hates slavery. So if what you say is true, then there must be a mistake or perhaps that warrior is up to something else. I'm sure there are more men like Slagar in the world. Besides, we don't know if Xerxes is even aware of The Dreaming or the crystals, so what use does she have gaining them?"

"You should ask your mom about that," Ashlyn said turning away from Markus to his relief. "Because what if that warrior went rogue? We would have a claim for her to decontaminate her army, and possibly join Levitika and Nineveh against the northern city."

"I will," the princess said brushing aside her bangs that have fallen upon her face. She turned to Markus. "In the meantime, nothing concrete is decided concerning you. For now, Nineveh is receiving the help it needs."

"Good, I'm glad," said Markus. As much as he had hated Nineveh growing up especially how the people had treated him and Ruth after his home had been placed under Black's protection, he was glad they were getting the help they needed to rebuild.

In the meantime, he had something else on his mind. "Do you guys have any idea what getting an auto-limb is like?"

"I never asked anyone who had one about it," said Ashlyn.

"Apparently," Esmerelda said as she took Markus and Ashlyn's plates on top of her own to set aside. "It's very painful."

"Oh joy," Markus groaned and at that moment there was another knock on the door. It opened to reveal a very tired-looking Vic. But his three eyes went soft and he had a small smile as he stepped inside carrying a large duffel bag with him.

"Hate to interrupt your lunch," he said dropping the bag on the floor and crossing the room whilst pulling out a measurement rope. "But I need some measurements before getting to work. How are you feeling Marky?"

"Dandy," Markus replied. "And don't call me that."

"Whatever you say," said Vic in a bored tone while digging through his pockets for some measuring tape.

"I heard that you were in the city?" Markus asked him.

"'ep. Helping with side paneling to homes, and I even did some work on some people and droids with damaged parts. The doctor is down there now working on the sick- Infested city this is..." he muttered as he measured Markus' left arm, one eye looking the tape up and down while the other two focused on the boy himself.

"He was in here patching you up, and then went straight down into the city with me. Been a long coupl'a days, it has."

"The same one who put my arm in the sling?" Markus thought looking back to the unkindly doctor grumbling as he fixed Markus' broken arm a few weeks ago. "Oh, the irony."

"That's what he said," Vic laughed. "All of this and I ain't gonna be able to get me Pluton-oil, oh well." He turned and smiled at Markus, winking with two of his eyes. "No matter. Least I get to work on you. Took down a Behemoth, eh, not a lot of people can say that."

"I had help," Markus said looking at Ashlyn who turned away smiling.

"All's well then." Vic turned and went to his duffel bag. He carried it over to the table and with one swipe of his hand knocked everything save the gauntlet with the crystal off the table. He turned to Markus who was giving him a dirty look, and then turned back to the crystal. He then looked at Markus again with a trouble-making grin on his face.

"With your permission Markus," he said. "I would like to try something new with the auto-limb I'm gonna make you. It has something to do with the crystals you need to find. With your permission, of course, I won't do it unless you want me to. But

I'll advise you," he picked up the gauntlet and held it to the light. "Never to wear these again. Slagar gave 'em to ya eh?"

"Yes?" Markus asked looking skeptical at the dealer.

"Well, Imma tell you right now, boy, ya got yourself some rigged armor here."

"What are you talking about?"

The mutant pulled the crystal out which flashed bright blue in the sunlight and tossed the gauntlet to the corner of the room. "Thing was meant to amplify magical entities, which in this case was your crystals, yes, but they also have a failsafe. Should you die, the gauntlets would cut off of you with your hand still in it."

"Uh, what?" Markus asked in disbelief.

Vic nodded. "Don't take offence, as I understand what Slagar is doing, he is ensuring that should you die, the crystals still have enough energy to resist potential users similar to you. But it is also designed to literally crawl back to the castle. My guess is they would go to the queen, but say Slagar had his biocode or someone else on the council on the list?"

"So it would move with my severed hand *in* it?" Markus demanded.

"That's disgusting!" Ashlyn said sticking out her tongue.

"And how do you know this exactly?" Esmerelda demanded with clenched fists.

Vic answered peering at the gauntlet some more, "'Cause I heard him talking to the queen about something considering how 'the gauntlet hasn't returned' while I was on my way up here. Looking at this guy here, that must be what they meant. They were trying to see if they could get it back, but I'm guessing it ain't coming back."

He sat it down on the table and looked at the teens more seriously. "Look, maybe Slagar had ill intentions with those gauntlets and maybe not. Can't tell for certain, can you? I ain't a fan of the guy, but he is loyal to the queen and that makes him both a friend of mine as well as an enemy. But until then, I wouldn't accept so much as a piece of bread from him until you check it thoroughly, and I mean it: *thoroughly*."

Markus looked to Esmerelda. "You think your mom knew about it?"

"If she did she would have told you," said Esmerelda. "She saw it before you left for Nineveh, right? My guess is she didn't know until Slagar approached her, which I am sure is going to make her really angry with him."

"Let's hope for the latter," said Ashlyn.

"Will you check with her though?" asked Markus. "For me?"

The princess said, "Of course."

Vic cleared his throat and said, "Marky, I have your permission then?"

"What will it do?" Markus asked, taking Vic's advise about being thorough.

"Think of it as a more powerful arm, that has a little bit of a kick in it," Vic winked again. "Auto-limbs are connected via nerve-endings, means immediate access to thoughts similar to that of movement. Also, you can trust me that it ain't gonna just pop off and take off without your permission."

Markus bit his lip and then shrugged. "Alright,"

"Great!" Vic said pleased and then remained silent after as he took out some parts and got to work tinkering on the table.

Markus began to rub his head, his dirty blonde locks turning into a rat's nest as he tangled his fingers into it. He would need a haircut soon but that was the last thing on his mind. "So Slagar has backup plans in case I fail. If I had died he would have gotten the crystal and who knows what could have happened?"

"I'll talk to my mother and see what that is all about. "I promise, Mark." Esmerelda promised.

"Thank you." He paused then and said, "Wait, did you just call me 'Mark?'"

"Don't like nicknames it seems," Vic grumbled his back still to the teens.

"Hey," Markus warned him but both his and Ashlyn's eyes were on the princess now.

"Well…" Esmerelda began to turn a shade of pink. "That *is* your name."

"Never heard you call me that before."

Esmerelda looked away embarrassed. "Sorry, guess it slipped."

"Don't be," Markus said quickly. "I just noticed."

"Okay."

"Anyways, before I interrupted us," Markus said peering over to Vic. "How long is that gonna take?"

"Coupl'a hours, give or take."

Markus nodded. "Alrighty then."

Esmerelda asked Markus and Ashlyn, "You both are done? I'll take the leftovers downstairs and go talk to my mom." She then turned to Ashlyn. "Will you come with me?"

"Yes, but can I actually meet you in the war room?" Ashlyn asked. "I need to talk to Markus."

Esmerelda's mouth went into an 'o' shape with understanding. She said yes and began piling cups and whatever leftovers onto the stack of plates she had made. When she was gone Ashlyn turned to Vic.

"Vic could you…"

"Nope," he said reaching into his duffel bag he pulled out a pair of earmuffs which he placed over his ears without another word. In a slightly louder voice he said, "Not gonna stop now, too delicate to do so."

"He's so strange," Ashlyn said shaking her head.

"You don't say." Markus said sitting up so that he could sit on the side of the bed next to Ashlyn. He turned to her. "What's up?"

Ashlyn pursed her lips. For minutes she had been silent to the point where Markus was becoming fidgety in agitation, anxious to hear what it was Ashlyn wanted to tell him.

Not knowing entirely what to do, he spoke up. "Listen I…" He sighed. "Thank you. For saving my life. I'm really sorry about you dad and… I wish I could have saved him. I tried, and… well… I'm sorry."

Ashlyn then turned furiously at Markus making him gulp, only to tackle him in a hug strong enough to crush the breath out of him. He let out a puff of air as she hugged him rightly around the shoulders. He felt pain in his stump but he ignored it, concentrated on wondering what had gotten into his friend.

"There's no need to be sorry," she whispered. "I'm just so glad you're alive."

Markus wrapped his one arm around her, rubbing her back as he felt tears spill down his chest. "Hey now, hey now, I'm here." He whispered.

"I'm upset I did not get to actually tell my father goodbye…" Ashlyn sniffed. "But when you were tackled, I was torn. I thought I was going to lose you both. He deserved what he got for what he did, but I still would have liked to talk to him one last time."

"I don't blame you…" said Markus, although he had *plenty* of reasons why he would blame Ashlyn, he was not about to bring those up. Not now.

"But now, seeing you here and well… I was more worried about you." She looked up at Markus, her eyes puffy and red. "I'm so happy you're alive Markus. That monster was going to kill you." She squeezed her eyes shut as if the memories of that day was flashing through her mind in constant flashes. "When we got to you, you were so cold and there was so much blood, I…"

Markus pulled her closer. "Hey. I'm not going anywhere." He said resting his chin on top of her head smelling the scent of lavender coming from it. "I'm still here."

"I'm so glad… Thank you, for saving my life again."

"Worked out for both of our benefit I guess," Markus whispered.

"Yeah," she agreed and while Vic worked none the wiser about what was being said or what was happening behind him at all, they remained silent just enjoying seeing each other safe and sound.

<u>Esmerelda</u>

Esmerelda was waiting just outside the war room with her back against the hallway walls for Ashlyn to show up.

She was looking out of the palace windows that had not been shattered during the battle watching as buildings were being rebuilt and parts of the Behemoth was taken away for scrap metal. More machines and vehicles flew in with civilians and supplies. Soon the city of Nineveh would be thriving and the thought of it made her smile. Her mother really was doing a good job, and one day she would be in charge and do just as she did. Be a good leader who cares for her people.

Her daydream was interrupted when she felt Ashlyn standing beside her. Her friend looked like she had been crying.

"You okay?" she asked.

"I'm fine, just happy I guess," Ashlyn smiled.

Esmerelda smiled back. "That's good."

"Are they almost done in there?" Ashlyn asked tilting her head in the direction of the door.

"They're still speaking." Esmerelda paused and then said almost abruptly, "You realize he's going to leave, do you?"

Ashlyn looked at her. "What do you mean?"

"Markus. I don't think he's going to listen to my mother. If he's determined to get to the Kaiken Isles-"

"He's hurt though," Ashlyn said suddenly, her eyebrows knit together in a scowl. "He's in no shape to go anywhere."

"I know, I know," Esmerelda said softly. "He knows it too, I'm not saying Markus is stupid, just headstrong."

"He's not allowed to leave," Ashlyn said. "Your mother-"

"I know," Esmerelda said again in a patient tone. "But you guys weren't supposed to leave Nineveh either in the first place."

"That was mostly me and Ruth talking…"

"Regardless, you saw how determined he was when he first told us," said Esmerelda. "I don't believe Markus is crazy enough to go even after Vic gets him a new arm. It'll take time, no doubt, but I'm worried he'll try to slip out."

"He wouldn't do that," said Ashlyn stubbornly. "Even if he was considering that, he would tell us."

"Would he?" asked Esmerelda. "He's kept it from us for quite a long time already."

"Everyone has secrets," said Ashlyn. "I'm not happy he kept it from us either, but I trust him not to just run off without a word."

"All right," Esmerelda said in surrender. "I'm just saying so."

Ashlyn laid her head back against the wall deep in thought. Esmerelda twiddled her fingers unsure of what else to do. "Maybe he will leave without your mother's consent, maybe he won't. Doesn't matter. He's our friend, and we just need to be there for him."

"I know," said Esmerelda, but even as she said this she couldn't help but wonder. *But how far is that going to stretch? Especially between you and I.*

Markus

While Vic was applying a new socket-rotator in Markus' shoulder, he was studying the crystal Ashlyn had managed to grab to take his mind off of the fact that metal was being fused to his shoulder bones. Vic was as he promised silent as he worked, but it still made Markus uncomfortable with how close the mutant was to him. Especially when he came back to double and sometimes triple-check measurements or pinch at the skin to fat ratio on Markus' left bicep and shoulder.

Still, he kept his focus on the crystal between his fingers, studying the many patterns and sides of the gem. It was lighter than Black's dark crystal, but Markus could feel the power between his fingers. There something in here, similar to that of Fethawit, but definitely different. Almost… inhuman. What had the spirit within go through since being trapped within? And who was it?

More importantly, why did it feel so closed off from Markus who should have no trouble speaking to the spirits of the crystals?

His mind then went to the battle, all who were killed by both The Angels and Xerxan armies. How many Ninevites were killed because of the Guards cowardice? How many Angels died in battle to free them and take the city… He then remembered Jacob being skewered by the warrior.

He turned to Vic. "Vic?" When the mutant didn't answer, he pulled off the earmuffs and Vic turned on him annoyed.

"What?"

"The leader of the assault- Jacob?"

"What about him?"

"What happened with him, is he…"

Vic scowled and looked back at his work, his soldering tool momentarily burning into Markus' split nerve-endings and causing him to cry out in pain.

"Dead," Vic said at last. "Buried him outside the city walls. That was his last dying wish the soldier who assisted him said."

"Oh my…" Markus laid back deep into his pillow. He did not know Jacob that well but he risked a lot to bend the rules and save the slaves. And Markus had not even thought of the young Angel until now, making the pain of his memory much greater to bear.

"He died for what he believed in," Vic said attaching some kind of rubber piece to a piece of metal. "He fought hard for Levitika, and did what he could to protect you. I know, I saw him while escorting a truckload of Ninevites out. Damn fine warrior he was."

Was. There was that word. Was. Not *is* anymore, but *was* as in no more. The guilt became much greater and Markus turned his head away in almost shame from Vic who didn't fail to take notice.

"Hey, hey, hey," Vic said turning around to look at Markus. "That man died for what he believed in. Don't blame yourself for what he did. It was his act and his alone.

He knew what he was getting into the moment he swore allegiance to Levitika. Don't blame yourself. This is war, Markus. And war is hell."

"It really is nothing like what you hear in passing," Markus said at last.

"Every veteran I ever met always tries to sugarcoat it," said Vic. "Every Angel who died in battle fought for a cause, and that was to take Nineveh and secure it for the good of Levitika and the rest of the Wastelands. Jacob knew that there was a chance he might not have made it back home to his girlfriend. He knew that the moment he strapped those wings on his back, and she did too. He died with honor."

Vic turned back around to continue his work. "There's an old quote that most Angels live by: 'Honor the dead, fight like hell for the living.' And he fought like hell for you, Ashlyn, his girlfriend, and pretty much everyone in both Levitika and Nineveh. Don't let his memory go to waste by blaming yourself. Just do your part and make sure his sacrifice in this first part of the war won't end in vain."

Markus looked back down at his crystal feeling still sad, but a little better. Vic's words played over and over in his head. He was right. This was war, and this battle was the first of many to come in order to end the tyranny of the north and bring the Wastelands together at last.

In this moment, Markus thought of Black, and how the Hunter had said no one truly chose to deal with all of this. No one chose to wage war against The Capitol and those who try to defy Levitika, but it was about how one chose to respond to it. He had comforted Markus in his time of doubt, and here was Vic of all people in his own way, reminding Markus of those important words of wisdom.

Though it sure would be nice to have Damion Black alive and fighting alongside them all, Markus knew exactly what the Hunter would say in this time of recovery.

He *would* fight, and he would keep going. He would do what he can, and he would do whatever it took to save the country and those around him. Markus would not let Jacob's death go to waste. 'Honor the dead, fight like hell for the living'. Helluva quote, but true to the end.

His thoughts were interrupted when he became aware that Vic had stopped tinkering on him, and was staring at him with a new auto-limb arm in his hands looking thoroughly pleased. Markus had to admit himself that the prosthetic arm was impressive; Bronze-metal fused with steel from the shoulder joint to the fingers. The flexible cables between the joints as Vic showed him bent and almost looked like a normal arm. What made Markus even more excited about it was the forearm of the arm. The backside appeared to have a stainless-steel plating on it, and the underside had flexing slots within similar to the ones in Slagar's gauntlets. Markus didn't need Vic to tell him what those slots were for.

"Titanium steel," Vic explained trailing his finger along the metal. "The arm is built to withstand most blows, but the steel plating is what will better protect you and the arm. It makes as a small shield in case you get into close combat. The underside *here*," he said turning the arm to show the slots. "Is what I had in mind: You're going to need an arm to work your magic from those crystals and you can't very well just keep 'em in your pockets can you? The arm works like normal, you will be able to channel energy through the special wiring that I have made. It is just like your old arm, but *slightly* better." He grinned from ear to ear when he said that last part.

"Wow," Markus said thoroughly impressed. "That's incredible."

"Also..." He pointed at the hand which Markus noticed was dotted with little black pads no bigger than an ant. "Rubberized sensors, so that your arm will be able to not only grab things but know how much pressure to apply. Once it is linked to your nervous system it will feel like a normal arm- Aside from the phantom limb you may feel on occasion."

"That's incredible," Markus said feeling a little more excited now despite having no idea what phantom limb was.

"I'm glad you like it," Vic said. "Now comes the hard part..."

"Okay?"

"I need to connect the nerves to the wiring before I can connect the arm. And I ain't gonna lie Markus boy, this part is gonna hurt like hell."

"Like how bad?"

"It's like pinching a nerve, like your whole arm is on fire."

"Oh."

"'Oh' indeed," Vic agreed. "But think of it as a shot. The faster we get it done the less pain you will have to deal with. Also, should we ever have to remove your arm to maintain or replace it, it won't hurt nearly as bad. I just need to make sure that you will stay still while I apply the wiring. If you stay still I can work faster and cause less pain. Less time, less pain. Got it?"

"I got it," Markus said nervously.

Vic smiled. "Excellent." He then reached into his pocket and pulled out a strap of leather. When Markus looked at him confused he explained, "So you don't bite your own tongue."

"Oh joy," Markus said taking the piece of leather and putting it into his mouth. He then gripped the side of the cot with his one hand while Vic slipped the arm half-way into the new socket. He then took up some wires and looked at Markus, who grunted that he was ready. And then he began to apply the wiring to the nerves within the shoulder.

It felt as if lighting was striking his shoulder it was so painful; he cried out biting hard into the leather strap and crying out past it. He felt as if his brain was going to explode and every cell in his body was on fire; he kicked hard at the cot but his body remained stationary. He would not move- anything to make the operation go by faster. Tears began to roll down his cheeks and his hand began to hurt from clutching the cot so tightly; still the pain did not dwindle and did not for almost a minute.

When he felt the pain finally subside he let the leather drop from his mouth. His teeth and jaws hurt, but the pain was nothing next to the agony of the nerves being connected to machinery. The leather had his bitemarks deep inside and he could see the crooked tooth he had near his molars. He looked to his right to see that the auto-limb arm had been successfully attached to his new shoulder joint. The scarring around the metal looked freshly healed from the cauterization, and the metallic arm gleamed in the dim sunlight through the window. On a whim, he tried closing his right hand, and to his astonishment the auto-limb hand closed. Intrigued he began to wiggle his fingers, which clicked as the fingertips tapped his palm. He began to extend and retract his elbow, getting a feel for the movement. Though he couldn't physically feel the auto-limb, the movement felt as natural as the day he was born.

He looked up to see Vic whose front was covered in blood and droplets of oil come over with a small glass of water.

"Here," he said. "Hold this. No, no, the *new* hand."

Markus did as he was told, the auto-limb arm moved and grabbed the glass like a normal hand; gingerly, careful not to spill the water within, and the hand did not crush the glass in its grip.

Vic smiled approvingly. "Good, good. It seems to be working great."

Markus reached out with his real hand to touch the auto-limb arm. In his head he felt the auto-limb arm like his real arm, but his real hand felt only cold soulless metal. This was not his arm despite feeling as if it was. Was this what prosthetics felt like? In your mind they felt like a part of your own body, but to your own touch felt as cold as any robotics. It was incredible and at the same time sad.

He looked at Vic with a grateful smile nonetheless. It was the first time he felt genuine appreciation of the mutant mechanic. "Thank you, Vic."

Vic smiled. "Yep, not bad I might say." He then reached down and picked up the Light crystal and handed it out to Markus. "Here, lemme see the dark one."

Markus handed it to him, and taking his arm Vic stuck the two crystals into two respective slots and they closed onto the crystals. Immediately Markus felt the presence of Abner and whoever was in the Dark crystal. Even with the auto-limb, he felt them as close as if he was holding them with his real hand. It truly was an incredible piece of hardware.

"I don't know what to say," Markus said. "I can feel them, I can feel my real arm, everything."

"Not too shabby, eh?" Vic said smiling bright.

"Unnatural, but cool."

Vic then busted out laughing. "Ain't nothing natural about a fake arm, especially one that can channel energy through the wiring connected to your nerves."

"True." Markus said tilting his head. "Thanks again, Vic."

Vic said, "Anytime."

Markus couldn't wait to show Ashlyn and Esmerelda his new arm. He hoped that their meeting with Elizabetha while important, didn't take too long.

Ashlyn

The discussion with Queen Elizabetha went as well as Ashlyn figured. After telling her about Slagar's gauntlets as well as another warrior was out there looking for the crystals she simple said 'thank you for informing me,' and went back to her map which she had laid out across the table of the war room. She didn't seem to care, and despite Esmerelda's efforts, her mother didn't seem to budge.

"I know about Slagar's gauntlets, he told me already. You don't need to worry about him and you shouldn't. I'm sorry, but I need some time alone to think."

The girls left the queen's presence at last. Ashlyn in particular was furious and she stomped alongside Esmerelda back to Markus' room. They wanted to see how their friend was doing but the queen's attitude and lack of urgency had put them both in a foul mood.

"I don't get it," Esmerelda said. "She knows not to trust Slagar or the other elders but she can't just act this calm- what if he tries to pull something?"

"Your mother is smart, I think she'll be fine," Ashlyn said this having to spit out the word *think*. "Besides, she's got to focus on the city right now, like she said before the more Ninevites learn to trust her and accept her as a gracious leader, then she'll have more support."

"People talk though."

"That's why you're here to make sure she doesn't wander off her path."

Esmerelda snorted. "A lot of good that did us."

Ashlyn decided it best to take their minds off of the queen and whatever mischief Slagar may or may not be involved in. "Forget it. Let's just trust her for now. Let's go see Mark."

Esmerelda nodded, still unhappy. "Agreed."

When they finally arrived, Ashlyn pushed the door to Markus' room open to see only Vic inside cleaning up his equipment. He flashed a smile at them. "You're back," He stated.

"Hey Vic," Esmerelda said looking at the empty cot.

"Where's Markus?" Ashlyn asked immediately worried and thinking about what Esmerelda had said earlier.

"Got up and walked out, said he was going to the city outside. Didn't say much."

"Did he say where?" Esmerelda demanded.

"Nope."

The girls looked at each other and in unison turned and hurried out of the room. As they sprinted down the hall they heard Vic shout after them, "You're welcome!"

They didn't say anything back. They just hurried to find Markus, and hope to whatever god was listening that he wasn't about to do something stupid.

<u>Zachariah</u>

Zachariah awoke with a start, the sound of children laughing echoed in his head.

He was slumped against a burnt tree on the outskirts of what looked like to be once a great forest. The burned landscape appeared to be a few weeks old, for fresh buds were now growing from the scorched ground. The tree that Zachariah laid against was ashy, and when he peeled himself off soot was now covering his backside. He stretched and began to rub the sleep from his eyes.

Dreaming?

"Yes," Zachariah said standing up.

Anything you remember?

"I was running, with a girl. I don't know who she is though."

I'm sure time will help you remember.

"Right." He turned towards the ruined forest and he began to walk on. As he began to cross the Wastelands he asked Akuta. "So who is this Abram?"

He is a monk whom I have met a couple of times within The Dreaming. He walks amongst the Nightmares and the Dream Striders, speaking, whispering, gathering information and giving as well. Many of times The Eldest would try to find him, but every time Abram would slip from his grasp. I was one of the few lucky of the brethren to find and speak to him. Good man he is, better company than the Nightmares.

"And you say he can help me?"

Hard to say. But no one knows about the bridges and gateways as he does. There was another, but he is no longer among the living.

"That sucks."

I only know from this side of the realm, Abram is the only one who knows both sides. Akuta paused and then said, *Oh how I wish I could walk as you are. But at least I can see all through your eyes. Been forever since I was able to see the world without straining myself or putting myself in danger.*

"Can you really be in danger in The Dreaming?"

Oh yes, just like good dreams or Dream Striders as I call them anyway, there are Nightmares. Mankind's greatest fears, regrets, agony, anger, all the negative feelings that overcome you while you are asleep. Yes, those feelings and senses are necessary, for they help guide us and shape who we are. But too much and you can be overtaken. And let me tell you, my Nightmares are chock full of the terror of my past, and I have none to blame but myself for that. There are things mankind shouldn't be capable of, and yet here we are.

"Who were you?" Zachariah asked passing by a crumbled building that appeared nearly a thousand years old. "Before you were trapped within, I mean?"

Oh a story that is. A long one at that.

"We got a long journey to go still."

Touche... I was once an officer in a city south from here. I fought many battles against The Capitol, as well as monsters and pirates with my sister, Sapphira. But when The Mad King found a way to open a portal to The Dreaming and unlock the secret of true magic, we were captured during battle and offered as sacrifices. And then lo and behold, I was trapped within The Dreaming, becoming a portable gateway to the land of dreams. Me, and a few others, most of them having served the Mad King all along.

"How many of you are there?" asked Zachariah.

Seven. Seven in total, all to see if an eighth would work. It had. The poor sod is lost, a minute god over a realm he has no business being in.

"So there is eight?"

No. There are seven of us, Disciples as we had been called once upon a time. The Mad King had a son who was deathly ill, and he turned him into a greater gateway with a greater crystal. The last I ever heard from it, it was in the hands of the Great Owl.

"Who?"

That is not important, not yet, anyway. The Mad King eventually became foolish enough to do the same to himself and extract enough power to make him the most sinister of all crystals Light and Dark.

"What is the difference? Between Light and Dark?"

Basically what the spirits struggle with. Some were legendary, walked in the light in search for justice and goodwill, as I once believed. Others were in it for their own selfish desires. And now they pay the price for it.

"It that what happened to you?"

Yes.

"And what of your animal forms?"

It's just something that has to do with The Dreaming. To be honest, I never quite understood it either. None of us had.

Zachariah was silent for a moment. And then, "You said The Eldest wished to escape as well as you and your brethren. How would he do it?"

The only way to do so is to open the portal he had once opened a long time ago, which he cannot do on his own. But just like me, he is capable of influencing those who walk among the world. And if he opens it, he will succeed. You see, to destroy our crystals, and sever all gateways is to find The Keeper, who is the only one capable to destroy them and let our spirits free. The Great Owl had been the first to understand the power of the crystals and through them, waged war against The Capitol. The city of Levitika was the first to rebel, and the first to achieve the unachievable. A living, magical island in the sky.

"Levitika..." Zachariah said in thought. "I've heard that fairy tale before..."

Believe me when I say it is real, my friend. I was there, I saw it just before the ship carrying The Mad King had been destroyed. It was The Great Owl who sacrificed herself in order to stop his reign of terror and scatter the crystals all over the Northern Wastelands. It was she, who apparently found within her time in The Dreaming a prophecy speaking of The Keeper.

"The Keeper... Who would that be, and what would that have to do with me?"

That is what I hope Abram will answer when we reach his island.

Zachariah nodded. "And what do you hope to achieve of this?"

Simple. Freedom, and that can only happen two ways. One, I become the sole owner of your body, or my crystal is destroyed and I die. And it is difficult when you are trapped within the realm of dreams where The Eldest rules and wishes to escape.

"Hopefully he never escapes. And we can find a way to free you, *without* having you steal my body. I still wish to know who I am and why I have come to be what I am now."

I am sure we will find out soon enough.

Zachariah then took out the Dark Crystal Lee had dropped. He could feel something tugging at his mind, but he could not tell what it was for sure. Was the spirit within here trying to speak to him? Zachariah shoved the crystal back into his pocket and continued his journey in silence.

Akuta, said no more, nor did he attempt to speak on Zachariah's thoughts.

Eventually after a few hours Zachariah saw a faint smudge in the distance lit with life essence bellowing above it like smoke, and as he got closer realized that it was a village. Which one he did not know, nor did he remember any names that he could think of. He pressed on, the village getting larger and more clear as he got closer.

When he first entered the village there was the sound of mingled chatter as well as a few dogs barking; there was the clanging of metal against stone, and the sound of children at play. In fact, as he passed an alley between two wooden houses, two young boys came out kicking a slightly deflated ball between them. Zachariah pulled his new coat tighter around his chest to hide his crystal heart. He nodded to the boys who waved kindly. Zachariah waved but kept going.

All around him people turned to take a weary glimpse at the traveler only to get back to whatever they were doing. A group of men were playing cards on a small wooden crate and sipping tankards of ale. One guy with an eye patch on his left eye and a cigar between his lips eyes Zachariah closely as he walked by but he ignored the glance. He walked up to a small window in the side of one of the houses where the smell of baked bread and spices emitted like a cloud. At the window writing something into a notepad was a woman with black hair that looked as if it was chopped off with a pair of shears. She looked up and smiled at Zachariah, her eyes as green as freshly grown grass.

"Hello," she said.

"Hello," Zachariah replied ignoring the sniggering sounds in the back of his mind.

"What'll it be?" she asked.

"Um," Zachariah scratched the back of his head. "Just water is fine but, I don't have any money."

The girl nodded, "One water coming up- on the house."

"Thank you." He turned and rested against the wall beside the window to take a better look at the village around him. "Miss?" he called inside just as she came out with a small glass of water. "What village is this?"

"Lakeshire," the girl said. "South of Xerxes." She looked at him more closely. "What's up with your eyes?"

Zachariah unknowingly tried to shield his face. "Um I, I'm not sure."

"Sorry didn't mean to sound rude," the girl said trying to smile. "I was going to say they're really pretty. I haven't seen purple eyes in a long time."

"Thank you," Zachariah said taking his water and chugging it in one gulp. Immediately he felt refreshed as if his insides were washed clean by the water.

"Anytime." The girl stuck a scarred hand out the window towards him. "Alma."

Zachariah looked at her hand, and then shook it. "Zachariah."

"Zach. Nice eyes for a nice name," she commented. "What brings you to Lakeshire?"

"I'm traveling south."

"Did you come from Xerxes?"

"No." In truth he did not know for sure nor did he know anything about the lands. If she named another place he would go with it."

"So you're from one of the northern villages then? How did you manage to get this far south?"

"Come again?"

"No one is allowed past the Xerxan border, it's how the government keeps track of all who are in their area. I swear they are no different than The Capitol."

"Is this village in their boundaries?" Zachariah asked in a serious tone.

"Yeah, they're the closest besides Nineveh, and so we get taxed to death for living outside the city walls. Soldiers come every once in a while to pick up prisoners or take people away, other than that we try to keep our own customs and try not to get involved with the cities affairs."

"Oh."

"Why do you ask?"

"No reason," Zachariah shook his head. "I was just wondering."

Alma looked at him skeptically. "Right." She nodded. She laid back her palms flat on the counter. "Well," she said with a smile. "Welcome to Lakeshire nonetheless."

"Thank you really."

"So where are you heading again?"

"Kaiken."

"Kaiken's in the west I thought you said you were heading south?"

"Oh," Zachariah said closing his mouth fast.

"So which is it?" Alma said smiling even more so.

"I'm going to Kaiken." Zachariah said trying to sound more confident than he was.

"You are definitely not from around here, are you?"

Zachariah said nothing.

"Don't worry I ain't a snitch, but best to be careful with what you say." She flashed another grin, this one more kind than the last.

"Okay," Zachariah said handing her his glass to which she took and placed it in the corner of the counter.

"So I'm guessing you aren't from any of the other villages either then?"

Can we trust her?

Hard to tell with this one past a face like that. Maybe we should keep our tongue in our mouth?

Maybe you should shut up. Zachariah pushed the thoughts from his head and cleared his throat before answering. "No."

She nodded biting her lip in thought. "You from the Capitol?"

"No. At least I don't think so."

Alma raised a crooked eyebrow. "Then where else could you be from? Not a lot of villages under the Capitol's rule could even hope to travel south. Not if they wanna be in trouble with Nineveh."

"I..." Zachariah shook his head. "I shouldn't say. It's best that I get going." He turned to go but he felt her hand grasp his wrist.

"Wait," she said pointing past him. He looked to see soldiers escorting someone towards the pavilion. "Soldiers. You wanna leave, act natural around here. You leave they might get suspicious."

"Outstanding," Zachariah murmured as he turned back to her. He leaned against the counter to make it look like he was a local there. "Why would they get suspicious?"

"Like I said, they keep tabs on all who live in their area. And ever since they keep getting their asses kicked in the south they are more worried about spies within their district."

Zachariah shook his head. "Wonderful."

"Yeah, ever since their new general took his seat war has been going on for a couple of years now between Xerxes and Nineveh. Everyone says it is safer within the walls, but you can't trust anyone in Xerxes. It's full of fools who hide their eyes from the danger in hopes that it is a dream. I don't even think the queen knows what is truly happening to her home."

"That can't be how it is," Zachariah said deeply concerned. "The queen was a strong woman, she led the district far into economics and technology. My own village was the primary plantation for wheat and corn." He stopped himself fast, surprised at the sudden remembrance of his village.

"Oh," Alma said smiling. "So you are from Mileshire- the farming area that is?"

"Mileshire? No I'm from..."

The sound of children at play and cows bellowing then sounded in his head including a few coherent words within the many sounds emitting from the dark matter of his memory; and among those words sprang the one he was looking for. "Gohan."

Alma gave him a suspicious look. "Gohan?" she repeated.

"Yes," he said confidently. He was sure that was the name of his village. *Well done,* he heard Akuta murmur.

"Um... Gohan is not a village anymore," she said. She leaned forward. "It was destroyed over three decades ago."

"Thirty years!" Zachariah gasped and he looked down at himself as if he expected to age suddenly. "But..."

Alma took a step back from the sudden shock. "Yes…" she said nervously. She had been looking at him closely too, perhaps wondering how old this stranger really was.

Zachariah was about to say 'that's impossible' or something along those lines when Alma's eyes suddenly went wide and she stepped back up to the window.

Realizing almost too late Zachariah turned away from the window and rested against the wall as usual when someone who he saw in an instant was a Xerxan soldier judging by the blackened armor with the red bat of Xerxes screeching to the heavens above. The man had his helmet off and he gave Zachariah a look that looked somewhat disgusted before stepping up to the window and demanding a beer. Alma silently complied to the soldiers demands. The soldier ripped the bottle out of her hands and began to chug his drink. He was about halfway done when he was shoved to the ground by another soldier who began to curse the man for not waiting. Beer foam escaped from the bottle to collect on the ground and the one who had been pushed began to curse the other back. All the while Zachariah and Alma both looked at the two soldiers as if they were lunatics.

"Enough!" someone shouted, and the voice made electricity flow through Zachariah's body and his eyes went wide with recognition.

He looked up to see another soldier walking towards them, this one obviously with higher ranks. Black power-armor etched in red with rocket boots and a power helmet with a blacked-out face shield that seemed to spark with electric holograms along the inside. Immediately as the man got closer Zachariah's anger boiled hotter. Despite standing as calm and as still as possible, he was very much ready to attack this warrior.

He's the one from the lab, the one who fed me to the wolves.
I know…

He kept his eyes low however as the man walked by him, his two guards making a hole for him to reach the window up to a very frightened Alma.

"Relax," he told her dropping a few copper pieces onto the counter. "For my guards rudeness."

Alma took the coins cautiously, almost afraid that they were going to burn her; her eyes never leaving the face or the two swords sticking out of the man's scabbards above his shoulders. She bowed stiffly to him muttering something along the lines of 'thank you'. The man then turned and stared at Zachariah for too long for comfort, and then he marched away, his guards following close behind. Zachariah took a step back out into the open, his eyes never leaving the warrior who looked to be heading to one of the three Dragonfly choppers parked near the town square.

Zachariah had thought for sure that the warrior had seen something in him, it was impossible to tell for certain when he couldn't see his face, but he had a feeling… a sort of probing coming from the man.

He didn't sense us… Akuta, did you feel that?
I did…

"Zach…"

He turned to see Alma staring at him with concern. "You look like you've seen a ghost."

Zachariah turned back to see the man getting on the hovercraft and when the vibrating wings began to hover, they took off at incredible speeds towards the clouds above. "It's because I just did."

<u>Ghost</u>

Ghost and his guards from Lakeshire passed over the walls of Xerxes in a little under two hours since they left.

The Gatling Lasers retracted when their sensors caught the frequency of their Dragonflies. They passed over the bustling city of many buildings and delivery tracks spider webbing across the streets below. Thousands of citizens, droids and soldiers walked beneath him and once even a delivery train carrying coal through the city and towards the castle thundered right beneath them. The Dragonfly carrying him and his crew followed the monorail towards the center of the city where the castle stood not quite as tall as the palace in Nineveh. It made up for it's height with it's immense bulk and gothic architecture with many towers and sky bridges reaching the skies above with the flag of the city flapping in the wind. Drones also flew around the towers scanning for enemy activity as well as many tank-drones scouring the streets nearby.

Ghost came up to the landing platform beside the castle and parked his Dragonfly on the ground and left it for one of the soldiers to see that it went below with the rest of the hovercraft and vehicles. He marched across the platform to the main hanger doors to enter the castle and make his way up to Queen Psyren's chambers.

He stormed passed many guards and servants on the way up the castle, the dark passageways lit with torches of green fire and the carpet red as roses. He marched up until he came across a pair of tall double-doors at the end of the hall in the highest tower of the castle. He knocked upon the door with a mighty fist and waited. After a while the door cracked open to reveal a petite woman in black, a servant girl. She bowed to the warrior and stepped outside, leaving the door open for him to walk inside. He closed the door behind him and walked over to the old woman sitting in a wheelchair watching the clouds that passed by her window.

He passed her bed which was surrounded by life-supporting machines and stopped beside her work desk which was littered with papers and notebooks. He touched one of them with his gloved hand and began to read it.

"It's been a long, cold, lonely Winter,
Sun never peeked his head out,
From behind the clouds,
The snow falls,
Dark,
Sun comes out,
The seasons drawing,
It's time for the cold to end,
And make way for Springs warm embrace.'"

Ghost looked back up at the woman still with her back towards him, which was concealed with the oxygen tank that was strapped to the wheelchairs top. "A beautiful poem your majesty."

"Thank you," the woman said turning her chair at last to face him. Her skin was deathly pale and her hair the color of winter, across her face was a mask lined with many pipes that led to a single tube that led to the machine and tank on her chair. The transparent plastic used for the mask had a thin coating of mucus across it and the sound of her breathing sounded hitched and hissy. Her bone-thin hands pushed the little joystick forward and her wheelchair etched forward a foot before stopping before Ghost who got down on one knee to become eye-to-eye with his queen.

"Milady," he said with a bow. "Has the pain subsided?"

"Only a little, the crystal you found seemed to have cleansed the air a bit." Her eyes lingered to the armrest opposite of the joystick where a small bright green crystal sat in a small slot glowing softly. Behind his visor Ghost smiled knowing the truth behind it. It was a crystal yes, but not one of The Seven as Queen Psyren believed, but merely a simple power gem that Ghost had acquired and stored some of the energy of his actual crystal within. This way, Psyren would be under the belief that she still had her actual crystal in her possession, when in reality the real one was back at the lab being inserted to another host for Project Arc.

"I am glad it works for you," he said. "I did my best to make sure it helped, I just wish we could have done it much sooner."

The Queen nodded, her own smile hidden by her mask but her eyes full of naïve kindness towards the warrior. "You have helped greatly since we have found you."

"All thanks owed to you, your majesty."

"Enough with the pleasantries please." She took a huge breath of air which made the machine hiss and squeal behind her. Her mask fogged up for a moment but went clear save for the mucus almost instantaneously. "What news do you have of the south?"

Ghost sighed. "There was a complication, milady."

"Complication, you say?" The old woman looked at Ghosts visor, seeing her reflection among the flashing lights reflecting from within. "Do tell."

"Veegar was about to surrender the city to Xerxes, but something came and took it back from us. The City of Angels had returned."

The Queen sighed. "So the rumors true then. Tell me everything."

Ghost told the queen what had happened in Nineveh, all but the most secret of details. When he finished she began to mumble about how there really was no need to waste countless lives all for a few mines.

"We have enough resources here and with the loyal villages," she reasoned. "Let Levitika keep the city, and let us just stay focused on keeping our own district safe. If Levitika or worse yet The Capitol should attack we must save any manpower we have until we are able to rebuild our army."

"I couldn't agree more, your majesty." Ghost then cleared his throat as he took hold of Psyren's wheelchair and turned her back to the window. He stood alongside her, taking in the view and he said, "With this mission being complete, albeit poorly, I'd like to speak about the matter concerning my personal agenda..."

"I did promise you men and vehicles," the queen said rolling back over to the window to take a look down upon her city. "However I can only give you vehicles and a few *droids* and nothing more. I need as many soldiers here and within the city limits. I can't risk being short-handed when my people could be in danger."

Oh how incredibly out of it you are. You don't even know what is happening, or who really is in control. "I understand," Ghost said standing up. "I will take just the one vehicle then. I don't need droids for this."

"What is it, anyway?"

"A family matter, up near the Bubbling Bog."

Queen Psyren looked to Ghost with concern. "That's very close to enemy territory… and aren't Lacertas in that area?"

"They won't be a problem," said Ghost. "I just need to make sure someone is okay there, taken care of. It won't take me long to do so, I just want to ensure they are safe and sound and they aren't having troubles with the Lacertas or Captain Ronin's fleet."

"He is a rather ghastly man, isn't he?" Psyren said shaking her head. "I remember when he was just a little sprout growing beside his father. Rotten apples don't fall far from the tree, don't they? Oh, how time passes."

"Indeed ma'am, indeed." Ghost bit his cheek in frustration. The lack of soldiers would make things difficult, but at least he had a plan B. Maybe the project would be complete and he could do *that*. If not, well there is always plan C. At the very least, Psyren wasn't being as pushy as she was when Ghost first requested some time away. "Is there anything else you need milady?"

"Just send Shasta in when you are done, please. Thank you Ghost, that will be all."

"Always an honor and a privilege your majesty." He bowed behind her grinding his teeth anxiously. B or C, which to go with…?

Ghost left the city, taking the next Railcar heading out to the fields where his personal lab was located. He had heard nothing since his departure to Nineveh and was anxious to see how the results were coming along. The Railcar bulleted across the city and through one of the tunnels beneath the walls where it stopped at a station in the nearby wheat fields. From there he took a Hoverbike further east. The air was still cold but his armor kept him warm, the landscape still thawing with the arrival of spring.

He crossed the lands for a few minutes before he finally came across the laboratory which he was upset to see some Hellhounds returning. No one was allowed to leave the lab until all research was experimented. So, what had happened? He went through the main hangar doors, parked his bike and began to make his way inside the massive underground building.

Many guards and scientists called out to him but he ignored them. He marched down the hall into the main tunnel network, where he saw disaster. The walling and platforms had been destroyed, bullet holes and dried blood stained the concrete and there were medical ropes leading down into the abyss in the middle which operated as a speed-release for Hellhounds. He crossed across the threshold and entered Dr. Lucas' lab, which the guard eagerly let him through without any lip. However, when he entered it to see all the machinery smashed and badly damaged, he was disappointed to see only his assistant- *what was her name? Kris? Kim? Probably Kim* –sitting at her desk across from Lucas' which was empty.

She sprang up and stood as straight as a plank of wood when she noticed him come in. "Sir," she said stiffly, her eyes puffy and red from crying.

"What happened here?" Ghost demanded. "I saw the damage outside." His eyes lingered to the glass container which sat empty and undamaged. Number 464 was gone.

"Number 464 escaped sir," she said a small squeak sounding in her throat as she spoke. He killed some of the guards and he murdered Dr. Lucas."

Ghost looked as calm as ever, but beneath his visor his face was clenching almost as tight as his fist; he felt as if he would crack his teeth he was biting so hard. But as quickly as his anger came, it disappeared like lightning. "Tell me, Miss…"

"Kim sir. Dr. Kim Song."

"Kim Song, yeah, that's right. Tell me Miss Song, was it a success?"

"Sir?"

"Was the bonding process a success?"

Kim Song looked confused at this question but she answered, "Yes sir, more than Lucas could ever hope for. He was extremely happy it was possible, until 464 escaped."

"No matter, it can be done. Do you still have the notes?"

"Y- yes sir, in fact…" She bent down and came back up with a thick folder about two inches wide. "Lucas came down here during the escape, when I came back down I saw these notes laying beneath my desk."

Ghost chuckled. "That's Lucas all right, brilliant until the end." He strode over and patted Dr. Song on the shoulder. "Congratulations doctor, you will now be in charge of Project Eleven."

Kim stared at him as if he grew two heads on his shoulders. "But sir, I am only-"

"You have his notes. You can perform the process, and the other doctors will assist you. I will make sure of that."

"Thank you, but… but sir, Lucas and the others-"

"Are dead," Ghost finished curtly. "Yes, I know, I understand that. But there isn't anything we can do about them at the moment- If you are concerned about four-sixty-four's crime I can promise we will find him and make him pay for what he's done. In the meantime I want the next subject operational as soon as possible, but this time make sure we do not have another escape. I want this one wiped clean- factory settings you understand?"

Kim Song nodded, still flustered by Ghost's callousness but agreeable nonetheless. "Sir, don't we need another…"

Her voice faltered as Ghost revealed the Dark Crystal he took from that pathetic boy who dared to stand against him. If he did not have his helmet on, Kim would be seeing him grinning from ear to ear with a sinister smile.

"I have one right here," he spoke softly but as cold as the ice in his heart. He placed it down on the doctor's desk and said, "Get started on it. I'll be gone for some time but I'll make sure our side is on the hunt for four-sixty-four."

"Yes, sir," Kim Song said nodding. "Sir, if I may request…"

"Request what?"

"Are you thinking of bringing four-sixty-four back?"

"If we can," said Ghost although he was considering as soon as the man is found have him killed and the crystal extracted. If they could do it once and a second time with this new subject, they could easily do it a third time. In the back of his mind, Ghost was also thinking about the strange man he saw at the bar where his men were bickering. He knew he felt something but it wasn't anywhere as clear as it used to be. He knew he wasn't losing his ability to detect other crystals, the boy in Nineveh being the most recent example, but perhaps there was something different once a crystal was bound with a biological host. That would have to be something Ghost would need to look into himself, in the meantime before he took off north he would give the camera footage on his helmet to his men remaining in Lakeshire, if that man was still there, he could be questioned and if that was 464...

Well, no loose ends, as Ghost believed.

What Remains

<u>Ashlyn</u>

It was several hours until Ashlyn and Esmerelda finally found Markus wandering the streets of Nineveh.

He was standing before an odd looking shack in The Narrows. The building's roof had caved in and the front had been blasted off. Esmerelda looked at the building questionably but Ashlyn knew it well: it was Markus and Ruth's old home. The cool evening wind blew past Markus kicking his hair up only to pass through the home and make whistling sounds through the wood and sheet metal. The little garage which once contained the hovercraft and workbenches where robots would be made, was in complete ruin and looking at it, Markus appeared devastated by this additional loss.

He did not turn to look at them, only stared at the destroyed building while rubbing an arm that was not his own. Ashlyn put a hand over her mouth, relieved that he got an arm, but now it was only auto-limb, a reminder of his injuries from that horrible day, and now he decided to come straight here, to his old home. The question was, why?

She walked forward first while Esmerelda followed. They stopped on either side of him, and he looked from side to side seeing their arrival. Esmerelda was staring at his auto-limb arm, and gingerly took its hand. She jumped slightly when the hand closed on her but calmed when she saw Markus' face looking at her. He returned his gaze back to the shack, and Ashlyn spoke up.

"You okay, Mark?" she asked.

"I'll be fine," he said his jaw clenched. "Just memories."

Ashlyn nodded and Esmerelda spoke with realization, "This was your home?"

"It *was*," he said releasing her hand. He looked down at his new palm and closed his fist. "So much had changed I just can't believe what was is now gone, I wonder what would Ruth say if she saw this place?"

"She would say thank you for the adventure beyond the wall," said Ashlyn. "Some good it did her."

"Stop." She turned to Markus who looked at her as calm as ever. "Don't do that."

"Do what?"

"You know."

He pursed his lips, and nodded. "Sorry."

She smiled and lightly punched his actual arm. "Don't be."

He smiled and looked back to the shack. "I'm surprised much of it is still left, I'm guessing someone broke it down after we left looking for something." He looked down to his auto-limb arm where his two crystals were- particularly the light crystal from his father. "Too bad for them."

Esmerelda looked up as Markus almost admirably. "You guys have really been through a lot haven't you?"

"Yep…" he muttered. He let his arm drop with a sigh. "Come on, let's get back to the palace."

On their way back to the castle Markus suddenly turned to a different street. The girls followed confused but soon saw why he took the turn. After a while of walking they came across The Drunken Badrat, the building had been scorched but it was still standing, and the droids and Angels were assisting in rebuilding the bar. Jim was amongst the workers and Kaltrina stood out front offering advice to her father. As they got closer she noticed them and hugged Markus tightly and shook hands with Ashlyn and Esmerelda. Markus introduced them all and waved up at Jim who was on the roof waving back.

"Things are looking good now," Kaltrina said. "The city is practically rebuilding itself without fear or prosecution. We might be able to make the bar look better than ever."

"That'll be good," Markus said.

"How's your arm?" she asked staring at his new metallic limb.

"Better," Markus said stretching it out for her to see. "Our friend Vic did a decent job."

"The one with three eyes?"

"The one and only."

"He's been a huge help on vehicles and droids, he actually stopped by for a beer before fixing our Hoverbikes."

"He's a good guy."

"Creepy at times though."

Markus laughed. "That sounds accurate."

"Listen, thank you for coming to see us." Kaltrina said. "We were so worried when you left and then the war and then out of the blue here you were it- it's good to see you, Markus. You too Ashlyn."

She looked at Esmerelda then and said, "And very nice to meet you. Any friend of Markus is a friend of ours."

Esmerelda bowed her head. "Thank you." She did not reveal that she was the princess of Levitika.

"My father would say hi too, but he's busy, as you can see." She looked up at Jim who was hammering a piece of sheet metal on top of the wooden roof.

"We'll come visit soon," Markus promised. "We need to get going, it's almost dark."

"You're always welcome here, just like before."

The teens said their thanks and their goodnights and then they left the Drunken Badrat, the sound of drills and hammers fading as they proceeded to walk back to the castle.

When they finally made it back to Levitika and inside the castle, the silence was killing Ashlyn. They had not spoken at all since they left Jim and Kaltrina, but she knew that they were all thinking the same if not similar things: How much had changed in the blink of an eye in Nineveh. What Esmerelda thought of it all was anyone's guess, no doubt perhaps sympathy in regards to what happened to her friend's old home.

They wandered the halls back up to the palace rooms when Ashlyn decided to break the silence at last. "Things are going to change, aren't they?"

"For the better this time," Markus said simply, although he didn't sound too upbeat about it either.

"I had no idea how bad it was here, before everything," Esmerelda said. "It's incredible that you both survived all of this."

"We had help," Markus said. "The few friends who were willing to help, anyway." His eyes lingered to Ashlyn who smiled at him.

"All the same, no one should have to deal with all of that," Esmerelda said. "Now I can actually see what you guys were talking about. I am determined that that needs to change. When a new governor will be elected, hopefully Nineveh will be a better place."

They arrived back in Esmerelda's room to talk a little more before retiring for the night. Markus wanted to put his new arm to use by helping in the city. Construction, the hospitals, anywhere he could.

"Are you sure?" Ashlyn asked. "You're still hurt."

"These are my friends, I'm not sitting this one out," he said. "Besides, no one should be trying to chop something off of me for now, right?"

Ashlyn looked to Esmerelda who shrugged and said, "He's got a point."

Ashlyn nodded. "All right. I'm tired, but Markus, you should hear about the meeting between us and the queen."

And so they told him about the extremely short meeting with Queen Elizabetha. He listened intently never taking his eyes off of the girls as they spoke. They told him about the elders exiting the war room muttering under their breath, and not long after Slagar followed, the old wizard grumbling and shooting dangerous glances in every direction "As if he was looking for someone to go at," as Esmerelda put it. They told him how they entered the war room where the queen was waiting, hunched over the maps on the table like a vulture. He listened to what they had found out about Slagar, including the information concerning the gauntlets, only to have her say 'thank you for informing me' before going back to her notes and maps as if they weren't ever there. Markus shook his head.

"She can't be *that* calm about it," he said.

"We can hardly understand it ourselves," Esmerelda said. "But I believe my mom when she says we shouldn't worry about it, not for now anyway."

"Well, all we can do now is what we previously planned, be careful who we trust in the branches outside her majesty," said Markus.

"Agreed," Ashlyn nodded. Markus had caught her staring at his auto-limb arm a couple times already, and this time he finally called her out on it. "What's on your mind?" he asked. Esmerelda just sat back watching intently.

"Nothing," Ashlyn said.

Markus raised an eyebrow but did not pursue the matter any further, which Ashlyn was happy about.

That is, until Markus began to speak about something else.

"One more thing that's been on my mind," said Markus. "I'm obviously not going anywhere until I'm fully-healed, maybe not even until Jim and Kaltrina have their business back. But either way, I have no intention on waiting as long as Elizabetha says."

"What do you mean?" Ashlyn asked cautiously.

"I mean, once I feel ready to leave for the Kaiken Isles, then I'm going to leave whether Elizabetha agrees with me or not."

"You mean to disobey my mother?" Esmerelda asked but not harshly.

"No, I intend to talk to her again beforehand. I won't disobey her unless I have to."

Esmerelda started to argue. "That isn't a smart idea, you-"

"Look," Markus said sternly silencing her. :I have to find out more about these crystals, and The Dreaming and how to protect myself and the people around me. And I can't do that here with limited knowledge. But yes, I plan to escape Nineveh and run off to Kaiken."

"My mother won't like that," Esmerelda pointed out. "The people might view you as a deserter, and Slagar could very well use that to his own selfish advantages."

"Even so, it can't be helped," Markus said. "We're just gonna keep beating this dead horse if we keep this up. I don't have a choice, and I think if Black was still alive he'd tell me I was right."

"You don't know that for certain," Esmerelda argued. "And besides, not to be insensitive, but he isn't."

"Because of *me*," Markus said looking Esmerelda in the eye. The princess's mouth opened and closed like a fish, trying to form words that wouldn't escape. "I'm not gonna be a victim of someone else with a crystal again, nor am I gonna allow anyone else to."

"Then you're not going alone," Ashlyn said trying to keep her frustration in check. She was glad that Markus was being transparent, but his determination only drove her more to fight to go with him. "I don't think you should leave at all, but if you are going, then I'm going too."

"No you're not," Markus said sternly. "It's not safe, there are pirates around the islands, much worse than the raiders out in the Wastelands. Besides, you don't have Eagle's Wings of your own and I'll need to fly in order to be quick about getting there. And as I said before, I need to be completely focused on Abram and whatever knowledge he can teach me about the Dreaming."

"I don't care, you and I left Nineveh together and we were fine there. I won't be a distraction- Yes, I know you never called me that but that doesn't matter. I want to go with you Markus, that's what friends are for."

"I appreciate it but I said no, Ashlyn."

"Why not?"

"Because I don't want you to get hurt."

Ashlyn's temper flared and she said, "Like you're the judge of getting hurt."

"C'mon, Ashlyn," Markus said with a groan.

"No, I'm coming with you."

"Not if I say otherwise."

"And who are you to say that?" Ashlyn retorted.

"Why are you being difficult?"

"Why are *you* being stubborn?"

"I'm worried about your safety!"

"Well I'm not going to just wait around here in hopes that you won't be killed!"

"Stop!" Esmerelda cried out tired of her friends bickering. "Enough!" She eyed Markus furiously. "You, Ashlyn only cares about you, and wants to make sure you are safe- Don't say anything! You plan to take no one with you, and she is willing to help!" She turned to Ashlyn. "You, Markus only wants you safe, whether you go or not is your choice, but think about how Markus feels about making you go with him back out into The Wastelands, particularly by the sea where more pirates and monsters lurk!"

Ashlyn tried to argue, saying, "I don't care though, I-"

"Well *he* does," Esmerelda said jerking a thumb in Markus' direction.

She then turned to them both. "I don't like the idea of you going either, Markus, but I'm not going to pretend that Black didn't have his reasons for wanting you to go, and my mother obviously agrees. That's why I don't believe she is never going to let you go once you are good and ready, and if you really need to go, fine. But you better come back one way or another. And Ashlyn, whether he takes you or not is his decision. It's not like he doesn't want you to go with him, isn't it, Markus?"

Markus looked down at his shoes and said, "No. If I could I would, I just don't want to just ignore her once we get there because I want to focus on Abram so that I can be trained as soon as possible to come back. Also, I stand by what I said about the Wastelands."

"Well, I agree with Ashlyn, that that part doesn't matter," Esmerelda reasoned. "You guys already traveled all across the Wastelands just to find us in the first place. You both are capable of defending yourselves clearly. So don't hide behind the whole 'I gotta protect you' spiel. Just say what you need to say: You wanna get there fast and out of there fast, and you don't want Ashlyn just sitting around while you are in The Dreaming."

She looked to Ashlyn then and demanded, "Is that really an unreasonable answer?"

"Whose side are you on anyway?" Ashlyn demanded. "It shouldn't matter what his reason is, letting him go out on his own is not only unreasonable, it just makes me feel like a rotten friend letting him go alone."

"Are you?" Esmerelda demanded back, sounding completely over Ashlyn's argument.

"You aren't a rotten friend," Markus told her.

"Then why are you pushing me away?" Ashlyn demanded.

"I'm not, I just-"

"Stop!" Esmerelda snapped, causing both Markus and Ashlyn to flinch. The princess looked so furious they both could see the potential in this future ruler of Levitika. "Jeez, what is *wrong* with you both? Markus, you have my blessing, whatever you do, as long as you promise to come back not just because you're the Keeper, but my friend as well. And Ashlyn, whatever he decides, a good friend would respect what he's trying to say and not be so bullheaded about it. The two of you, figure it out, because I'm done listening to this argument if you guys are just gonna go back and forth."

With that, Esmerelda turned on her heel and stomped towards her bedroom door. She did not look back nor was she gentle in slamming the door, leaving both Markus and Ashlyn staring dumbfounded at the door as if expecting it to start cracking down the middle.

Doesn't she realized she just stormed out of her own room? Ashlyn thought. She turned to Markus who was hunched over with his head supported by his new auto-limb fist. She was still very frustrated with him, but she realized that Esmerelda was right. They really weren't getting anywhere here, and Ashlyn felt that it was only herself who was to blame here.

"I'm sorry," she said.

"No, I'm the one who should be sorry," he said shaking his head. "I'm so worried about putting you and the city in danger I can't help but leave, but I am also worried about your safety and don't want you to come. I don't want to take you there just to watch me meditate."

"At least I would be there with you if you ever got into trouble," said Ashlyn. "I might not be able to do magic like you do, but I can at least be there for you, right?"

"I know," said Markus. "If I didn't think time was of the essence or believed that it should just be me going to Kaiken, I would gladly have you join me again."

"But you won't," said Ashlyn. "That your final say?"

Markus nodded. "I need to do this alone, Ashlyn."

Ashlyn shook her head. "You're selfish, you know that?"

Markus looked at her reproachfully and said, "I'm trying to do the best I can here, Ashlyn."

"Good for you," she said and she started for the door. She was about to throw it open and stomp out, perhaps look for Esmerelda or perhaps just straight to her room. What held her back was the bitterness she felt in her throat at her last words. She knew Markus was looking at her, but she didn't move still. Not until she turned around to look at him and say one final piece.

"I'm not helpless, you know. I'm not going to die, and I'm never going to stop supporting you. You're my friend, Markus, and for what it's worth, there is nowhere else I'd rather be than by your side. Whether you take me or not... Whether you decide to go alone or not when the time comes, I'll always support you."

Markus stared at her for a long time before asking, "I have to do this, Ashlyn. My mind is made up. Can you support that?"

"I guess I'll have to..."

"I will be back," said Markus perhaps simply to assure her. It sure felt like it, anyway. "I have to."

Ashlyn nodded. "Yes, you have to. You better."

She left him then before she said something she would regret. She was furious with him, but at the very least she could understand his reasons. She didn't like it, didn't want him to go at all, but as the door slammed shut behind her brisk pace slowed to a stop and she hung her head in frustration, her hands clenching and unclenching.

"Selfish, stubborn… brat," she said as tears began to roll down her cheeks. "Why do you have to make things so difficult…"

Whether she was talking about Markus or herself, she couldn't answer for sure, not now, anyway.

Zachariah

Zachariah stood in the shower which poured rainfalls of cold water over his body as he stood still in the middle of the four-sided box that served as the stall. The wood was stained by being sprayed with water many times, and Zachariah was surprised at how much dirt floated down the drain between his feet.

On his chest the crystal began to glow slightly. *So what will you do now, Zachariah?*

"Do you have to ask?" Zachariah asked running a hand over his head, feeling the suds in his locks collect on his fingers as he combed them through.

Well I do know what you are going to say, but I want to hear *you say it, and I'm sure it will help if you heard yourself say it.*

"I'm going after him," he said simply.

Oh the classic chase after the bad guy in revenge and ignore the important task at hand, said Akuta bemusedly. *I won't tell you what to do, you are in control of this body of yours, but I have to say I believe we should keep going to Kaiken.*

"No. He knows who I am, and I'm going to find out."

Alright, suit yourself, but what will miss Alma feel? What will her family think seeing you run off like this? Have you even put any thought into the family?

"They're not *my* family, and I will only bring trouble to Alma and her father," Zachariah said turning off the water and stepping out into the cold just outside the side of the house Alma had taken him to. As he dried himself Akuta continued. *Oh so you* do *care for the girl and her family, you're not in love with her are you?*

"Are you serious?" he demanded. He couldn't believe the nerve of this spirit.

I'm just pulling your leg, Akuta lied. *But seriously though, all joking aside as well as Miss Alma and her kin, do you* really *believe that this is the right path to take?*

"Yes," Zachariah said tightening his towel around his waist. "I do."

Alright fine then, I'll let our new friend know about our change in course if they're willing to listen. We should leave soon though, we might have already lost too much ground between us and him.

"Agreed." Zachariah said walking back inside the house to get his clothes back.

When he was finally decent he had time to think as he sat on the leathery couch in the living room. His clothes smelled of lemon soap and Alma's father was kind enough to offer him a better pair of boots. He wished he could do something, *anything* to thank them. But at the same time, he knew he had to leave and soon. The trail of the warrior would soon go cold, and then he would have nothing to go off of, only guesses. This could be his only chance to find out exactly who he is and why they did this to him.

Part of him wanted to continue east for Abram, but his anger towards the warrior and his horrible intentions were far more influential for revenge against those who slaughtered his people and village only for him. He wanted to not believe that Gonan was gone, but he knew it was true for Alma's eyes held no lies. Therefore, the man had to pay for his sins, and Zachariah was determined to make the man pay in full.

"What are you thinking about?" Zachariah jumped to see Alma in a pair of cotton pants and a tank top, her hair loose and wet over her shoulders. She cocked her head at him as she leaned in the doorway, behind her stood her father who happened to be the smoking man with the eyepatch from earlier in the village square

"You look like you're thinking hard," the old man said.

"Sort of," Zachariah admitted.

"Are you okay?" Alma asked pinching the side of her pants almost nervously.

"I'm fine," Zachariah said looking back down.

"I heard about your village," her father spoke. "But if I am correct the village had been gone for over thirty years. And you don't look forty to me."

Zachariah shook his head. "No, I guess not."

"So what, you crazy or something?"

"Dad!" Alma exclaimed mortified.

"I wish I was to be honest, sir," said Zachariah honestly.

The old man grunted, stepping past Alma to take a better look at his guest. "I don't find it hard to believe that Xerxes would experiment on humans, so if that part is true I have no trouble believing you, boy." He eyed Zachariah closely. "I don't know what they did to you, and I am sorry for your losses and whatever torture you endured, but I need to ask you to leave. In the end, my daughter's safety becomes a priority over all others."

"I understand, sir," Zachariah said relieved on how easy the decision was to make. "I plan to leave as soon as possible, but I can't help but wish to repay you somehow. You both did so much by helping and feeding me when I had nothing."

The old man smiled for the first time since Zachariah arrived in Lakeshire. "Just make sure you make it out safe. Knowing that you made it safe without harm to you or my family is enough payment for me."

Zachariah stood and bowed his head to the man. "Once again, I thank you both. I will leave in the morning."

Alma's father smiled while she wore a worried expression on her face. "We will make sure you have food to take with you. Try to sleep tonight, okay?"

However, Zachariah could not sleep. The voices of Akuta and another were silent, but his mind was spinning like the clock upon the wall of the living room. He sat on the couch with his fist curled beneath his chin. He had hoped he was not a burden upon the family, and wished he could do more. It was when he felt the presence of someone sitting beside him when he stirred.

Why are you awake? asked the weasel who stood on his haunches, his forepaws on Zachariah's lap like a housecat.

"The family was good to me," he said. "I'm wishing I could do something for them. They deserve so much more, but I have nothing."

Akuta smiled like a fox, or in this case: a weasel. *Come.* He hopped off the couch and began to slink down the hall. *Follow me.*

Zachariah rose wordlessly and followed Akuta down the hall. Soon they were just outside a door where heavy snoring was seeping from beneath the space between the door and the floor. This was Alma's father's room.

"This is creepy," Zachariah muttered under his breath careful not to be too loud. "I'm not going in there."

No need, Akuta said climbing up his pant leg and perching on his shoulder. *What I want you to do is let go, I'm going to show you just what else you can do with that crystal in your chest.*

"Let go?" Zachariah asked confused.

Yes, let yourself float away from your body, from this world. Let yourself feel weightless and open, and place your hand over your... heart.

Zachariah did as he was told, at first nothing happened he merely stood there with his hand right over his crystal. He closed his eyes and tried to relax but nothing happened. He was about to say something as he opened his eyes and gasped at the fact that he was no longer in the hallway of the house, but somewhere *else* entirely.

He appeared to be standing upon rock overlooking a vast galaxy of stars and planets, thin strips of clouds etched across the starry sky and comets zipped past him in flashes of purple and pink. He was marveling at this amazing sight when he was forced to leap back as a creature flew right in front of him; a ghastly creature that slunk like a black eel with thousands of little tentacles beneath its belly and a large and dumb eye that seemed to roll back to stare at him; its teeth were as long as a man and just as thick shining bright white. It flew past him without giving him a second thought. Zachariah jumped once more as Akuta suddenly appeared beside him in his spirit form.

"Is this going to be a normal thing with you!?" he demanded.

"You made it," Akuta spoke ignoring the question. It was strange, hearing the spirits voice both in Zachariah's head as well as his ears.

"What in the world was that?" Zachariah pointed in the direction the creature departed.

"A Nightmare, don't worry it did not seem to recognize you. Little buggers float around here always looking for someone to torment. However, that one didn't know you so it couldn't bring your fears to life."

"Where are we?"

"Haven't you guessed?"

Zachariah remained silent but apparently feeling that the matter was miniscule Akuta walked forward. "Each star represents a single person in the world, and in a realm as vast as this, there are nearly billions out there. You can now understand why I am so reluctant to stay here for the rest of my existence."

"Why did you bring me here?" Zachariah asked.

"You want to leave, but you also want to thank the family for doing what they did, yes?" Akuta looked back to him. "Well, I happen to know where their dreams are being concocted. Come." And with a leap he jumped off the rock and Zachariah bent over to see that there was nothing down there, only more stars below him. Reluctant, he stepped back, only to jump once again as Akuta floated back up to eye level. "You coming?"

"Must I?" Zachariah asked not trusting his ability not to plummet into eternity or whatever lied beyond The Dreaming.

Akuta made a sigh and it looked like he was rolling his eyes from afar. He floated up to Zach and took his arm. "Come on," and before Zachariah could protest, the spirit pulled him off of the little rock island he was on and the two began to soar through The Dreaming. He had almost cried out, but Zachariah was merely stunned by the vast beauty of this realm of dreams.

They passed many 'stars' as Akuta called them, and more strange creatures beyond imagination floated nearby, some like the Nightmare from before were just as grotesque and unreal, while others appeared more friendly, primarily taking the form of small fairies and other animals. They crossed the vast space until Akuta stopped before a small star that glowed bright purple. He released Zachariah letting him simply float beside him.

"Take a look," he gestured to the star.

Zachariah edged forward and saw within the star was a vision almost like from a monitor, of the old man sitting alone in the grass playing a guitar. What struck Zachariah was the fact that he no longer had an eye patch, and this man was much, much younger than Alma's father.

"He dreams of the past," Akuta said. He looked behind then and Zachariah turned to see a Nightmare in the form of a black dragon coming towards them. An unsightly creature whose scales shone like obsidian, it's wings appearing slimy and membranous. From it's massive maw a rolling tongue slithered out like a worm, the end snapping like a claw.

"To drive away the Nightmares," said Akuta. "You must bring out the good of the man's past. The man has suffered a lot, so you will need to dig for it."

"Dig?"

"Reach for the star," Akuta told him.

Zach placed a hand over the star and as his palm got closer to the light his crystal began to glow brighter, and when he was just about to touch it, he gasped as he created a bridge between his mind and the man's.

He saw flashes of the old man's life flash throughout his head. A time of war as the man had been a Xerxan soldier, encounters with bandits, getting his eye gouged out by pirates, losing his wife to the pox; There was so much pain in the man's life it was hard for Zachariah to not release and escape the gruesome images.

But then he *did* see something within the cluster of memories that looked to be happiness, his little girl Alma at the age of six, dancing beneath a blue sky that was dotted with white clouds; the sun shining against her pink dress and the grass crushed beneath her feet. She was giggling and her father laughed with sheer delight as if nothing else in the world mattered to him. Zachariah reached for the memory, and took it, grasping it like a precious stone. When he brought it back, he implanted the memory into the man's dream, and then released to return to Akuta.

When he came back to his body, Akuta was right beside him looking into the star smiling warmly. "Oh look," he mused.

Zachariah saw the old man strumming his guitar under the tree, his eye patch gone and his fingers playing a perfect tune as his little girl danced before him laughing and demanding him to look at her. He looked so happy that he was in tears. Zachariah felt a warmth in his heart that wasn't there, and smiled.

His smile faltered slightly as the Nightmare dragon stopped beside the star, sniffing it and then snorting in indignation. It eyed Zachariah with a sinister glance, as if he was lunch. Not knowing exactly what he was doing Zachariah lifted his hand up, his crystal glowing bright as well as his purple eyes; a small spark of purple lightning began to appear between his palm and his fingertips and the dragon backed off slightly: suddenly afraid.

"In this world, you have control," Akuta explained. He looked back at the man watching her daughter dance in the light. "Not over everything here, especially should The Eldest ever find you. However, since you are now a bridge between the two worlds, you have as much control over your destiny here as you do in the real world."

"That's incredible," Zachariah said as the dragon turned tail and began to fly away towards another star. He let his hand drop, the energy depleting from it and the light in his eyes and crystal dimming.

"Come," Akuta said holding out his hand. "There is still one more we need to visit. We must be fast, before we are discovered."

They crossed the void once more, and Akuta brought Zachariah this time to a light blue star, which was beautiful but something else caught Zachariah's eye: the Nightmare that was caressing the star like a long lost child. It was humanoid with black wings like a bat on its back with the face of a cat. It hissed at them as they got closer, swiping its clawed hand menacingly. The malice in it's eyes were human however, and Zachariah felt sick looking into them.

"We will need to remove the Nightmare from the star without waking her up," Akuta said drawing his sword. "Steel alone will not keep the monster at bay, I will need your help."

"What can I do?" Zachariah said ready for action.

"Besides The Keeper, you are the only link between the worlds, break the creature and he will simply leave. But if you are to fail, he will use *you* as a gateway and enter the real world from which you came."

"That can happen?"

"It's happened once," said Akuta. "I'd rather not have it happen again."

"Outstanding," Zachariah said clenching his fist which spewed purple lighting from between his fingers. Not incredibly sure what he was getting into, he advanced on the Nightmare, who released the star and began to float between him and it.

It hissed at him again, extending his claws just a little more which shone black as ebony marble. It then spread its wings out all the further to make it seem bigger, and opening its maw it produced a deep guttural roar that seemed to shake the entire void and echo across the heavens. From afar, or so it seemed, Zachariah heard the faint whispers of a man. Akuta who levitated beside him suddenly turned pale and held his sword at-ready. "He cometh..." he whispered, and Zachariah was shocked to hear fear in the spirit's voice. "If we are to give the lady a proper goodbye, we must best the Nightmare and do it fast."

"What else do I need to worry about?" Zachariah said edging to the right of the beast while Akuta took the left.

"Far worse," the spirit muttered and the Nightmare lunged at Zachariah.

He grabbed the beast by the head and twisted so that it would be forced downward. The monster, outraged of being put into a headlock, clawed at him taking away parts of his clothing and flesh but the wound closed up in an instant. Zachariah then released his energy into his hand and the monster grunted as purple lightning zigzagged across it's loathsomely slender body. It hissed again and swatted at Zachariah with a single wing before Akuta stabbed the creature in the back. When he pulled out the blade black smoke belched from the wound.

Zachariah seized the opportunity to get a firm grip on the forehead of the beast, it gasped but then grabbed his own head with a single clawed hand, and the *real* battle began; it brought his face towards it's glowing red eyes and the two grappled with each other's minds, trying to break the barrier down and seize control.

Zachariah held his ground as the monster searched his mind for something, while he looked into the beast. But there was nothing to see, only sheer darkness clouded the black matter of the Nightmare's being. He felt the pain the monster felt as it was stabbed again and again by Akuta, but it was only when the spirit joined the bridge between man and beast was when Zachariah was able to break into the monster's mind just as a flash of his mother covered in blood filled his vision. Zachariah then seized the monster and with a flash of his eyes, the beast's head exploded in a flash of black smoke. The form of the Nightmare trembled heedlessly as it began to flap away only to fall down into the night sky, a trail of smoke following it as it appeared to disintegrate into dust that was caught by the winds of this realm and was carried off forever.

Zachariah began to pant as that last image of his dead mother lingered in his mind. "What was *that*?" he asked Akuta who appeared at his side, his sword now returned to it's scabbard.

"The Nightmare was in your head," the spirit said broodingly. "Trying to find what you are afraid of. Your regrets, anger, and darkest fears." He stared at Zachariah. "Had it succeeded you would have been paralyzed in your own nightmares."

"Lovely," Zachariah muttered as he went towards the star to take a look inside.

Within the bright light there was Alma, all alone in the dark as rain poured upon her. She was on her knees before a massive serpent with fangs that curved long and venomous below its thin lips; its golden eyes gleamed in hunger as it began to flick its long red tongue over her. Immediately Zachariah seized the star and entered her dream.

At first he was where she was, cowering as the serpent coiled around her. He was about to go find a better memory to help her when he saw the serpent turn towards him hissing menacingly. Alma turned and saw him and began to scream for help with tears rolling down her eyes as she reached out towards him.

"It's only a dream, he called out as he felt the rainwater smack his face. "It's only a-"

The serpent hissed and lunged at him, its fangs piercing his torso, he gasped as he was pinned to the ground by those fangs.

What happens in the dream happens to me! he realized.

His eyes began to glow as he felt magic seeping into his body from his crystal heart, and seizing the snakes head he released his energy which made the serpent jump back in pain as electricity arched across his head. It hissed angrily and released Alma before wrapping its body around Zachariah who all too soon felt the very breath in his lungs get squeezed out. He gasped and tried to bring his arms up but it was no use, they were pinned against his body and the snake was now eye to eye with him, and in its throat began to hiss in a short-burst pattern- it was laughing.

"Okay," Zachariah said eyeing the creature dead in the slit-like pupils. His eyes glowed brighter purple and in the monster's eyes, he saw fear. What was it seeing? It released him and slithered away frightened at whatever it had just seen. Zachariah hunched down where the snake dropped him and began to breathe again, and when he had just gotten his breath back it was crushed out of him once more as he was tackled into a hug by Alma who kissed him hard on the lips. The sky then went from gray to bright blue, and the sun came up as well as the flowers that shot out of the ground like the hands of the dead.

When their lips departed Zachariah sat there gaping like a fish out of water while Alma blushed brightly. "You saved me!" she cried out, sounding like a princess being saved by a knight in some fairy tale.

Is this still a dream? Zachariah wondered still dumbfounded.

Scared out of his mind he pressed his palm against Alma's forehead, and reaching as far as he could he took the one thing out that could distract her. Immediately the scene changed, Alma now stood alone in a field of grass next to a rushing river. She turned to and fro frantically, looking around for Zachariah who was gone. Disappeared. She began to choke up as if she might cry.

"Alma?"

She spun around and gasped. Tears began to spill from her eyes and she ran over to the figure who enveloped her in arms wrapped in linin.

"Mom…"

"Yes honey, I'm here," the woman said her hair blowing in the light breeze. "It's okay," she said brushing her daughter's hair. "I'm here."

Zachariah watched from the star this time, smiling at the sheer joy that was on Alma's face. He ignored the look of gleefulness that Akuta was giving him. "Didn't quite go as planned eh?"

"Not at all," Zachariah said and closed his eyes.

When he opened them he was back in the house, standing in the hallway as he previously was. This time, in front of a different door entirely as if he had slept-walk, and perhaps he did.

He nodded at the door and then turned around, Akuta in weasel-form stayed hunched on his shoulder. *You are leaving now?*

"I need to."

They will most likely worry about you, seeing you gone and all.

"I have to go, as long as I am here, I'm putting their lives in danger. And I lost a lot of time anyway, I need to catch up to that warrior."

We still going down the path of revenge then?

Zachariah opened the door and walked out into the cool night, the moon shined a bright silver across the land, and the animals the family kept were aroused by the sound of the door closing.

"You don't need to say it like that." Zachariah said walking up to the nearest horse and petting it's nose gently, the beast's glowing red eyes stared sweetly into Zachariah's as if expecting a treat.

Why not? Asked Akuta. *That is what it is.*

"That's enough," Zachariah turning and soon began to walk back north where the warrior and his men were heading.

On foot even? I swear it is going to take us forever to get there!

"I'm not a thief," Zachariah said dismissing the suggestion.

Fine, fine. No skin off my non-existent bones if you lose ground on the guy. Zachariah stopped in his path. *That's right, think about it: do you really want to lose the guy again?*

"A horse won't catch up to them."

Who said anything about a horse? There was a mechanic shop with a bike near the garage out in town.

Zachariah bit his lip in thought.

Come on, Akuta mused. *Who's going to know?*

Zachariah thought about it for a moment, and then grunted something that sounded like 'okay'.

Ten minutes later, he was back in the Wastelands heading north to the city of Xerxes where the warrior who condemned him to experimentation and the slaughter of his people was. Zachariah and Akuta did not talk throughout the night, but their passenger who bounced around in Zachariah's pocket began to whisper once more, incoherently, but still tried to speak as the night dragged on. He however ignored the whispers, his mind being in two different places as he rode on.

He kept himself distracted by the image of Alma's overwhelming happiness, and although he knew Akuta was watching, no doubt enjoying it, it brought Zachariah some comfort that he had done at least something good while he was in Lakeshire.

Deep down, he also kind of hoped he would see her again, but he didn't believe it was possible.

<u>Markus</u>

Markus' night was unrestful, and he found himself tossing and turning all throughout, the bed seeming to outright refuse him comfort.

It wasn't a matter that he wasn't tired however, nor that it was difficult sleeping when he only had one arm, his auto-limb haven been removed and sat on the nightstand beside his bed as if it were a pair of glasses waiting to be used the following morning. He had a lot on his mind, thinking about the weeks to come and the adjustments he would have to make in order to get used to the metallic arm, and all throughout, helping rebuild Nineveh and continue to train. At the end of it, he would have to convince Elizabetha when the time came for him to seek out Abram.

That, and also between here and there, there was Esmerelda and Ashlyn to consider.

Unable to bear the silence of his room, he got out of bed and exited the bedroom; careful not to awaken the sleeping guard who sat hunched in a chair by his door. He hoped the man was not caught by security, a lot has happened in the last two days and everyone was tired.

Well, everyone except him, anyway, or so he thought.

When he finally made it to one of the palaces balconies overlooking Levitika and now having a clear view of the high walls of Nineveh, he was surprised to see Esmerelda standing there leaning against the guard railing; her nightgown glowing in the moonlight and her hair loose and billowing in the light breeze. She wore thick boots and a coat over her nightgown to stay the cold, which by the sight of it made Markus wish he brought his own coat, for his long-sleeved nightshirt and cotton pants let the wind through it and chill his bones. He was about to turn and go back inside when Esmerelda turned startled but relaxed as soon as she saw who it was.

"Hey."

"Hey, sorry, I didn't mean to scare you." He stepped onto the balcony and joined her by the guard railing and looked beyond the wall at the bigger wall that encased Nineveh. He had only seen it twice, both of them brief as he had been escaping the first time and couldn't afford a good look, and the second was as they were converging in for the assault. Seeing the high walls now and knowing what lied behind, made him really feel much smaller than he ever had in his life inside.

He heard Esmerelda say something but didn't catch it. "I'm sorry, what?"

"I said, 'can't sleep?'" She said not looking at him but kept her eyes on the walls as well, perhaps trying to imagine living behind them.

"No. I'm guessing the same for you?"

"Pretty much," he said resting her chin on her hands.

"I'm sorry," he said.

She looked up at him curious. "For what?"

"You know what."

Esmerelda's eyes hardened but not in a way that made Markus feel she was mad. "You don't need to apologize to me. You know that, right?"

"I feel like I should though," Markus argued looking back at the walls. "You deserve to know, even if we don't agree."

"I have a strong feeling we'll be disagreeing on a lot of things," Esmerelda said simply, likewise returning her gaze to the walls. "Especially as time goes on and you learn more and more about The Dreaming. In a way, you kind of reminded me of the Hunter Black."

"How do you figure?" Markus asked looking at the princess.

"He hardly knew anything about the crystals when he first came to Levitika. But when he became more exposed, when it became more clear that he could harness that sort of power, he began overstepping boundaries."

"Black? Overstepping?"

Esmerelda nodded. "He and my mother argued a lot. The way he wanted to do things were very different than what she wanted. She even threatened to excommunicate him and take the crystal herself. When he said that wouldn't work and she knew it, I remember her breaking down and crying."

"When was this?" Markus asked curious, as far as he was concerned, Black had always been in Nineveh, at least when he and Ruth were still living there.

"It was a long time ago, before he left for Nineveh. I was still a kid then, but you don't ever seem to forget your own mother seeming so hopeless. At any rate, at the end of it, she learned to trust Black's judgement and as he had promised, he came back. He came back knowing more than he had before, and he even brought you guys. I guess what I'm trying to say, you're reminding me of Black during that time. That's why I'm saying you and I might be having plenty of arguments and I've accepted that. I can't pretend I know everything about the crystals anymore than you can pretend being prepared to lead a whole city one day."

Markus nodded, understanding. "I can't imagine that kind of pressure..."

"It isn't fun, but it'll be worth it. As long as you and Ashlyn stay my friends."

"How could we not?"

At this, Esmerelda smiled. "Good."

Markus cleared his throat and said, "So, you and I, we are good?"

"No matter what you have to do," Esmerelda said. "As long as you come back."

"Of course."

"Then we are good." She looked at Markus then and said, "Are you and Ashlyn good?"

"I don't know," Markus said honestly. "She's pretty upset with me still. Last we talked, we had somewhat agreed that I had to do what I must, but it didn't feel like much was truly resolved. I don't blame her, but... I have to go alone."

"It's her choice," Esmerelda said her eyes staring up at Markus. "Whether she chooses to stay or go is her choice alone. You can't expect her to sit around, especially given all you two have been through."

Markus nodded. "I just want her safe. I want her here, either to train or to just be close to you. I just have this feeling that I have to do this alone."

Esmerelda nodded. "That's what Black told my mother, when he said he had to return to Nineveh."

Markus looked at her.

"You need to tell Ashlyn that," said Esmerelda. "You have to let her know that your decision is because you feel it to be right. She trusts you, that much is very clear. But if she decides to join you, don't push her away. Convince her all you want, but if she decides to go, is there really any harm in taking her?"

Markus thought about it and said, "No, I suppose not."

Esmerelda nodded. "And don't worry so much about me here. I'll be fine. In the meantime, we have enough on our plates to keep us busy. Whether Ashlyn goes with you or not, I'll be fine."

"I'm not gonna stop trying to convince her I need to go alone, you know that, right?"

"I know. Just prepare yourself when the time comes."

"Okay."

He remained against the railing with her, staring up at the stars that seemed to stretch far and wide across the sky. The crisp cold made him shiver but not nearly as bad as before. It was just harder to keep warm with only one arm, and if Esmerelda was uncomfortable with him not having his auto-limb on, she didn't comment on the subject.

"Did you know there was a time when you could barely see the stars at all?" Esmerelda asked all of a sudden.

"No, I didn't."

"There was a time the stars shined as bright as this, and then many years later, when mankind began to really industrialize, the sky would remain dark completely for many years. Even the moon was sickly yellow."

"I can't imagine that."

"Me neither. But it seems that all these years, even though it changed our world completely, it's made the sky more clear again. It's beautiful."

"Yeah, it is," he agreed.

She continued to stare, and then spoke. "You aren't going to tell us when you're gonna leave, are you?"

Markus looked at her helplessly. "I wasn't planning to. I'd be lying if I said the thought hasn't crossed my mind though."

"You are undecided then?"

"No, I decided I would tell." But even as he said it, Markus felt like a liar.

"A little advice from another girl," Esmerelda said standing straight up. "Girls hate it when guys run out on them."

Markus looked at her, seeing how bright her hazel eyes shone towards him. "Even if it means to protect them?"

"*Especially* then," she whispered. She closed her eyes and turned her head away. "I'm sorry, I shouldn't have said that."

"No," Markus said grabbing her attention again. "I'm glad you did."

"What- Why?"

"Because I plan to leave in a few days."

She turned on him suddenly, her eyes wide with alarm. "What? But you aren't fully-healed, you haven't even gotten used to your new arm yet!"

"I can't waste time," he said looking down at his arm. "I'm not planning on leaving tomorrow or anything, there's a lot I wanna do here too still, but yes, I'll be leaving as soon as I can, just as I said earlier. I've made up my mind."

Esmerelda's expression hardened then. Her hands were clenched into fists and they were trembling. "Fine then. As I said, I won't stop you. But you better talk to Ashlyn. Soon."

"Of course I will," said Markus. "I'm not that kind of guy, Esmerelda."

"I know," she said stiffly. She looked away and said, "She's really attached to you, you know?"

Markus looked at her. "Well, we've been through a lot and-"

"You know what I mean, don't play dumb."

"I'm not! I..." Then he did realize what Esmerelda was saying and the night cold did nothing to prevent the heat now suddenly rising in his cheeks.

Esmerelda smiled at him coyly. "There it is."

He looked away suddenly embarrassed. "I just want you both to be safe, and you both are better together than separated."

"She won't like it," Esmerelda pointed out.

"I know."

"And you know that if she's determined, you can't stop her."

"I... I know."

Esmerelda nodded. "Either way, it's gonna be you or me who's gonna have to deal with her. And I'll just say if it's me and if it's in any way just to comfort her from whatever decision you make be it in her best interest or not, you better come back."

"I already promised I would," said Markus no longer feeling red and now capable of looking at her.

"I know," said Esmerelda simply. "Because I promise you that if you hurt Ashlyn just to keep her from coming with you, when you get back, you're gonna have to deal with me as well."

Markus tried for a smile. "That a threat, your highness?"

"Nope. It's a *promise*, Markus."

He nodded then and said, "Then I guess we'll see what happens. Either way, I promise I'll be back. As soon as I am done with Abram, I'll come back."

Esmerelda took a deep breath and said, "Okay."

"I, uh... I better try to get some sleep," said Markus wanting to point back with his right hand but as he lacked one now, resorted to his left. "You coming in, or...?"

"I'm gonna sit out here a bit longer. Don't worry about me."

"All right," said Markus. "And, Esmerelda?"

She looked at him. "What is it?"

"Thank you, for talking to me," he said. "I... I actually really appreciate that. You're a good friend, to Ashlyn and to me."

Esmerelda smiled and said, "Well of course, you two are the only true friends I have here."

He left her then, letting her stand out there in the cold. As he passed Ashlyn's door he paused and thought of knocking. Risk waking her up and telling her his plan, make his statement here and now, and see what happens then. Then perhaps if she really must come, they could at least prepare.

Perhaps, even to try to clear the air of some things.

Not yet, he decided, and he moved on.

Ghost

It was time to go, Ghost had a lot of work to do on his way north, but as promised he stopped by The Queens chambers after telling Dr. Kim Soul what he expected out of Project Eleven.

"I want it done and operational by two weeks' time, and I want no mistakes. I cannot risk losing this one like you all did the last, so wipe it clean and start from scratch."

"Yes sir," Kim had said before running off to prepare the body.

Now Ghost was knocking upon the door of Queen Psyren's chambers, and when a really weak "Come in," sounded on the other side, he pushed it in and entered.

The Queen was in bed reading a book, her mask pumping more of her medicated oxygen into her lungs, the machine above her beeping profusely. Ghost came around to the side of her bed and she sat her book down, whether she was smiling or not he could not tell.

"You made it," she hissed.

"I always try to keep my promises ma'am," Ghost said.

"Won't you take off that mask Ghost?"

"It takes too long ma'am, and I would prefer to leave as soon as we are done without distractions."

"Very well. Will you still be able to stop by The Southern Harbor before you head to Kaiken? We cannot let those sailors think they can get away with treason, if we lose the harbor then we will lose our supply of fish and minerals from Kaiken. We lost enough as it is."

That was a low blow.

Ghost simply said, "I will be able to ma'am. I will make sure those sailors know their place soon enough. I plan to return in about two weeks if things go according to plan."

"Excellent, because according to our intelligence, The Dark Queen has been preparing a preemptive strike upon the northern walls."

"Does she now?" Ghost said with little surprise. "Do not worry, your highness, I will make sure this city will see through it until the end."

"That is why I can count on you," the Queen said weakly but happily.

Ghost nodded his head. "Milady," he said before he departed from her presence.

He took off with a single Cargo Hellhound heading off for The Southern Harbor, unaware of the man on a Hoverbike following him across the Wastelands below.

It was time to begin this. It was time for the end.

Markus

The next few days were riddled in chaos, a good chaos but hectic all the same.

With the surplus of Ninevite metals from the mines work had begun on reconstructing damaged buildings or completely demolishing them altogether for spare parts. The Gatlings and other damaged defense weaponry were replaced and then repaired and as for the ruins of the citadel itself, it was perfect as a base of operations for the rebuilding of Nineveh, and whenever Queen Elizabetha and her council were not in Levitika, she was often there working closely with the Ninevite people.

With the help of Levitika's scientists, production of Hellhounds in the Ninevite factories had begun immediately, as well as a surplus of droids which would be used in the war. The people of Nineveh while glad to be rid of Baron Ovid and General Veeger, had been hesitant to trust the Levitikans with many even refusing to believe that the island that shouldn't have been able to just appear out of nowhere outside the walls could really fly. Nevertheless, the aid they were being given including medicine from the doctors and scientists was enough to convince them who the good guys were, and in return assisted however they could for the war effort. Those who were injured were treated regardless of their status, and as for the Ninevite Guard, it was disbanded with the guard either having been arrested and brought in for questioning with the rest having escaped and were now in hiding in the city.

Markus had found using his auto-limb arm as simple as using his real arm, the only difference was he felt no pain when he struck it with a hammer, or some other silly mistake he made while helping refurbish The Drunken Badrat. Jim was doing alright, in fact Markus did not think he had seen the old man any happier than he already was. Kaltrina was doing good as well, she had joined Ashlyn and Grim as well as a handful of citizens to learn about gun safety as well as how to use a Photon Rifle. During his time assisting Jim, Markus was surprised when the old man came to him suddenly saying he found something in the streets the night before.

It had been his Eagle Wings pack, the pack having been completely ruined and the wings themselves in critical condition, missing most of it's bronze feathers. He had thought he had lost it after being attacked by the Xerxan Leader along with his staff, both of which he had thought he would never get back.

"Found it on the way home," said Jim. "Looked familiar, so I made sure to snag it before a scrapper could."

"Thank you," said Markus genuinely and already thinking of how he could fix them, make them even better than before.

"No," said Jim shaking his head. "Thank you, Markus. "I certainly don't deserve your kindness with everything you have done both in the last few months but when you and Ruth were here as well. Your sister would have been proud of you, Mark. Your father too."

Touched by the old man's words, Markus hugged Jim and he felt like a little kid again. Only this time it felt different, and Jim perhaps having the same sentiment, hugged him back, grateful for his aid as well as him being alive.

Vic was working on new lines of droids as well as a few Behemoth bots that would only be reduced to twenty feet rather than their usual forty. As for the City of Angels itself it laid in the clearing between Nineveh and the mines with it's citizens going back and forth and assisting the miners to supply as much Radio-Bronze as possible. At some point Esmerelda had told Markus that the city would undergo reconstruction as well, it was to be used as a mobile air base when it was time to move north. Markus had asked Esmerelda if her mother would be okay in using her old home as a weapon, and Esmerelda simply said, "She would not answer when I asked her that myself."

By the end of the fifth day Nineveh seemed to have jumped out of a book the city looked so beautiful, the trashed streets were paved and cleaned, the rotting buildings were demolished and replaced with new buildings that seemed to fit better within the city. The walls were fixed after removing the drill, and the newer defenses were up and operational. There was still so much to do, and Levitika was still unfinished but that would have to wait, for tonight was to be a celebration The Queen had announced on the new Info-Monitor that replaced the many bullhorns that littered the city during Baron Ovid's reign. Her face, appeared on the screen one afternoon after a pleasant little jingle was played throughout the city, and she spoke to one and all in a clear and proud voice.

"Citizens of Nineveh, today marks a new day for your city. The Baron and his Guard are no more, a distant memory that will never resurface. As usual please inform your local superior should any unregistered members of the old guard is out and about. We are not to criminalize them, but see if they are willing to forget the old ways, and embrace the new.

Furthermore, tonight, we will celebrate the rebirth of a new Nineveh, a city with hope, a shining city upon a blessed hill. Even now Xerxes fears our new city, for now it is a safe haven for all who come and live amongst us. Tonight, we will drink, dance, and eat until we can eat no more. There is still much work to be done, but within less than a week, you Ninevites had rebuilt your city to its greatest glory- one that shall never falter under the wings of a tyrant again. Blessed are all who stand with me and my fellow Levitikans, for we have lifted the yoke from your city and we shall do everything in our power to bring its entire glory so the world can see Nineveh and see why they call it The New Beginning. Soon the yoke will be released from the entire country, and oppression, dictatorship, and sheer evil will never claim us again."

With her speech over the entire city rose as one, chanting over, and over, "Long live the Queen! Long live the Queen!" It was a bittersweet moment, but Markus did not think that Elizabetha could have planned it better. And then, leaving the busy streets of Nineveh having finished his current duty for the day, he went to the old town square to meet an old friend.

Her tent was taken down but he managed to catch up to the old woman as she was packing up her stuff into a cart that was to be pulled by a cybernetic horse. He called out her name and she turned to greet him. Madame Zerona smiled that toothless grin of hers as he came up to her. Standing up she was a lot shorter than when Markus and Ashlyn met her before escaping the city. Her wrinkled face had not changed much, and her clothing were somewhat modern compared to the robes she had worn before.

"Markus, you truly did return."

"Hey, Madame Zerona," he said. "Are you leaving?"

"Yes, to my new shop just down the road a bit. This area is going to need new shops, and I don't want to endanger someone else's opportunity. Besides, everyone knows my name, those who need Madame Zerona will find me."

"I'm glad to hear that," Markus said.

"How ails young Ruth, if I remember her name correctly?"

Markus' smile disappeared somewhat. "She didn't make it. She died before we made it to Levitika."

"You poor thing, I am so sorry," Zerona said with saddened eyes. "I *thought* I saw something, but I just couldn't tell for certain."

"Well, there's nothing I can do for her now but just keep going; keep breathing." He looked at the old woman. "Those were your words, weren't they? Never give up?"

"My words *exactly*, my memory has not failed me yet."

Markus smiled. "Right."

Zerona tried to smile. "What about your friend, Ashlyn?"

"Well…"

In truth, Markus had not spoken to Ashlyn since she had stormed out of Esmerelda's bedroom a few days ago. In fact, it felt that after that night, Ashlyn had been avoiding Markus as if he were the plague. She was never around when he tried to find her, and wherever he did see her, she was always preoccupied and whenever she saw him, she would turn away as if ashamed of him. Even when he would go to her room and knock, only silence would answer and he would feel like a complete idiot standing at the door and saying all sorts of things in order for her to come out. Sometimes it was as simple as 'please can we talk,' and sometimes as complicated as the many different ways he had learned to say 'sorry' and 'I hope you are okay' just to name a few. Even when they were out and about helping Nineveh, Ashlyn was always with a different group and never seemed to want to join Markus or vice versa.

"She's doing good," said Markus. "She's going through some stuff, and I don't seem to be making it any better."

"Well whatever it is, I hope you two make up. Nothing is worth losing those you care about, even if an argument seems petty. Never lose your values, but don't undermine hers."

"I'll try to do that."

Zerona nodded satisfyingly. "Also, as you walk The Path, make sure you are treading carefully and keep those you love close. Those crystals that you now carry in your metal arm, they are much more than meets the eye, right?"

Markus cleared his throat. "Well, um…"

"There is no need to lie," Zerona said with a smile, those dead white eyes seemed to be drilling into Markus' very soul. "Like I said, I see and hear a lot of things. How do you think I am able to make a living off of fortunes?"

"Wait, I thought you said you don't do fortunes?"

"Don't I?" She winked.

"Okay, now I know you are messing with me now."

"Who me? Never." Zerona cackled which made Markus laugh. "Well, I am glad you made it safe and came to see me Markus. You have been in my thoughts the last few days and it does me good knowing your journey, despite it's hardships, was a success. Once again I am deeply sorry for your loss."

"I'll be fine, thank you."

"Come visit anytime, I will see you in the streets tonight hopefully, today really is the day of celebration is it not?"

"Yeah," Markus said smiling. "Indeed."

<u>Ashlyn</u>

The massive funeral for all the unburied took place a few hours after the announcement. While many buried their dead with their families, Ashlyn was burying her own father in a grave that was dug by a droid who had long since left to assist another.

For a long while she stared down at the body who was wrapped in cloth just lying in the hole of dirt, a small mound to bury him beside him like a little mountain. She made a small prayer to whomever might be listening, and then spent a majority of her time just staring down at his lifeless body. She could not see his face, nor did she want to. It was better that way.

"I hope…" she found herself saying as tears rolled down her cheeks. "I hope if you're not burning in hell, that you see Kira and Mom, and… and…" She paused again, wiping at her nose which began to run as bad as her eyes. "I hope they can forgive you better than I can."

At last she began to shove dirt into the hole. With every shovelful, the dirt piled upon Veegar's body like a small mountain, which gradually filled the sides and after several long minutes which resulted in blisters forming on the palms of her hands, Ashlyn's father was completely swallowed by the earth and she filled in the hole some more, patting it down with both shovel and the soles of her boots in order to pack it in and add some more. She did this for a while longer before finally stopping and setting the shovel aside for someone else to use. She stood before the fresh mound of dirt that would now forever serve as Veegar's grave.

She never found out if her mother and sister were buried. For all Ashlyn knew, their bodies had been one of the many hung along the power lines as a warning to all potential witches and those who were associated with them, or perhaps just burned on a pyre with their ashes haven been lost to the winds long ago. At any rate, she had never expected to bury her own father, and though there were a lot of things she wished she could have said to him, or better yet have her revenge herself, burying him was like burying a bad memento of a terrible time. It was painful, grueling, but when it was done it was as if a weight had been lifted from her shoulders and she felt a little better.

She felt all the more better, when she felt a cold metal hand land on her shoulder she looked to see that it was Markus who gave her a small smile. Her momentary frustration resurfaced for a moment, but to see him here having found her, made her ever so grateful for him and she smiled back at last, just happy that he was here now.

He looked back down at the body and frowned. At last he said, "I'm sorry I couldn't save him."

"Don't be," said Ashlyn. "You had quite a bit on your plate, and… I think it was better this way."

"What do you mean?"

"If I killed him… what sort of person would I be?" she asked him honestly. "I never thought I would ever do such a thing to anyone, let alone my own father…"

The tears returned with a vengeance, and Markus reached out and put his real arm around her and pulled her tight, letting her rest her head in the crook of his neck; leaning against him. He smelled of sweat and dirt, and yet this familiar scent was more comforting than ever, and she let it all out and allowed him to comfort her as such.

"No one would have blamed you," he told her. "But I understand what you mean. I can't imagine that. I'm sorry. Not just for him, but for everything."

"Shut up," said Ashlyn softly. "Don't say anything else anymore, not about him, and not about what I've been avoiding you for."

Markus chuckled, his chest heaving slightly and pushing against her momentarily. "So you were avoiding me?"

"Just a little..."

He stroked her back, and it felt so amazing. It was amazing just to have him back. "Will you be okay, though?"

"I will be soon. I stand by what I said, but still, he is my father. Although he will never have the pleasure to know that." She was silent for a few minutes, and then, "Mark?"

"Yes?"

"If you had not stopped the Behemoth, I would have shot him." At this tears began to spill from her eyes. "I would have killed him..."

"Shh, shh," Markus said pulling her deeper into his hug. "It's okay. It's okay."

"Thank you," she whispered. "Thank you."

He held her as she cried, and she never felt more at peace than standing here in this moment right now; feeling his arms around her drawing her close, the smell on his person as she breathed, and the sound of his heartbeat as she rested her head against his shoulder, her ear above his breast. She then reached up and took his auto-limb hand in hers and pulled away at last, never letting go as she looked at him with reddened eyes.

"Thank you," she whispered. "For... for coming back still."

He smiled and nodded, and then after taking one last look at the grave, he suggested that they return to the city. Focus on something else.

She agreed that it was a good idea.

Markus

By sundown the gates of Levitika was opened and a plethora of food came charging out the door to line the many tables around the main steps of the massive building. Food and drink was brought by the citizens as well, by the time everyone had arrived there seemed to be enough meat and baked treats to feed the Capitol- twice!

With both Ninevites and Levitikans in the same space, the whole area was packed, and the famous fountain in the center of town was chock-full of people dancing and singing and playing instruments in terrible but heartfelt harmony. Fireworks were shot off of the palace rooftops, flowers of light blooming in many different colors and patterns scattered across the sky like beacons, illuminating the whole city below. Fight Circles were made here and there with usually the toughest men or in most cases droids wrestling each other, and a few shop owners brought carts full of goodies and toys for the children to play with- with the refreshment of supplies they were able to craft many toy cars and drones that were soon zipping between the legs of many dancers who took over the entire streets. It was a chaos worthy of celebrations of old, and both Markus and Ashlyn were glad to be lost in it.

Music was being played by a group of men on the steps of the palace, guitars, flutes and drums charmed the city with their alluring notes. The Queen stood upon the new balcony over the main doors of the palace, dancing with Slagar and drinking some of the wine to everyone's surprise. When it came to speeches the whole city did not seem to be getting enough of her, and Markus who was in the streets below her with Ashlyn really had to hand it to Elizabetha, she knew how to celebrate, and it even seemed that Slagar was in good spirits.

"Who knew he was such a big drinker," said Ashlyn handling a goblet of her own. "Did you see how many times he went for that barrel up there while dancing with the queen?"

"A shock he didn't fall over," said Markus with his own goblet.

The two of them had gotten a chance to speak after returning to work a few hours ago, and after a while and a few but minor harsh words, Ashlyn finally forgave Markus for making his decision how he saw fit, and respected him for saying that if she really wanted to go with him, he wouldn't stop her. She said she didn't know for certain, as she had spent some time thinking about what he had said and promised she would have an answer for him prior to him leaving.

"I still don't want you to go," she repeated. "But I understand."

"Thank you, Ashlyn."

And that was the end of it. No sooner than this conclusion for now happened, was when the party started. They stuffed their bellies, played a few games with those out in the fields, and even sipped a goblet or two of fresh mead and wine which made their heads spin with delight.

At some time Slagar and Queen Elizabetha disappeared from the balcony. Soon after the hypnotist was spotted dancing in the streets below, and by the time the two teens had realized this, Slagar had eventually caught up to Markus and pulled him aside, the smell of liquor mixed with elderberry wine heavy on his breath.

"Markus, uh… I gots somzing to tell 'ou…"

"Come on," Markus said as he and Ashlyn led the old wizard into a chair near the food tables. It was near an old shop and then Slagar went into a short rave about how good the sweets used to be when he was a child.

He then said to Markus, "I-I-I… y'know, I don't likes zou very mush…"

"You don't say," Markus said looking at Ashlyn helplessly. She had shrugged and he told Slagar, "Why don't you take it easy here, okay?" He thought of taking the goblet out of the hypnotists hand but decided against it.

Slagar then broke into a cracked song being played by a nearby bard and Markus and Ashlyn took their chance and left Slagar to enjoy himself. Markus only relaxed when the two of them were far enough away.

"That was interesting," said Ashlyn taking a sip from her cup.

"That's *one* word for it…"

As the music intensified Markus found himself spinning around with Ashlyn who was laughing as she spun like a top around him. The two danced together trying to keep up with the ever-changing crowd. They only stopped twice for a sip of someone's ale or water and a bite of cattle brisket. They were in the middle of trying a Caramel Roll when the music ceased and all raised their heads to The Queen back in the same position on the balcony above them.

"Citizens," the Queen said in much control as if she was sober. "I have an announcement to make." The citizens soon were silent, anxious to hear whatever news their new leader had. One man played an obnoxious note on a lute and a sharp slap and a cry sent the crowd roaring with laughter for a moment and then it quickly died down as Queen Elizabetha repeated herself.

"I have decided to let the true hero of Nineveh be revealed!"

"Oh no..." Markus muttered under his breath and covering his face while Ashlyn looked at him in amusement.

"Without him, we would not have been able to penetrate the great walls, without him we would have never been able to take down the Behemoth of mass destruction, and without him, we Levitikans would not have rushed to your aid in time. I would like him to come up to the staircase and be recognized, Markus son of Johnathon! Come!"

The crowd cheered and began to clear away from the staircase, waiting their new hero. Markus had no intentions to go at all. Ashlyn however, had other plans pushing him towards the staircase and before he could turn around and disappear into he crowd again, but was soon too late for many hands seized him and pulled him up until he found himself on top of the stairs being stared at and cheered by all who could see him. He had lost his goblet in the carnage and wished he had it still. Not knowing what to do and nervously, he waved which was a cause for more cheering.

The Queen continued to speak. "This boy has suffered much, but still he stands tall, ready to battle the forces of evil, and with all of our help we will all rise victorious in a new world order where all men are equal, and all war shall cease! Citizens of Nineveh, The Prophecy has begun, and The Keeper has returned, Markus!"

The whole city clamored and cried to the heavens above, fired up by the final speech the queen had made for the evening. While everyone drank a toast to Markus and their new future that seemed so close now, Markus slipped away into the crowd, hoping not to embarrass himself as he did so and find Ashlyn as fast as possible.

"That was cheap," Markus muttered to Ashlyn who sat beside him on the rooftop of a nearby building overlooking the street flooded with the dancing crowd. They had climbed up the downspout and were perched along the ridge like pigeons with fresh goblets in hand.

"Gotta hand it to her," Ashlyn said still smiling with amusement. "She knows how to rally a crowd."

"I was talking about you," he nudged her.

Ashlyn shrugged laughing. "What can I say, you're a hero of another city."

"Everyone keeps calling me that…" He looked away. "So how come I still don't feel like one?"

Before Ashlyn could answer or joke, someone said, "Found you two," and they both looked to see Esmerelda climbing up and sitting beside Ashlyn. The princess was in a beautiful gown of white and yet she climbed onto the roof like a thief, smiling from ear to ear her cheeks red from the wine she had at the castle.

She grinned at Markus. "You looked so cute up there."

"Oh, shut up," Markus said laughing along with his friends.

"Well, your mom's got the crowd now." Ashlyn said to Esmerelda.

"Does she ever," Esmerelda agreed nodding proudly. "Sorry I couldn't join earlier, there is a lot going on."

"Seems like it," said Markus happily. It felt good to finally wind down and actually celebrate something. With everything that had happened and everything to come, it was good to just be here with Ashlyn and Esmerelda.

He wished this night could last forever, but deep down he understood that tomorrow was going to be a new day, like always.

At some point after midnight the crowds soon dispersed, leaving the new Street Bots to clean up the garbage and food. Soon everyone from Nineveh was back in their respective city and in bed dreaming with a sense of peace that have not been possible for a long time. Markus led Esmerelda and Ashlyn back at the Levitikan castle to their rooms before heading to The Queen's chambers; as Elizabetha had requested for him to see her before bed.

"This might be the time to talk to her," said Markus.

"You're going to tell her you're leaving soon?" asked Esmerelda surprised. "I thought you would sneak out."

"I promised I wouldn't."

"You promised Ashlyn and I you wouldn't leave without telling us," Esmerelda argued.

"I think he's doing the right thing though," said Ashlyn. "At least your mom wouldn't be surprised if he were to disappear."

Esmerelda couldn't argue and after a few more minutes, departed to her own room and Markus told Ashlyn goodnight before leaving her and heading straight for Queen Elizabetha.

He knocked upon the chamber doors and Queen Elizabetha answered still in her party dress. She smiled. "Markus, come in."

"Thank you," he said and stepped inside.

"Take a seat," she offered her chair at her desk which Markus took while she sat upon her bed looking dead serious now as she eyed him. "We need to talk,"

Uh oh, does she know? "About what ma'am?" Markus asked.

"It's about Slagar."

Whew. "Okay," Markus said hunching over. "You were told then?"

"Yes, I am sorry I did not say anything sooner, I had to make sure preparations were made to earn the Ninevites trust."

"Well you have succeeded," Markus said with a smile. "That was quite the party."

The Queen offered a small one before continuing. "Went pretty well, I'd say. Anyways, about Slagar, as far as I can tell he has not *tried* anything, it was merely a failsafe to get the crystal back in case you failed. I cannot rule this as a good thing or a bad thing, but I cannot bring it up at all. Already he has most of the support of The Elders, and they are watching, listening for anything to use against me and use it upon the crowd."

"Then why not just banish them?" Markus asked. "Just get rid of them!"

"We need Slagar and his magic and expertise in warfare. He is a useful ally, and The Elders wish to only keep the secret of Levitika safe."

Markus knew she meant The Eldest's son deep in the heart of Levitika. "It all sounds too complicated, ma'am."

Elizabetha shrugged. "It's politics. You're always going to have one group who are only in it for their own selfish needs despite their necessity."

"Makes sense."

Elizabetha nodded. "It's beena hectic past week, but how have you been, Markus? Esmerelda has told me briefly that you have spoken with some old friends back in Nineveh."

"A few, anyway," said Markus. "Some didn't make it, others, well, they never liked Ruth or I back when we lived here, it's complicated."

"Understood. You are well, then? How is your arm?"

Markus flexed his auto-limb saying, "Getting more used to it. It's easier than I thought, although there is an itch in my arm that needs to be scratched, but..." He tapped on the metal with his fingernail to emphasize.

"I see," Elizabetha said nodding. "You feel well then?"

"Much better," said Markus. "Ready for action, so to speak."

Elizabetha nodded again. It occurred to Markus that the queen might still be a little intoxicated, but she handled herself so well it was a miracle anyone could function as smoothly. "And I assume that includes your quest for Abram of Kaiken?"

Markus didn't even hesitate. "Yes. I plan to leave really soon, one way or another while things get wrapped up here."

Elizabetha sighed. "You are so much like your father, you know that?"

"Am I?" asked Markus genuinely curious.

"He was very eager to go back to Nineveh, despite having his family here at the time. In the end, no one could dissuade him. If Johnathon was alive today, he'd be very proud of you."

Markus smiled. "That means a lot, thank you."

"I have just one request," said Elizabetha. "Tell me before you leave, understood?"

"I will."

"Then we are in agreement, and I believe that is everything," Elizabetha said standing up. "Do you need anything from me?"

"No ma'am," Markus said standing up as well. He bowed his head. "Thank you."

"Anytime," she said. "You have a good night, Markus."

"I will," Markus said leaving The Queens presence and heading for his room; his mind buzzing with a million thoughts and when he finally reached it, his mind was made up at last.

It was time.

It was now or never, because in the pit of his heart and through the whispers in his ear from the crystals, there was a storm coming, and fast. Whether he liked it or not, whether the others like it or not, he had to make it to Abram soon, or else he would lose his chance to be prepared for the next assault.

Now or never.

Markus

"Will you come?"

Markus asked this of Ashlyn who was sitting on the edge of the bed. She was wearing a nightgown and she was staring up at Markus who was already dressed up for the journey ahead. A fresh pair of pants and leather boots and a coat which he had acquired out of one of the Angel Armories along with a pack of cartridges for a Laser Pistol he had as well. He had told her that he was going to leave tonight so that he could reach Kaiken in a timely manner, and hopefully make it back to Nineveh before any plans for Xerxes gets taken into effect.

Ashlyn had listened, had been disappointed to see Markus looking ready to leave, but she her stoniness softened when Markus essentially told her that he was offering her to come if she wanted.

"It would take longer," he said. "You need a long time to train before you use Eagles Wings and I can't carry you, but if you want to come, I won't stop you."

Ashlyn pursed her lips in thought and she said, "You're not pulling my leg, are you?"

"After all you put me through?" Markus smiled when Ashlyn glared at him. "I'm kidding, I'm kidding, what I put *you* through, I mean."

Ashlyn relaxed and said, "I want to. But... I don't want to slow you down either. I know we can cover good ground together with a Hoverbike, but..." She paused for a long time and then looking back at Markus she shook her head.

"I've been thinking about everything, and I've decided that you are right and should get there quickly. Quickly, and hopefully learn all that you need. I was the selfish one, thinking you were just doing it to protect me, all this stuff about The Dreaming, it's beyond me. The best place for me is here."

Markus couldn't help himself but laugh. "So after all of this drama..." He shook his head. "You sure you don't want to come?"

"I'll see you off," said Ashlyn. She looked like she wanted to say something else rather than what she said next. "You are leaving soon, then?"

"Yeah, I was gonna go pack and ask you to start yourself, but as it is..."

Ashlyn nodded. "Go do your thing. I'll meet you later."

After packing a small pack of water, food and a as well as the ammunition and Laser Pistol, Markus strapped on his leather boots and looked in the mirror as he strapped on his pack which was outfitted with a brand new pair of Eagles Wings he also got from the armory. His own pair still sat on his nightstand as he didn't have time to work on it and after testing the ones used by the Angels, he felt comfortable enough with them.

Lastly as he had lost his staff, he hesitantly hooked Black's sword to his belt. When the fight for Nineveh had begun he didn't even think about using it, and yet it was the only weapon he could use and it felt right to do so. Some part of him believed that perhaps Black's spirit was guiding him as he had in the brief moments they shared while in Levitika, and he decided he would wear the sword proudly like a badge of honor.

He was about to turn away from the mirror but instead paused and inspected himself further. He noticed that he had lost a lot of weight since he escaped Nineveh, and he noticed his shoulders were more broad and muscular, no doubt from the last two months of intense training. But what caught his eye more was his upper lip, which had a slight shadow to it. First he needed a haircut, and now he would be shaving soon.

Am I really getting that much older? he wondered as he left his bedroom.

Sneaking past the guards Markus managed to make it outside, and cross the street to the main garage a few blocks away. There was only one instant when he thought he was caught and for the first time since his battle with the Xerxan warrior, decided to attempt to use magic again. He imagined the gas torch on the far wall opposite of him and the soldier suddenly erupting brightly and placing his auto-limb hand on the wall and 'feeling' the rough textures through the fingertips, he pulsed and felt the flow of energy pass through him and the crystals and into the wall.

Surely enough and scarily enough, it worked. The light from the gas-fed torch suddenly turned bright red and enlarged like a blossoming flower. It startled the soldier who cursed and hurried towards it to turn it off, allowing Markus to slip by undetected and escape the castle feeling pretty proud of himself to say the least.

Good on you, Vic, he had thought. *It works.*

From there he managed to steel a Hoverbike from one of the nearby hangars and as silent as possible, he moved it to the nearest manhole. As they had planned, Ashlyn was there waiting her body clad tightly in an overcoat.

With her, was none other than Princess Esmerelda, looking somewhat disappointed but smiling nonetheless.

"Figures she should know," Ashlyn explained.

"Glad you did," said Markus kicking out the kickstand for the bike to settle on it's side.

"What about your Eagles Wings?" asked Ashlyn.

"There isn't enough fuel on the boosters for it to get me there and back in a timely fashion. I plan to take this to the coast and from there fly to Kaiken if I can unless I can cover enough ground tonight."

Ashlyn nodded. "Understood."

Markus turned to Esmerelda and said, "I'm sure Ashlyn filled you in?"

"Enough, anyway," said Esmerelda. "I'm just glad you two finally made up."

"Yeah," said Ashlyn looking at Markus. "Same here."

"Think your mom's gonna be pissed?" Markus asked.

"What do you think, genius?"

Markus shook his head. "I'm sure she'll understand, she already knew I was gonna leave soon anyway, I just don't wanna waste anymore time and get this done as soon as possible. The sooner I get with Abram and learn more about this whole thing, the sooner I'll be back and a better help than before."

"Will you be okay though?" asked Esmerelda.

"I'll be fine," said Markus. "I just gotta make sure I play it safe once I reach the coast."

"You do that," said Esmerelda. "The Kaiken Isles are full of pirates, and Captain Ronin is the worst of them all."

"I'll be careful and I'll be back before you know it. Hopefully before anything is done with Xerxes."

"If so hopefully we can let you know."

"Yeah, maybe I can swing by Xerxes on the way back."

"Good idea," said Ashlyn.

Markus then took a mighty exhale and said to the girls, "Well, I best get going." He was looking at the manhole cover as he said this, not looking forward to going in. The last time he went through a sewer pipe he wound up in a warzone, and the time before that he was escaping with Ashlyn and Ruth from maniac Hunters.

"All right," said Esmerelda, and the princess stepped forward and wrapped her arms around Markus' waist. He hugged her back and when she pulled away her eyes were shining but tearless. "Be safe out there, okay?"

"Of course." He turned to Ashlyn and shrugged. "Last chance. You sure?"

"You got a spare bike?"

The two laughed and then they embraced. Ashlyn's chin was right on Markus' good shoulder and she whispered softly, "Come back soon, okay?"

Markus gave her a squeeze and the released her. "I'll be all right and I'll be back soon. I promise."

Their parting words finished, Ashlyn and Esmerelda helped Markus open the manhole cover for him to get in. The Hoverbike was longer, which was an annoyance getting it down the manhole but he soon managed. When he landed at the bottom he was glad to see that the sewers were clean, although not *entirely*. He looked up at the girls looking down at him through the hole as if he were trapped in some underground dungeon and said goodbye one last time.

He traveled down the pipes guiding his bike beside him as quickly and quietly as possible as water slushed around his feet and rats squeaked at the intruder that had entered their home. Behind him, he heard the manhole cover clunk back into place and he paused momentarily, thinking about leaving the two of them behind and then he moved on.

Eventually his eyes caught the faint moonlight through the bars of the exit pipe, which he lifted open and held up with a stray piece of wood before dragging the bike outside. He silently closed the grate and got onto his bike; he drove off into the night heading north.

As he drove off the land beneath him blurred past as he drove while the starry skies remained as motionless as ever. As he officially started a new journey, he looked back and saw the two cities side by side becoming smaller and smaller until they were nothing more than two black dots on the horizon. It made Markus think of his friends again and while he was glad they were safe, a heavy burden laid on his heart for he was almost all alone and out once again in the harsh Wastelands heading in a single direction, guided by the voice calling to him towards The Great Sea and from there, The Kaiken Isles.

Come to me.

By the time the sun had risen from its slumber and was almost halfway to it's highest point in the sky, Markus could see the vast waters of the sea in the distance. He was very tired having partied with everyone earlier only to be on the road again immediately after. Many hours had passed and his journey had allowed him to avoid the Xerxes limits using first the South Twin Lake and then the North Twin Lake for reference as to where he was, keeping it to his right so that he knew which direction would send him towards Xerxes.

For a brief moment he thought of turning there anyway, but he knew that would accomplish nothing and so he moved on. By the time he had reached the North Twin Lake which was misty in the arrival of dawn, he knew that if he turned immediately left he would end up in the Southern Harbor operated by Xerxes, but he had the sensation that he should travel north just a little longer and he trusted Abner's direction and he moved on.

At last he felt the sudden pull that once guided him on his first journey with Ashlyn and Ruth into the Northern Wastelands pulling him to his left and he continued this path until at last he could see the sea in the distance. It amazed him how huge it was, for he had never actually seen the sea and had always wanted to when he was a little kid. He decided to stop and make camp for a quick breakfast or brunch and found a place to park near what looked to be an old statue that had long ago fallen, its face weathered down and completely unrecognizable as a human face.

After he had a small fire built, he went to the beach and looked down along the shore. He saw lots of washed-up artifacts and garbage and among them, crabs. They scuttled across the sand, some as small as the size of his hands and others even bigger. Some ranging from full-sized dogs and others much, much larger. Deciding to save his bread, Markus thought of cooking up some of those large spider-like green legs that the creatures were scuttling on.

Then he got an idea, and dropping down to one knee, he placed one of his hands onto the cold sand. Drawing energy from his crystal, he 'pulsed' with but a single thought that reverberated through the thousand upon million grains of sand.

Come here, I will not hurt you.

One crab about the size of Markus' hoverbike stopped its advance towards the splashing waters and completely changed course, scuttling right towards Markus while the others also seemed to pause but continued on their designated paths. Markus watched in awe as the crab he had picked approached him and stopped to inspect him with those beady little black eyes standing out on thick stalks with wavering whiskers.

"Well," he said grabbing the crab by the back of its shell and picking him up as he stood with a grunt. The thing weight heavily but it did not thrash and did not resist. "That's convenient."

In a matter of minutes, he had gotten a pot of sea water boiling and with a brief apology to the crab for deceiving it, Markus tossed it into the water and allowed it to boil. It felt dirty, tricking the creature with his telepathic magic, but still, crab was no different than deer or any other animal he had eaten he was simply using the tools he had just like many Hunters of old. There was no point in trying to deceive himself with the details or 'honor' of what he had done, and the end of the day, he had to eat and it was either him or it.

When the crab was ready he broke it apart and allowed it to sit in pieces in the pot that was now off the fire and now sitting beside it to cool. Wishing he had brought some butter or some other form of oil to dip the crab in, Markus spent the time looking out over the waves that were crashing into the beach, admiring its tranquil beauty. Above him, he watched the skies full of clouds and creatures of the air flying overhead. Ahools and Eagles were finally free to fly in the sky for winter had lost its hold on the land and it was now the time of new beginnings, and for all animals to officially awake in the midst of the new season. He was surprised to see a few of these creatures dive into the waters like pelicans only to come up with thrashing fish or one of the other crustaceans Markus had seen on the beach.

In the distance far beyond the hills to the east he saw a herd of immense bison with thick coats of brown fur and horns that curled like goats, all of them moving north in search of fresh grass, their younglings bellowing beside them. Their bull, which Markus could tell even from the distance had eight horns on its head, kept its head on the swivel in search for any and all predators. Markus decided that he should follow their example as he prepared to eat instead of sightseeing. When he, Ashlyn and Ruth had crossed The Wastelands there was little to no animal life, however in the wake of spring all beasts of air land and sea were awake, and many were sure to be hungry.

Eating one of the large crab legs, Markus once again wished he had some butter. But the salty water added plenty of flavor to the meat and he enjoyed pulling out strand after strand of the rubbery and yet satisfying muscle. He was about to dig into a second one when he felt a presence approaching him. Keeping a hand at his belt where his gun hung, he waited, watching in the direction the presence was approaching. In his auto-limb, both crystals began to glow brightly, especially Abner's though the spirit was as quiet as ever.

When whatever it was finally broke over the hill dividing the beach from the rest of the Wastelands, Markus relaxed but kept a sharp eye on the man who approached him.

He was a short and gangly man wearing a tattered coat and pants and carrying a backpack on his shoulders. He wore a stocking cap and his face was covered in dirty gray hair leading down to a goatee that reached down to his chest like an old goat's. The man had a walking stick to help him descend the hill of sand and he nodded at Markus with a warm smile.

"Greetings, my friend," he said with a raspy smoker's voice. "A lovely day on the beach, wouldn't you say?"

"It is," Markus said still remaining cautious. "Who are you? A traveler?" The last thing he wanted to deal with was a caravan of people- or worse, pirates.

"Something like that," the man answered now stopping within a few feet of Markus. "Could you spare some of your meat? These old bones haven't packed on anything in the last few days."

"Go right ahead," Markus said scooting back. He knew he wasn't going to be able to finish anyway, and he didn't want to be anywhere near the man just to be safe. "Help yourself."

The man thanked him, drawing closer and taking a seat opposite of the fire. After setting down his cane and his pack, he reached into the pot of warm water and with careful fingers gnarled with arthritis, removed a leg. He cracked it open, and sucked the succulent meat right out of it.

"Mmm," he hummed in delight. "That's good. Thank you."

Markus said that he was welcome. "You said that you were a traveler?"

"Of sorts. Am I to assume that so are you?"

Deciding not to answer Markus instead asked, "Why are you out here on your own?"

"I like to travel," the man said running a clean hand through his long and dirty goatee. "I've seen a lot during my travels, but there is still so much more to see."

"No offence, but I don't think it's safe for a man your age to be wandering around the Wastelands alone..."

The man chuckled at Markus. "I appreciate your concern, but I am not worried. I have nothing of value to any in this world anyway. Besides, if anything, I think it should be *you* who should be cautious. You don't get auto-limbs for nothing." He said this while staring at Markus' prosthetic.

"Guess you're right," Markus said cautiously.

"What is your name, son?"

"Pete," Markus answered not wanting to give his real name. "And yours?"

"I go by many and yet none."

This made Markus feel like he was talking to a physical being of a much older Abner. "And what does *that* mean?"

"Could mean everything, could mean nothing."

Convinced now that the man might be senile or simply crazy, Markus decided it wasn't going to get him anywhere asking all these questions. "All right then, what do *I* call you then?"

"Hmm..." the old man said cracking open another segment of crab and popping it into his mouth. As he chewed he said, "Which to choose. Maybe... Jon?"

"Jon, then," said Markus. "Pleased to meet you."

"And you," Jon said finishing up his crab leg. When he was finished, he discarded it into Markus' own pile and the two removed another leg and began to eat again. Markus looked at the man's pack, and asked him what he was traveling with.

"Books, writing material, that sort of thing."

"No weapons or food?"

"Nothing that I don't need."

Markus was confused and asked if the man was crazy. "I mean, it's dangerous to be out here unarmed and without food."

"I ran into you, didn't I?" Jon asked finishing his second leg and now starting his third. "You shared your food with me. And I've never had issue with any man or beast here, so I'm not worried." In the middle of his meal, Jon reached into his pack and removed a small wooden box. He sat it down next to him, and asked Markus if he liked music.

"I do…" Markus said. "But I'm still-"

"Give this a listen." Jon told him as he opened the box. From within, an eerie and yet relaxing tune sounded from within. The little gears inside chimed against the little musical pieces inside to produce a soft song that Markus immediately fell in love with.

Listening to it, his thoughts had gone to his sister and her final resting place. He thought of his father, who died back in Nineveh. He thought of Aventis, and anyone else who had left this world and gone to the next- wherever that was. He then thought of Jim, and other people who he still had. He thought of Kaltrina, and Esmerelda, and the rest of the Levitikans who he had left behind. He thought of Ashlyn, and how much he missed having her nearby. The two had been inseparable since their arrival in Levitika, and though he had started to miss her the moment he left Nineveh, he found himself more grounded within that feeling.

Before he knew it, the music had stopped and Jon had closed the lid on the wooden box. "This had been a gift for a friend," Jon said. "When he no longer needed it, it was returned by another friend who was just like you, Markus."

Markus felt his heart stop and his hand returned to his belt again.

"Calm down, I mean you no harm." As he said this, Jon himself showed no sign of alarm or ill towards the now alert Markus.

"Who are you, old man?" Markus demanded sharply.

"As I have said, I am Jon."

"Don't play with me. *Who* are you?"

Jon tossed his third leg away and sighed contently. "Where would I even begin to try to answer such a question?" he asked himself and after thinking about it for a few seconds he said, "I am merely a storyteller, writing stories to share with others across the many worlds beyond."

Markus' eyes narrowed in thought. "So, what, you're some alien author?"

Jon gave a polite chuckle at that. "You're a funny one to be certain."

"I'm serious."

"So am I."

"All right then, who do you serve?"

"No one but myself, and my books."

"Whose side are you on then?"

"I am on no one's side. Well, actually, that is not quite true. I am on everyone's side but also no one's. I am neither good nor evil, I simply exist for the sake of making my books contain the stories of those who are worthy to share. As for why such a business is in the Northern Wastelands, I am writing another, basing it on the war as of now and what you and the others will play in it."

Though he still didn't quite understand, another thought came to Markus and he revealed his Crystal from his arm. "Are you one of… *them*?"

"No," Jon answered. "I have no connection to them either here in the here and now, nor the dimension from which they are from. I have nothing in common with what happens with them. I am merely a traveler, and I watch and write. I serve no one but myself, and the natural order of the worlds I travel."

"What exactly do you mean by 'worlds'?" Markus then asked.

"Exactly as I had said."

"But…"

Jon looked out towards the sea with that warm smile that somehow felt like it had a light shimmer of sadness to it as if he was thinking back on something he missed dearly. "I have nothing much to offer you in thanks for your hospitality. But what I can *tell* you, is that the power you seek, it is one of the many worlds that we live in. Here and now, and The Dreaming."

"I thought you said you didn't know anything about it?"

"That's simply because that is a place I have yet to travel to."

"Do you have a crystal?" Markus asked, wondering if Jon did, how he would go about retrieving it.

"No. As I said, those mean nothing to me."

"That still doesn't explain who you are or why you know this stuff."

"Do all questions need answers?"

"Well, yes, that's how we learn about the world."

"Ahh," Jon said with a wink. "So you know everything about the ocean then?"

"Well, no…"

"Do you think you can know everything about the ocean and all it's mysteries?"

"That's impossible."

"Same as the stars above," Jon reasoned. "This world has managed to stretch beyond all the way to the planet Mars, whose colonies are just as wrought with ruin as Earth. But what other questions are out there, and will mankind ever truly understand them?"

Markus was stumped at this. "I guess you have a point, but what you say still doesn't make any sense. No one can go to 'different worlds' and expect to be considered human."

"No one should be able to alter reality, and yet here you stand."

Markus said nothing. The old man had to be crazy, there was no other way to put it and no further point in asking anymore questions.

"Imagine the sea," Jon then said pointing out towards the waves. "It gives, it takes, it moves, it shifts, but it still remains. While the dry land of this planet have been ravaged by the Falling, the sea still remains. Despite all that has been dumped into it and how much it has suffered, it remains. As with everything in this world and all, things change, new things arise, and not everything can be explained. Just like you, and how your journey will lead you to much hardship, but quite a story it shall be."

"I appreciate you saying so," said Markus said looking out towards the sea. He considered it's vastness, all that was hidden within it's depths. He looked up at the sky and thought of the vastness there as well. There was obviously more worlds out there, he knew that, but the way Jon was saying the things he had said, it made him wonder.

And yet, maybe it was no different than himself. Maybe the mysteries of the universe are just as vast as The Dreaming, if not more so. There was a lot of parts to this, and because of that, maybe that could be considered the key to understanding his power. Maybe, without giving Jon too much credit, the old man was right in a sort of way. Maybe this was what it was like becoming something more. More than just mere magic, but something else.

Markus turned to Jon. "Sir, I–"

But Jon wasn't there. He was gone; vanished as if he was never there. His tracks in the sand and where he had been sitting remained, but other than that, he was gone. There was no sign of him leaving, nor did Markus sense him anymore. He was just gone, like a dream upon awakening.

He searched all around, not convinced still, and when he could find no trace of the old man, he gave up and began cleaning up his camp. He thought about what Jon had said but in the end pushed it aside. It didn't matter what some old man out in the Wastelands said be it in riddles or not. Markus had plenty of riddles of his own to solve, and he couldn't stick around for everything.

He has a point, however, he heard Abner's voice clear as day.

"Well, well," said Markus as he mounted his bike, his pot washed clean and now back where it belonged. "Where have you been?"

Consoling our friend here, and listening.

"Well, what did you think?" asked Markus and putting the bike in gear, continued along the coast to the north where the crystals guided him. "Was he real, or something from The Dreaming?"

I cannot tell, Abner admitted. *But he is right, your story is far from over, Markus.*

Markus ignored the spirit and Abner never spoke up again, and he proceeded north. He followed the pulling sensation, his auto-limb seeming to hum with the essence from both the crystals, and something beyond the horizon where the sky met the sea.

Jon… said a voice in Markus' head. It was not Abner, and it was not Abram whom he had assumed was the one who had called to him much earlier in the night.

Markus glanced at the dark crystal joined with Abner's, and wondered what it all could mean.

<u>Ashlyn</u>

"Do you trust him?"

Esmerelda asked Ashlyn this the following afternoon, as they made their way downstairs where some men were waiting to train some more civilians about firearm safety. With everything that has happened in Nineveh, Elizabetha wanted to arm the citizens just as the Levitikans were. Giving them the right to bear arms was one thing, it was training the responsibility that was another. While hardly anyone had weaponry and would have to acquire some themselves as the Angels couldn't just give away their own, it would take some time but at the very least the citizens would be well versed and even potential soldiers wanting to fight for the good of the North. Already many men who had lost homes, families, businesses, wanted to take the fight to Xerxes at the very least and so were lining up at checkpoint stations asking to enlist, Kaltrina from the Drunken Badrat had been one of them.

Upon being asked by the princess this question, Ashlyn turned to her friend confused. "What?"

Esmerelda asked once more, "Do you trust him? Markus, I mean."

"Of course I do," Ashlyn answered incredulously. "I trust him with my life." Ashlyn said. For a while the only sound between them were their footsteps echoing throughout the halls until she asked, "Why?"

Esmerelda made a 'hmph' sound in her throat. "I'm still peeved that he would just leave like that. But I know he's doing it for all the right reasons, it's just you know him better than I do, and I was just curious."

Ashlyn nodded. Although she wasn't so sure about that minute little 'hmph' Esmerelda had released. "Well, I trust him to do what is right in the end. He has a lot on his plate, and I'm sure he wants to prepare himself better. After what happened with losing his arm, he's been acting more... I dunno... not elusive, but more..."

Esmerelda suggested, "Maybe just quiet? About The Dreaming in general?"

Ashlyn nodded. "He didn't talk about it much after Black showed him much about it, but then he ceased talking about it altogether after he lost his arm. I thought it was strange because he would talk about wanting the spirits inside to speak to him all the time, and then all of a sudden..." She shook her head. "Nothing."

"Maybe he thinks we won't understand?" Esmerelda asked.

Ashlyn shrugged. "Either way, he isn't here to ask him anyway. We just gotta trust him to come back."

"I'm surprised you didn't go with him," Esmerelda said looking at Ashlyn more serious. "You were pretty dead-set on going. Why did you refuse?"

"Because I don't want to slow him down in the end, and also, my place is here for now. The least I can do is continue to train and become a better fighter."

"You're serious about that then?"

Ashlyn nodded. "I didn't undergo training both with the Angels and been practicing at Vic's for nothing, you know."

"I noticed you've been spending a lot more time at Vic's than the Angels," said Esmerelda.

Ashlyn looked at her friend. "Is that a bad thing?"

"No, like I said before with you and Markus, just be careful. Vic has proven useful, but he still doesn't like the government."

"Neither does your mom," said Ashlyn.

"That's slightly different. My mom tries to work with the council and the elders, Vic does not. I'm not trying to say don't trust him, just be careful, like always."

Ashlyn shrugged it off and said, "All right."

Esmerelda glanced at Ashlyn and said, "I'm just looking out for you."

"I know, thank you," said Ashlyn with a smile. In the back of her mind she wondered if it was Vic Esmerelda didn't trust, or her. Because she had been spending a lot of time at Vic's shooting range, she liked the peace and quiet of the range despite the gunshots and she liked testing some of Vic's weaponry. She had gotten better at rifles but still miserable at pistols of any sort. Even fully-automatic weaponry was beyond her despite her best efforts. Ever since she just barely missed the witch Lameika in the Grand Hall back when the attack on Levitika took place, she had wanted to become better. She tried to balance this as much as she can learning how to read with Esmerelda.

As it was, Esmerelda didn't bring Vic back up again and the two continued to the training grounds to work on their shooting together. Despite her mother's desire to not feel the need to be armed, Esmerelda had trusted Ashlyn to be discreet as possible in showing her proper etiquette. It was difficult with so many Angels in training taking notice of the princess sticking around, but it was not impossible at least. Ashlyn did her drills under the command of a brutish woman with a gruff voice, and by the time she was instructed to begin rifle training again, her arms felt like gelatine from all the pushups. All the while Esmerelda watched and encouraged her.

When it was time for Ashlyn to attempt to use a pair of Eagle's Wings, it proved to be much more difficult. She had not been trained on it before, and the neuro-link that strapped to the base of her skull stun horribly and it made the conscious thought of moving the metal wings on her back much more difficult. She had spread them out but couldn't bring them back down, or she could flex them before her and couldn't unflex. She felt ridiculous and at the same time envious of Markus, but the lady who was coaching her had assured her that it sometimes took months for some Angels to get used to them.

At this time, Grim came barreling up to Ashlyn. The mutant's uncanny gray skin made him appear like a ghost as he came before her and he dismissed the coach and then told Ashlyn to take the Eagle's Wings off, all the while Esmerelda watched at the sidelines curiously.

"Come to the palace, now," the soldier said in a stressed but angry tone. He looked to Esmerelda and said, "Your highness, the queen has requested your presence as well."

Esmerelda approached them by the time Ashlyn got the wings off, grateful for their absence. "What's going on, Grim?"

"As if you don't know. Word is your mutual friend is missing."

Ashlyn and Esmerelda looked at each other. Neither of them had taken the initiative to tell Queen Elizabetha that Markus had left so suddenly, both having never talked about informing the queen nor feeling as if it were their responsibility. Nevertheless, they followed Grim not to Elizabetha's castle, but the Nineveh Citadel.

When they finally arrived at the citadel which had been relatively repaired in small increments over the past few days, they were led up into Elizabetha's newest Throne Room, where she was standing at the large war table sitting in the middle of the room that was cleared of all the old banners of Baron Ovid and the few columns that had been damaged in the battle were replaced with new beams just to keep the ceiling from falling down. Slagar was with her, and by the motions of their hands and facial expressions the discussion wasn't a pleasant one.

What also occurred to Ashlyn Baron Ovid's throne was missing. Elizabetha might have gotten rid of it with the intention of replacing it once a new leader was placed for Nineveh.

Her thoughts were interrupted by Elizabetha's peering eyes that seemed to flash in anger. If looks could kill, this was one of them. She said something to Slagar and he stormed off scowling bitterly. By the time Ashlyn got and Esmerelda approached the queen, Elizabetha suddenly turned around and walked over to the window, watching the busy streets below. She was silent for the longest time which made Ashlyn shuffle her feet nervously. When she finally did spoke the queen's words were cold and grasped every fiber of the girl's attention without effort.

"Where did he go?"

Ashlyn swallowed a lump that suddenly formed in her throat and Esmerelda said, "He's left for Kaiken, Mother."

"I am *aware* he has left," said Elizabetha still with her back to them. "He was to tell me when he plans to leave so I can prepare. He has defied my orders and the council is on my tail about it. What makes it worse, is that you two are admitting now that you knew, and you have said nothing." She was shaking her head, her reflection in the glass window scowling angrily.

"I'm sorry, your highness," said Ashlyn.

"No, I should be sorry, Mother," said Esmerelda tilting her head in shame and looking down at her boots. "I should have been the one to inform you. Ashlyn was just looking out for her friend."

Ashlyn stared at her and Esmerelda glared back. A simple wordless message: Keep quiet.

Elizabetha took a deep breath and then exhaled through her nose. "Why did you keep this from me?"

"Markus seemed very adamant on getting out fast, not wanting to waste any time, including yours. Also, I didn't think of telling you as I thought that if he was leaving, he must have told you."

Elizabetha turned about-face like a soldier, her face stern and looking more furious than a vengeful angel. It made Ashlyn nearly wilt under her gaze and Esmerelda had clenched her eyes as if expecting a blow.

"So was it to let him go without anyone knowing, or did you believe he told me? Which is it?"

"I thought he told you…" said Esmerelda.

"Wait," Ashlyn said to Elizabetha. "She-"

"Ashlyn, I admire your courage for my daughter, but do not speak." Elizabetha had not taken her eyes off of Esmerelda and she said to her, "You thought, and you did not check in to confirm? What is it I have always told you about assuming anyone knows anything?"

Esmerelda gulped and said, "A ruler does not assume unless she knows for certain."

That wasn't quite the phrase Ashlyn knew about assuming but she wasn't about to speak out just yet.

"That's right," said Elizabetha. "It ensure there is no miscommunication or ignored details, especially in consideration to the council and the citizens. It may not affect you in any way possibly, but it could mean everything to another. Regardless of his reasons, Markus should not have gone alone without telling me something. That way I could have a clear case with the council, and as it is, they are not happy. They are already causing me much grief."

"I am sorry for instigating that grief…" Esmerelda said sounding like she was about to cry.

Elizabetha sighed again and then at last turned her blue eyes upon Ashlyn at last. "Did he take anyone with him?"

"No, your majesty," Ashlyn answered.

"Did he *take* anything with him then?"

"Just a bike and some rations as well as the crystals and his weapons. Whatever else I'm not so sure."

Elizabetha nodded. She had turned back to Esmerelda and said, "I'm not going to scold you for this. I just need you to understand our position now, and you must learn this before you become a leader one day."

"I understand," said Esmerelda.

"Slagar is already beginning to question my authority because of Markus' rebellion. It won't be long before he gets The Elders to side with him. It was a mistake letting him go like that, but it can't be helped now. What's done is done. All we can hope now is that he comes back safe with the information he needs before we begin the liberation of the country."

Both the girls nodded mutely.

"Hopefully the spirits and the Great Owl will be on our side still," Elizabetha said at last and then she smiled softly at Esmerelda and opening her arms out to her daughter, asked her to come to her. She did so, and the queen embraced Esmerelda warmly. "I'm just trying to make you understand, okay?"

"Okay…"

They let each other go and then Elizabetha turned to Ashlyn. "There is another matter of which I have summoned you for, Ashlyn."

"What is it, your highness?" asked Ashlyn.

"I've been hearing about your shooting becoming better. Both at the castle's range as well as Vic's. In fact, Vic had high praise for you. Told me your aim is impeccable."

Ashlyn tried to suppress a small smile of appreciation as well as a slight hint of shame. "Thank you."

"We have compared some notes, and Grim and I both agree that you have a good pair of eyes. Have you had them inspected ever?"

"No, I haven't."

"I'd like to get your eyes checked. If the stats are as good as your aim is, then it would make sense. The reason I want to, is because I would like you to accompany Grim on a small-team mission."

"Okay," said Ashlyn hesitantly. "What sort of mission."

"We will not begin our invasion north until we are better prepared, but we need more information on the primary target as of now: Xerxes. We need to know what the city is like, what the people and security are like, as well as the conflict with The Capitol and why Queen Psyren was so determined to take Nineveh almost without prisoners. To be personally blunt, that does not sound like the Psyren I have heard of before, and so we have no information as to what it is like in the city, what position they are in and all that. This would be critical in understanding our enemy's needs, and hopefully work with them to take down a common enemy."

"So what does this mission have to do with it?" asked Ashlyn.

"There will be an infiltration of Xerxes. A small squad who will pose as citizens and spies." She grinned at Ashlyn's look of shock. "Let me explain: Your team will head for the nearest village of Lakeshire, and gather whatever supplies you need to make it seem like you are returning to the safety of the city walls, from within you will live among the people, earn the trust of the citizens and gather as much information as you can without alerting the soldiers."

"Mother," Esmerelda spoke up equally surprised as Ashlyn was. "Is that a good idea?"

"I believe so. If Ashlyn's sight is as good as Vic and I expect, I think that would be very resourceful for reconnaissance. I do not know what kind of force they have, so the selected few must be careful until you have a better understanding of how things work. We need to know how the war in the north is going, what they think of the queen, and if they would think about joining forces against The Capitol. Every week someone will leave and report to an officer who will stay in Lakeshire and report it back here. All you need to do, Ashlyn, is play the part of a daughter or perhaps a friend, mingle with the citizens, and get what we need without putting yourself in danger."

"Why me?" Ashlyn asked at last. "No offense, your highness, but I don't know anything about reconnaissance or any of that stuff."

"All that will be arranged to make sure you are prepared. Also, your history as a thief and evading the law fits some of the criteria we have set for this sort of work."

"What if something goes wrong?"

"We have that arranged as well," Elizabetha assured Ashlyn. "If we are able to succeed in reaching an impasse and a resolution for it, then we can earn a powerful ally for the Northern Wastelands. Grim knows what to do should your squad be discovered, and from there you will be returned back safely. On that, you have my word."

Ashlyn was thinking about it. Esmerelda noticed this and asked her friend, "You aren't considering this, are you?"

"I do want to do my part," Ashlyn admitted. "But I'd be lying if I were to say I was nervous."

But she was also thinking about something else. How much closer she could be to Markus, and if there was a slim chance that perhaps she could slip away and see him in Kaiken, or if he swings by Xerxes as he had promised, maybe they could see each other sooner. Esmerelda was saying something to her mother, and all Ashlyn caught from Elizabetha was "… her decision, I will not force her to go."

"I don't need to think about it," Ashlyn said at last. "I will go. I've always wondered what Xerxes was like anyway, and if this will help our cause, then even better."

"Are you nuts?" Esmerelda demanded. "You're just a kid!"

Ashlyn looked at Esmerelda. "A lot of the Angels are kids the same age as me, Esmerelda."

"That isn't the point, I'm not saying you are incapable of it, but-"

"I want to do my part, Esmerelda," said Ashlyn. "Besides, I don't want to just train and train and wait around. I want to *do* something."

Esmerelda looked to her mother helplessly. "Mother…"

"It is her decision, daughter," said Elizabetha calmly. "I wouldn't have even suggested such a thing if I did not believe she could do it. What her test results will bring will ultimately decide whether she can go or not, but if she wants to go and is able…"

Esmerelda had ceased speaking to her mother and was looking at Ashlyn shaking her head. "This isn't because you let Markus go, is it?"

Ashlyn felt both ashamed and angry at this accusation. "No, and quite frankly, I don't need you to tell me what I can and can't do either, Esmerelda."

The princess threw up her hands and said, "Fine. Put yourself in danger too."

She started to go away but Ashlyn had grabbed hold of Esmerelda's arm. The queen had raised an eyebrow but otherwise did not intervene.

"Don't start that with me," said Ashlyn sternly. "I want to do my part here. If I can aid the Levitikans better, then I have to. Markus is doing his own part, and so is everyone else in the Angels including you. I'm not helpless, Esmerelda."

Esmerelda glared at Ashlyn but she did not resist, and because of that Ashlyn let her friend go. "You do realize you are going into enemy territory, right?"

"I've *lived* in enemy territory," Ashlyn argued. "First chance I had to do something greater, I took it. I know this is right. Even if it does have anything to do with Markus, you can't argue that I want to serve my knew home as best I can."

Esmerelda still hadn't stormed off yet, and so that had to be a good sign. The princess still looked mad, but her eyes were shining. "I don't want you to go too…"

Ashlyn tried for a small smile. "Then I guess that means I better come back too, right?"

Esmerelda glanced at her mother and looked back at Ashlyn. "You sure you want to do this?"

"Positive. Worst case, Grim will protect me, right, Elizabetha?"

"That is the plan, yes," said Elizabetha.

Esmerelda still didn't look happy but at last she nodded. "I understand. But you aren't allowed to leave without telling me either. Okay?"

Ashlyn nodded smiling. "Of course. What are friends for?"

Esmerelda finally smiled back and shook her head. "You remember when I said you could pass as royalty when you first came here?"

"Yeah, I remember."

"Well… you still do. But you also have a fighting spirit for sure. I wish I was as brave as you are."

Ashlyn smiled and gently slugged Esmerelda's shoulder. "C'mon, you're brave in your own way, and when we are all back together, we can share all of our stories together. I'll stick to my reading lessons too, I promise."

Esmerelda laughed then and said, "You better, because I'm not going to teach you all that again. Also…"

"What?" Ashlyn asked, noticing that the queen was smiling at them.

"If you don't come back, I'm never going to forgive you, especially if I have to explain it to Markus."

Ashlyn laughed and said, "No pressure, right?"

Ghost

Ghost stopped and parked his Hovercraft just a few meters .of the Bubbly Bog, a desolate bayou just off the coast of The Great Sea; a bulbous wart in the otherwise desolate of the northwest part of the Northern Wastelands.

The trees were tall and covered with moss that had been frozen since the winter, and were now thawing to add to the thick sludge that had collected in the bog. Legends told that when the bombs fell long ago, that this was the place where one of them had landed, right off the coast. Over the many years it had created it's own little pocket of an ecosystem, and the radiation within had been potent enough to kill many if they had not mutated along with the plants. If he were not wearing his suit, where he stood now, he would have suffered from poisoning, and should he venture further, he would not have been human anymore. He would be no more human than the monsters that now called this bog home.

Dismounting from his craft, Ghost drew one of this katanas and began to enter the bog.

The bugs buzzed around him but he paid them no heed: in his suit he was safe from all temperatures as well as bug bites. From the looks of the mosquitos the size of livestock, to create snakes slithering among the writhing vines in brilliant neon colors, he kept a wide berth of them all and cut down whatever came his way. At one point a carnivorous plant began to reach out towards him with great vines coming from the base of the tree it was connected to, and Ghost cut the vines away before casting a spell on the ground to tell the plant that he was not food. It left him alone as he pushed on into the thick of the swamp.

He kept his head on the swivel however, for whom he was looking for could not be far. He saw glimpses of glowing eyes within the darkness of the trees, most of them however were golden and cat-like, not at all what he was looking for. But every once in a while he would see the flash of slanted eyes of a dull golden brown. They were close by, and they were watching him. He saw one lingering closer and closer to him and he whipped out his Laser Pistol and jammed the barrel right under the chin of a Lacerta who growled and flashed his teeth at the unwelcomed guest who had entered his bog. It was a hulking creature, standing nearly ten feet in height and it's back was covered with thick spines. The creature hissed at the Hunter Ghost having recognized the weapon.

All around him, Ghost saw more of the giant lizards coming out of the brush hissing and wielding spears and mangled swords of twisted metal. Their green skin seemed to change color as they emerged, their eyes slanted and tails waving to and fro in anxious hesitation to attack their intruder. A whole pack of them, no doubt having caught his scent the moment he had entered their domain, and while all of them were similarly reptilian, none were completely identical due to the heavy concentration of radiation which buzzed in Ghost's helmet in great warning symbols.

Ghost merely smiled beneath his helmet. "You really are easy to track," he said to the creature he now held hostage. "All I had to do was follow the movement of the trees and water, I can see how a lesser creature can easily be overcome by your band, however I am not like other creatures."

"What do you want?" the Lacerta hissed indigently, it's voice raspy and gruff as a forked tongue tasted the air and tasted no fear. "Your kind ain't welcome to our home."

"I am aware, but I come with a proposition for you."

"A what?"

"A proposition, I wish to offer you a job and you will be paid."

"You have nothing that we want," the lizard growled as he gently pushed the gun away with a claw. His band seemed to relax but were all ready to lunge if their leader gave the word.

"I can give you land," Ghost offered. "Better land than the swamp, a warmer place perchance. This bog is after all far north, it takes longer for the cold to thaw I could imagine."

The lizard cocked his head, and Ghost was happy that he was grasping his attention. The jagged teeth that stuck out of the creature's lips were large as it smiled at him. "I doubt you have anything of the sorts, man-meat."

"What I offer had more sunlight, and far from the prying eyes of humans and other mutants," said Ghost keeping his pistol and sword on either side.

"Your people, hunt us like animals," the monster hissed. "You come in vain, human. Here, we will eat your bones."

"What is your name?" Ghost asked trying a different approach.

The Lacerta hissed indignantly. He was tense, and appeared ready to strike at any time and if he were to, Ghost would be ready. He did not fear this monstrosity.

"Why would my next meal care about my name?" it demanded.

"I don't. But that is how you make conversation."

The Lacerta squinted at Ghost as if trying to see him through the suit. "I am known as Ripjaw by my people, tin can."

"Ripjaw," Ghost nodded amused. "Okay Ripjaw, let us think about this. How many are in your tribe?"

"We are fifty strong, what is left."

"And how many warriors?"

"Thirty."

"Okay, so as for the remaining twenty, wouldn't you do anything to keep them safe, find them a better home where they can have a better chance at peace and happiness? Being so close to the Capitol and yet having little choice other than the Southern Sands, why stay here?"

"What kind of question is that? Of *course* I would do anything for our mates and hatchlings. But the cities don't let us go that far, they shoot us down, wear our skin as boots and armor."

"And you eat human beings," said Ghost. "As it seems, this is not a safe place for you as well."

Around them some of the Lacerta warriors were hissing and snapping their jaws. One of them even called out to Ripjaw to just tear the whelp limb from limb. Still, neither Ghost nor their leader looked away from one another. They stood together as equals in the thick of the swamp.

Ripjaw grinned again and said, "And yet you have a solution?"

"Let me repeat myself: If you and your band can assist me on a little visit, you can keep the island. I will of course make sure you are well equipped, and when the job is done, I will leave you in peace, and I can guarantee that no humans there will harm you. I of course must warn you there is a *slight* chance some of you might get injured, possibly killed for the man I am looking for will not go easy. But it is *definitely* worth the risk."

The Lacerta made a strange humming in his throat as he thought about Ghosts' proposal. "And what guarantee do I have that this island you speak of will keep my people safe? Well sheltered, and more importantly fed?"

Ghost said, "The food from the sea has to be better than whatever you must eat here to survive."

Ripjaw considered Ghost for a moment and then another rumbling sound came from his throat similar to that of a croak about to be released. "I don't trust you."

Ghost holstered his weapon and held up his free hand. "May I see your head, please?"

Ripjaw tensed but did not retreat. "What trickery is this?"

"None. I just want to show you something."

He placed his hand on the creature's head, only slightly sure Ripjaw would just bite his hand off. As it is the Lacerta allowed this to happen and Ghost pulsed, releasing a memory of the place he had in mind. Ripjaw relaxed only slightly but then pulled his head back and hissed as the instant memory was sent to him and he hissed at Ghost.

"You're a witch," growled the monster.

"Maybe, maybe not," said Ghost feeling the energy of his own crystal in the confines of his suit. "But, what do you make of what I have to offer?"

Ripjaw growled but by the look in those intelligent brown eyes, Ghost knew he was considering it. "I need to discuss it with the rest of the tribe."

"Of course you do, by all means." Ghost nodded. "I will wait here for your answer."

He took a seat upon a rock and crossed his legs. He looked up at the lizard who looked at him skeptically. "Time is of the essence my scaly friend, if you are not going to help me then please let me know so I can go."

Ripjaw growled. "We'll be back. But you ain't going nowhere one way or another." He nodded to his crew who all but one left in the darkness of the swamp. The one who stayed looked to be female by the hue of her belly skin. She rested against a nearby tree, her eyes never leaving Ghost who waited patiently.

After a good hour of uncomfortable silence, Ripjaw reappeared with his band of warriors. The Lacerta approached Ghost who stood up awaiting the leader's response.

"Alright tin-can, we got a deal," Ripjaw growled.

Ghost nodded contentedly. "Excellent."

"On one condition."

"Fine," Ghost said expecting such. "What is it?"

"I am in charge of this clan, so I will tell them what to do. You however have no say."

Ghost shook his head smiling. He placed a hand on the lizard's shoulder. "Oh Ripjaw…" He pulsed and the Lacerta stiffened as his eyes began to glow blood-red. He gasped as Ghost entered his mind and searched within his consciousness within The Dreaming.

"*This* is whom you will serve," Ghost said and immediately Ripjaw began to quiver and shake as if he was looking at something horrible. "I answer to The Master, and so you will answer to me. Do as we say, and I can guarantee that you and your clan will be safe on your new island- your new home."

Ripjaw looked at Ghost his eyes still glowing. "Witchcraft…"

Ghost chuckled amused. "Tell me Ripjaw, what do you fear the most?" He dug in deep, and suddenly Ripjaw fell to his knees crying a guttural scream. His warriors stepped forward about to attack Ghost but their leader cried out at them in a desperate snarl.

"Get back!" He held his hands up over his face, cowering beneath them he began to mutter, "Go away… go away…"

"You know how to make them go away my friend." Ghost said. "Who do you serve?"

"No one… Ahh!"

"Who, do, you serve?" Ghost asked again. He pulsed again which made the lizard stiffen and go rigid with fear.

"Ghost!" the leader cried out. "We follow Ghost, and The Master above him!"

Ghost released him and as the monster fell on his hands and knees gasping he said, "Fail, and I will make sure He tortures you until your last dying breath." He then turned to the rest of the tribe who growled and hissed at him. "Your leader just witnessed The Master of a new age, fail and you will all see what he saw. Succeed, and you will have a new home away from the prying eyes of humans, and rich in hunting and fishing grounds."

Ripjaw stood up behind Ghost muttering curses as he walked up alongside him. He seemed more collected now but he still appeared shaken up by whatever he had seem. "What say you boys? Shall we hunt?"

The lizards began growling affirmations in excitement of their new home. Ripjaw looked over at Ghost with such loathing, but he growled, "Where to?" frightfully despite his demeanor.

Ghost waved his hand over his head and began to march back where he came. "To my ship, and then we cross The Great Sea."

Markus

Markus had seen many islands out on the waters as he traveled up the shores, however as he flew across the mighty blue his Hoverbike having been stashed at a grounded ship along the shore, his eyes scanned the few smaller islands as well as the larger islands in the distance. It was more difficult to pinpoint just which of these islands Abram could be on.

C'mon, Abner, help me out here, he said to the spirit.

The sensation of direction intensified momentarily, the gravity trying to pull him back down to earth driving him in the direction of an island full of lush trees and a small hill, the island itself being in the shape of a horseshoe. He banked right liking the feeling these Angel Eagle's Wings had and like an eagle himself seeking sanctuary, he dove in the direction of the island.

When he finally reached the island, he swooped and landed within the trees which were scraggily excuses for pine incapable of surviving out here. The Eagle's Wings retracted back into his pack and he stretched his body, looking at the waves of the sea and listening to the sounds of the island among the minor popping sounds in his spine.

It was beautiful, and Markus could tell that it was warmer out here on the sea. The air smelled and even tasted salty, and the breeze made it more so with the sun fully exposed with not a single cloud in sight, save for further out beyond the sea. It was a good change in Markus' opinion. In the sea he saw the life essence of many fish and sea creatures, as well as a Waterbeast that glided beneath the shifting whitecaps. When he turned to look within the forest he saw even more animal life, though the creatures that he saw shaped held no recognition compared to that in the Wastelands, and in the far distance deep within the trees he saw the faint outline of a person walking around.

Markus knew that had to be Abram, and hoisting his pack, started to hike in the direction of the essence in the shape of a man.

He soon became within earshot of some whistling, it was not however the birds that sung up in the trees upside down like bats, but the distinct raspy pattern of a person taking a breath between tunes. He soon came out of the tree line and into a clearing in the center of the island where a miniature cove was present, the waters within the horseshoe shape which crashed against a shore of black sand. He stopped to observe what was within the clearing just before the shore. About ten small cabins constructed of pine logs sat around a large garden area filled to the edge of an old fence with corn, lettuce, tomatoes, strawberries, and melons. There was also a small shack not far from the cabins where a cauldron and stove sat and smoke was seeping through the roof. Markus walked into this clearing, his auto-limb hand resting on the pistol on his hip.

What surprised him was that there was no sign of life now here, and yet he could hear minor chatting among the cabins. This confused him, as he should have been able to detect any signs of life, and yet this minute community appeared to be a ghost town.

"Hello?" he called out. He walked towards the nearest house a little faster only to slow down in case someone was nearby. He looked all around still calling out. "Hello? Anyone here?"

He came up to the house and up to the door and knocked upon it. "Hello?" His final knock had pushed the door opened, and carefully he pushed it further in which revealed a darkened room lit by only the light that shined through the drapes of the windows as well as a small candle that rested on a table in the center of the room.

"Hello?" he called inside again. "Sorry, but your door was open, is anyone home?" When he heard nothing he pulled the door closed and stepped back outside. He pursed his lips in thought. He turned walked back into the clearing, he huffed as he laid himself upon the grass and laid on his back. His sword scabbard sat across his lap and his pistol stayed close to his hand just in case. Someone should have heard him by now, and yet there wasn't a single soul in sight save for the essence he had seen when entering the woods.

He was about to sit back up and consider his options when he heard something running towards him and as he was just getting back up a large Werecat the size of a small rhino jumped right on top of him with a loud and solitary, "MEOW!"

"Gah!" Markus stifled a cry as the mutated cat's weight crushed the breath out of his lungs and cracked his back. His arms were pinned under the cat's body so he could not protect himself by the fiendish tongue that slapped his face like a dog. The Werecat had a thin white coat and his eyes shined blue as the waves of the sea. Of course, Markus did not see any of this yet for his eyes were closed and he was gasping for breath as the cat licked his face again, and again, seeming to almost try to drown him.

"Get off me, you moggy son of a-!" His words were cut off as his mouth was practically scraped off by the sandpaper-like tongue which proceeded to drool contentedly. He gasped for air when able with a, "Gah! Someone help!"

"He will get off if you ask nicely," he heard an old voice say amongst the slobbering kisses.

"Just tell him to get off of me!" Markus cried.

"Just say 'please get off'."

"Please, for the love of Pete, get the hell off!"

Markus gasped as the weight of the Werecat left his body and he crawled away gasping for breath and pulled his weapon too late as he felt the steel of a sword against the back of his neck. He froze in place the Werecat completely forgotten despite being right in front of him sitting upright and licking a massive forepaw.

"Who are you?" he heard the voice ask.

Markus swallowed and raised his hands. "I'm sorry, I, uh, I'm looking for a guy named Abram."

He felt the touch of the blade leave him and he felt a tap on his auto-limb arm. "I see you got some crystals with you. No doubt you know what they are..."

Markus turned his head to take a look at the man. The man was tall, almost six foot with a slender body and broad shoulders which made him he look like a large 't'. He also wore baggy pants and a cotton shirt under a long brown trench coat. His face was clean-shaven but his hair which was tied into a ponytail was white and hung down to the small of his back. His eyes, which were steel gray flashed alert and careful.

Behind the old man Markus saw some people who had come out of their homes. Children hid behind their mother's dresses, and men before them staring at Markus with both looks of welcome, and fear. For some reason, Markus couldn't see any of their life essences and it made him wonder if they were all ghosts, for the man who held him hostage was the only one with an essence that was bright and full of life, not anything like his age should have revealed.

"I recognize that sword," the old man said removing his blade and holding out a hand to help Markus up. Markus happily took it. When he was back on his feet the man asked him, "Where did you get that? And the crystals?"

"I was given them," said Markus his mind already reeling with excitement despite his face being all scraped raw and slobbery. "Are you… by chance Abram?"

The old man smiled and nodded. "That would be me. And you, you must be Markus."

Markus glanced at the people watching and then his eyes returned to Abram. "Then… why would you ask me why I have the crystals if you know me? Also, how do you know me?"

Abram shook his head. "A test, nothing more."

Markus narrowed his eyes, already having plenty of his fill of tests and riddles for the last three months since this whole thing began.

"It is good to finally meet you," said Abram warmly. "Damion has showed me images of you."

"Damion? Images?"

Abram tapped the side of his head. "The boy can still send a good picture of his memory when he is asleep. Such a fine apprentice he was. How is the fine Hunter doing anyhow?"

Markus swallowed. "I am sorry sir, but he is dead. He was killed during a raid against Ninevite troops."

"Old Ovid could not ever pass up a chance at power could he? I am… sorry to hear that." Abram looked away as if remembering a sad memory. But he soon brought his attention back to Markus. "And now you are here, so I guess that answers my question to why you are out here."

"Yes sir, I was told to seek you out."

"By Damion Black."

"Yes, that is correct."

Abram nodded. "That would explain why he told me these things. I wonder if he predicted this to be… Oh well. Hopefully his soul rests in peace. Come, I am sure you are hungry and thirsty. I will pour some tea and we can talk."

Markus followed, remembering to wipe his face as the Werecat sprinted past him to catch up with his master. As he walked by, the people watched him with intense interest, in fact one boy about a few years old ran up to him despite his mother's warnings. He had black hair and brown eyes and a smile with many gaps between his teeth.

"Hi, I'm Mylo," he said smiling still. "Who are you?"

Not knowing what to say or do Markus merely replied. "My name is Markus. Nice to meet you, Mylo."

"Are you a friend of Abram?" His eyes flashed with excitement.

"I guess you could say that." Markus locked eyes with the mother then and he jutted his chin towards her. "Your mother's worried, you should go to her."

"Okay," Mylo grinned. "Nice to meet you!" He said as he ran back to his mother. One by one the villagers returned to their duties, while some of the younger women stole glances at Markus as they departed. The mother of Mylo nodded thanks to Markus who waved sheepishly at her.

He then heard Abram clearing his throat and he turned to see the old man waiting patiently by his front door. "Come," he said to Markus who quickened his pace.

"I apologize for Daryl's affection," Abram said pouring some tea into some cups while Markus sat on a couch chewing on a muffin as the Werecat laid beside him, taking up more than half of the couch in the process with it's muscular bulk. "He just loves visitors. He didn't bite you, so I figured you weren't a pirate, but I had to be sure, Markus. I've had plenty of unwelcome visitors here since I lived here."

"It's okay," Markus nodded as he observed the back wall which consisted of an entire bookshelf filled to the top with many, many books. "Who are all those people out there?"

"They live here on the island with me. They live here and count on me to protect them from pirates. As long as me and Daryl are here, we protect them, and they give us food and shelter."

"They seem like nice people."

"Indeed they are, you will have to meet them after we are done here. I am sure they would love to meet you after your training."

"Training?"

"I can't have you distracted, at least not yet. The people here don't get many visitors, but they understand the urgencies of some situations. They will be patient until I am done with you. But we will discuss that later, for I am sure you are tired and only want to talk for a little bit."

"You have a lot of books," Markus pointed out.

"Oh, yes," Abram sounded taken aback by the odd question which Markus didn't blame him for. He was nervous and didn't know what to say. The old man continued, "I like to read, and keep a hold on my research." Abram handed Markus his tea and then taking a seat in a rocking chair across from his visitor.

"So, tell me about you, Markus. Your journey, and what you know thus far. And if you can, I would like to know how Levitika is faring as well as Elizabetha. I haven't seen the girl since she was very young, and I would also like to know how every detail as to how Damion died. Go on, speak."

So, Markus told Abram everything. From his escape from Nineveh to the battle in the sky. He told the old man about Ruth, and his friend Ashlyn. He told him about all that Black had taught him upon arriving in Levitika, about him being part of a prophecy and being The Keeper. What he had heard about The Eldest, and much more. All the while Abram never moved nor took his eyes off of Markus. He only moved when he took a sip of his tea, and even then he never took his eye off of the boy.

When Markus was done, he was surprised to see that the room was darker, and the sun outside the window was now beginning to set. He had been talking for over two hours, and he developed a heavy thirst in doing so. He sipped his tea which had gone cold as Abram sat nodding and mumbling to himself.

When he finally did speak to Markus, his voice was soft. "Incredible. Already you have endured much, and without too much knowledge. I am impressed."

"Thank you sir," Markus said. In truth, he really didn't know what to say. Beside him, Daryl was sleeping soundlessly like the cat he truly was.

"And now I am to teach you the rest of the history of the crystals and how to properly use magic, huh?"

"Yes sir, I was hoping that you would."

Abram raised an eyebrow. "You hoped? I thought that Damion had requested you to, or had I misheard?

"No, sir, you heard correctly. It's just a lot has happened since, and I want to become stronger in order to find the other crystals and destroy them as Black told me."

Abram nodded. "Well, I suppose I could try. I have not taught anyone since Damion. I must warn you though, the history of The Eldest is a dark tale, and the art of the crystals is even darker."

"I know about The Eldest, sir," said Markus. "I know how the crystals were made for him, as well as the one he put his son into."

"Perhaps," Abram mused. "But that doesn't mean you know everything. Like I said, it is a grim tale. Those crystals are not just dangerous, they carry with them more misery than their own master."

"I'm not afraid to learn, sir."

Abram cocked an eyebrow. "Not afraid huh? Well, we shall see."

"Sir, Black also told me to tell you something."

"Oh?"

"He said you could teach me how to destroy the crystals. I have hunches why, but I do not know for certain why."

"That we can save until tomorrow, when we begin." Abram stood out of his chair, groaning as he stood up. "Damion has taught you swordplay, so I can move on with exercising the most important muscle: your brain."

"Okay," Markus said setting his cup down and standing up. He had expected nothing less considering what Black had taught him back in Levitika. "Sir, I have so many questions I need to ask you."

"All in good time. You have told me much to think about, and I am weary. The news of the warrior you described worries me, and I need to sleep on it. You need to sleep too, I want you fresh and ready to go at the crack of dawn, understand?"

"Yes sir."

"Good. Also, Damion has taught you on how to meditate for The Dreaming, yes?"

"Yeah," Markus said remembering. "Taking hold and grounding myself, control my emotions and all that."

"There is much to it than that but I am glad he did so. I want you to that again tonight before you retire. You might as well get used to the island and every soul here."

"Um, sir, about that, I couldn't see the life essence of the people here..."

"That is because I have hidden them on purpose," said Abram. "Meditate, and when you are capable of sensing them beyond my veil, then perhaps you will be ready beyond your imagination."

"Oh, okay..." Markus said doubtfully.

"Do your best, and after that, sleep. All answers will come in due time. The couch is all yours and blankets are in the pantry. Help yourself." And as he walked away, Abram muttered something along the lines of 'goodnight' as he disappeared down the hallway mumbling to himself with Daryl now fully awake suddenly, following close behind. Markus was then left standing alone in the room, happy he had found Abram, but was now wondering what exactly he was getting himself into.

He was also wondering where Daryl slept, and why in the world that Abram had a *Werecat* of all things as a pet.

<u>Ashlyn</u>

Ashlyn had just finished packing with the help of Esmerelda when a servant knocked on the door. She had made a quick stop at Vic's earlier that morning and now it was nearing noon, just about the time to head to Xerxes to meet up with the rest of the squad.

"Grim and her royal highness is waiting for you at the gates," the owner of the knocking called out through the door.

"Thank you," Ashlyn called out whilst returning to her packing. She was wearing her travel coat and her hair was up, whereas Esmerelda looked like she had just woken up as the princess was still in her nightgown.

"Feels like I am losing you both now," Esmerelda said with a sad smile. "At least I know you won't be alone."

"Thank god for that," Ashlyn agreed. She was sad to leave Esmerelda as well but as she had promised she had some worksheets to work on her reading and writing skills.

"You stay safe out there, okay?"

"I will. Do you know much about Xerxes?"

Esmerelda shook her head. "Not really, they all call it The Industrial City, so I am guessing they are good in the terms of technology for the time. Not as advanced as Levitika's but still. It takes a lot for a city to be called that nowadays, even the Seifkr Empire down in the Southern Sands doesn't have anything like that, although there was rumor of another city but those who speak of it can never find it again."

"Another Levitika, maybe?" Ashlyn asked jokingly.

Esmerelda laughed at that which made Ashlyn feel better. "I doubt that very much, but then again, who am I to judge considering not a lot of people Levitika existed anymore in the first place."

Ashlyn nodded. "Well, Xerxes sounds interesting. Color me curious."

Her packing complete, Ashlyn looped her arms through the straps on her pack. Esmerelda stood up and walked over to her and before the two of them left together, Esmerelda placed a timid hand on Ashlyn's shoulder.

"I'm serious," said the princess. "Be safe out there."

"Of course," said Ashlyn. "You take care of yourself too, okay? Keep your mom safe."

Esmerelda huffed bemusedly. "If anything she might need to keep me safe..."

"Why do you say that?"

Esmerelda shook her head. "Just princess duties and expectations, nothing serious."

"If you say so," said Ashlyn, and she promised to be safe again, which seemed to set Esmerelda somewhat at ease and they left together at last.

By the time they reached the new gates of the city the sun was exactly at it's midpoint in the sky, the clouds casting great shadows across the city which like

Esmerelda, seemed to barely begin to wake up as well. It would seem the festivities two nights before had tired many out, not just the princess. Ashlyn couldn't blame any of them, as the work had continued nonstop ever since.

When they reached the gates Grim was waiting on a bike talking to Slagar. He was wearing a black coat and had a large rifle strapped across his back and a sword at his side. The saddlebags on the bike contained additional supplies needed not only for the trip, but infiltration once they arrived in Xerxes. Elizabetha was standing off to the side waiting for the arrival of the girls, and she smiled at Ashlyn and her daughter as they got closer.

"How did you sleep?" she asked.

"Fine," Ashlyn said shouldering her pack. "Is Grim ready?"

"He's just wrapping things up and then he'll be ready." She bent down and gave Ashlyn a hug. "You stay safe, okay?"

"Yes ma'am," Ashlyn said hugging her back. It felt as if she were hugging her own mother, and although this pained Ashlyn she was grateful for the queen's kindness. When she was released Ashlyn turned to Esmerelda and hugged her as well. "Love you, girl."

"You too," said Esmerelda still embracing her. She squeezed Ashlyn's shoulders and said, "You *better* make it back. If Markus gets here before you, he might freak out."

Ashlyn laughed as she pulled away. "That's a possibility."

Grim the called out, "Ashlyn, you ready?"

"Yeah, coming."

She said goodbye to the royal family one last time and then jogged over and hopped onto the bike taking the seat behind Grim. She wrapped her arms around his waist as she waved at Esmerelda who looked sad once more as she and Elizabetha waved in return and then Grim kicked the bike into gear, sending them speeding off into The Wastelands heading north.

Ashlyn watched behind her as the gates closed, shutting off everyone she was going to miss dearly inside, the last person she saw before the two doors met was Esmerelda who was smiling sadly. She wiped her eyes really quick however; she would not cry now.

She leaned over and called up to Grim, "How long until we reach Lakeshire?"

"Couple hours if we keep at the speed we are going." He called back, "Are you sure you are ready for this? Cause if you have any doubts, it's now or never."

Yesterday Ashlyn believed she wouldn't be ready even with her test results. She had 20/20 vision according to the doctor and when tested on movement and coordination specifically through various scopes, she was given one of the top scores and was highly praised for her effort. When she turned it into the queen, Elizabetha had likewise expressed her astonishment and work was done to get her prepared for the trip. Esmerelda had stayed with her as she felt the jitters begin and she had been grateful for the princess' company. She almost gave in and told the queen she wasn't ready, but as it was she got ready this morning anyway and here she was now.

To back out now didn't seem like a good option.

"I'm *not* ready, but let's do it!"

Grim smiled. "Let's do it!" he barked and gunned the bike, propelling them forward much faster and across the crisp but warming Wastelands.

They had made it to Lakeshire in a matter of hours. They used their fake trader's passes to get in touch with some of the locals and grab a bite to eat as well as gather whatever other supplies they needed. While Grim was loading what they needed into a small cart that was to be towed behind them, Ashlyn went to a nearby vendor to get some food. The girl at the counter looked upset about something, her face expressionless as if she were zoning out trying to focus on something that wasn't there. Nut her eyes immediately softened at the sight of a customer and she smiled broadly which felt authentic enough.

"Afternoon. What will it be?" the girl asked. "Thirsty, hungry, or both?"

"You wouldn't happen to have any jerky, would you?" Ashlyn asked.

"The best in the country," the girl said. "Depends on who you ask as well as what kind of meat. We got beef, chicken, some Leaper Dragon, the works. You ask, we might have it."

"Beef is fine," said Ashlyn.

The girl nodded, disappearing for a moment only to return with a couple of strips. Ashlyn took two and paid for it with a few coins Grim had given her.

"Thank you," Ashlyn said shoving one strip into her pocket for Grim and began to chew on the other. It was tough but it was tasty enough. A good snack before moving on to the big city."

"That's a fine weapon you got there," the girl said admiring the pistol at Ashlyn's hip. "But I'd be careful if I were you. Xerxes got some strict gun laws, and the soldiers that pass by like to think that Lakeshire is part of it."

"I'll keep that in mind," Ashlyn said as she covered the gun with her coat. "This is a nice village you have here."

"It has its perks," the girl smiled. "It's outside the walls at least."

"Why do you say that? Wouldn't you feel safer *inside* the walls?"

The girl shrugged almost distractedly. "Perhaps, if Xerxes wasn't so strict and heavily taxed. A lot of the folk who live here year-round don't like the big city and would prefer to farm. Keeps the city fed and keeps money in our pockets."

"Isn't it dangerous out here though?"

"We have our own militia, and the soldiers pass through here on the regular. Though not many patrols come here as often as they used to, with The Capitol apparently making threats and all."

"The Capitol is threatening Xerxes?" asked Ashlyn.

"Oh yeah. Been threatening. Saying they are overstepping their boundaries. Queen Lamia and Psyren apparently never liked each other, and tensions are high."

"Think they are going to attack? I heard Nineveh was hit pretty hard by the Xerxans."

The girl looked about nervously. "That's right, but keep your voice down. Some of the people here are supposedly spies for Xerxes. They like to rat out people who speak bad of the city and the queen."

"Got it."

"But, yes," the girl continued. "Because of that, the threats keep getting worse and worse. If The Capitol somehow thinks Xerxes is now an easier target, they'll come knocking on the door and eventually ours as well. At least we will get a warning and we can clear out somewhere."

"Where would you go?"

The girl shrugged. "We'll cross that bridge when we get to it."

"I guess that makes sense."

The girl nodded. "You new to the trade route? I don't remember ever seeing you and your…" She nodded her chin in the direction of Grim and their new cart.

"My father," said Ashlyn. "We are meeting some others just outside of Xerxes. Might go in the city, might continue East, not sure."

The girl nodded. "Careful with them. Not all Xerxans are bad, but you know how it goes."

Ashlyn who knew very well that was true, agreed.

The girl reached out to shake Ashlyn's hand. "At any rate, welcome to the route. Name's Alma, it is a pleasure to meet you, miss…?"

"Kaltrina," Ashlyn said remembering the fake name on her pass. "My father is Robert."

"Kaltrina, I like that."

"Alma is a good name too."

Alma smiled. "Thank you. So tell me, not that it is any of *my* business, why do you and your father want to return behind the great walls? There isn't much desire for traders in the city, unless something's changed."

"We have coffee from the Southern Sands to sell," said Ashlyn, referring to the story she was to memorize on the way here. "Hard to come by nowadays, and the cities pay a hefty buck for it. You should have seen our stocks after Nineveh."

"Coffee, eh? Yeah, that oughta do it," Alma agreed nodding. "Did you already speak to our trading postman?"

"My father should've."

"Good, good."

"Anything we should be aware of should we end up inside the city?" Ashlyn asked. "I'm still fairly new to this, and don't know much about the area."

Alma nodded sympathetically. "Only real good advice I have, don't speak of The Capitol or the war going on. The soldiers don't like civilians speaking about it. If you're religious, keep your trap shut. Also, if you speak ill of Queen Psyren, be it her politics, choice of leadership among the soldiers, or her illness, then that's gonna get you into a lot of trouble."

"Queen Psyren is sick?" Ashlyn asked.

"Oh yes, been all her life. Dunno what it is, but it is just now catching up to her in her old age. She still tries her best for her country, but the weaker she gets the more influence her generals have over the people. I don't like Psyren anymore than most folk, but I doubt the queen even knows what is happening to her own city and outside the walls, if you know what I mean."

"Oh my," Ashlyn said deeply troubled. "That cannot be good."

"No it isn't. But as long as I still have some life in me," Almas eyes seemed to be looking past Ashlyn, looking at all of the people around her; the men playing cards, the children in the street, everyone in her village. "I will do what I can to protect my family. My district is important to me yes, but in the end, family is what is most important."

Ashlyn thought back to her dead family, and then eventually becoming part of a new family with Markus and Esmerelda. It made her miss her friends even more. "Yeah," she agreed sadly but not unhappily. "Family."

Alma sighed. She returned her attention to Ashlyn. "Do you have any other family besides your father?"

"No, they were all killed during the war with Nineveh."

"Oh, I'm so sorry. Wait, if you just came from Nineveh having traded with them…"

Realizing her mistake Ashlyn was quick to rectify. "I used to live in Nineveh as a child. My family was murdered by the Guard. I was then smuggled out of the city with some other children, I only just came back with my adoptive father."

Alma's mouth opened and then shut like a trapdoor. "Oh, I see. That explains the lack of resemblance- No offence of course."

"Don't worry about it. He's been good to me."

"That's good, that's good… How is Nineveh then now? From what I heard, another army came through."

"That's right," said Ashlyn. She pretended to laugh bewilderedly and shook her head. "And you're not gonna believe whose."

"Who?" asked Alma, immediately intrigued.

"Levitika."

Alma's eyes widened and then narrowed within the span of a second. "You're pulling my leg."

"I promise you, I'm not."

"Wait, wait, Levitika," Alma gathered. "The Levitika? The City of Angels?"

"The only one I ever heard about," said Ashlyn.

"You're kidding!"

"Nope," Ashlyn said shaking her head. "Saw the Angels and everything. Traded a few things with them as well. They were planning on invading Nineveh for the sake of freeing the south. They were in battle with both the Xerxans and the Ninevites, but while we were there, they were helping rebuild the city. Apparently they are trying to build a new government there."

Alma looked away, thinking hard about this. "But if they do exist, then that means… you've seen the floating city?"

Ashlyn nodded. "Couldn't believe it at first."

"I don't blame you… but if they are invading Nineveh… Does that mean…" She looked at Ashlyn suddenly. "Do you think they are trying to take over the North?"

"I don't know," said Ashlyn. "What do you make of it?"

Alma pursed her lips in thought, her fingernails drumming along her countertop. "I honestly hope that Levitika is not our enemy. If they took over Nineveh, are they planning to invade? Honestly, I hope it stays far from here. We cannot fight two enemies at once. Xerxes has suffered heavy losses, and we cannot afford to lose anymore with The Capitol at our throats. I may not be a fan of Xerxes, but The Capitol is far worse."

Ashlyn wanted to tell Alma what the plan was. Give her some shred of hope that it was going to be okay. But the mission was still going, and she could not afford the risk of compromising her and Grim.

So, she nodded. "Me too. I can only imagine what it's like to leave your home. At least my home goes with me."

Alma laughed at that, which seemed to set her and Ashlyn both at ease. "Yeah, indeed."

Shortly after, Grim was done packing everything in, the cart now to be drawn by two cybernetic horses which must have cost a fortune. Ashlyn said goodbye to her new friend and they continued their journey north. They both spoke of what they learned and had ridden a couple of more miles until they finally reached the walls of Industrial City of Xerxes.

Not standing nearly as tall as the walls of Nineveh, but definitely far more protected with many Gatling Lasers along the top and Drones patrolling the skies above, it looked as if the walls were that of a giant fortress rather than a city. After riding along the walls, they soon found the main entrance to the city which consisted of a small tunnel that seemed to go under the walls themselves rather than through. They drove inside and immediately the soldiers were upon them, checking their luggage and doing background checks on the badges. Any weaponry purposefully left out by Grim was confiscated and Grim signed his name with a fake signature to get them back.

"Thank you for your cooperation," said the lead man who watched as his men took the few guns Grim had. "When you leave the city, just make sure to sign out and your weapons will be returned. However, if there are any banned weaponry, they will not be returned at all."

"Would have been nice to know beforehand," said Grim gruffly.

"I'm sorry sir. I understand life out in the Wastelands is hard, but Xerxes has no intention of takins risks. You want to trade with us, you follow our rules."

Ashlyn never said a word as the men in black checked her own bags of clothing. The weapons that Grim had packed with the intention of using, haven been concealed in a compartment which he had installed in the cart, courtesy of the people of Lakeshire.

She was disgusted as one soldier checking her clothes picked up a pair of underwear and snickered to his buddy. Ashlyn did her best not to grow red as Grim continued to talk to the man in charge.

"So that's coffee, flour, scrap metal… Wait, the list has a lot of personal items here. What are you planning to do, move in?"

"Maybe," said Grim. "It has become dangerous outside, and I had brought what I needed should my daughter and I decide to become full citizens."

"You understand the documentation for illegal aliens in the city?" asked the soldier. "All you get is a pass for now."

"I know well of Xerxes' citizenship laws," said Grim. "Is it still the DCOX Building?"

The soldier nodded. "You've done your homework. And you understand the housing taxes as well?"

"I do. God willing, we'll make enough trading our wares."

"Do you plan to work in the industry or open a business?"

"Why so curious, sir?"

"I'm not. Just trying to get all the information I need for potential citizens."

"Fair enough. I'm not completely sure. If we stay, I'd rather remain in retail. My old bones ain't much for factory or soldier work."

Ashlyn had to suppress a smile. Grim might look old given his mutations, but the man was dangerous, dangerous enough to train Markus at any rate.

"Might I suggest this one here… Hold on…" The man took out a piece of paper and jotted down an address. "It has been abandoned for years but the building is still in good condition. Could be used for both housing and work. I am sure the neighbor would be delighted to sell it. But you still fall under the tax bracket of both home and business. Just to warn you."

"Thank you," Grim said taking the paper and shoving it into his pocket without reading it. "You've been very helpful."

The soldier shrugged. "Things get boring when shops close down and we can't find a place to get a drink or something. Another suggestion for you, at any rate."

He then backed away from the cart and whistled to his men. "All clear. Open it up."

Before the carriage, the large set of doors on the side opposite of which Ashlyn and Grim had entered outside the walls. Light shined through the dark corridor and with a wave of thanks Grim drove up the ramp and into the light. Ashlyn gasped as she and Grim found themselves in the main streets of Xerxes.

It was simply stunning. It was a far cry from Levitika's ancient marbled architecture, or Nineveh's height and military might, but Ashlyn could see why Xerxes was known as The Industrial City. Buildings of stone were built on a massive hill, some built on top of one another and some even built along the walls of the city. Tracks and tubes zigzagged between the buildings, and along them sped many carts and supply-pods that sent goods zipping all throughout, as well as cable cars between skyscrapers containing a multitude of passengers. Drones both aerial and terrestrial moved throughout the city, their cameras on the lookout for criminals and other sources of information. The streets were of paved asphalt, which like the tubes ran throughout the city and should this caravan of two entering the city kept following the road, they would eventually end up in the center where the spectacle of Xerxes could be seen.

Standing in the middle was a great gothic castle of stone and steel, appearing straight out of a storybook. The towers stood a little shorter than the walls themselves, with many pointy roofs and gargoyles keeping watch over the city. The building seemed to stretch wide in the center of the city, with many more houses and stone structures built against it. The castle seemed to have been the heart of the city, there for all who wandered the streets below; the thousands of citizens both old and young walking around in many styles of clothing both rich and poor.

Some were mutants with deformed or interesting body structures, some had auto-limb limbs or parts, and some looked human but judging by their black eyes they were actually androids that looked like humans. Normal androids that were made of pale metal still walked through the streets among the humans but the human-like androids which were commonly known as R.U.R. models, were more impressive than any droid Ashlyn had ever seen. Human flesh over a mechanical skeleton, the very few remnants of the A.I. War prior to the Great War which ended in nuclear fallout.

Vendors and shops were alive with activity as many visited friends or bought supplies. The majority of buildings however were immense factories, whose stacks belched black smoke into the air. From shafts built into the high walls of some of them, drones came in and out often with supplies. It seemed almost amazing that people could live in such comfort behind the walls that were under constant threat of The Capitol.

Or so it seemed. It was hard for Ashlyn to put her finger on it, but something was wrong. Something was *off* about this city. It wasn't just the mass of soldiers and Drones that seemed to be watching them, no, it seemed like the whole city was under an anxious spell of silence. Yes many were talking but in hushed tones and always looking over their shoulder as if someone was listening. Even as Grim drove the cart carefully down the streets the feeling of being watched never left Ashlyn. She felt that even the rats that were scampering along the sidewalks and slinking through the sewage drains were watching her as well. She felt naked: exposed out here in this city. It felt wrong, who was watching them and why? Grim obviously felt it too by the way he was constantly looking everywhere, peeking behind him or taking quick glances down the alleyways that they would pass. The drones made him tense the most.

Ashlyn knew she didn't have to say that the sooner they got to their new temporary home, the better. "Where are we meeting the others?" she whispered.

"Don't worry about that right now," said Grim. "Keep a lid on it for now."

They were passing by what looked like a canning factory. Drones carrying nets full of animals most of them mooing or bleating in displeasure only to disappear into some of the shafts. As they passed, Ashlyn caught notice of some nets directly beneath the windows of the factory, and she asked Grim what those could be.

His expression darkened. "Those are suicide nets."

"Suicide nets?"

The mutant soldier grunted. "Keeps those who jump out of the windows alive."

"But why would they..."

"Don't worry about that right now. Just understand that not everyone may be happy with their job, especially in a city that seems to never cease working. Xerxes doesn't like losing workers. They like to keep them alive."

"There are a lot of people out and about though..."

"Yeah," Grim agreed. "So why do none of them appear jolly?"

He had a point. But seeing those suicide nets along the sides of the factory made Ashlyn nervous, and seeing more of them on other factories as they delved deeper into the city made her stomach clench, making the jerky she had eaten in Lakeshire threaten to come slithering back up. The idea that such a net was necessary made her wonder what conditions the workers might be in and how long they had to endure it day in and day out.

Another thought which made her sick to think about and quickly shove out of her mind the moment it came, was how many times had *that* happened for such a precaution to take place.

When they finally arrived at the building where they were to meet the others, Grim and Ashlyn hopped off the cart to look it over. It was an old building that was for certain, but the building appeared to be in good shape- apart from the broken windows of course. Someone was already out on the wall using a grapple line connected to the roof in order to repair the windows.

"Gabriel!" Grim called up to the man replacing the glass. "So far so good."

"Grim!" a startled Gabriel said. He was a young man with short brown hair that looked hacked down with a pair of blunt scissors but lean and fit as he hung off the side of the building like a rock climber. "You scared me. About time you showed up! Who's the girl?"

"This is Ashlyn," said Grim. "The sharpshooter."

"Nice to meet you!" Ashlyn said to Gabriel.

"A pleasure!"

"Silva inside?" asked Grim.

"Yeah," said Gabriel smiling broadly. "She's working on the plumbing now. She lost the bet."

"What bet?"

"Tell you later."

Grim turned to Ashlyn. "Watch the cart for a bit while I meet with Silva. Might as well make sure we are set."

"Oh, okay," said Ashlyn and she moved to the cybernetic horses while Grim rushed inside. She petted the mechanical horse's flank and although most of it's body had been replaced with robotic parts, the horse sputtered happily at her touch.

She watched as people, droids and Drones passed her down the street, usually slowing down to take a quick glance before continuing on their way. But still the feeling of being watched still plagued Ashlyn, and it made her sick to her stomach. She took notice at some security cameras connected to the buildings and sometimes mounted in clusters on tall poles above the streets. She hoped Grim would not take too long, she didn't want to be out here longer than necessary.

It wasn't long before Ashlyn felt a hand upon her shoulder and she looked up to see Grim smiling satisfyingly. "Get your stuff first. There is a room ready for you. Then come out and help me out."

Ashlyn grabbed her pack and hurried inside, glad to be out of the suffocating atmosphere that she just couldn't comprehend.

The shop itself was dusty and had many booths and seats that had cracked leather with a layer of thick dust that seemed to have fallen everywhere. The shop would need a decent clean-up soon. Ashlyn then followed a flight of stairs to the living quarters of the building. While it was just as dusty there was no furniture in either of the two rooms which consisted an empty space as soon as you reached the stairs and then there was the bathroom. Ashlyn took a peek inside to see a moldy shower and cracked tile on the floor. The toilet looked more clean than anything in the bathroom and that was saying a lot, mostly because of the woman working on it.

She was a petite woman, older than Ashlyn but definitely an adult. She wore overalls similar to that of what Gabriel was wearing outside and her skin was as dark as night. On her head was a backwards cap and she turned around from her work as if sensing being watched. She smiled brightly at Ashlyn with perfectly white teeth.

"You must be Ashlyn," the woman said standing up and wiping her hands on her overalls. She stepped over to the sink and began to wash her hands. Miraculously, the water coming out of the dingy thing looked clean. "I'm Silva," she said coming to Ashlyn at last and shaking her hand. "Pleased to meet you."

"You too," said Ashlyn.

"How old are you?" asked Silva.

"Fifteen."

"Fifteen… and you got a high score on your aim?"

"I guess so."

Silva smiled. "Excellent! I've heard good things about you."

"Thank you," said Ashlyn.

"Your and my room is just down the hall," said Silva. "To the right. Make yourself comfortable, I already have my cot."

"Okay, thanks."

Ashlyn left the woman to continue working and she entered the room in question eyeing the two cots on opposite sides of the small room. One cot was covered in a blanket with a small pack and a neatly stacked pile of clothes on the floor and other stuff packed underneath. The other was empty, and Ashlyn placed her pack on top of it before peeking out of the window at the end of the room to look out back into the alleyway. It was not a pleasant view but it let in at least *some* sunshine.

She hurried back out to see Grim had dropped his stuff near the entrance and had already gone back outside. Ashlyn hurried out to help him bring in the supplies they got in Lakeshire. After a few trips many bags and barrels were stacked in the corner of the room, and Grim had now taken a seat against the far wall by his stuff.

"Well, we're here," he said. "You met Silva?"

"Yeah, she seems nice."

"Good. What are your thoughts on Xerxes now, now that we're here?"

Ashlyn shrugged but she was looking out of the floor story windows nervously. "It's like a whole new world."

"Yeah. All of those Drones… it's amazing yet unsettling. Many of them were watching the people rather than the walls. This place seems to be under constant surveillance."

Ashlyn nodded. It explained the constant feeling that someone was watching her. "All the people seem so quiet too. I don't know- they just don't strike me as the people of an 'industrial' city. They seem more careful, as if expecting something to leap out and pounce on them."

Grim grunted. "I kinda figured, but I didn't know it would be this bad. But this is what we are dealing with now, and there isn't any turning back just yet."

"Okay," Ashlyn nodded still keeping her eyes outside in the streets below.

Some kids were playing with a hoop but other than that, the entire block seemed quiet, like there was a density in the air that was heavy and tense, like something bad was going to come down at anytime and anywhere. Ashlyn looked behind her to see Grim laying on a nearby booth staring up at the ceiling with his hands over his chest. He tapped his six fingers as if he was deep in thought.

"Grim?" asked Ashlyn.

"What?"

"Do you have any family? Like in Levitika or outside the city?"

She knew that Grim had come from the Wastelands before joining Levitika, and she knew so little of the man. She wondered why she hadn't met him earlier, and if they were going to kill some time might as well use it to get to know him. Him, and Gabriel and Silva of course.

"Not anymore," Grim muttered softly closing his eyes. "They all died out in The Wastelands. Pirates attacked us, and I was unable to save my wife and boy. Little rascal didn't even get to see his sixth year."

"I'm sorry."

"Don't be. It was my fault for not getting there on time, and I will never forgive myself for it."

Ashlyn nodded and looked down at her feet. She looked back up towards Grim. "What was your son's name?"

"Sitka." Grim said.

"Your wife?"

"Sheila."

"That's beautiful."

"Yeah, it always lifted my heart to hear that name, as well as hearing her voice. She would sing to Sitka every night to put him to sleep, and I always used to listen."

"She sounds wonderful,"

"Indeed she was," Grim opened his eyes to look at Ashlyn. "She would have liked you."

"Thank you sir.... Grim? Is that your real name?"

"No."

"What is your real name? If it is okay me asking?"

Grim sighed. "I buried my name when I buried my family and left my home."

He refuse to say anymore, and Ashlyn did not push him further. After a while, he got up saying he was going to try to sell off the cart and the horses. "See if the others need help. Might as well get used to the people you are working with."

Ashlyn did as she was told, feeling more alone than ever before.

Markus

Markus' morning consisted of many small puzzles and exercises given to him by Abram. The man wouldn't even present to him the slightest opportunity to ask any questions that had been brewing in his head all night.

The moment he was awakened was when Abram opened his guest bedroom door and knocked on it as if it were an emergency. "Up and at 'em. I want you outside in five."

"MEOW!" the Werecat Daryl agreed behind him.

The morning was dark still and very cold, and a light mist was just barely started to fade off the island as in the far distance the sun was just barely beginning it's ascent. Markus, shivering and with only one arm capable of warming him up, was immediately put to work by Abram.

Compared to Damion Black's training, Markus thought that he preferred the deceased Hunter's method much better. There was no combat training, no meditation, nothing that involved magic of the sort. Abram just put him through multiple rigorous exercises and forbade him from using his crystals to alter his body in a y way shape or form. Once when Markus attempted to do just that whilst doing pushups, a mental weight crushed down upon him forcing his face into the dirt.

"Try that again," Abram challenged him sternly. Markus knew that Abram had a crystal in his possession, but the man had not taken it out nor had he reached towards Markus or even the ground to pass whatever spell he had used to him. This alone was enough to make Markus do as he was told, despite his arms feeling like rubber, both his actual arm and his metallic one

He performed his other tasks, from sprint laps between the cabin and the gardens several hundred times, to stopping to break only to assist in the weeding of that morning's same crop. Immediately after just as the sun was fully exposed on the horizon, Markus was instructed to jump into the water within the cove and swim all the way to the edge of the island's horseshoe points and then all the way back. It was only this exercise that he was allowed to use magic should a particularly predatory fish take an interest in him. By the time he was back, his lungs were burning and his body felt like a jellyfishes, and he took his momentary reprieve to ask Abram who was petting a sleeping Daryl what all this was meant to accomplish.

"So you can understand your physical limits," answered the old man. "I've met a few crystal-bearer's who attempted to alter their bodies beyond the point they were capable of. Some were minor, like torn muscles or shattered bones, but others took on permanent psychological or even physical damage, their bodies no longer human. You doing this is no different than your meditation; understanding your body so that you don't push yourself beyond the limit and attract unwanted attention."

"When you say no longer human," said Markus still panting while on his back on the shore. "Do you mean... possessed, by chance?"

"That is a possibility yet. Mostly from Nightmares, but also, the one whom you have come to train against. Now back up, Markus. I want you to take this axe and fall a tree. Once the tree is downed, reach out to me using your mind."

He said this while a consciousness seemed to brush against Markus' own. It was surprising and Markus backed away startled at first but then the conscious sent a warm sensation of calm across his mind. Some telepathic link that he understood immediately it to be Abram and the old man smiled approvingly. "Do not keep me waiting or I'll have you fall another."

Markus groaned as he sat up but he took up the axe and did as he was told. He chose the pine tree that looked the most dead but he felt Abram's conscious brush against his own and he knew that wasn't the one he wanted. He went to the next, and again he was tugged in another direction. Thankfully, the old man didn't take him to the widest and most healthy tree on the island, but the one he was assigned to was still pretty large and without stopping except to drink some water from his flask, it took him about half an hour to fall the damned thing.

Finally, after he reached out to Abram, the old man came and congratulated him on falling the tree, only to tell him to sit upon stump he had created.

"You have done well. This is not the end of your testing of your physical abilities. You must understand what your limits are, but never be afraid to push yourself in the briefest of ways. You do not want to cast a spell on your body to make yourself stronger, only for your muscles to tear out of your skin, for example."

Markus didn't dare ask if such a thing had happened before.

"For now, it is time to begin exercising your mind. I understand Damion had done this before, and so we shall do the same but at a greater level."

Markus who was as excited as ever, finally took his seat. He sat cross-legged as he had been taught to by Black, and once he was in position, Abram nodded approvingly.

"Now, same as Damion has taught you. I want you to sit here and listen to the entire island. Every single life essence that is in existence here and around it. From the trees, to the ground, to even the coral reefs just off the coast. Reach out and become familiar with it all, and when you can hear no more, want you to come to me and answer this: All is one, and one is all. What am I? Do not come back inside until you do so." He then turned and started to go.

"Abram wait," Markus called out making the man stop. "What will this teach me exactly? I mean to ask Black, but..."

Abram turned his head and Markus noticed sympathy and sadness etched in the wrinkles of his eyes. "What do you sense when you take in the energy of the crystals?"

"Little whispers of the life of others. Animals, people, droids, it's like I can see their life force."

"That is correct. With the crystals you are able to see in the darkest of nights, for the life of the world around you cannot be hidden from your eyes. You have already proved your strength from the exercises I have made you do: you no doubt know that the crystals give you a physical advantage here in the real world. But you still have yet to prepare your mind for the dangers of using such powers. You have gained control over the spirits within, but you are still helpless to their influence."

"Abner has helped me from time to time though," Markus pointed out.

"Abner has good intentions yes, but his anger, his misery and regrets, are still powerful. He was chosen to be trapped within The Dreaming for his suffering, not just his expertise."

It is true, Markus heard Abner speak. *I am still haunted by my failures, my fears. Sometimes I have no control over my rage when you let yours out, just like on the Leviathan, but I have to say that it was Fethawit's anger as well that combined with mine.*

"He speaks the truth," Abram said as if he heard Abner's own voice. "Even when it is difficult for him to communicate to you, for he would risk putting himself as well as you in danger, he speaks the truth."

"From The Eldest," Markus reiterated. "The Eldest like all the spirits within the crystals, will try to always find you. You've experienced this back in Levitika, but that was only a mere taste of what the demon is capable of. He always lies in wait like a hungry lion, patient and eternal, waiting for some chance to escape The Dreaming without being let out."

"But, sir," said Markus. "The Eldest was taken away, the crystal, I mean. When you say 'let out'…"

Abram nodded grimly. "It is possible, but that is nothing we can change for now. The stronger you become, the less eager he will be to come to you. Even though his crystal is gone, he still has great influence on The Dreaming. Therefore, you must prepare yourself. This particular sense of meditation is to test your alertness and make sure you can protect yourself from the physical dangers of the world, whilst always being aware."

"Haven't I done enough already?"

"We shall see. Now begin." And he walked away without another word.

Bitter, Markus placed his hands on his crossed knees and took a deep breath. See until he could see no more? He had already done this, what more could he prove? He knew as well that in order to do so, he would need to really allow everything he felt to be felt, every pain to be pained, every joy to be treasured. Once his mind was clear of the clutter as Black had once said, it would be easier to become more aware of everything. It had been difficult since Black's death, but Markus was willing to try.

His vision now darkened by his eyelids, and he allowed whatever he felt to come to him. His grief for the loss of his arm, the grief he still carried from Ruth, and the anxiety he felt when Black had given him the task to find and destroy all the crystals The Eldest had ever created. He tried to, but the pain became too great and it overshadowed the few moments of happiness and pride that he had come to accept as his way of comfort from his friends and those back in Levitika. He would see minute flickers of life behind his lids, from the birds in the trees to the few bugs scampering around the one he had fallen, but again and again they would blink in and out like distant stars and he grew more and more frustrated and decided it best to just return to the world he himself had created in his mind. He had accomplished seeing the whole island of Levitika before doing this, and so believed that this would be no different.

So, he felt himself slip free from his physical form and then discovered he was back in the place that he knew he would be the happiest, and safest.

His shack from Nineveh, in a vast sea of wavering green grass. This time there was a small garden right off the small garage where all his father's and his own work laid resting. He was happy to even see his own father tinkering with something on the workbench, his back to him and Ruth close behind, healthy and well. In the garden, Ashlyn was picking something and when she turned to look at Markus, her smile became alight and she waved him over. In this dream-like state, Markus approached his friend and crouched beside her to see what she was doing.

"This was a good idea," she told him. "It's a nice place."

"It is," he agreed. "I'm going to go talk to Ruth, real quick."

"Okay," said Ashlyn. "I was thinking... maybe you and I can head to the river and fish. Just you and me?"

"I'd like that," said Markus and he left Ashlyn there and started for the garage.

When Ruth saw him she stood up and ran to him. She hugged him and he hugged her back, feeling her warmth and comfort which had been lost since her death in the Burning Plains. As quickly as that memory came it was washed away by this false place and Markus felt himself relaxing. On the edge of his vision, he began to see little minute flares of life as if this whole place was haunted by ghosts, but Markus wasn't paying attention to them. Instead, he looked to see his father turning away from the bench, his beard and hands slick with oil which he wiped both of them somewhat clean with a rag.

"Hey, champ," Johnathon said smiling. "What took you so long? It's been a while, the girls told me you've been gone for a bit."

"I was," Markus said. "Now I'm back..."

He hadn't expected to see his father and the overwhelming gratitude to see him alive and well here caused the speckles of light appearing in and out of his dream to immediately vanish. He approached his father and gave him a hug, relishing in the sensation of safety and comfort as Johnathon wrapped his arms around his son.

"I've missed you..." said Markus.

His father squeezed him tightly saying, "I've missed you too. You've gotten so big..."

"I know," Markus said. He lifted his face up to look at his father. "I-"

Terror struck him in the heart. His father was no longer grease-stained with his eyes bright and kind. Instead, Markus was hugging a skeleton in the rags that his father would often wear while working. The skeleton's hands suddenly raised up and began to shake Markus' shoulders, causing him to scream.

"Mark?"

Markus turned his head to cry out at Ruth to get away and he screamed as he saw her mouth now covered in blood and then she coughed and more began to spill upon the floor. She was clutching her belly and was looking at Markus imploringly.

"Mark... help me..."

"Gah!" Markus cried out and he shoved the skeleton away which immediately burst into a cloud of dust collection upon the floor. She rushed to Ruth and then she suddenly fell back, the floor behind her now an opened grave which she fell in and before Markus could plunge in after her, the ground swallowed her up with an audible snap. He clawed at the dirt floor and screamed out for Ashlyn to help.

When Ashlyn arrived, she was looking at him with a look of disgust and disapproval. "You lost them again..." she said.

"No, I didn't, I-"

"You lost them like you lost my father," Ashlyn said now angrily approaching Markus. "You son of a bitch, you took away my chance to kill him myself!" Her fury was so intense it was like a heatwave, and Markus now desperate to end this nightmare once and for all, screamed out and clenched his eyes shut.

When his eyes were back open he was screaming still but he covered his mouth almost instantly as to not draw any attention. He listened to the silence of the small forest expecting someone to come running and demand what was happening, but for several long minutes nothing happened and eventually the bird who had been startled by his cries, began to tentatively resume whatever conversation they had.

Markus bowed his head and began to cry. This wasn't fair. He finally had a place of comfort and now it was snatched away. A safe place for him to reside while doing what he was told to do. Could he not have a moment's peace in this world? Did he have to endure every single feeling he felt in his heart?

"Yes," said someone behind him. "That's what makes us human."

Markus raised his head in shock and he turned around his legs untangling with one foot now touching the ground. He gasped as standing before him, wearing his leather armor and cloak but weaponless, was The Hunter Black.

"B... Black?" Markus said in a hoarse whisper.

The Hunter Black was staring at him intently just ten feet away from the stump. Had his eyes always been silver orbs? Markus found himself unable to remember what color the Hunter's eyes were. The Hunter then began to approach him, and Markus got off the stump and stumbled back, scared out of his mind.

"Are you... you're dead..."

"Perhaps," said the Hunter Black. "Obviously, you remember me fondly."

Markus couldn't help but laugh. It was better than screaming. "How are you here?"

"You brought me here."

"No I didn't, I-"

"Subconsciously, you do," Black said patiently. He had stopped approaching and was now close enough to the stump that if he wanted to, he could step upon it. "You do it every time you try to run away."

"Run away? What-"

"You know what I mean," said Black sternly but in a way, not unkindly. His voice held that calm demeanor it always held, especially when he had trained Markus for the brief time they had upon arriving to Levitika. "Markus, you cannot keep doing this. You cannot keep going to that place no matter how much you want to."

"But, it's my mind," said Markus defiantly. "Why can't I daydream a little, have a happy memory that I can actually be a part of?"

"Because it isn't real, that's why."

Markus opened his mouth but immediately shut it again. Shame overwhelmed him and he looked down at the ground as if expecting a scolding.

"Markus, look at me."

Markus did as he was told. Damion Black was smiling softly at him now and he was taking a seat on the stump. "Come here, sit with me."

Markus shook his head. "You're just in my head. You're just a memory, aren't you? You're just…" He swallowed the lump that had grown to the size of a tangerine in his throat and finally admitted, "You keep coming because I feel guilty about that place…"

"In a way, yes," said Black softly. "Your memory of me brings me every single time, and you've known about it all along."

Markus swallowed again and nodded bitterly. He felt tears welling in his eyes and he angrily brushed them away.

"Come here," Black said again. "If this really is just a memory of me, come here and speak with me."

Markus numbly approached the Hunter. He sat down on the very edge of the stump which dug into his butt as he sat as far away from Black as he could. Upon reaching him, the familiar smell of leather and sweat he had remembered Black for came to mind and a sense of calm came over him.

"I don't think I can do this," he admitted to Black at last. "What you told me to do… I don't think I can do it. Even with Abram's help, I… I…"

He felt Black's hand fall upon his shoulder. He tensed for a moment but then relaxed as Black said, "I wouldn't have told you what to do if I didn't believe in you, Markus."

"But I don't believe in myself."

"I know. That's why you try to create a false reality in your head. I'm not here to scold you because of it, you're only human. We all do it from time to time. What makes the difference is understanding that it isn't real, and cannot be. You understand it, I know, but you don't want to."

Markus sniffed and said, "It's just too hard. What I feel about what happened to my family, to Ashlyn, and… and to you. It's all too much, on top of being what the world needs to be."

"And what do *you* think you need to be?" asked Black.

"I don't know…"

"Yes, you do."

Markus was silent for a long time. At last, he said, "I want to do some good here. I want to make those around me happy and safe. I want… I just want to be happy."

"So do a lot of people in the world," said Black. When Markus turned to look at the Hunter's memory, the man said, "But what will make you truly happy, Markus?"

Markus sighed and said, "I guess… I guess I just want to make things right, or as right as I can, anyway. I… I also just want my family to be proud of me."

Black nodded. "Well, you did the right thing, coming here. The reason you are here is to prepare yourself, not just open old wounds. But if you keep trying to escape to this false memory of yours, then you will only be tearing open new ones as well as the old. I understand why you do it, but you must remain focused on yourself. True healing is not by pretending something that is not, it is experiencing that healing, just like I taught you. The pain doesn't go away, but the closure will make it easier. And you pretending nothing happened to your family, will only make the reality of it more difficult to bear. Do you understand me?"

"Yeah," Markus said stiffly. "I do."

"Good," said Black now patting Markus' shoulder before releasing it. He looked around the forest and said to Markus, "I remember when I first came here. I was a very angry man."

Markus looked at him. "You were?"

Black nodded. "I come from a hidden city in the Southern Sands. I had no family, and life was difficult. I used my anger to strike fear into the hearts of others. My rage made me dangerous, and my reputation became one associated with evil. When I first found Fethawit, my rage only grew. But then I found this place, and Abram taught me how to ground myself, accept what has happened has happened, and that what has happened to me was not my fault. I couldn't change what I had done, but I was able to live with it and move on, as many people need to."

Markus realized something then as the Hunter was telling him this. "This... this is supposed to be my memory of you, isn't it?"

Black nodded. "Yes, but who is to say I didn't leave little traces of myself behind when I passed on?"

"So you are dead?" asked Markus. "You're not a... a..."

"A ghost?" Black offered and then shook his head. "No. No one truly dies, until that person is no longer remembered. You remember me, as do may others. Sure, their memories of me will be different compared to yours, but, a small part of me will always echo through time, as well as The Dreaming."

Markus said realizing this, "You left some of you behind still, didn't you?"

Black nodded. "Make no mistake, my soul is no longer part of this world. But, your memory of me keeps me alive and well. I am here, because you need me. And I will always be here, as will others."

"What do you mean?"

"As you become stronger," said Black. "The memories of those dear to you will always be there for you, will always watch over you, and will always guide you as long as they are the true memories that you have of them."

Markus looked away, bewildered. "That's... hard to believe."

"So is a lot of things," said Black and when Markus turned to look at him, the Hunter was gone and he was alone on the stump. And yet Black's voice echoed all round him, "But nothing is impossible, when one truly puts their mind to it."

He was all alone, he realized. He looked all around and then in his head, the voice of Abner was whispering to him, *He speaks the truth, Markus.*

"I know."

So what then?

Markus took a deep breath, and then positioning himself back on the center of the stump, he closed his eyes and began to *truly*, begin his meditation.

<u>Markus</u>

It was tough at first, but heeding the memory of Black's word, Markus allowed himself to come completely undone, and surrender to the thoughts and feelings that always plagued him.

It was painful, the memories of his sister and father seeming to crash down upon him like a great tidal wave, but Markus endured it, his face now soaked with tears as he let what he felt come out at last. He allowed himself to think hard on his act to save Ashlyn and his failure to stop Veegar, and after grappling with himself as if he were in a wrestling match, he came to terms that he couldn't have done more than what he already done. As for his arm, he instead thought of how grateful he was for Vic for building an auto-limb not just to replace it, but to assist with the handling of the crystals. He thought of all that has happened in his life, and where he was now. He thought of how many kids his age had managed to do all that he did and was still standing? He thought of how many people in the world had friends such as Ashlyn and Esmerelda, and Markus' pain and fear of disappointing them while still very much present, slowly evaporated just a little to make way for the gratitude of having such people in his life.

Little by little, his sensation of dread and grief and fear and anxiety, while still a part of him, loosened his joints and muscles and he became relaxed at last upon the stump and through the darkness of his eyelids, he could finally truly begin to sense the life of the world around him.

All the flickers and whispers of light throughout the forest, the birds in the trees and the insects in the ground and among them. Even the trees himself he felt pulsating with life, constantly reaching deep into the earth for a chance to find water, as well being the hearths of the life in the forest itself.

Beyond the forest, he could see even through the influence of Abram's spell over the village, the people who were out and about working on their daily chores and jobs in order to keep this community alive and thriving. He saw boys assisting their fathers and learning from them, girls with their mothers either cooking or sewing clothes. He even saw in one woman, a second life slowly being woven together in her belly. At the edge of the village, even Abram and Daryl who were sitting inside speaking to someone, or so it seemed. In the garden, not only did he see the life essence of the insects crawling about, but the life of the corn, the tomatoes, and more.

Beyond the clearing on the other side of the island, birds and foxes scampered and flew between the trees, and within the trees and beneath the dirt were a great many insects and moles. Curious, he expanded his gaze further still, looking far out into the waters. In the sea he saw a great many species of fish and sea creatures. He saw crabs along the shore looking for food, he saw minnows swimming among the sharks that were corralling them like sheepdogs herding sheep. Beyond he saw Waterbeasts crawling along the ocean floor. Beneath the floor itself he saw spider-like creatures crawling beneath the depths. As the sea stretched further, the floor got deeper and deeper, he saw the brilliant shades of the coral reef which shone like diamonds in the great depths, and more creatures of various shapes and sizes swimming among them. Markus thought if he kept going the ocean would just keep going, giving way to more terrifying creatures of the dark.

Beyond the sea, to the north the Kaiken Isles were rich in pirate life, in fact he heard melodious music and swordplay as the many forces laughed and fought amongst each other. On the other side where the continent sat more life was visible in The Wastelands.

More animals and bugs were crawling across the earth, and a great many more were in the sky. Ahools heading north, Dragonflies and Slugs basking in the sun, and BloodBoars racing across the plains. In the Lagoon to the south, Badrats slinked along the shores amongst the Walruses bathing in the sun, their single tusk and four eyes glistening and alert. Beyond the lagoon Markus could see Nineveh and Xerxes, and within the walls were the many voices and souls of thousands of civilians and soldiers. Markus wanted to pull back, for he did not want to invade the privacy of their minds, but he found himself unable to contain himself. He felt himself, drifting away in a sense, but he was curious as he thought he felt something familiar seeming to draw him in closer to the industrial city.

However, beginning to feel lethargic, he felt himself return to his body when he felt a hand upon his shoulder and he came back to himself in a gasp. He looked up to see Abram standing next to him, looking pleased.

"You can see very far," said the old man. "I am impressed. I am also glad you did not venture too far, the further you stretch the more vulnerable you are to prying eyes of strong forces. Hence why I came running."

"I'm sorry," said Markus nervously. He wondered if Abram was capable of sensing that, if he could also sense his struggle earlier, and his memory of Black.

Abram shook his head. "Don't be. You know your limits on how far you can look, and manage to come back safely. You truly do have good sight, and I never once doubted that you were indeed The Keeper."

Markus asked, "Everyone keeps calling me that, yet I never truly understood what it meant."

Abram sat beside Markus on the stump in the exact same spot as his memory of Black had sat. "It means you are the owner of the crystals you find. The spirits within are able to pick and influence who they want, but you on the other hand can create a bond between yourself and them. I suppose that is why the warrior had a hard time breaking your spirit and taking the crystals and had to resort to taking your arm."

Markus touched his auto-limb arm at the remembrance of the fight. "It was a horrible moment. I felt like everything was caving in on me. It was like... he took what I remembered of my past and... and..."

"Made it a nightmare?"

Markus nodded without shame.

"That is what fear will do. Fear is an important factor in the human mind: It protects us, helps us to avoid danger, and our instincts keep us out of harm's way. Too much however, and you become a victim of it, you are controlled by it. The warrior used all of your fears and collected them all upon you as he got to work breaking through the barriers of your spirit. Had he succeeded, you would be under his influence, and you would have lost your crystals. Thankfully, you only lost one. I can only hope Fethawit is okay."

"You talk like you knew him," Markus asked.

Abram grunted but ignored the question. "The new dark crystal you have there, I recognize her presence. Her name is Nokama. She was killed during the sacrifice for The Eldest."

"I need to ask you something." Markus asked.

"Go ahead."

"What is the difference, and the point? Between dark crystals and light crystals, they both work similarly, but why are they different?"

Abram nodded as if he was expecting that question. "Difficult to understand. The Light Crystals are the same as The Dark, the spirits within suffer in agony, forced to relive the burdens and failures of their lives, their sins. Unlike the Dark Crystals however, they were blameless and honorable. They believed their actions were just with all their hearts and minds. Heroes during the war. The Dark Crystals, were the ones who worked with The Eldest of their own free will, before the Mad King turned on them and sacrificed them to make the crystals."

"Why exactly were they made?"

To Markus' surprise Abram reached into his pocket and pulled out something glowing bright orange crystal. The old man looked down upon it as if it was a mere child he was holding, and he spoke, "When The Mad King realized the existence of The Dreaming there was only one portal to the realm, where all of the nightmares and dreams of the souls who die go to be collected among the realm. I believe you heard of the location as well?"

Markus thought long and hard back to the discussion with Elizabetha nearly months ago. And the name did come up eventually, and even as he said it he felt his heart go cold. "The Well of Souls."

Abram nodded. "It was there where he attempted to save his son and preserve his life. Instead, he created a crystal which now resides in the heart of Levitika, as you no doubt noticed."

Markus nodded.

"The Mad King was desperate to find another way. He began to experiment on many people, attempting to create crystals out of them in order to gather enough power one day to completely destroy the barrier between reality and The Dreaming. He wanted to do this so that he would let his son be freed, but his mind became corrupted with the influence of the Nightmares that plague the realm."

"Like, legitimate nightmares are… alive?"

"Spirits, actually. Because of this, he kept going. Eventually, he found a pattern and begun to create the twelve crystals that were ever truly known in the world. Only seven became the true gateways to The Dreaming, and those seven are the spirits who had been committed what had been called, The Second Death."

"How do you know all this?" asked Markus.

Abram's brow darkened. "Because... I was the one who helped The Mad King create them."

"Wait- You?" Markus asked incredulous.

Abram nodded. "Long ago."

"But that means..."

"Yes, I am very old," Abram said bemusedly. "But that isn't important. When The Great Owl began her rebellion of Levitika, I had helped someone escape The Capitol with two of the crystals. You can imagine one of them."

"The Eldest's son?"

"Correct. That was the very beginning of the great change in the new world. I will get more on that later, but for now, we must return to the cabin. There I can tell you more. I know you have much more to ask, and I will answer it all in due time. For now, let us return." He stood and started to go.

"Abram, wait," said Markus.

Abram turned to him.

"Can I ask one question at least. You said that all the spirits both light and dark were sacrificed. You called it the Second Death. What does that mean?"

Abram shook his head. "Later. Come."

He started to go, and Markus left his stump to follow. For a brief moment, he felt watched and he looked back over his shoulder to see a figure sitting on the stump again. The figure waved goodbye, and like a true ghost, faded from sight. Markus looked around for a moment, but then hurried to catch up with Abram.

When they arrived back at the cabin, they entered the living room where Daryl was still sleeping on the couch. The Werecat opened one eye and Abram stroked the large cat between his ears before sitting down on the couch with him and instructing Markus to sit in the chair opposite.

Abram then lit a pipe and took a long drag before exhaling a puff of smoke into the air. "Now," he said. "The Eldest. Listen closely, and you will know the whole tale."

Markus leaned forward in his seat, eager to learn more about The Eldest, the crystals and what this Second Death was.

"When The Mad king was alive, he ruled the entire country with an iron fist, many leaders bravely rose to fight him, and for a long time he was held back in the north where his accursed Capitol stood strong and proud. The war lasted for ages, and as The Mad King got older and older, he began to study upon an old kind of magic known as Dreamcasting. From there, he wondered if it was possible to draw the powers from The Well of Souls itself. During this time, his son was ill, and you know this part of the tale and what has come after. The people whom he experimented on to replicate what had happened to his son, ended in many failures. Children would come up missing first, and then average citizens."

"He sacrificed children?" asked Markus in horror.

Abram nodded. "Many children were brought to me, the Mad King thinking that as his son was a mere child, then children were the key. Came to discover, that it was not. It only got worse as he began to give me newborn babies to work on. By then, I was beginning to realize the depths of the man's evil. But I could not stop, for I would be killed and my family tortured. They are long dead now, and I am the last of my lineage."

Markus was dumbstruck. He couldn't imagine anyone having to do such a horrible thing, let alone live with it.

Abram continued. "When we finally found a pattern, The Mad King began to collect the greatest warriors in all the land. Mercenaries, Hunters, even Generals. He soon came to create twelve in all, but even then it was not enough for the evil one as only seven were capable of being created and lasting with the power he needed to break open The Dreaming.

"But as I mentioned earlier, he was growing old, and he would soon long be dead. However he had no intention on giving up his power or his life. So he ordered the crystals to be brought together as one, and through one last Second Death ritual, we created the ultimate crystal, The Eldest. From there, we planted it into a new robotic body for the Mad King, and he continued to live for many, many years. Because of my exposure to The Crystals, I was cursed with a long life as well. I was able to witness all the atrocities The Mad King could accomplish, his dream of tearing open The Dreaming to find his son, now a long forgotten goal."

Markus moistened his lips, his mouth feeling as arid as a desert now. "Sir, what is this... Second Death?"

Abram was silent for a long time, just puffing away at his pipe and absently stroking Daryl's large flank. The Werecat was purring but he never took his eyes off of his disturbed master.

At last, Abram said, "The crystals were mere gems of which we cast into the Well of Souls. We would later retrieve them. No one knows how this volcano had become a gateway to another dimension, some believe when the bombs dropped it tore something in the fabric of nature, but for all my years studying it, the answer never became clear. As for the crystals themselves, we discovered this only on a hunch when the Mad King demanded a cure for his son's body. At the volcano, when we first created a crystal, we had cast it into the volcano and then it levitated out of the well, as if we were in space. We took it, and under the Mad King's orders..."

Abram paused for a second. No longer smoking his pipe or petting Darly. The Werecat groaned and nuzzled closer, and still Markus waited, dreading to hear what was to happen next considering the name of the ritual.

"The crystal was still hot," Abram said. "And taking a knife we carved a hole into his son's chest, and removed his heart. He died then and there. The crystal was then placed in the cavity, and his body began to quake. We had thought that the power of the crystal was healing him, and instead, his body was dissolving, becoming absorbed until all that was left was the crystal was left. Now a fully powered source of energy from The Dreaming itself, fueled by the soul of the son and all who followed him. This is what we called The Second Death, Markus."

<u>Markus</u>

Markus couldn't believe it.

He had heard of old rituals that took place in the world centuries before the Great War and nuclear fallout, but he had never heard of such a horrible way to achieve power. Regardless of The Mad King's earlier desires, it had clearly become far more warped if he was willing to do it again and again long after his son died a second time and became trapped in The Dreaming. It was no wonder Black wanted the crystals destroyed. They were an abomination of nature, and the creation of them nothing short of demonic, especially considering The Eldest had made one for himself.

"What happened after?" asked Markus trying to keep the conversation going as to not think about The Second Death.

Abram had refilled his pipe and lit it, now puffing little rings of smoke into the air as he continued his tale. "The Mad King sheltered his son's crystal like a treasure, used it along with his own and The Seven in order to take further control of the Northern Wastelands. Soon all was under his control, and none could stop him. My family had long since perished, and there was little else for me left, and yet I was forced to remain in the Mad King's service. Until I found someone to take the son away, as well as one of the crystals, where they ended up in Levitika.

"You remember the legend of the Great Owl who led Levitika to rebel against The Capitol. Over the course of months the city had broken free, but The Eldest did not want to surrender. He flew for the city itself, and did battle with the Angels as they called themselves at last in order to retake Levitika and make an example of those who rebelled. But The Owl was an intelligent leader and had grown very powerful with the assistance of the newest leader, Pilate. Together, they prepared the city and The Great Owl cast a spell to lift the city into the skies, using the Eldest's son to fuel the island and keep it afloat. Still, The Eldest pursued them.

The battle lasted long, and at last The Great Owl faced The Eldest, only to eventually meet her end when she unleashed her secret weapon from the island. The Shi Ray, which obliterated The Eldest's fleet, and even the Mad King himself. The Eldest's body had been destroyed but the crystals which they found scattered across the countryside, survived and the spirits within, restless and bloodthirsty. The Eldest being the most dangerous, they attempted to destroy it. But even after tossing it back into the volcano and blasting it many times with many kinds of weaponry and sorcery, nothing could destroy it nor its brethren."

Markus nodded, remembering this part of the story back when Elizabetha had told him.

"It was then decided that The Eldest would be kept safe within the new Levitika, and the few crystals found were divided amongst the leaders and scattered across the country, even to the new ruler of the Capitol, Queen Lamia, who was just a newborn child at the time. Eventually, the power the leaders had were not enough and they all went after one another, fighting for more land, more people, and for the crystals. Soon, it became too dangerous and Levitika was forced to flee into hiding among the mountains, and with them, The Eldest. But as the war for power continued, soon there cam the prophecy that was whispered from The Dreaming through the crystals about The Keeper who was to save the world from The Eldest once and for all."

"The prophecy concerning me," said Markus.

Abram nodded. "Spoken from the very mind of the Eldest's Son himself, as written...

"Angels of Eden will fall,
From the depths, nightmares will crawl,
Nightmares from the past meet new,
The Eldest's strength, and fear grew.
Gateways must be shut, destroyed,
Both by Dreaming, war, and droid.
The Seven that closed the gate,
Can no longer stay in wait.
The one who can speak to all,
Can prevent the worlds great fall.
Whether locked up, or set free,
The Eldest rules all we see.
Through fear, despair, and hate,
He shall bring all from his wait.
But before The Night shall fall,
The Keeper, shall free them all.
And to the end of this tale,
Whether trapped or free, He shall fail."

Abram stood and left Daryl laying in the couch. He went to the kitchen sink and poured him and Markus some water before returning to the boy and giving him his glass. He sat down, pipe now smoldering in a tray on the table and he drank heavily before continuing.

"In my opinion, the spirits of the gateways could not have been more ridiculous by speaking in a prolonged riddle. But even then, we waited. Until all who had a crystal was told that The Keeper has awakened. That was when Levitika finally came out of hiding, ready for battle. And lo and behold, a young boy has come, whose heritage is as ancient as the legend of the Great Owl herself."

"Wait a minute," said Markus setting his now empty glass down on the table. He was still thirsty but he wanted to ask, "Back in Levitika, Queen Elizabetha said my father was to birth The Keeper, and that he and the queen were half-siblings. When you say the lineage goes back to the Great Owl, does that mean..."

Abram smiled. "You are related to the Great Owl, yes. How exactly is unclear, for Johnathon was a bastard, and his lineage unclear. And yet the moment you were born, the crystals became agitated, especially The Eldest."

"Hence why my father fled for Nineveh," said Markus bewildered.

"That's right," said Abram. "And now you have been assigned the task to find an destroy the crystals after destroying The Eldest. However, that will not be easy given the circumstances of our country. Queen Lamia of The Capitol and her legion of droids and the darkest of magic ever concocted since The Great War, will stop at nothing to take back what her ancestor had created, including the crystals themselves. That must not happen, as The Eldest and the crystals I helped him create must be destroyed, and seal the doorways between our world and the land of dreams so that no one will ever have access to such atrocities again."

"But the Nudushi Volcano is still active, right?" asked Markus. "Wouldn't that mean the whole volcano needs to be destroyed as well?"

Abram smiled nodding. "And so how do you suppose that could happen?"

Markus thought about it for a moment. At last he said, "That the crystals, all of them, must be destroyed inside the volcano with a final spell."

"Exactly," said Abram proudly. "No one else can do it except The Keeper, who is the only one who can tap into every type of crystal in existence."

Markus stared at his empty glass on the table, and then he stood up and walked over to the nearest window to look outside of it. He digested all that he was told, thought about what he himself had experienced in The Dreaming as well as the presence of The Eldest. The Mad King was still the greatest threat, but if Queen Lamia and others were trying to get ahold of the crystals, more terrible things could come to be. But something else was missing. Why were they struggling for all of the crystals when The Eldest was obviously the one they wanted?

"Why hasn't anyone else tried The Second Death?" asked Markus.

"I'm the only one who knows about it," said Abram. "When I escaped The Capitol, I destroyed all my research. If anyone attempted to, they would all end in tragedy."

Markus nodded. "And what about The Eldest?" he asked. "Levitika lost it and whoever took it is nowhere to be found. What is stopping them from using it?"

Abram stood up and joined Markus by the window, looking out into the late afternoon. "The Eldest will not submit to anyone, it merely influences others to do his work for him. All he needs is a powerful subject, and go from there. His brethren want to die, to pass on to the next world beyond this, but he needs them to come back from The Dreaming. He realized his mistake by taking on another body that would not last. And from what I hear from Lucius here…"

Abram then displayed orange crystal in his hand like a magic trick. "The Eldest has gotten stronger, and has learned much in terms of magic and The Dreaming. He needs both the power of Light and Darkness to escape his prison. If he succeeds however, then the world will unravel as he begins his judgement upon the country, and eventually the world."

Markus nodded feeling more scared by the second. He clenched his fist as he spoke. "And it is my job to destroy the crystals and set the spirits free, and prevent The Eldest from coming."

Abram nodded. "It will only slow him down, for the crystals are not the only way he could escape. What they are we do not know for sure. But Lucius is doing what he can, as well as Abner to find out. For all we know, destroying the gateways might stop The Eldest entirely. But then again, we cannot risk more being made as well as more opportunities for The Eldest to escape The Dreaming."

He looked at Markus. "That is where you come in, Markus. You are the only one who can cross between both worlds, and you are the only one with the power to destroy the crystals. There are many out there who can use the crystals and use magic, but they cannot enter The Dreaming, or in the very least escape it they make it. You are The Keeper, you are destined to destroy the Gateways, and destroy The Eldest and bring this country together as one."

Markus nodded and resumed looking out the window deep in thought. This was a lot to take in, especially on the first day. But deep in his heart he knew it to be the truth. He was still nervous, still scared of his capability, and the constant nagging question of 'what if I fail' still plagued him.

He thought about what his memory of Black said. *What do you think you need to be?*

"I believe I know the answer, to your riddle."

Abram looked at Markus smiling. "I was hoping you might. What is it?"

"I am one. And the world is all. Every single life on this planet makes up the vast ecosystem, it builds, it dies, it grows, all giving to one another in perfect harmony. I am just one single person, but I am part of something much bigger. The animals, the plants, the thousands of people on the continent, the entire world is made up of many 'ones' so in a way, the world is one. The world is all, but it is also one."

He turned back to Abram. "Am I right?"

Abram smiled and nodded. "That is how The Dreaming is. It is like the world. Millions of dreams and memories brought together in harmony. Now, you are ready to begin your training on Dreamcasting, as well as the understanding of the realm of dreams itself."

The Ways of Dreamcasting

<u>Markus</u>

Markus was now standing in the middle of the field with Abram standing a few yards away. It was now the late afternoon and the sun was about to begin it's disappearance casting marvelous colors of orange and purple across the sky like a water painting.

Markus was shirtless and was now barefoot, and the grass tickled his toes as he dug them into the earth. The light breeze swept cool and clear around his body and the sun while nearing it's lowest point, felt warm against his skin. A few of the villagers were up and cutting firewood from the tree he had chopped down, and a few of the girls about Markus' age were folding laundry, stealing glances at him every chance they got. All the while Markus stood before Abram who had his hands behind his back as he began his next lesson for the day.

"Dreamcasting is simply bringing your imagination into reality," the old man said now walking around Markus. "When you are asleep, your brain is capable of creating worlds unlike anything you have ever seen, and in a way make it seem like you are actually there. The human brain really is the most spectacular organ ever created. But anyways, your dreams come from both reality and your fantasy, what you see and think each day, in a way, what you also daydream. Dreamcasting, is about letting your imagination become reality. We are only capable of using ten percent of our brain, but Dreamcasting requests us to use a little bit more, which in turn performs the miracles we know today as magic."

He paused in step directly in front of Markus though Abram's eyes were straight ahead as if eyeing something in the distance. Before Markus could turn to see what it was, he said, "Tell me Markus, what is the difference between Witchcraft, and Dreamcasting?" He then turned his eyes back to the boy, eyeing him tensely.

Markus scratched the back of his head as he tried to recall what Black had told him before. "Witchcraft is based on the influence of the four major elements on the planet, right? Earth, wind, fire, and water?"

"That is correct. Witches are able to perform many different spells but each witch has their own elemental ability they are superior in. For example your witch friend from The Leviathan, she was no doubt a water-element. But she was still able to cast spells in the most unnatural of ways like some witches who are capable of signing deals with spirits."

"What kind of spirits exactly?" asked Markus.

Abram shook his head. "More ancient and more evil than what we will be discussing about today. Pay attention now. Dreamcasting is based on who you are inside, your imagination and dreams are what brings true magic to life. You are by no means a witch, alchemist or wizard. You have to potential for *true* magic. That is the difference between Dreamcasting and other magical properties."

Markus nodded, heeding Abram's words.

"Now then, I want you to do a very simple task now: I want you to make this seed grow." From his sleeve Abram revealed a small black seed before throwing it into the dirt at Markus' feet. Markus stared down at the spot where the seed landed and then he looked up at Abram deeply confused.

"How?" he asked.

"Use your imagination." Abram said with a grin as if that was the obvious answer.

"Okay, um, can we start with something that could be actually possible?"

"And what would that be?"

"I don't know, um maybe something that doesn't include forcing something to grow at an irregular pace?"

"This exercise is to teach you how to expand your imagination. Making something grow or shrink is easy if it is a plant, but how it looks depends on what you put into it."

"Okay, um, this is a living thing, how can I defy the laws of nature?"

Abram smiled. "Exactly."

"Come again?"

"The first lesson is not forcing something to grow against the laws of nature, but to know your limits. Magic can be used in many ways, but one of the ways of self-control is knowing what should *not* be attempted, such as making an animal, plant or person's growth accelerate. It is one thing to alter a mind and body, it is another thing forcing something to mature beyond their own limitations. There are laws of nature for a reason, and yes, your imagination can break these laws, but to avoid damage to the person or thing, it is usually best to not do it. You can change, or influence what is already there, but as for making something physically grow or age, that would be against the laws of nature."

"I see," Markus nodded. "So, how am I supposed to do it?"

Abram pointed to a nearby dandelion not far from where he stood. "That dandelion must be removed from my lawn, however I do not want you to kill it. Tell me, what could be a better alternative?"

"I'm going to guess change it?"

"Precisely. What is your favorite flower?"

"I don't have one, to be honest I hardly ever look at flowers."

"Then might I suggest picking one that you saw when you took your journey through the country? When you blurred the line between reality and fantasy in order to see as far as you did, you did happen to see flowers, did you not?"

"Yes."

"Then pick one of them," Abram said sitting down on the grass. "Just focus on the dandelion and picture your goal in your head, and using the energy of your crystals, change it to your liking."

Markus walked over to the weed and sat before it staring at it with such concentration it began to hurt his head. What was he going to change it to? *And how in the world am I going to be able to do it?*

This wasn't at all like making himself stronger or faster, this was something else, a different life force and item altogether. How was this supposed to work? He frowned at the weed and thinking back to all he saw while he was traveling through The Dreaming, he wondered what to at least try to make.

He *did* remember one flower he saw on the island however, just before he passed the shores and began to explore the vast waters of The Great Sea. It looked like a small white rose among a bundle of similar buds. What color they were he did not know, for color had less definition when he used The Sight, but he felt confident he could wing it. Now would come the hard part: Actually committing the act itself.

He took a breath and began to build up some energy from the crystal which began to glow as he stretched his auto-limb arm towards the weed. He pictured the flower he saw in his mind over, and over, and over again as he stared at the plant and taking a slow exhale he pulsed.

Bright blue lightning arced between his fingers and shot out towards the weed. The dandelion began to twitch and turn, it soon lost all of its color and the yellow tufts began to turn ashy gray and fall as something else seemed to sprout from the very stem. The small white rose sprang up tall and from the weed's leaves sprouted more rose-like buds of purple. Markus took a breath when he opened his eyes to see the flower, and he thought it was beautiful. He looked up to Abram to hear what he had to say.

The old man pursed his lips as he walked over and bent down to observe the flower. He peered at it with keep eyes and leaning forward he took a sniff of the new plant before him. He then smiled. "It is still a dandelion, I can tell by the smell, but you have completely altered its appearance and made something much more pleasant to the eye. Well done."

Markus smiled, and then frowned as he had a sudden thought. "Abram?"

"Yes?"

"You said it was still a dandelion, but only looked different. Are you saying that you cannot *create* life?"

"That is right. Creating a living organism, or even bringing back the dead is against the laws of nature, and is considered a taboo for even most wizards. Of course, that never stopped witches from attempting such feats, but it is frowned upon and should never be attempted for any reason whatsoever. There is but only one being capable of creation, and to attempt to ascend to such a level would be dangerous and foolish."

"Got it," Markus nodded understanding what Abram was saying but not understanding just who exactly he was talking about.

Abram nodded and waved his hand. "Now, the seed."

Markus looked back to where Abram had tossed the seed. He looked back at his teacher and said, "But I thought you said not to forcibly mature something?"

"I did," Abram agreed.

"Then how-"

"Help it mature," said the old man patiently.

"Help it?"

"What do plants need?

"Sun and water."

"And?"

"... A, uh... dirt?"

Abram nodded. "Alter the environment around the plant. Make the soil richer, make sunlight, and of course, water the seed. Once the seed begins to sprout, then you have done your part."

"Wait a sec," Markus said shaking his head. "Don't plants need time as well?"

"All living beings do," Abram agreed.

"Then how-"

Abram waved his hand dismissively. "Don't overcomplicate things. Use your imagination, make the seed feel welcome and safe. Make it grow in it's own pace."

Markus still didn't understand how this was going to accomplish anything, but he turned about and returned to the seed as he was told. He stooped before it and digging a small hole with his fingers, he then pushed the seed into the earth with his thumb and then buried it.

He then thought about the earth, thought about the soil here on the island. Placing his hand on the ground, he considered the good soil that is mixed with the sand here, and thought of bringing it all here for this little seed. Seeing that this was probably not a good idea, he decided to stand and leave the seed, Abram watching him the entire time. He went over to the garden and took a handful of the soil used in the boxes the garden was planted in. He then took a pail and pumped some water from it. He returned to the seed and placed both the soil and the water on top of the place he placed the seed and then he replaced his hand upon the wet earth and took a deep breath, and pulsed.

Blue energy sunk into the earth, and he imagined the earth and water coming together around the seed like a comfortable cocoon. He warmed the earth with his hand, and through his link with the seed which was faint, as delicate as a newborn baby. He sensed it's eagerness, it's need to break out of it's shell, and through this link he said, *It is safe. Come on out.*

He heard something crack within the earth and he waited there for several long minutes, constantly feeding energy into the soil and before long, a small green stalk broke the surface, poking right between two of his metallic fingers. It bloomed two little leaves and removing his hand from the ground, Markus hovered it directly over the plant and looked out across the sea towards the sun. He imagined it's heart, it's sunlight, and looking back at the plant he pulsed again, this time casting a sort of werelight from the palm of his hand which shone down upon the plant like a halo. The plant quivered and shook, but still it grew, and when the plant was about a foot in height with several bright green leaves sticking from the stalk, the bud that was accumulating like a bulbous little sack, suddenly opened releasing at first a pungent smell that became fragrant, and what stood before him was a little white rose that he had meant to transform the daisy.

He looked at Abram, both tired but surprised that he was able to accomplish such a feat.

Abram was smiling and he nodded satisfyingly. "Good. Good. Now, come with me," he said this before turning about and walking away. Markus quickly stood up and followed his master.

He took Markus to a nearby creek, which seemed to cut through the island as if it broke in half. Daryl was already there, appearing to be drinking from the creek but upon approaching the Werecat, Daryl was simply eyeballing what was in the creek itself. Small green sea fish swam through the rippling waters, while some even circled one another in small pools that have formed near the sides of the creek. Markus leaned over the water, seeing his reflection in the water, to his eyes he saw only a stranger. That seemed to be the case whenever he looked at himself in any reflection, his hair was longer, his torso leaner despite his muscles being more defined than ever. *Have I really changed that much?*

"Your next test, will be to catch a fish," Abram declared. "But you appear to have no pole."

"No problem," Markus said eyeing a fish with green scales. "That's easy."

"If you are thinking of doing what you did to the crab on the mainland, that isn't what I want you to do."   Markus looked at his teacher confused. "How'd-"

Abram tapped the side of his temple with a small smirk. "I picked it up easily enough the moment you thought of it. I want you to try catching a fish a different way."

"A different way," Markus said looking at the water. "Right…"

He eyed the closet fish to the streambed. It was a dark blue with a lighter underbelly with little whiskers sticking out of the sides of its small head. It appeared to be fighting against the current, which kept it stationary a few yards from Markus. Having an idea, Markus raised a hand and stuck it towards the fish and pictured the water and the fish rising out of the water. He concentrated harder and pulsed. Lighting struck out and a sphere of water shot up out of the water- however only a rock sat in the center like the nucleus of a cell. Markus went red as he let the sphere drop back into the water. Abram chuckled as he stroked his chin. Markus frowned and attempted it a second time- this time there was only the sphere and nothing else. A third time, a leaf. Getting frustrated, he was about to do it a fourth time when a hand grabbed his wrist. He looked up to see Abram squatting beside him scolding.

"You need to remain calm and collected when you attempt such spells," he said stern but not unkindly. "You let your anger get the best of you, your frustration. Anger is important, it pushes you, makes you push beyond your boundaries and makes you stronger, but too much and it can overwhelm you and control you. Just like during your battle in the sky. If you allow yourself to succumb to such emotions, you leave yourself open for the spirits within the crystals to lose control of their own demons as well. And you do not wish to do that, do you?"

"Sir," Markus said trying to remain cool. "With all due respect, it made me stronger. I was able to withstand the radiation, survive the explosion and destroy the Leviathan. How can it be a bad thing? Besides, this isn't the same thing."

Abram shook his head. "That's where you're wrong, Markus. That state you were in is very powerful. In fact, that is what I like to call The Dream State. It means you are at your most powerful in the real world as you are in The Dreaming. But in the state, you are at your most vulnerable. If you are killed in this state, you will not only destroy all the gateways to The Dreaming, but all of your anger, fear, and doubt will fuel The

Eldest's power, and he would be able to escape without the need of the crystals. He would become you."

Markus looked down almost ashamed. "I... I see..."

Abram released Markus' hand and added, "This catching of fish may seem different than the heat of battle, but the lesson remains the same. That is what makes magic so dangerous. You need to control yourself, train your body and mind to control your feelings and only use the right amount and never succumb to the evil dwelling in your heart."

Markus looked back up. "Evil in my heart?"

Abram nodded though he no longer appeared stern or upset. Only carefully calm and assuring. "The human heart is the most powerful source in the universe besides the brain. While the brain controls the body and mind, it is the heart that makes us who we are. Everything we feel, we feel in our heart. And if there is anger, or resentment, or hatred, it remains in your heart for a long time. That is just who we are. We all have a little bit of that deceit within us, what defines us and how we use our magic, is how we use our hearts. How we let it control us, and how we in turn control it. Your heart is the key to complete control both physically, and mentally."

"I never thought of it that way," Markus said thinking about his time on the Leviathan, how desperate he had become, and what had resulted in it.

"That is how you learn," Abram said smiling. "Do not dwell on it, only learn from it and don't slip up. Now try again, and this time, take your time. Your mind is a muscle, it needs to be trained and worked to bring it to its full potential."

"Okay..."

Markus focused on the water, and in a more calm matter- or at least as calm as he could- he raised his hand and pulsed, letting the energy flow through his body and the crystals. A fifth sphere of water came from the creek, this one too was empty. He growled but calmed himself with a steady breath and tried again. And again, and again, every single time pausing to breathe for a few seconds before attempting again.

On the eighth try he almost tossed the sphere back into the creek before stopping himself just in time for he saw a small green fish swimming around in the sphere. He laughed at his success and looked at Abram a look of pure exhilaration and victory.

Abram nodded, smiling contentedly. "You get stronger with patience," he said. "Through patience you can learn much, much more. Keep this in mind in all your training, all your meditations, and every time you cast a spell. It will save you a lot of stress, and a lot of problems."

He took out his own crystal again and raised his hand towards Markus' sphere, and the fish came out of the sphere and began to twist and turn as if invisible hands were holding it. He hovered the fish directly towards Daryl and the Werecat leapt for it, snapping it in a single bite and proceeded to chew noisily.

"I believe," Abram said as his pet ate. "It is time for our own dinner as well. Shall we go then?"

"Sir?" asked Markus.

"What is it?"

"How did you learn how to use the crystals? Was it because of your time helping create them?"

Abram frowned and Daryl looked up at his master cautiously. When Abram finally answered he said, "No, it's because I finally answered the call for help."

"What call?"

Abram shook his head. "Another time. Come. I am hungry."

He started to go, and Markus watched as Daryl followed close behind, looking like a feral Werecat ready to pounce on him. After a moment, Markus hurried to catch up and walk with Abram and Daryl back to the cabin. He did not dare to ask Abram more questions about his time with the Mad King again, although he thought he could hear a faint voice coming from the old man which wasn't his own, but perhaps belonged to someone else.

He saved me…

Elizabetha

Elizabetha was eating lunch with her daughter on the balcony of the Nineveh palace. The sun was high up which gave off plenty of heat for the workers who were applying the finishing touches on the newly-built city.

Far beyond the wall The Angels were doing repairs to Levitika's walls. Soon it would be in tip-top shape to take into battle if need be. It had been several days since Markus' disappearance and Ashlyn and Grim meeting with the others in Xerxes. As she ate her lunch, Elizabetha just couldn't help but wonder about the boy. Even as The Keeper, he was so much like his father...

His mother would have been proud of him though...

That wasn't all that was on her mind though. She had not told Esmerelda yet, but had sent a message to the queen of Xerxes via voicemail delivered by a Guardian Owl. She would only hope that she would gain at least an audience with the queen, and also give Grim and Ashlyn a little more time to make sure everything was in order and begin their recon of the city. If the queen or some other leader meant Nineveh and Levitika harm, it would need to be handled quickly and a settlement declared for Xerxes as soon as possible. She would like to avoid bloodshed, but if Queen Psyren refused to cooperate, then they would have to fight. They would need all the support they could if they planned on taking The Capitol and removing Queen Lamia from the throne.

She looked up from her stew and eyed her daughter. It had been a long time since she and Esmerelda had eaten together just the two of them. There was still so much to do, and Esmerelda had been studying well on her spiritual texts and history. History was important for any leader, lest they be doomed to repeat it. She had sat down on many meetings between her mother and the council, but Elizabetha worried that it would not be enough. The others felt it too, especially Slagar. He in particular had been very adamant on saying that Esmerelda was not ready to lead just yet.

"She's still far too young," the hypnotist would say.

Elizabetha in turn would remind Slagar of the vows he made to their family, and should Esmerelda become next to wear the crown, he would serve her until the next one. Whether that be in Levitika or some other country, it would happen sooner than he thought.

It would happen far sooner than Elizabetha herself thought...

There were times where she wished she was never born into royalty. Sometimes she wished she could choose a different life. As it is, however...

She broke away from her thoughts and turned to Esmerelda who had finished her bowl and was now glancing over some topics that Elizabetha wanted her to look over, specifically concerning Nineveh. She had answered well but her mind seemed elsewhere. She smiled at her daughter, deeply proud of the woman she was becoming.

"Esmerelda," she said softly as she stood up from her seat. "Come to the balcony with me. Leave your stuff."

"Oh, okay," Esmerelda said standing up quickly. As she followed her mother to the Nineveh balcony overlooking the city, a servant quickly moved in and began clearing away the dishes.

They stood together there for a long time, Elizabetha breathing in the cool afternoon air while her daughter leaned over the railing looking out beyond the walls, as if she was a simple girl looking for someone who had been off to war for far too long. It made Elizabetha regret having Esmerelda be one of the only children in Levitika with such high standards. The girl had needed friends growing up, and she wondered if she had met Ashlyn and Markus too late.

Especially considering the position those two were in.

"Esmerelda."

Esmerelda turned to her mother standing straight up. "Yes, Mother?"

"I have something important to tell you."

"What is it?" Esmerelda said turning completely around so that she was facing her mother.

"It is about your father."

Esmerelda's eyes went as wide as dinner plates. The subject of her father was always a touchy subject for her- in fact, it pained Elizabetha just as much. Esmerelda opened her mouth and then closed it only to mumble. "What about him?"

"Do you remember what I said about him? How he left us?"

"Yes, I remember," Esmerelda said stiffly.

"Well, you are becoming a woman soon, in fact you may be inheriting Nineveh very soon. The people look up to you, they see you as the Hope of Nineveh, did you know?"

"I thought Markus was?"

"No, no. Markus is the 'Savior' as they put it. But he is not a king, nor do I think he will have the chance unless he marries into royalty."

Esmerelda nodded. "Any girl would be lucky to have him."

"Are you disappointed?"

Esmerelda shook her head, completely unfazed by the question. She was as composed as ever, and Elizabetha was impressed with her daughter. "No, I'd be very happy for him. He's part of my family after all, and I love him like a brother."

"That is good," said Elizabetha carefully.

"Thing is," Esmerelda said. "I don't know if Markus would marry into royalty if anyone asked him to."

Elizabetha nodded. "I see the way he looks at Ashlyn."

Esmerelda nodded. "Those two like each other. I can tell."

"That's right. But, let us not worry about the possibilities of their future. I want to talk to you about yours."

"Okay," Esmerelda said looking back to her mother.

"Since you are my daughter, many believe that you will be the new ruler of Nineveh when we move on. In fact, I am considering putting you in charge here."

Esmerelda looked at her mother with a skeptical look. The talk of becoming a ruler was never her favorite either. She showed no surprise or fear, only an acknowledgement that showed just how much ruling truly meant for her.

"What does this have to do with my father?" her daughter asked.

"Well, you deserve to know the truth about your family."

"The truth?" Esmerelda asked with concern in her voice.

"Yes. I lied. Your father didn't really left us. In fact, he came back."

Esmerelda looked confused. "What do you mean?"

"Your father is-"

"Your highness!" a voice said behind her which made her stand to turn and see that it was one of the servants.

"Yes, what is it?"

"A message, from Xerxes!"

Elizabetha went ridged with excitement but contained her joy. A reply this early? This was good news- no, this was *great* news.

She turned to her daughter and smiled, Esmerelda returned with equal ecstasy. "Give it to me," she said accepting a small scroll from the servant downloaded from the response sent from Xerxes. The servant bowed and departed as she began to read aloud the letter from Queen Psyren, reading each word letter by letter to ensure that she would not misread it in any way shape or form.

Dear Elizabetha,

Your occupation in Nineveh is quite amazing to hear. However, with the now decreased number of troops in my army, my council are against the idea of parley over dinner. However, I remember you when you were just a little girl, and to object to such a notion would shame my name for the last of my remaining days.

Therefore, I accept your invitation, but must insist you join me here in Xerxes at my castle. I am in no condition for travel, and appreciate you offering to come here instead of the opposite. I shall expect you in three days, and we may eat and catch up and then discuss what exactly we must do for the good of our districts. We will discuss this over our meal, I hope to see you soon.

Sincerely,

Psyren Xerxes.

Elizabetha grinned and turned to her daughter. "She has accepted."

Esmerelda grinned like a fox at the news. "You didn't tell me you were planning on meeting Queen Psyren. Is that safe?"

"It will be," said Elizabetha. "She could have easily dejected my offer, considering what had taken place here. However, this answer means that she is willing to listen given that we have returned for good. I doubt she would have agreed if it were anyone else but Levitika. There just might be hope for them yet."

Esmeralda nodded, realization dawning on her beautiful face. "That explains why you were mentioning me ruling Nineveh..."

Elizabetha nodded. "Are you nervous? Disappointed?"

"No, I feel I've been training for this my whole life," said Esmerelda, and how sad of a truth that really was for Elizabetha. "But, do you think I'm ready, Mother?"

"I wouldn't be discussing this with you if I didn't," Elizabetha said with a wink. "We must end this lunch now, I'm afraid. I must discuss this with the council immediately. You will join me if you want to."

"Okay," Esmerelda said, her precious smile returning.

"We will continue our talk later, this cannot wait." And with a turn Elizabetha ran inside excited to tell Slagar and the rest of the council about the splendid news about the future of Nineveh and Xerxes.

"Mother, wait!" Esmerelda said as she caught up to her mother. "What about my father though? You said this was important to know."

"I did," said Elizabetha.

"It wasn't... It wasn't Black, was it?"

Elizabetha shook her head. "Once, I believed he was, my daughter. But you were born from one of the old lords of Levitika. When I rose to power, he had perished of his age."

"You married an old man?" asked Esmerelda.

"It is not uncommon in positions such as ours. That is why I wanted to talk to you about Markus as an example. You do not have to make the decisions I made in order to retain your leadership. You are smarter than I, and I believe you deserve much better than that."

"Are you... ashamed of having me then?" asked Esmerelda, and this caused Elizabetha to stop in her tracks and turn her entire attention to her daughter who stopped as well. "Because... I wasn't born out of-"

"Stop that now," Elizabetha said, stooping down and taking her daughter by the shoulders. "You are the greatest blessing in my entire life, Esmerelda. The most precious thing that ever came out of my life. I was always so hard on you because I want you to be better. Now I know you can be. If you are up for it, I will declare Nineveh to be yours, and you may lead as you see fit. You will work closely with me and Queen Psyren, and one day, you will rule a district of your own, be it Nineveh, or whatever you may call it. Your father would be very proud of you, I know that too."

This made Esmerelda beam and she said, "Okay," and that seemed to settle this matter.

They moved on, eager to share their news with the council as one. No longer was it just Elizabetha with Esmerelda listening and learning. They would do this together, and one day, they would be ruling as equals.

After discussing everything with The Elders as well as Slagar, who remained silent throughout her entire announcement, Elizabetha waited patiently for their comments or 'advice' as they would call them. She knew to play her words carefully and in turn listen carefully and really think about her peers words. They were all part of a snake, and Slagar was the head. She would need to be careful. They all stood before her as she for the first time sat on what remained of Baron Ovid's throne. It felt uncomfortable compared to hers in Levitika but she sat still and tall as the men before her whispered amongst themselves. Beside her, Esmerelda stood tall and proud just as she always taught her, and she stared these men down as the lioness she was born to be.

"I do have, a few things I would like to request Your Highness." Slagar said taking a sip of wine. This was becoming troublesome, Slagar had only started drinking more since the battle with Ovid's Leviathan fleet.

"Yes, Slagar?" Elizabetha said drumming her fingers against the armrest.

"Considering that we just wiped out a huge chunk of Xerxes army, I would like to have us all under the impression that they still might not be happy with us, and we should exercise the utmost caution."

"I agree," one of the Elders said. "We cannot let you very well go alone."

"See?" Slagar gestured with his wine. "You should have offered to send any of us. After all, we are far more disposable than you."

"You know that is not true, Slagar," Elizabetha said sternly. This was just another one of his tactics to make her look bad. But she and Esmerelda just had to put up with him for a bit longer, if this kept up and his record got any longer, well, the hypnotist would need to find someone else to counsel.

And after that, perhaps the council itself would all need to be replaced too, given how often they all looked at him rather than their queen.

"Also," said Queen Elizabetha. "I do not plan on going alone to Xerxes."

"Oh, we know, your daughter and a few guards." Slagar nodded. He sat his glass down on the table he was sitting at and walked closer to the queen. "With all due respect, Elizabetha, I would rather not let you go at all."

Let? Elizabetha thought without speaking.

"However, I do agree that this could be a wonderful opportunity to at least try and form an alliance with Xerxes. Save us some manpower as well as droids. Psyren as well, especially if we plan on moving north. However, considering that they could possibly still hold a grudge against us, I would rather have you bring me along or more than a 'few' guards."

Most of the Elders looked at one another in surprise. Elizabetha was likewise impressed by this. Slagar willing to put himself on the line was never something she thought the man capable of, and yet...

"Also," Slagar continued. "I must advise that Esmerelda not go with you."

"I never said she would," said Elizabetha. "Which brings us to another topic. She will be in charge here in Nineveh and watch over both here and Levitika in my absence."

Everyone was looking at one another. Slagar's face was neutral, but the red tinge that had bloomed across his cheeks seemed to deepen into a dark maroon. Once some of the Elders began to voice concerns about how much responsibility two cities would be for a young girl, Slagar raised a hand, his eyes flashing bright and he called for silence. Once the room settled, his spell was lifted and he said, "Let her highness explain, please. Go ahead, my queen."

Elizabetha nodded, content. "Princess Esmerelda here has grown up well, as you all have witnessed. She has trained well, and I believe will be a competent ruler in my absence, as well as your guidance. That being said, she will be in charge over both cities until I return, and when Levitika is to move north again, she will rule over Nineveh permanently as we proceed with our revolution for the Northern Wastelands."

The Elders said nothing to this, only glanced amongst themselves.

Elizabetha continued saying, "That being said, Slagar, I will take your guards but I would like you to stay here was well. If something were to indeed happen then I need you to take over the preparations for the war and ensure that my daughter becomes ruler when all of this is over."

Slagar frowned but he nodded. "As you wish."

"I will however take Kahun as my escort and advisor as we speak to Queen Psyren."

The oldest Elder shuddered under his long white beard and his hood covered his obviously surprised eyes. "M-m-me ma'am?"

"Of course," Elizabetha said. "You are the oldest- and I must say the wisest. You have a good judge of character, and I need to be on my guard while I discuss everything with Psyren and her council, even if she was once a good friend."

"I must agree with that," Slagar added.

"Hear, hear," another Elder claimed.

Kahun grumbled beneath his beard but reluctantly agreed. "As you wish."

"Good. The meeting will take place in three days as I have said, and there is still a lot of work to do. So let us discuss mode of transportation- I do not plan to fly our own weapon to dinner."

<u>Esmerelda</u>

Esmerelda left the palace after her mother informed her that she would be staying in Nineveh while she was visiting the queen of Xerxes. She thought the meeting went well, all things considered, but the princess' mind was still restless and buzzing.

She was scared, but knew this was coming long before she ever met Markus and Ashlyn, and earlier still before she ever heard of the prophecy about The Keeper. All in all as she was being raised in order to achieve her role as a leader despite how much she disliked the very idea of ruling or leading a district into war. The thought of dealing what her mother always dealt with made her sick to her stomach. She didn't want to have to worry about everyone in the district- Esmerelda only wanted to worry about the people who mattered most to her in the world. Her mother, Ashlyn, and Markus...

She passed through the city streets as many people walked past her without realizing who she was. Esmerelda had taken her cloak with her to obscure her figure and face so that she would not be stopped by one of the citizens. She did not want to be hailed as the princess of the new queen. She wanted to just walk down the street like a normal person without care or worry. But that was the problem: She did care and worry. In fact, she did so quite a lot, and she wanted to see Vic and see if he was busy. Despite the rumors that often plagued the mutant, she felt that the only person outside the castle who might have a remote chance of understanding her was him. Especially as her two only friends were out and about now.

They're doing their part, and I'm about to do mine...

He was supposed to be working on a new bar stable at the Drunken Badrat Ashlyn and Markus had mentioned. Esmerelda figured it would not hurt to actually get to know the world those two knew before they left.

After walking for a bit, she finally came across the refurbished Drunken Badrat. The buildings walls were free of bullet holes and laser burns, and the new sign was lit and alive with new lights and paint. The picture of the Badrat laying on its back with a drink in its hand made Esmerelda chuckle with amusement. She placed a hand on the door and pushed her way inside.

The inside was as rustic as ever, with leather seating in the booths and handmade wooden tables and chairs set around the center of the bar. The bar in the back was of fresh polished wood and the shelving behind it were lined with new drinks that were made during the time of rebuilding. The man Markus told her about named Jim was behind the bar pouring a drink for a mutant with a third leg. Esmerelda passed one of the waitresses and took a seat upon one of the stools before the bar and waited for the tender to see her. When he did, he leaned forward his glasses catching the light of the new lights above their heads.

"Can I help you honey?"

"Are you Jim?" Esmerelda asked pulling back her hood. "Markus told me about you."

Jim's eyes went as wide as his smile did. "Well, well, Princess Esmerelda. This is an honor." He bowed his head respectfully.

"Thank you, but could you not like, announce that I am here?"

"Yes, of course my apologies. What brings you here?"

"Gossip. Trying to get my mind off of things, I heard Vic was here earlier?"

"Great guy that one is, he left 'bout an hour ago."

Damn. "Oh well," she said. "Could I bother you for a water?"

"But of course!" Jim ducked behind the bar and after the sound of a faucet letting loose water ceased, he came back up with a clean glass of water. Esmerelda took it and took a sip. She thanked him to which he nodded.

"How fares your mother?"

"She's fine. She is discussing the plan concerning Xerxes."

Jim nodded. "A good woman she is, and a good leader. Well, we will be ready to assist. I hear we got plenty of battle-droids in production now but we may need more *human* soldiers." Jim pointed over to a woman with long black hair. "My daughter over there is determined to join the fight if it comes down to that, but I convinced her to wait until we get conformation about what is going to happen before she signs up."

"We may not even have to fight," Esmerelda said. "But we'll see."

"I hope we don't, at least not yet. I am upset about what the soldiers did but hopefully they can make up for almost destroying our city."

"I do as well." Esmerelda said taking another sip. She wiped her mouth with the back of her hand before asking her next question. "Jim, what was it like? Before Markus and Ashlyn left, I mean?"

"Hmmm." Jim rubbed his chin and his eyes appeared to have darkened as if remembering it was a memory he would have rather long forgotten. "Where to start?"

he said. "Well, life here was always difficult under the rule of Baron Ovid. He was always one for control, and if he did not have it in some areas, he would enforce it usually through methods of fear and torture. The influence of his Guard was enough to have everyone submit to their iron-fisted rule. They would take what they wanted without explanation. Money, property…"

Jim's eyes lingered to Kaltrina who was serving a customer. His eyes began to well up in tears as if some unhappy memory had just resurfaced. But as quickly as it came, it was gone and he continued to tell Esmerelda. "Even women. Anyways, making a living was hard, and after Markus and his sister's father was killed under the orders of Ovid, he took up delivering packages throughout the city. He hated his job, but he did what he had to, to make Ruth feel better. The Guard never stole from them for the man who killed their father made a deal that they were not to be harmed."

"Black," Esmerelda said already knowing.

"Yes, it was… most unfortunate." Jim shook his head. "The sonofabitch was a monster, and everyone knew it. What he did to those kids and placing a 'protection order' on them… that only made things worse. Kaltrina and I tried our best for them, but we couldn't do much 'cause of the public, and the old Guard didn't care much for us either. After the kids started leaving, that was when things got worse for 'em. When Ovid sent in the witch and her gang of Hunters to chase him and his sister out, along with Ashlyn."

"What was Ashlyn like?"

Jim shook his head morosely. "Ashlyn was… an orphan, and lived on her own out in the streets. Stealing to feed herself and whatnot. I actually caught her a couple times stealing bread from our cabinets a few weeks after her mother and sister were killed by The Baron's second in command. But there was nothing we could do to help her. She was a wanted person by The Guard. And if they found her in our bar or home, they would have executed us and hung us up in the streets with all who dared defy The Barons rule."

"That is awful," Esmerelda said thinking of just how horrible a place this was before her mother and all of Levitika came in. Markus and Ashlyn really did have it rough, didn't they? She looked at Jim once again. "What was Markus like?"

Jim raised a single eyebrow. "What do you mean?"

Esmerelda shrugged. "What was he like? Like, his personality, who he was known for, that kind of stuff."

Jim nodded, still giving her a funny look. "I see. Well… He was always the silent type. After his father was killed, he took over the role of a guardian over his sister and did everything he could for her. He was always willing to help my daughter and I, and my old partner Aventis. We were like his second family I would like to think."

Jim shook his head then. "Lotta good we did them though… Otherwise he always kept to himself running errands, working on his robots, or taking care of Ruth. He would do anything for that girl, as if nothing else in the world mattered. In fact, I barely believed the day he and Ruth left he left with Ashlyn… I remember being so worried for him and Ruth, and praying that they were okay. That somehow, they would find the city we thought was a myth. But somehow deep inside, I knew he was still the same stubborn child he was before he left. Angry at The Guard, at the man who killed his father, and desperate to save his sister."

Jim lowered his head. "It is too bad he wasn't able to save her in the end. Another thing that has never changed about Markus, is that he always blames himself for things he is unable to prevent."

Esmerelda nodded remembering how he was after he made it to Levitika, as well as after the battle. He always came off as stone-faced and straight to the point, always making plans and backup plans. But inside, he was just as broken as anyone else in the world. Their own personal demons haunting them despite trying their very best for those around them.

She thought of what her mother said about her friends earlier, and though she wished they could have had a better childhood, they were stronger because of it. Perhaps that's why, in some way, Esmerelda envied them both.

She looked back up at Jim who was now resting against the bar with his chin against his fist. "What was Ruth like?" she asked. She was always afraid to ask Markus this for fear of hurting him, but she wanted know just what kind of person she was.

Jim sighed. "Beautiful, innocent, and very sick. She tried so hard to make others smile when she was younger, when she was diagnosed with her illness, we were all heartbroken but could do nothing to help her without getting The Guard involved. She was Markus' last hope. I guess you could say back then she was all that was keeping him alive." He smiled. "And now he realized that he isn't truly alone. I guess even he can learn some things."

Esmerelda frowned and looked down at her clasped hands. "Yeah, indeed."

Talking to Jim, understanding where her friends came from, in a strange way steeled Esmerelda's resolve. As much as she was nervous about becoming a new ruler, she was determined now because no child should ever experience such a tragic beginning. Sure, they were stronger for it, but no one should have to deal with such horrors.

When she became queen of Nineveh, things would be different, she vowed internally. She wouldn't allow anyone to deal with that ever, ever again.

It's the least I can do, she thought. *This can be me doing my part in this whole thing.*

Ashlyn

Ashlyn placed the last stool into place before another crate that was to be a table for the new coffee shop. She and the others had worked the last few days cleaning up the place and fixing it up, ready to pose as a legitimate business in Xerxes.

Near the counter, Silva and Gabriel were installing machines to grind and then brew the coffee beans, and Grim was writing down an order of additional ingredients they would need. Cream, sugar, whatever else one would want in their coffee. He was grumbling about how expensive it was going to be, but Queen Elizabetha had supplied them with enough money to buy a whole farm if they wanted to. Unfortunately, the currency didn't quite match the pace of all the taxes that went over Ashlyn's head, but she could tell were quite crippling for most other people.

Her current task complete, Ashlyn turned about and surveyed the coffee house. Many stools and crates were placed throughout the ground floor for people to sit at, and the main counter where the grinder and filter would be was almost complete, for Gabriel was connecting the filter to the main water pipe of the building. Ashlyn placed another candle on top of the crate to give it a more 'formal' look.

"Do you even know how to make coffee?" she asked Gabriel and Silva, both of which had been part of the Angels and she had gotten to know them slightly over the last few days of working with them.

"How hard can it be?" Gabriel asked without looking back.

Silva looked back at Ashlyn and winked at the girl. "We got the beans, and we got the grinder and everything else, it can't be too difficult. Considering the price we'll be selling it, here's hoping no one is expecting gourmet. Are you done over there, by chance?"

Ashlyn gave the warrior a thumbs up. "All set."

"Good. Can you go upstairs to our stash and bring me down my nine-banger please?"

"My rifle too," Gabriel added, again not looking back.

"Sure thing." Ashlyn looked to Grim.

"I already hidden my weapons," said Grim.

"Where?" Silva asked. "I didn't see you poking about?"

"How do you hide weapons from those who might search for them?" Grim asked looking up from his clipboard with a broad smile. "You sit them right in front of everyone, right under their noses."

Silva rolled her eyes. "Whatever."

Ashlyn chuckled and crossed the room and ran up the stairs to the room where her and Silva's bed were set beside their packs. They managed to get some old mattresses from a vendor down the street as well as some extra blankets. Ashlyn crossed to the center of the room and pulled up one of the floorboards, and between the insulation and the boards were their stash of guns and recon equipment. She reached past her photon rifle and pulled out Silva's nine-banger; the shotgun-like pistol was heavy but she kept her grip on it as she closed the floor back up. She then proceeded to Grim and Gabriel's room and after finding the loose floor board there, soon came back downstairs with the rifle cradled in her arms as well.

When she returned downstairs she sat the gun on the counter, to which Silva took it and taped it under the countertop. She asked Gabriel where he wanted his and the man said to do the same thing on the far end. Ashlyn watched as the concealed weapon was tucked under the counter, and if Grim had hidden some around the shop as well, that meant that if anything were to happen, they would be armed and ready to make a quick escape. One of the tasks Ashlyn had been put in charge of was ensuring some getaway packs were ready near the back door leading out to an alleyway should they need to abandon the shop because their nationality is discovered.

"Not gonna happen, I think," said Gabriel one evening as he cooked a brief meal of dehydrated noodles. "Silva and I had been here for almost a week just to purchase the place, and we haven't had too much trouble. Only thing is we keep getting asked to work in the factories and constantly requested our passports to show we aren't full citizens."

"That alone is gonna come with it's own set of problems," said Grim. "Immigration will be on our asses more than ever now that Ashlyn and I here."

Most of this Ashlyn only listened partially, feeling as she had no say in the preparation for this. Still, it was interesting to see the precautions they were having to take in order to prepare for everything and anything.

"So, what now?" Ashlyn asked presently, now leaning against one of the walls. The room was set, all their gear stowed, the coffee machine was almost set up and the sign out front was in place. 'Chuck's Coffee' the sign read, which was Gabriel's alias as he was the one on the building's lease.

"Nothing that I can think of," Grim replied setting his clipboard down on one of the tables in order to help move a crate of beams over to the grinder. He poured some into it and started it up, by then Gabriel was off the machine and Silva was filling the tank with the waterline.

When the beans were grounded, Gabriel used a measuring cup to pour the contents into the filter. As the machine hummed and began to work, he turned to all the others smiling confidently. "I believe we are all set for business tomorrow if this works out."

"Finally," Silva sighed contentedly as she flopped into a nearby booth.

"Ashlyn," Grim said turning to her. "If you want to head for the roof to practice your swords play, I'll join you in a sec."

"Is that safe?" Ashlyn was worried about the drones and whatever surveillance tech was being used in the city. That, and unlike Markus she never practiced with a sword, only guns.

"We'll be fine," said Grim smiling. "I have a jammer device that Silva's matched the frequency of the drones. It'll give them blind spots of the rooftops while we are up there. As long as we turn it off beforehand and don't use it too often, we'll be good. We'll practice in the shop as well once we get into the groove of things here."

"Makes sense," Ashlyn nodded getting back up. "Alrighty then." She crossed the room back towards the stairs. "I'll get started."

"I'll join you in just a minute," Grim said as Ashlyn ascended up the stairs. As she did so, he went to Silva who already had the jamming remote ready for him and he took it and turned it on.

"Now that we're alone," Grim said more seriously to Silva, glancing over at Gabriel who was now watching the extraction of the brewing coffee. The other soldier didn't need to hear what Grim was going to talk to Silva about. "What exactly did she have in her bag?"

Ashlyn took the time to practice her stance and her thrusts using a wooden sword as she danced along the rooftop of the new coffee shop, performing what she saw other Angels do and simply focusing on maintaining her balance.

The rooftop of the shop was the tallest on the block but the other buildings towered far over her head, especially that of the Xerxan Castle. Down in the streets below, people were still milling about, some driving carts or other hovercraft, hardly anyone talking to one another. It reminded Ashlyn of how droids behaved, incapable of sparking true conversations with one another other than responses to commands of their masters. With so many other shops nearby as well as restaurants, she had expected there to be much greater conversations even greater than Levitika itself. And yet the people far below spoke in hushed tones to one another if at all, and all conversation ceased when a patrol of Xerxan Soldiers came marching by or a drone flew overhead.

Ashlyn ignored this and proceeded to just work on her form, fully confident about Grim's jamming device keeping the rooftop as invisible to surveillance as he claimed. The concrete roof clicked as she thrusted forward and her boots clapped against the man-made rock. Her hair which was tied into a ponytail bounced past her face as she attempted each move as flawlessly as she could in remembrance from Markus' training with Black and Grim. She was soon able to stop guessing however as Grim came up the roof hatch with his own wooden sword in hand.

"I can hear you down there," Grim said walking up to her. "You are too loud."

"Sorry," Ashlyn said feeling absolutely foolish.

"No don't be, it takes practice." He got into a stance and waited for Ashlyn to mirror his form before he continued, "I cannot show you everything I taught Markus as he is obviously very gifted, but I will make sure you know the basics of defending yourself in case we need to."

"Hopefully we don't need to," Ashlyn said making sure her feet were positioned the same way as her teacher.

"Good. Now, if I step here…" Grim crossed to the left while Ashlyn crossed to her left as if they were the hands of a clock going around each other and making a perfect circle. With every step he took, she mirrored almost perfectly, never crossing her legs or placing just part of her boot onto the ground, ensuring herself remaining solid.

"You have been watching," he said, smiling.

Ashlyn shrugged smiling back.

"Your footwork is good, but try landing your feet a little differently. Instead of being flat-footed, move your foot as you land. Heel-to-toe. In a way, you are almost gently placing your feet on the ground and you reduce sound. Not only with this give you more balance, but it will make you more silent should you have to sneak away. Now, I want you to swing at me and I will block your attack. I want you to pay attention as I do so."

"Okay," Ashlyn waited, and then using both hands took a swing at Grim's side. She had to remind herself not to go too softly for she knew he would scold her for doing so.

Grim immediately side-stepped and swung upwards, knocking Ashlyn's sword off course and forcing her to barrel right past him. She spun around fast and caught his counter-attack with the hilt of her sword.

"Not bad," Grim muttered as he shoved his student back and came at her again. He had moved in pretty close and nearly collided with Ashlyn, who swung sideways and knocked the sword aside and then swung once more, nicking Grim in the thigh. The soldier grunted as the wood smacked him.

"Very good," Grim said blocking Ashlyn's attack once more. "But let us see if you can be faster. Keep your knees bent."

This time he came at Ashlyn without mercy, for every time she blocked an attack another would come up fast to take its place. The relentless barrage of swings made Ashlyn's arms turn to spaghetti and she felt as if her legs were turning to lead. But still she pushed hard and accepted the blows that Grim landed on her, and in turn tried to score as many as she could on him. All the while Grim coached her on form and even demonstrated how to position herself at varying strikes.

After an hour, Grim stopped her mid-swing by gasping her sword with his free hand.

He panted, "That's enough, we'll practice more tomorrow after our first day."

"Okay," Ashlyn said letting herself plop down onto the ground with a sigh. Her face was beading with sweat and her ponytail made the back of her head and neck extremely humid.

She looked up at the sky which shined with a beautiful streak of pink like spread plankton over a pond overhead. Among the few clouds flew a hawk, its tail streaming behind it like a banner. Ashlyn watched as the bird turned and dove down towards her. She gasped and covered her head as the bird swooped over her, only to turn back around and land gingerly on the railing of the shop, immediately beginning to groom it's feathers. It peered at her and Grim with beady eyes and squawked before taking flight once more and flying off into the clouds.

"Damn bird," Ashlyn swore as Grim walked over to where the bird had landed. He took a seat with his back against the railing making it look like he was resting, but the reality was he was reaching down for the small note the hawk had dropped before taking off. He shoved it into his pocket and grinned at Ashlyn who did not fail to notice.

"Be nice," he said to Ashlyn. "That bird is going to be visiting us as often as it can, courtesy of our queen."

"Yeah, okay," Ashlyn said feeling foolish once again. It was weird being bossed around by adults again more vigorously.

Grim looked like he wanted to say something else to Ashlyn, and she had given him her full attention, ready for whatever was to come. In the end, he smiled and said, "Come on, I'll make us some dinner. Gabriel and Silva should be back with the rest of the supplies and groceries.

With that he stood and Ashlyn followed him back to the roof hatch to head back downstairs.

Gabriel had gone up to take a nap while Silva likewise retired to her room to read after Grim politely declined her offer to help with dinner, instead having Ashlyn assist with the cooking. The kitchen in the back of the shop was small but thanks to Gabriel it was functioning properly, and as Ashlyn cut the potatoes and the bell peppers, Grim was stirring some ground beef that was sizzling in the pan they brought from Nineveh along with some garlic and a good amount of black pepper. Ashlyn worried about the amount going in, thinking it would overpower the meal that Grim was calling 'Poor Man's Hash.' When the vegetables were cut he transferred the meat into a small bowl and used the accumulated fat to sauté the peppers along with some onion, telling Ashlyn to take the potatoes to the other range and par-boil them. She did as she was instructed, turning the other range on and then setting the pot of salted water and potatoes onto the glowing coil and then snagging a lid to cap it and cook it faster.

As Grim cooked he asked Ashlyn to grab him the wine he had Gabriel bought as well. At first when she gave it to him she thought the solider was going to drink it, but after the vegetables were softened up considerably with some fond forming at the bottom of the pain, he poured a shot or two's worth of wine into it, sending a great plumage of steam as the vegetables and fond were scraped off. He then added the ground beef and continued to stir it.

"Once those potatoes are just barely able to be poked through, drain them and we'll fry them," said Grim.

"Okay," Ashlyn said getting another shallow pan and filling it with another chunk of fat. She sat it beside the pot which was now a rolling boil, she asked the old mutant, "Were you a chef before you were a solider or something?"

Grim laughed at that. "No, I just enjoy good food. The chefs at the castle let me play around in the kitchens from time to time. It's just something I enjoy to do."

"It smells delicious," Ashlyn said, her stomach having been growling ever since they started this process.

"I sure hope so," Grim said with a wink. After a minute his expression turned serious as he focused on his own pan. "Ashlyn, I want to ask you something, and I want you to be honest with me."

Ashlyn looked at the soldier, confused and a little scared at first. "Sure, what's up?"

"Do not take this the wrong way, I'm not asking in order to scold you or anything. But, did you bring Buckweed here?"

Ashlyn's heart stopped in her chest. She thought about her personal pack and the contents inside, and she wondered if Silva had smelled something or if Grim was poking around. Neither of which she wanted even dare ask. When she didn't answer at first, Grim looked at her with a softer expression.

"C'mon, Ashlyn, you can tell me."

Ashlyn looked away, ashamed in a way. "Yes..."

"Where did you get it?" he asked.

She hesitated.

"Ashlyn."

"I got it from Vic," she said in a brash tone. She hadn't meant to, but she felt embarrassed and ashamed of it.

"Vic, eh?" Grim said nodding. "Makes a lot of sense. You realize that is illegal in Levitika, right? Hell, that's illegal in a lot of places."

"I know..."

Grim looked at Ashlyn again and she was afraid she might begin to cry. He glanced at the pot and said, "Check your potatoes, please."

She did so without a word, poking the potatoes with a fork to check their tenderness. They felt good enough and so she began to drain them through a strainer in the sink, her back facing Grim.

"How long have you been doing it?" asked Grim.

"I don't know..." She didn't dare to look back at him.

"Did you use to do it while in Nineveh?"

"Sometimes..."

Grim grunted. "Can't say I blame you, all things considered. When your clothes were changed upon making it to Levitika the first time, you thought you lost what you brought there, didn't you?"

Ashlyn turned and looked at the mutant who nodded. "How do you know that?"

"I'm part of the security force in the castle," said Grim. "It's my job to catch contraband. The only reason we didn't arrest you was because it was a small batch, and you had not been caught with it in the castle since."

"I've..." Ashlyn faltered, looking at the potatoes as if they could save her.

"Done it while you were training at Vic's range?" asked Grim.

She didn't answer.

"Ashlyn, look at me, honey."

Ashlyn did so, tears welling in her eyes.

Grim shook his head. "Don't do that. I'm not trying to give you a hard time. I'm talking to you about this because you're on this mission with us, and we need to be on the same level. Quite frankly, I don't care what you do in your free time. You never brining that crap to the castle has been proof enough that you respect Elizabetha's laws and don't want others to know anyway. But you bringing some on this mission is problematic. Do you understand?"

"Yes..." said Ashlyn, her voice just a mere whisper.

"Good," said Grim. "That stuff may not be as dangerous as other drugs, but it can become a problem if not cared for. I won't ask why you do it nor am I gonna ask you to explain why you brought it. I've done that stuff too, after my own family passed away."

Ashlyn looked down at her feet feeling weightless with this sense of guilt.

"But I am going to tell you that as long as you are in Xerxes with us, you need to be clear-headed and prepared for anything. We need to be highly alert, and as you will be caught and arrested if you smoke that stuff out in the streets or try to do it on the roof without my jammer, the whole mission will be jeopardized."

"I'm sorry," Ashlyn said.

Grim had lowered the heat on the pan and approached Ashlyn. He placed a hand on her shoulder and turned her around to face him again. He smiled softly as if he were talking to his own daughter and just wanted what was best for her.

"Don't be sorry," he said. "Be smart. I understand the need for comfort or even numbness, but we can't have that here. I'm not going to bring this up ever, and you'll never hear about me reporting you to the queen. That's not how I do things. What I am going to do, is respectfully ask you never to touch that stuff, and the first chance you get should you go out into the city, get rid of it. I'm counting on you to be focused, and so are Gabriel and Silva. Can you do that for me not as a fellow soldier and leader of this mission, but as a friend?"

Ashlyn wiped at her eyes of the minimal tears and nodded softly. "Okay, I can do that. I'm sorry, Grim."

"Don't be sorry," said Grim patting her shoulder. "Be smarter than that. Now..." He turned and placed the pan full of fat onto the same heated range that the water and potatoes had been boiling in. "Fish those out and get to frying. Our team needs to eat."

"Okay," said Ashlyn, and she carried out her tasks as she was told while Grim took a can of tomato paste and mixed in a little molasses into the frying pan of meat and vegetables. He never brought up the Buckweed again, and Ashlyn was not only grateful for that, but was more eager to follow his instructions as he had set out for her.

Dinner was delicious, the Poor Man's Hash being equally sweet, salty, and very filling. While Ashlyn and the other two Angels ate, Grim read the note the hawk had dropped off to them on the roof. They all sat together at one table covering each side, and Grim sat opposite of Ashlyn. As he read, Ashlyn noticed his smile getting wider and wider until finally he slammed the paper onto the crate with a laugh, startling no one at the table as Gabriel and Silva were watching as well.

"Well?" asked Gabriel eagerly.

"It's a go," Grim said smiling broadly. "Elizabetha is coming to Xerxes!"

"Wait, what?" Silva asked surprised.

"Really?" Ashlyn after swallowing some beef and potatoes.

"Yes, in three days she will be having dinner at the castle. What we need to do is find out where the dining hall is, and if possible hack a drone to take video of the meeting."

"Sweet!" Gabriel said clapping his hands together. "I've been wanting to get my hands on one of those drones.

"Hold on," said Silva to Grim. "Isn't this too soon?"

"Doesn't matter," said Grim. "The queen is coming whether we are ready or not, it's our job to get into position and prepare for the meeting. While we run the shop, we'll take turns plotting our infiltration. I'll go out tonight and see what I can find and then we will discuss it in the morning before we open."

Silva still looked nervous but she nodded and said she would be sure to map out the city this evening as well.

"Good," said Grim. "We'll set up sniping positions around the castle as well once we find out the meeting place, and while Gabriel is controlling the drone, Silva, you and Ashlyn will monitor what is going on and ensure the queen's safety."

"What about you?" asked Ashlyn.

"I'll be looking for a way to infiltrate the castle and be there when the dinner takes place," said Grim. He winked and added, "Trust me. If the dinner does not go exactly how Elizabetha plans we need to be prepared for anything, be it a quick extraction or an escape.

"Agreed." Silva nodded. She looked off to the side as something- a thought came over her like a cloud.

"What' troubling you?" Grim asked.

"Nothing, sir."

"Lighten up," Gabriel said poking Silva in the shoulder with a long index finger. Silva glared at him and this only made him laugh. "We've done this a million times, it'll be a walk in the park."

"I know…"

Grim was staring at Ashlyn now. She hadn't realized she had been zoning out until he did so and she felt embarrassed by it. "What do you think, Ashlyn?"

"I think it's a great plan," she answered.

"But…?" Gabriel mused.

Ashlyn shrugged. "It just isn't the same without Markus," she admitted. She had spoken how close she and her friend had become in leaving Nineveh, as both Gabriel and Silva were intrigued by the story of how they arrived in Levitika in the first place.

Ashlyn shrugged again. "I don't know, I just miss them. He, and Esmerelda.

Silva looked at Ashlyn sympathetically. "You were pretty close the princess, I remember. She's a sweetheart, isn't she?"

Ashlyn smiled. "Yeah, she was."

Grim offered a small smile. "Hey, keep your chin up. Markus has a good head on his shoulders. I am sure he'll be back before anything happens. And don't worry about Esmerelda. That girl is tougher than you think."

"I know," Ashlyn said. "It's just…" She found it difficult to say. Did she miss them so much that she was worrying something would happen to them? Did she have no faith in her friends? Her…

"They're your family Ashlyn," Grim said speaking her thoughts. She looked up at the soldier with wide eyes. "And family always comes back. No matter what. Markus will be back, and Esmerelda will be with you when all of this is over. Let's just make sure we are set to go here, and be prepared for whatever comes next."

Ashlyn smiled and nodded at Grim. "Okay. Thank you Grim. That means a lot."

Grim smiled and then took the last bite of his own meal. For the first time in Ashlyn's life she felt as if she was talking to someone who was actually meant to be her father. Grim spoke to her with the reassurance a father should give his child. Even in the kitchen though he didn't treat her as if he were her father but instead a friend, that tenderness and care only solidified her appreciation of the mutant general, and for the first time, Ashlyn felt her heart torn in three different ways.

Not only was she afraid for Esmerelda and Markus, she was afraid for Grim and these two other Angels, and hoped everything would work out here in Xerxes- that everything would be alright.

Markus

"Do you think of them often?" Abram said out of the blue while Markus was working on casting a ball of light in the palm of his hand.

The sun was about to set, casting it's ever beautiful colors across the sky and the sea glistened for as far as the eye could see. They were on the beach and Abram was sitting in the sand while Markus was attempting to cast an illusion that there was a Badrat in his hand. He had not yet told Markus that it indeed looked like a Badrat, and had only asked a question that took Markus off guard and forced him to release the spell. His eyes and the crystals in his auto-limb dimmed to their natural color and he turned to look at Abram.

"Think of who?" he asked, confused.

"The people you've killed of course," Abram asked.

Immediately images of people falling from the sky, people being stabbed of beheaded in Nineveh, as well as the witch Lameika's brother, Lee who he watched fall to the valley below during the battle against the Leviathan.

Markus scowled, the question offending him both in retrospect as well as for causing him to think on that more. He always tried to never think about that- to try and forget the faces of people he had killed in that battle. It was easier to forget them for there were too many explosions and many fell from the sky, he never had to look them in the eye when he killed them. During the fight in Nineveh, however, he had watched people get shot and stabbed and other times reduced to piles of hot ashes. He saw the pain in their faces, the agony that it was the end for them. All these memories came rushing him like a flood, and all that he tried to forget came rushing back.

Markus looked down at his feet and muttered, "I try not to."

"Why is that?" Abram asked tenderly- almost carefully as if he did not want to upset his student. "Keep in mind, Markus, you did not murder those people, no matter how much you believe you did."

"You were reading my mind."

Abram nodded. "You are not the only person who regrets killing in war."

Markus nodded almost numbly. "Why do you care about that?"

"Because you do."

"I try not to think about all that."

"And yet you do."

Markus looked at Abram and the old man said, "There is no shame in thinking about those men and women who died in battle. If you took pleasure in what you did or think it a game as most people do, then that would be a different story. Still, you are young, and you never once thought of killing anyone on purpose, except for one person."

Markus knew exactly who Abram was referring to. "That was different then. I was a kid, I didn't understand why it had to be."

"It is," Abram agreed. "But war is different. War changes people, and not often for the better. The fact that you think of those who had fallen, means you do consider them as equals still, and not some obstacles to get past."

Markus nodded, and after a long time of thinking about it and Abram patiently waiting, he said, "I see them every time I close my eyes. The battle in the sky, I was just focused on making it to the Leviathan alive, I never thought about the people falling around me. In Nineveh, when I saw the faces of all who were killed, whether they be enemy or foe, I see them. But the faces of those I killed with my own hands, I can't forget them no matter how hard I try. I wonder if they left families behind when they died, what their last thoughts were, and in the end I just feel sick. The thoughts make me almost afraid to remember the faces."

Abram rose from the sands and stepped out of his shoes. He waded into the waters and upon approaching Markus, placed a hand on his student's shoulder. Markus looked up to see the old man smiling.

"It's okay, Markus. There are reasons we remember those we kill if we had little choice. I can feel the guilt on your heart, so let us speak plainly as men who had to do things we aren't proud of. Tell me, you fought in Nineveh, because why?"

Markus frowned in thought but then replied, "I did it to save as many people as I could. I fought to protect Ashlyn, the queen, Esmerelda, and others. But I still feel like I failed some of them."

"You cannot blame yourself for something you had no control over. You did your best, and your cause was great. You fought not only to survive, but to protect. You killed, so that others could live."

"But does that make it right?" Markus asked. "I still killed them. And now I cannot forget the faces of the fallen."

"I once met a general during my time in the Mad King's courts," said Abram looking out at the sea. "He was good at doing what he did because he was completely numbed by it. He saw war not as a necessary evil as most good men do, but as a game. He often believed that life itself was a game of stakes, and man's greatest trait of divination."

"Why divination?" asked Markus, curious as to how such an awful thing where lives were often lost or destroyed could be taken as casually as a game of chess or poker.

"Because to him, war was god."

"I don't understand..." said Markus.

"And thank the Lord you don't," said Abram nodded respectfully. "In his eyes as well as many in the world, war is the ultimate game. In a way, he is right, for war had been around long before mankind had ever existed, and has altered the world many times over long before The Fall. And still, no matter how many wish for war to never resurface, as long as there is man, war will endure. But in his case and many, this separates themselves from man, because in the end they see mankind as nothing more than pawns, obstacles, and nuisances. War endures not because of men, but because men love it. And those who love it, shall worship it as the god it had become in their hearts. Such men… they are no longer men," Abram says again almost bitterly. "Such men, are now monsters."

He turned to Markus, who was mesmerized by this sudden rant. As far as he was concerned, Abram was a man who had seen his share of the worst of mankind, not just in the creation of the crystals, but of what war makes of men.

"I tell you this not to frighten you or make you feel hopeless," said Abram. "I tell you this as a way to look at your position through different eyes. Do you think that this war Levitika is waging against the Northern Wastelands is justified?"

"Of course I do," said Markus.

"And do you believe it is right? Despite the sacrifices that will be made because of it?"

Markus thought about this looking out at the sea, and at last he said, "I just wish so many didn't have to die."

"You take no pleasure in those you have killed and perhaps will have to in the future."

"No," Markus said shaking his head. "I don't think I could stand myself if I could- "Anymore than I already do," he added.

Abram nodded. "Your humanity is what defines you, not just the actions you present. You do not fight because you enjoy it, you fight because you have to. War might be a great evil, but sometimes it is necessary. And you keeping those who have fallen both friend and foe in your heart, means that you are not a murderer as you believe."

"Then what am I?" asked Markus.

"It makes you a warrior." When Markus remained silent Abram continued, "A murderer, is not what you are. A murderer kills without reason or conscious. He doesn't care about the faces he sees. You do. That does not make war any easier, but you fought so you could protect others. The reason you cannot forget is because you are not meant to forget. Not yet, anyway. Maybe there is something you are to learn from your experience. I am saddened that you had to witness such things at a young age, but you are mature to keep going. You try hard for your friends, your family. And that is what makes fighting in war worth it. To protect those you love."

Markus looked out beyond the sea and sighed. "I still feel awful."

"Give it time, but don't forget those faces. Yes, it is tragic for them. But in the end, you need to consider, what is more important? The life of a soldier that is trained to kill you no matter what, or whom you wish to protect and preserve?"

Markus grunted clenching his fists. "I want to believe all life is the same. It doesn't matter who you are, a life is a life, and a person is a person."

"All men are equal then?" Abram asked.

Markus nodded. But then he looked to Abram feeling nervous. "That's the wrong way to think of it, isn't it?"

Abram shook his head/ "No, in fact, that is the answer to this riddle."

Markus looked back to Abram confused. "What riddle?"

"The riddle of who you are when it comes to war," Abram answered. "All life is equal, no matter what race, rich or poor, good or bad, all life is equal in a sense. Does that not mean some deserve to die, absolutely not. Some *do* deserve death. But the fact that you are able to look at your enemies as human beings is important. Yes, war is hell, but it is those who are able to come out of it and still think of their fellow men and foes as human as they are, are those who do not belong in war. You fight to protect those you love, they fought to destroy. You claimed your right as Keeper not because of some sense of bloodlust or even self-righteousness, but because you believe it is the right thing to do when you think of those who you protect with your life."

"But don't they think they are doing the right thing as well?" asked Markus. "If that's the case, then who is really in the right?"

"Think about this," Abram said. "Say one nation begins to conquer and destroy and occupy, because they believe that is God's will? Say a second one, just as strong and influential, rises as well to push back and reclaim what was stolen in their own name, because they believe that God was on their side. Who is in the right?"

Markus thought about this and shrugged, saying, "No one?"

Abram shook his head. "The answer is more simple than that. The one who is in the right, is the one who will write the history afterward."

"I don't understand…"

"History is won by the victor. When the Mad King first rose to power, it was at first because he wanted to unite the Northern Wastelands. His cause was to eventually find peace within a nation that was originally only occupied by men and women who desired more than what they had. In the end, his reign survived long enough to create a more terrifying evil and he became relished within. And yet his reign remained, as he had made history and therefore it is written by him. Same goes for Levitika and the Great Owl, who waged war against him because they wanted to change the course of history. We can both agree that it was for the greater good, but in the end, war is the defining factor. The best answer, is that war is fought for the sake of one's endurance. Be it for wanting the better or for the worst, at the end of the day, neither is right, nor wrong."

"Then who defines what is evil and what is good?" asked Markus. "If that's the case, why should we assume that the Mad King was evil in the end, and Levitika is the side of good?"

"You don't," said Abram. "Good and evil are indeed opposing forces, but neither side has gray areas. Those who fight for the side of good, not all are doing it just for that. Some, are just trying to protect their homes and their families. Same goes for those of opposing armies. At the end of the day, there is only one true fact: War will forever endure, but the wars that we fight within our own lifespans, those are the only ones that matter in the present."

Markus stared at Abram for a long time before asking him, "Why are you telling me this? Really?"

"Because I want you to think of this war for the Northern Wastelands and your mission to close the gateways to The Dreaming, not as the true divine way, but a necessary evil. And the fact that you answer with such confidence that all men are equal, means you are not lost in war's embrace. And I pray that as you continue your journey, you will never grow to love war. That you will only do it, if it will protect the people you love and the liberties you believe in."

"But is that right to think?" asked Markus.

"What do you think?"

Markus sighed and shook his head. "I just want to protect my friends, and I want to make the world a better place."

Abram nodded. "Two worthy goals. And hopefully you will always do your best to uphold such values."

Markus looked down at his hands, his real one playing with the fingers from his auto-limb. "Do you really believe I have what it takes Abram?"

"If your family does, I don't see why you should not." Abram looked down at his student's auto-limb. "You've suffered so much, and sacrificed a lot to save the ones you care about. A heart like that, has no way of faltering even in the face of war and all that is to come."

"But the body is weak," Markus pointed out.

"And the heart is the most deceitful thing in the world," Abram countered. "But, what the heart can overcome with the help of both body, mind, and soul, then it can do no wrong."

"Like when you are in The Dreaming?" Markus asked.

Abram smiled, a small twinkle seemed to flash in his eyes. "Precisely."

Markus grinned to himself. He then went serious and asked Abram, "What about The Eldest?"

"What do *you* think?"

Markus pursed his lips. "Well, he was human once right? But all the stories I hear about him tells me about how truly evil he is, regardless of his original intentions. What he did to his own people, and sacrificing his servants." His hand went down to the crystals. "Even Abner. It is hard to picture him as once being somewhat of a 'decent' person. Does that makes sense?"

Abram grunted. "Well, there is his childhood to consider, as well as how he was raised but there comes a point where someone is no longer a child. The child inside The Mad King is very much gone, I'm afraid. Just like the child in you might be gone. Actually- that is not quite right. The child that we all were once lives in us until the day we die. All the good memories and the bad as we take those steps of being merely children will live on in us forever. But there comes a point, Markus, when the child grows up. But some don't grow up, still enjoying their games."

"Like war..." said Markus.

Abram nodded. "Correct. Yes, the spirit that once kindled the child is there, but when you become an adult, you are no longer completely the person you once was. And I am afraid that in order to gain full power from The Dreaming, The Eldest gave up the one thing that actually made him who he was- he sacrificed his past."

Markus nodded, thinking about the story of his son now being used as a makeshift battery in order to keep the city of Levitika afloat. He thought about his discovery of the Second Death which had plagued him along with the faces he had seen lost in the battles he had survived. Regardless of The Eldest's original intentions, he had lived long enough and had seen enough to strive to become more than he already was, his original goals lost to the idea of complete control.

And all the people The Eldest had murdered, just to become the monster everyone tells Markus he is...

"What made the Seven so special?" asked Markus. "The spirits now trapped in the crystals we have now?"

"That is one of the things I have wondered ever since we discovered how to create the crystals," said Abram. "When the Mad King had first discovered the Well of Souls, he had been approached by men who had worshiped the volcano, and told him the things they had heard how to save his son. When his son was turned into a crystal gateway, he strove to find a way to save him, and in the end he murdered those whom he believed deceived him, and proceeded to try to make more in an attempt to bring his son back. Hence, the continuation of the Second Death. So many lives were lost, children who was believed to be the most ideal of imaginative creatures and even newborn babies, all lost and then moving on to just anyone the Mad King felt able to get his hands on, even going so far as to wage wars on his own kingdoms in order to gather sacrifices."

Abram looked down at the waters that sloshed about his and Markus' ankles. The memories of what had become of The Eldest's desperation seeming to weigh on the old man's shoulders like the earth itself.

He continued, saying, "What made the seven so special out of the twelve that were capable of surviving the Second Death? I believe it was the same reason The Eldest was able to transfer his soul into a crystal, and therefore transfer it again into his artificial body. Not just because he wondered if there was a way to transfer one's soul into another body, but because there was little left of him left to truly remain. The spirits trapped in the crystals, just like I had mentioned when it comes to those who fight in war, all had lost some part of themselves in the process up to finally agreeing to the Second Death. They had wanted it, believing that they would be able to come reborn in ways of power rather than be used. In the end, they were all betrayed just so that The Eldest could keep it all.

 And in turn, he has become the monster of The Dreaming, this time without boundaries or guilt or conscious."

Markus frowned. "That's harsh. To just give up who you are..."

"That is the problem with power, I am afraid," said Abram. "For some, they are content with the power they already have. Just like with war, they are content with serving their country, protecting their loved ones, and that is good enough. For some, once they get a taste, they... how should I put this? They crave it, they need more."

"They grow to love it, just like war," said Markus.

Abram nodded. "And instead of going the natural path of learning such things, they are willing to sacrifice anything- anything in the world to achieve even the darkest of powers no one should ever mess with."

"So, The Eldest is indeed gone then? There is no hope in bringing him back? Does he not deserve to live?"

Abram smiled. "Oh Markus, your naïvetés for believing in the value of life is admirable. All who live deserve to die, and all who have died deserve to live as a wise man once said. But there *does* come a point where there is no hope of saving someone no matter how equal we believe them to be. Whether it be in battle, or in spirit, some people are far from gone. The Eldest is no longer a human bound by humanity, but a monster, an evil being twisted into the very fear that could destroy the world whom he had grown to hate."

Abram took Markus by the shoulder and began to lead him back to the shore. As they trudged through the waters he said, "And if he manages to escape, there is no telling what horrors wait for us beyond the gateway. Years and years of being trapped in there, you know what it does to your friend Abner and his partner in your arm. The Eldest is sure to have gained much more knowledge more terrible than we can ever imagine. There is no other way, Markus. The Eldest cannot be set free. No matter what. Who he was, what he once believed in, doesn't matter anymore. It is gone. All that is left is the hollow shell of a beast."

Markus nodded, understanding as they stepped out of the water and continued to trudge across the wet sand to where their boots sat. "I still find it sad though. It all still feels like a big game to some…"

"That is what makes you special. You care despite knowing that you have to do what is necessary for those you care about. Your love for others is what separates you from The Eldest, and that is how you can beat him and make sure he stays in his prison forever."

Abram then took out his crystal, which was glowing orange this time and held it out to Markus. "You are the only one capable of stopping him, Markus. And now, I will teach you what no one else can do: For your final test for tonight, I want you to free the spirit trapped within this crystal."

What is Mercy

<u>Markus</u>

Markus stared at the crystal, and felt a conscious touching his own, almost as if a child was begging him for something. Amidst the sounds he was hearing, he caught but a single word: *Please*.

This was different than the consciousness of The Eldest. This spirit, despite perhaps having done such atrocities in their lifetime in a way, was repenting in exchange for mercy. This spirit who had contributed to the most awful of things a human being was capable of, wished nothing more than to be set free, and to never again be used as some tool.

He looked up to Abram. "What do I do?" he asked.

Abram smiled. "To destroy the gateway, you must sever what ties the soul to the crystal. And I must warn you, what ties each one is one of their darkest fears. You know how to manipulate the human mind now, to cast illusions. In a way, you are capable of entering their minds through The Dreaming and finding out their darkest secrets and fears. The crystals, well, let's think of them like human minds. Deep inside this crystal, is the entrance to The Dreaming, but only through the very thing that the soul within in tortured with to sustain the power of the crystal for many years."

Abram extended his arm, offering the orange gem to the boy. "Take it Markus, and I will guide you best I can. I am incapable of such a leap, but you- you are The Keeper. You are the one to set the man inside here free. I have faith in you."

He dropped the crystal into Markus' receiving hand and immediately the bond seemed much stronger now as he stared into the glimmering stone. He looked up at Abram who continued to speak. "Close your eyes. Imagine you are trying to find the source of your enemy's fear, but instead looking to help a friend. To ease the pain, to set him free. End the war that has been raging inside of it all these years. Abner will help you, as well as your new friends. Enter The Dreaming, and do what you must."

Abram's voice soon faded, and Markus felt as if he was floating. He took a deep breath, preparing himself for whatever was to come and at last, he closed his eyes, feeling the sensation of fading away and when he opened his eyes after a few short seconds, he gasped.

He saw that he was no longer on a beach, but on some kind of rock island in the vastness of space. Stars twinkled and shot past him in a flurry of colors and more rocky islands seemed to float throughout the space between the stars. What caught Markus off guard the most however was the giant jelly-fish like creature floating overhead. Its jelly glowed bright purple and its tentacles that shot lightning of similar color were long and black. It even looked like there was a single golden eye within the jelly looking down at Markus as if it was hungry.

"Now I have officially, seen everything," Markus muttered to himself.

"Not quite," a voice said behind him and Markus jumped at the sight of Abner right behind him, his armor shining dimly in the starlight. The owls on his shoulder pads seeming to be in the middle of a great scream.

"Did you have to do that?" Markus asked the old warrior.

Abner smiled. "It is good to see you again, Markus, and to speak with you again. I am sorry I could not speak to you about all of this before, but I hope you can understand my reasons why."

"I do," said Markus. He looked all around and said, "We should figure this out before The Eldest sniffs us out."

"Agreed." Abner then looked behind him. "There are some people I would like you to meet before we continue."

"Meet?" Markus asked and Abner stepped aside for him to see. There were indeed two people behind the old warrior, and Markus figured they were the spirits of the other crystals.

The one he recognized as Nokama was a short woman with long black hair that reached down to her hips, and at her hips were two blades. She wore a simple leather outfit with broad shoulders and black boots; and her eyes gleamed like a cat's above a pair of high cheek bones. The other one Markus assumed was from Abram's crystal, for this man wore a fur clock of white fur over what looked to be power armor. His face was hidden by a bandanna and his hair was dark and cropped as if someone just attacked him with a pair of scissors.

"You already know Nokama from her presence it seems," Abner said. "The man here is Essau."

Markus bowed his head. "It is an honor to meet you two," he said.

Nokama raised an eyebrow. "The boy has manners. How quaint."

Markus bit his lip to keep himself from saying anything. He looked back out into the vastness of space. "So, this is The Dreaming?" he asked.

"In all it's glory," Abner said stepping up beside him. "Every dream that every living creature has is formed here, and each star represents a single person."

"Incredible," Markus said shaking his head in wonder.

"Indeed," Essau appeared opposite of Abner. He breathed in deep and turned to his companions. "Once again, I thank you for allowing me to go first."

"The kid needs us apparently," Nokama said not even looking at Markus as she said so. "So we might as well see what we have in store for us."

"Nokama," Abner said calmly but sternly. "Do not hold it against the boy. He needs us in order to free the others. We shall be last. I have foreseen it."

"Hopefully The Eldest doesn't foresee us first," Nokama muttered but she said nothing else.

Abner returned his attention to the boy. "Markus, Essau was the first to be bonded to a crystal. He is the oldest of The Seven."

"Oh," Markus said amazed.

"If anyone deserves to be freed of this curse first, it is him. Now please, Essau if you would, lead on."

"Right." And Essau leapt off the rocky island only to float in the air beckoning for Markus and the others to follow. Markus looked to Abner for an explanation.

"Come," the spirit said and taking a leap of his own he joined his companion along with Nakoma who waited impatiently for Markus.

He took a deep breath and leapt off the rock crying out, sure that he was going to fall- only to be suspended in the air as if something was holding him up. He grinned at Abner who nodded and beckoned him to follow. Markus found it easy to follow, all he had to do was think about following and his body seemed to float after the spirits. They passed many stars and creatures of elegant beauty and terror, and Markus caught up to Abner to ask him, "What are those things?"

He was pointing to another monster- this one appearing to look like a giant piranha with tentacles rather than a tail.

"They are the manifestations of what you call Nightmares. They are spirits that bring out what humans fear the most and when they are dreaming, apply them to the dream."

"Are they dangerous?"

"Only if they feel threatened. But we are usually here, and you are not. But since you are with us, I don't believe we will have any trouble- yet."

"There," Essau said pointing down and Markus looked to see that it was another island of stone, but this one had something that resembled a giant alter of blackened stone; a bright orange light seemed to shine out of the alter like a portal.

The four landed on the island which was also being circled by many bat-like creatures like imps that screeched at the newcomers with distaste. Essau walked closer to the portal and seemed to be looking inside the light. He approached this beacon as if it were the most beautiful, and yet most terrible thing imaginable.

He said as if speaking to the light itself, "So many memories, so much pain, it will soon be all over…"

Markus walked up beside the spirit and peered inside.

In the mandarin light he saw images of people being shot and stabbed, and he realized he was looking through the eyes of Essau. More scenes of bloody battles took place until one came up that chilled Markus to his very bones. He watched as a woman and child were cowering in the corner, begging for Essau to stop. But they were soon cut down by the sharp end of an axe that Markus saw just in time to turn his face away. When he looked again, he saw the warrior bellowing like a raging bull, an infant clutched in his great hands and he hurled the screaming baby towards the ground at his feet, and Markus thankfully turned just in time before the child was murdered.

"Yes," the spirit said beside him sadly. "I was a monster, and I deserve a place like this. To remember all of the horrible deeds I have committed in the name of The Eldest. I gave up everything, believing I could gain immortality as promised. Instead, I was forced to serve still as a prisoner, trapped in this own hell. I…"

Essau raised his head towards the 'sky' where the beacon of light disappeared into the vastness of the void beyond. Markus looked up to see only to look back at the warrior, now seeing him crying.

"I am unworthy," said Essau, his voice strong despite the tears rolling down the man's cheeks. "Forgive me, for I am unworthy…"

He was not speaking to Markus, but at the same time, it felt like the spirit was.

Markus was about to ask who it was when he felt something- like a buzzing in his ears that sounded somewhat like a guttural growl. Abner suddenly went pale and serious- Nokama remained stone-faced but the color drained from her face as well.

"He is coming," the old spirit said.

Markus didn't need to ask Abner who he meant. He had felt this presence before, and it was accumulating in his own head, as if threatening to swell it to the point of bursting.

"Markus," said Nokama impatiently as her eyes scanned the horizon. "Whatever you are about to do, do it now!"

"How?" Markus asked in a frenetic tone. He looked at Abner. "Tell me what I need to do!"

"We will help you," Abner said placing a hand on Markus shoulder which caused his own crystal to glow brightly. "Nokama, come."

The other spirit came, and she too placed her hand upon Markus' opposite shoulder, her own crystal glowing brightly.

Abner looked as Essau, whose back remained to them as he stared into the beacon of light. "Are you ready to pass on Essau?"

"Yes," Essau said and turning to face them he bowed to Markus. "I shall never forget you, Keeper." And walking backwards towards the portal he leapt and the orange light seemed to suck him inside, and he was gone. The light now dimming to a dull gray, and then black as shadows.

"Now," Abner said his eyes glowing brightly. "Hold out your hands." Markus did so with his palms facing the alter. "Now, let us give our friend peace at last."

Markus took a breath as he felt something tugging on him and he looked down to his auto-limb arm to see that both crystals were glowing. He focused all of his energy on the portal and pulsed. Arcs of bright blue lighting shot from his hands and entered the portal. The island itself began to shake and the Nightmares above screeched and flew off into the realm, but Markus noticed none of this. For he felt himself seeing through the eyes of the late Essau.

He felt his body pouring energy into the portal but in his eyes Markus saw everything that haunted Essau here in The Dreaming. He watched through the warriors own eyes as he butchered soldiers who dared opposed him either through a shot of a nine-banger or by the sharp end of a power-axe. Blood seemed to fly like rose petals in front of him as each soldier and citizen fell. Markus cried out as he watched a small child scream before being shot by Essau.

What is this? Markus cried out in a soundless scream. *This isn't what I wanted, I want out of here!*

Be strong Markus, the voice of Abner called out somewhere in The Nothing. *We are almost done.*

I... can't!...

The scene shifted and Markus watched as the body that was not his kicked down a door revealing a screaming woman who took their daughter across the room only to cower in a corner as the body marched up to them, his axe which was dripping crimson in hand.

"Essau!" the woman screamed out her hair a mess and tears dripping down her face, she tried to shield the child who was balling behind her. "Stop this right now!"

But even as she begged, Markus watched helplessly as the hands that were not his raised the axe. "Sorry honey," the voice that was no doubt Essau's said as the axe came down. Markus tried to pull back on the arm's but it was too late, for the axe came down and cleaved both the mother and daughter in two.

Markus cried out and he found himself on his knees in complete and utter darkness. The horror he had witnessed had broken him down and he began to sob. He soon felt a presence next to him and he looked up and stood furiously as he saw that it was Essau. Both of them lost in the black of the warrior's sin.

"I do not blame you for hating me. The crimes I have committed are unforgiveable. But during my time here in The Dreaming, seeing myself doing that day after day, night after night, there was nothing I wanted to do more than to tell them I am sorry."

Essau looked away ashamed. "I am a monster, which is why I was sacrificed for The Eldest's gateway. I deserved such a punishment. But now I am ready to finally meet my maker, and if He wills it, apologize to my wife and daughter." He turned back to Markus. "I do not expect you to look at me like some poor unfortunate soul. But I do thank you for officially letting me be free from this world, and so that I can have my chance to end up where I deserve in the next."

Markus swallowed, realizing his mouth was dry and nodded. "I hope you find peace in the next journey," he croaked stiffly still angry for what he had witnessed, but he truly hoped that Essau would find peace at last, anything to destroy this gateway and prevent the monster that would give such an order to Essau would never be free in the world again.

Essau smiled as his figure appeared to glow a bright white, and the whole darkened room appeared to be lit up in brilliant light that was blinding, and Markus covered his eyes as the light shined brighter and brighter until all was white as snow, and Markus saw no more.

"Well done," said a man's voice that was neither Abner's voice, nor Essau's, not even Abram's.

Markus cried out as he returned back to the real world, and in his hand the orange crystal cracked as if he crushed it like a pebble. A bright light shot through the crack, and a whisper of light that looked somewhat like smoke seemed to float out of it and rise into the night sky; waving above it slightly as if unsure where to go, only to disappear from view after it reached a height that Markus and Abram could see no more.

Markus looked back down at the Light Crystal and saw that the light and glow dimmed until the stone itself looked as fragile as glass, and as dead as a broken light bulb. And before his eyes Markus watched as the crystal seemed to disintegrate into dust in his very hand, only to be carried off by the wind never to be seen, or least of all used again. Markus fell back on his side exhausted and began to sob.

Abram placed a hand on Markus' back, calming him in a patient and kind matter. For a long time the only sound that was heard was the crashing waves above

Markus' cries of anguish. All that he had witnessed, he wondered if Essau truly deserved peace at last, for his soul to move on to wherever one goes once they truly die.

To his surprise, Black's voice said in Markus' mind, *He has repented. He is forgiven.*

This calmed Markus somewhat, and Abram though still concerned for the boy's wellbeing was smiling as he held him still. Eventually the sobbing stopped and Markus pushed himself back up wiping his eyes dry.

He shuddered and sat there beside Abram trembling and feeling as if he would vomit, but he held onto himself and did not let go even after the sensation finally faded away like an illness finally being lifted.

"Are you okay?" the old man asked with intense concern in his eyes.

Markus shook his head. "It was horrible," he eventually whispered. "He... he killed his own family, Abram..."

"I know," Abram said. "He had told me when I acquired him. What he did was a horrible deed, his bloodlust unquenchable until all he wanted was one thing. But, he made up for it in the end."

Markus stared at his teacher incredulously. "How?" he demanded. "After what I saw, you can't possibly expect me to believe that he 'made up' for that act."

Abram sighed patiently as if he was dealing with a small child rather than a teenager. "After he massacred his homeland, Essau went to The Mad King and demanded his reward which was promised immortality. But The Mad King told him what his true intentions were and Essau in his anger slaughtered many of The Eldest's soldiers. He was the one who delayed the Eldest's transformation, until he was eventually captured and taken to The Well of Souls to be sacrificed for the creation of his crystal. But as he was trapped in The Dreaming, all he could see and remember was the sin he had committed against his own family. He never forgave himself for that, and it is good that he never forgot his deed. For in the end, he realized what he had done and tried his best to stop The Eldest. And that was his greatest deed in his life he could have ever done for others. It by no means excuses him for the atrocities he had committed, both before and after murdering his family, but he tried to make it right in life, and in his Second Death, he repented. That is not something many people can do. And besides, who are we to judge, once one is truly spiritually dead?"

Markus while still disgusted by what he saw, understood what Abram meant and nodded, sniffling and wiping at his tear-stricken eyes. "I still feel sick when I think of that. I still see it happening again, and again." He lowered his head into his hands and shook it violently. "I can't take it Abram, I don't want this in my head..."

Abram sighed sadly. "I am sorry Markus. I had no idea that it would require you to see such horrible deeds from Essau's point of view." He rubbed his student's back hoping to comfort him more. "But you did what you could, and you were strong. I am proud of you, and I know Abner and Nokama are as well. You saved Essau, and stopped one gateway from helping The Eldest escaped. In the end, it was all for the greater good."

Markus nodded and wiped his face once more. "Will this burden go away?" he asked.

Abram nodded. "Just like the faces you try so hard to forget, it will all go away, eventually. When peace is obtained for you, and you are meant to. Do not dwell on them, let them take their course and eventually they will be gone. If you think about it, it will take longer for it to go away. Think not of the man you laid to rest and his sin, think of the deed you have done for the greater good."

Markus sighed. "Just like war..."

Abram nodded. "Exactly." He was silent for a moment in thought and then continued, "Think of it this way: You showed pity, to release Essau from his torment. You saw what he had done, but it was pity that stayed your hand and allowed you to show mercy and release him from his torment."

Markus took a shaky breath and eventually the trembling stopped. He took another deep breath, and sighed. "Thank you, Abram."

Abram smiled kindly. "You're welcome, Markus. You really are a strong man. You are indeed The Keeper."

"Even if I didn't want to be?"

"Even then. I have met many people in my life, but there's something special about you."

Markus couldn't help but chuckle at that. It helped to take his mind off the barbarism he had witnessed. "Thing is, I never *felt* special. Even Black said being special had nothing to do with it."

"There are other kinds of special, Markus," said Abram. "Your heart is pure, and your strength knows no bounds when you put your mind to it. I can see it when I see your memories of working in your garage working on stuff most your age wouldn't even touch. I certainly wouldn't be able to fix an old Behemoth. That really wasn't my direction of knowledge."

Markus tried a small smile. "Thanks."

"Being The Keeper isn't all you are. It's who you are that makes you unique, and I believe that is why you were chosen. I have no doubt."

Abram stood then and approached Markus, reaching out and helping him to his feet and then he began to walk back to the cabin. "Come. Let us sleep and rest. You are tired and weary, and need to rest. We will continue our training tomorrow."

Markus followed not saying a word as in the back of his mind he heard two voices speaking as one. *You did it. Thank you, Markus.*

But Markus didn't feel like he deserved thanks anymore than he deserved to witness the cruelty of Essau. It made him wonder what all the other spirits had done in order to obtain what they believed to be immortality. In particular, he wondered what Abner had done, and as he wondered this, he felt the spirit's consciousness fade away as if ashamed, and he only felt more disdain for him.

Perhaps sensing this, Abner while walking with Markus back to the cabin proposed this question. "What is the opposite of war, Markus?"

"I don't know," he answered. "Peace?"

"No, not quite," said Abner. "War is often waged for the sake of peace, as Levitika is doing so now. Peace is a goal, not the opposite."

"Then what is it?" demanded Markus.

"Mercy," said Abner. "Forgiveness. Forgiveness of oneself, and others. Mercy defines who remain men after war. Did Essau deserve mercy? That is not for us to decide as he no longer has influence over the world. Only the one who seeks to use the power of his corrupted soul has influence, and though you could have used his crystal for yourself or simply surrender it to The Eldest, you have instead showed him mercy not just for him, but for the good of others."

"But does he deserve peace in the end?" asked Markus. "Does he deserve to rest in peace?"

"That is no longer our concern," said Abner albeit not absently or out of cruelty. "We have done our part here on earth, and the rest, well, that is beyond us. Look not at the person who assisted the madness of a tyrant, but the good of his sacrifice at the end of his life, and his spirit."

Markus said nothing, but he thought about this all the way back to the cabin, and longer still.

Ghost

Ghost was resting in the pilot's seat of the Hellhound while his new crew of Lacerta's were huddled in the cargo hold behind him, the door was shut and all was quiet and he found it peaceful to just drive the hovercraft across the landscape as the stars hung overhead. He had always enjoyed driving vehicles or flying various hovercraft, and seeing the little lights twinkling as the moon glowed bright, lighting up the passing Wasteland far below the craft was his own peaceful pastime.

Heaven knows how much peace he truly needed.

It reminded him of his time in The Dreaming, although not as horrible or as vast he remembered it. He would have rather fly in the skies above than dive into the minds of man again, for the horrors he had witnessed was almost enough to drive him mad. But The Master needed him there, and he needed to find as many of the gateways as he could. The tests were almost complete for Project Eleven to move onto Project Human Arc. Just a few more tests, a few more weeks and then the task in Xerxes, and everything would be set for the release of The King.

If only he hadn't been interrupted when taking the arm of that boy... that damned boy...

Thinking about The Keeper caused Ghost to clutch the steering column of the Hellhound so hard that his knuckles cracked within his armored gloves. Thinking about the boy and all he represented had filled him with such rage upon seeing him that he could hardly contain himself when addressing him. That boy was about to ruin everything if given the chance; he should have slit his throat rather than flee upon getting shot at rather than have him bleed out of his shoulder. He knew that the boy was not dead however, he had seen him in his restless dreams. The dreams that were presented to him by The Master.

The defying welp lives, The Eldest had told him. *You should not have tried to kill him.*

I had no choice, Ghost had said. *We needed the other crystals. You need-*

His thoughts were interrupted when he heard the unmistakable alerting beeps from his wrist-monitors, and after clicking a few buttons on his suit, a hologram appeared above his arm with the face of Ghost's old comrade. A grizzled face with a patchy beard and many, many scars with what looked like a telescopic piece in place of his left eye. The man in question was sitting in his respective quarters, the walls blacked out and covered in many notes in many different languages.

"Quickshot." he said to the man in greeting. "How is it going back home?"

"Right as rain, Ghost," Quickshot said in a thick accent. "Miss yer cute lil' arse though. 'Ow's yer trip going?"

"Mind yourself," Ghost said impatiently.

"Arright, arright, don't get yer panties in a knot, sunshine."

"I'm busy," Ghost said impatiently. "What is it?"

"I 'eard from a reliable source that Queen Elizabetha plans to meet with darling Psyren for dinner in a few days," Quickshot said raising up his hand which was playing with a single bullet. A .50 caliber that had the name of some girl etched into the side. The name was 'Lorretta,' and the Hunter Quickshot was curling this massive bullet between each finger as he continued. "They plan to talk of parley considerin' the war between the two. Rumor also has it that they have spies in Xerxes as we speak."

Ghost growled in his throat. "Dammit, why now of all times?"

Quickshot shrugged. "You know 'ow the old lady gets with old friends."

"This cannot stand..." Ghost's outrage boiled inside his suit, and for a moment he thought of letting it all out then and there. To hit the steering column or end the call and scream. But what good would it do to lose his temper, especially in front of someone who would take nothing but pleasure out of it?

Calming himself, breathing slowly, Ghost thought about the report for a moment, and then spoke once again. "Is your brother back from The Capitol?"

Quickshot raised an eyebrow. "Yeah, so what? He came back like... yesterday at mid-day. Why?"

"I sense an opportunity," Ghost said with a cruel chuckle. "Tell him to get ready. Those spies will no doubt be around when the dinner takes place. I want him to take care of them, however he sees fit. Tell him to get the information for all new citizens within the last week, and he may begin his hunt."

"And what about me?" Quickshot asked greedily for a piece of the action. "Don't tell me you forgot about your dear friend..."

"Take up a place far from the castle, and get into position to where you can track the queen's movements. When dinner is finished you are to follow her and eliminate The queen of Levitika. Shoot her, stab her, I don't care. Just make sure it is done within our city, and so we can use this to bait The Levitikan's to attack. Without their queen their government will collapse, and soon enough the city itself. We will destroy them and Nineveh both."

"And what about 'er 'ighness?" demanded Quickshot. "Should she 'appen to notice her guest of honor being butchered like that?"

"Do it beforehand if you can, but should you be spotted by anyone, report to the queen that you work for me. Say it was for her protection, and if she resists... restrain her."

"On what charge?" demanded Quickshot. "I don't like the idea of winding up buried underneath the castle, mate."

"My charge," said Ghost. "One of her advisors, Harker, he knows of the queen's illness. He understands our position should she seem unfit to rule. Report to him that as my stand-in, that you see it fit for Queen Psyren to be under evaluation until my return."

Quickshot whistled in admiration. "You've been busy, mate."

"Always," said Ghost with a touch of pride, ebbed with an eagerness to end this call.

"Heh, heh, brilliant," Quickshot laughed. "Just brilliant, mate. Say no more, me brother and I will take care of it all. When will you be returning?"

"A few more days. I have unfinished business in Kaiken. When I return, I expect Xerxes ready to defend itself, it is time to get this war to keep going. We need the city weak if we are to move forward with the plan."

"Roger dodger." Quickshot then turned to his left and whistled sharply as if calling for a hound. "Oi, Siddy-boy? You hear? We goin' hunting!"

A voice that sounded behind Quickshot both light and sinister chuckled. "'Bout time, brother."

Quickshot returned his attention to Ghost. "Say no more, mate, we'll take care of it."

"I am counting on you, my friend," Ghost said in a soft but cold voice that made Quickshot's cocky little smile waver and fade like a dying leech. "We already had enough setbacks with Nineveh and Project Ten. I don't want any more distractions. We need to have everything ready as soon as possible. When I am done here, we will be one step closer to our goal. I don't need you two screwing anything up."

"I'm offended, Ghost," Quickshot said trying to save face. "You think-"

"You mess this up," Ghost warned the Hunter. "You fail to kill every single spy reported to be in Xerxes, you fail to kill Queen Elizabetha, or you fail to keep Psyren under control, and it won't be the justice system you'll have to worry about."

He didn't need to say anything else. Quickshot knew very well what Ghost was capable of, and in the light of the holographic projection of the Hunter, Quickshot looked as pale as porcelain. He gulped and nodded briskly.

"Right, right, mate. We don't fail, we swear on our mother's-"

"Swear to *me*, Blake," Ghost said. He waited patiently, the silence that followed hanging in the air like a dangerous thundercloud.

"I... I swear to you, Ghost," said Quickshot.

"Good," Ghost said, satisfied. "Now get to work and be ready. I'll contact you when I am returning."

Quickshot opened his mouth, but whatever he was about to say was cut off as Ghost killed the connection and the hologram went dark as the call was terminated. Ghost closed his gauntlets and returned his attention to his course, in the far distance he saw a good spot to land and rest. He would reach the island within a day or two if all goes well. He probably could have just made a straight shot towards the island from the swamp, but he wanted these Lacerta he was carrying as cargo to rest and eat and be prepared for battle. With his influence, they would destroy his enemies and all he had left tied to his past.

Ghost was happy; everything was going according to plan. But Ghost was always one to be aware of setbacks and complications. Because like his old man used to say: 'Some things just go bad. You either learn from them and move on, or let 'em slow you down.'

And Ghost couldn't have agreed more. A lot has gone bad, ever since he first encountered The Dreaming, and had lost so much in the process. But that would all be over with soon. Something better was on the horizon, something far more important.

However he decided to take it nice and slow this time, and enjoy the view of the ocean as soon as they reached it. He had all the time in the world at this point.

Rushing would not help him like last time. And with each passing moment it brought him closer and closer to his goal.

This time would be different. This time, Levitika and all of the Angels would pay dearly for what they had done to him. They would all pay, including the boy.

The Keeper...

He was with his old master, Ghost knew it. And if he got the chance, there would be nothing to protect him this time. This time he would not hesitate, he would not be discouraged.

This time, the boy would pay for what he did as well.

<u>Markus</u>

After a frightful night's sleep that consisted of murder and bloodshed, Markus found himself sitting outside watching the sun rise over the waters of the sea, his eyes dark with deep circles under his lids.

Daryl was laying beside him sleeping soundly as Markus stroked the large cat's flank. As he petted the Werecat's head he saw images as Daryl slept. Images of good food, fresh grass, tall trees to scamper in and watch the forest below, and Markus realized he was seeing Daryl's dream. The image went from smelling all of the plants to drinking cool and clean water from a brook. Daryl then turned and saw a female Werecat, and began to bound towards it. Markus released the cat's head cutting off the image before anything explicit could be seen.

"Don't need to see that," he said to himself. He heard a noise behind him and turned to see Abram coming up to him with a bowl of soup. He sat down beside him and offered the bowl. Markus who was very hungry, accepted it gratefully and ate ravenously.

"I see you have recovered since last night," the old man said looking across the sea.

"A little." Markus said between bites. He wondered if Abram could sense his thoughts, now that his personal crystal was gone forever, along with the spirit of Essau's whose very name sent shivers down the boy's spine.

"How was my cat's dream?" Abram asked while smiling at Daryl who continued to sleep.

"For him, fantastic. For me? Not so much..."

Abram laughed. "Cats, even Werecats, dream about the things they love as often as humans do. They have nightmares, good dreams, and more. Dreaming is never limited to just humans."

"Easier to understand," Markus pointed out. "Not as complicated, I guess."

"This is true," said Abram nodding. He turned to Markus who sat the bowl down now empty. "If only Daryl knew how to protect his dreams and thoughts from the prying eyes of others."

Hearing this, Markus looked at his teacher who was grinning. "You mean..."

His teacher nodded. "Today, I will show you how to defend yourself against attacks like what you dealt with in Nineveh against the warrior you have told me about."

Eager to get his mind off of Eassau and whatever else he might end up exposed to on this journey to close the gateways, Markus grinned broadly. "All right, let's do it!"

Abram nodded and stood up. "Come, then," he said, and Markus followed.

"From what you had told me," said Abram. He and Markus taken their empty bowls of breakfast and discarded them into the sink by the door. Daryl meanwhile remained sleeping outside. "It appears that the warrior casted an illusion while he had you down. He dug into your memories until he found your fears and unleashed them upon you while he tried to break the bond of the crystals in your possession. That is a common attack for those skilled in using the crystals. They use a bridge-like bond using The Dreaming between the two minds to cross over and pick and prod at their enemy's minds, making it possible to unleash their fears upon them."

"So that was what Black was doing…" Markus realized thinking about what he had seen back on the Leviathan.

Abram nodded. "Damion was always good at that, it made his name feared throughout the entire continent, not just the Northern Wastelands."

"You knew him that much personally?" Markus asked.

Abram looked to Markus, amused. "Knew him? I taught him everything he knows, remember. Him and two others but that is beside the point. He was always capable of casting strong illusions on his enemies to make them doubt themselves as he struck them down. He was one of the best I've ever trained beside your father."

This got Markus' attention immediately. "You trained my father?"

"After he found Levitika he traveled with Black. The two worked together for many years. It was your father who was an expert in building barriers around his mind and protect himself from those who tried to use The Dreaming to enter his mind. It might even prove just as easily for you as it was for him. But, I digress. Barriers are used to protect the mind, like a second and third skull beneath your own. It traps the intruder, snares them, and you are able to grapple with them and either send them away, or take them over and enter their own minds and use their tactic against them. To place a barrier, you need to have a simple thought. An unbreakable thought, something that your enemies cannot understand. If they cannot understand, they can't get in. And most of the time, they will only understand fear, and pain. So in turn that leaves…?" He looked at Markus waiting for the answer.

"Memories that cannot be broken…" Markus started, studying Abram's face for some clue that he was on the right path. However, his teacher remained stone-faced, so Markus still quite uncertain continued. "It cannot surely be good memories could it?"

"Why couldn't it be?"

"Nothing could possibly be that simple."

"You're right. It isn't that simple, however you are on the right track. Yes, it is the good that you remember. Family, friends, love, heck just having fun are the braces that build up the barrier. But to build the barrier itself you must let yourself be open, and allow your mind to build up the confidence it needs to withstand even the strongest of doubt and fear. That is how you build a barrier."

"There's a problem with that," Markus said looking up at the sky in thought of how to explain it should Abram asked.

Unfortunately, he did. "And what might that be Markus?" Abram asked with a sullen expression as if he was both confused and sad.

Markus shrugged. "The past is gone, so what good does it to focus on it? Whether it be good or bad? I taught myself not to dwell on the happiness of the past, because the present is a fight for survival, while it ensures some chance for the future."

"Hence your false reality you had grown accustomed to?" asked Abram.

Markus looked at his teacher. So Abram did see that when he was tasked to let everything in, perhaps even the memory of Black himself. He nodded.

"Well, that is one way to think of it," Abram reasoned. "However, that is a negative way of thinking. Remember when I told you that sometimes there is a reason you shouldn't forget those who you have killed in combat?"

"Yes?"

"Well, that applies to all memories good or bad. They shape us, mold us, transform us into the person whom we are meant to be. But if we fight negativity with negativity, what good will it do? Opposites are what makes the world the way it is, and it can only get better if we do not fight the bad with bad, but with good. Love, peace, happiness. Letting what hurts hurt is one thing, allowing inner peace to heal us after, is all the rest."

"Okay," Markus said understanding but not quite sure of himself.

"If a person dwells on the bad all he gets is bad. But if they rely on hope for good, then they will overcome even the most difficult of tasks. And one of your tasks happens to be protecting yourself from those who wish to control you, steal the crystals from your bond, and kill you."

Abram then looked Markus dead in the eye. "What do you believe Ashlyn is hoping? That she never sees you again, or that you come back?"

"That's kind of harsh," Markus said.

"It is an example. When you are gone, what do you think she is thinking about when it comes to you? That you *will* come home, or that you *might* come home?"

Markus looked down. "That I *will* come."

"Exactly. We do not know what the future has in store. But those who believe in bad, will get the bad."

"But sir, shouldn't one consider the bad?" asked Markus. "Be prepared?"

"What good is preparing if what will happen will happen no matter how much you know?" asked Abram.

"Then isn't hoping for the best just false hope?"

"If it is false then it is not truly hope is it?"

"Abram," Markus sighed patiently. "If I absolutely truly believed I could fly without wings or rockets, and I attempted it, what good would come of it?"

"There is a difference between believing in something and being an idiot," Abram said simply. When Markus didn't answer Abram told him to sit with him on the couch and the two sat together while Abram continued speaking.

"Faith is believing without seeing, hope is *trust* that something will happen. If there is doubt there is no faith, and without faith, how can there be hope?"

Markus had to admit he was stumped on that one.

Abram continued, "Even if the hope does prove false, it is then a matter of how you react to it. Because let us be realistic here: you are right. Sometimes we can hope for things to happen and they don't. You were thinking about your father, and your sister, weren't you?"

"Yes..." Markus admitted.

"You hoped that he would survive the fight against Black. And to your disappointment, all your hope fell when he did. Did it not?"

"Yes."

"Then why did you keep going? Why did you continue to fight for Ruth, and even risk your life to save her?"

Markus shrugged. "I wanted something to believe in."

"Precisely!" Abram said smiling brightly. "Yes, it is unfortunate that your father did not make it. But look at all the opportunities it has given you. You became a loyal and loving brother, and did your very best to save Ruth."

"A lot of good it did her though."

"Ahh but think about the positive in it. Yes, it is a tragic- a horrible tragic that your family is gone. But that never stopped you from carrying on, did it?"

"I *wanted* to give up," Markus said.

"Ahh but you didn't, did you?" Abram said with a smirk. "Tell me Markus, why didn't you give up? Why did you keep going despite all that has happened within the last couple months?"

"I don't know..."

"Yes, you do," Abram insisted. "Look deep inside yourself, Markus. Why do you think you never gave up?"

Markus blew a puff of air out of the corner of his mouth. "Honest truth?"

"I would hope." Abram said softly.

"I had nothing else to lose at that point after Ruth was gone. And then everyone came down upon with me with the whole prophecy thing and telling me to keep fighting. I agreed at first because I figured it would be a mistake, and I would die anyway. But as I got closer to the people of Levitika, and closer to Nineveh before we invaded it, I found myself fighting still. I just kept breathing. I just felt this- this feeling in my gut that I had to keep *breathing*. Because..." He found himself unable to continue. Luckily, Abram put his thoughts into words.

"Because you never know what could happen in the future," the old man guessed. "You were hopeful?"

After a long pause, Markus nodded. "Not a day goes by when I don't think of my family. Not a day goes by when I don't think about anyone who has died either because of me or close to me. So many times I wondered if it is worth it, especially after last night if I'm going to be honest still. But as we kept going, I found myself wanting to survive. I wanted to keep fighting to protect the people I loved. The people around me."

Abram nodded. "That is why you still have hope. You never know what the next day will be, but you push on through the present so that you can make it there with those you care about. Our hearts may be deceitful Markus. But if they are tamed within their cages, they can guide us and never let us down."

"But everyone expects so much of me," Markus said. "What if... what if I'm not good enough?"

"What do you hope for?" asked Abram.

"I don't know... I just... I just want to be happy."

"As do many," said Abram. "I do not blame you for being unsure, what you are dealing with, who you are, it's more than what a lot of people can do. And yes, a lot do expect so much from you. I do as well. But here's the good news, you're not alone.

You're never alone Markus. You have me, your friends, and The Queen. If that's not a family then I don't know what is."

Markus felt something push against him and he looked down to see Daryl looking up at him with big eyes almost expectedly, unblinking as if demanding something. He then felt a little better to the point that he smiled and reaching out, he scratched the Werecat under the chin and Daryl's eyes shut with satisfaction.

"You know what? You're right, old man."

Abram laughed out loud, a rich bark that shouldn't have belonged to a man as ancient as him and yet it was strong and bold. "'Old man'? Heh, when you're old as I am you won't look as good." Abram winked. "Now enough of this tender-talk. It is time for you to defend yourself."

"So how do I do that?" Markus asked ready for anything now.

"Just remember the good, all the good times and bad times of your past. As you would during meditation, leave nothing behind closed doors to yourself. When you are attacked mentally, look back to all who held you up when you were down, all the times you laughed, and all the times that made you feel alive and free. Because with the memory of all who love you, you are never standing alone against those who wish to harm you."

"Can it really be that simple?"

Abram said, "In the heat of the moment, people tend to not think about the good. They only think of the here and now."

Markus nodded. "I guess that makes sense."

"Tell me Markus," Abram said placing a hand on his student's forehead. At first, Markus wasn't afraid. Abram had no crystal, what could he possibly do?

Then he felt something like lightning pierce through his skull as Abram asked, "What do you fear?"

Markus then saw a flash of light that blinded his vision, and all had vanished.

He found himself in utter darkness, which soon ebbed into shades of dull orange and red, the colors blending like oil to a scene he knew all too well. He found himself within The Fiery Plains, fumes filling his nostrils with poisonous gas, and the sound of crows cawing overhead. Markus suddenly went rigid as he heard a familiar coughing sound behind him, and turning slowly around he was dismayed to see his sister Ruth on the ground, crawling towards him as blood dripped from her fragile lips.

"Ruth!" he cried out running towards her, panic unlike any other coursing through his veins in the fear of failing her yet again. This felt nothing like the nightmares he had or the illusion the warrior of Xerxes had placed upon him. This felt all too real, too terrible.

"Ruth!"

She disappeared in a whisper of black smoke before he could reach her however, and the figure of Abram appeared where she once was looking sullen for a moment, only to change once again in a flash to the lizard-like monster they fought before roaring at him. Markus instinctively went for his blade and realized that he did not have it. Backpedaling he began to scream as the Lacerta Slitzar roared at him again, her purple tongue wriggling like a worm past her sharp teeth.

"Control yourself," Abram's voice said from nowhere in particular. "You are letting your memories- your fears take over as you see this place again."

Markus then squatted down and lowered his head as if he was trying to curl up into a ball before the monster. "I can't..." he gasped, finding it difficult to breathe. "I just can't..."

"Yes, you can."

And Immediately Markus felt the heat of the ground beneath him cool and he opened them to see ice now accumulating on the otherwise sulfuric ground. It shattered beneath him and he fell through the 'ground' before landing somewhere else entirely, somewhere that was freezing and covered in snow.

He looked up to see that the lizard had gone, and he was no longer in The Fiery Plains, but in Nineveh. He then looked at his hands and saw that he was now wearing a coat he had not worn in many years. Was this the past?

Looking at the buildings around him, it sure looked to be that way. But something was very different than before. There was no people either in the streets or in the buildings, and the bodies that were hung on the wires high above were also gone. He was all alone, or so it had seemed.

A blast of ice splattered against the back of Markus' neck which he realized was snow, and he whirled around to see his little sister when she was just a few years old grinning from ear to ear like a fox. She was wearing a dirty pink coat and her blonde hair was in two braids. "Gotcha!" She cried out laughing hysterically.

Markus was at a loss for words and merely stood there as the snow melted off his neck and dripped down his back. Was this really here?

Ruth frowned and cocked her head to the side, another snowball pressed into her palm but now seemingly forgotten. "Hey, what's wrong?"

Markus dropped to his knees unable to hold himself up or the tears back. "I remember this... The first time you came out into the snow..."

Ruth smiled, not seeing the tears from the distance she was at. "Yeah, and it's incredible." She dropped the snowball she was going to throw next and rushed for Markus and tackled him in a hug that had enough force to knock him onto his back while Ruth hugged him around the neck. "I love this weather!"

"Aren't you cold?" Markus said still not believing that she was really here. It was the only thing he could think of to say.

"Not at all!" She was up again and twirling about like a dancer in the snow and Markus sat up and watched her. It was like watching a rerun of some security footage, and he just couldn't believe how real this all felt.

Markus nearly choked at the remembrance of asking her that exact same question many years ago, and her giving that exact same response. It was at this very moment when-

"Hey, you two!"

His heart stopped in his chest. Ruth was laughing and rushing past him and he turned about to see his father coming home from the mines. He was wearing a thick coat all covered in suit and he scooped Ruth up into his arms upon her making contact and spun her about in the air laughing and showering her with kisses.

Markus stood up, disbelieving.

His father was watching him as he held Ruth in his arms and he was smiling tiredly but warmly. "What is it, Markus? You sick?"

"No… no, I…" Markus shook his head. Unsure of what to say. "I'm just glad you're home."

Johnathon laughed. "Same."

Markus started to approach his family, and Ruth said, "I love you, Daddy."

"I love you too, sweetheart. You too, Markus."

"I…" Markus said hesitantly as he felt something very wrong here.

"Love you too, bro," Ruth said smiling. "I didn't forget about you!"

Before Markus could say anything however, both his sister and father erupted into black smoke, their figures having been cut away like a burst bubble, and stepping out of this smoke, Markus was distraught to see that coming out with his two katana swords, was the Xerxan Warrior who had taken his arm, and nearly killed him. His electronic bug-like helmet sparking with light from within, but the many codes and sensors that were blinking and whirring inside were almost forming the shape of a human skull.

"You're nothing to her," the warrior said as he approached Markus who stood frozen in place, his limbs refusing to make him run away and he realized he no longer had his auto-limb, just his one remaining limb of flesh and blood.

"You're nothing to your father," the soldier added. He was dragging the tips of his katanas through the snow, leaving little trenches within. "Think about how much of a disappointment he feels about you knowing you got her child killed…"

"No," Markus said shaking his head vigorously. "No, that's not true. That wasn't my fault!"

The warrior raised his katanas and struck out at Markus and he instinctively held up his only hand as if to block the blow.

"That's not true!" he repeated, thinking about the times he and Ruth had shared here together, how happy they had been with their father. All the wonderful things they had been a part of together. Birthdays, working late but coming home to one another, just glad that they were alive together. Ruth learning how to read by her father, who also taught Markus how to build and play with some mini-battle bots.

Because those were the memories that mattered. If he just remembered the good, the bad seemed less scary.

The katanas passed through Markus, and the warrior dissipated into shadows which spread across the vision of Nineveh, leaving Markus alone, now wearing the same clothes as he had back on the Kaiken Island, his auto-limb retrieved, his heart no longer burdened with what he had lost being used to torment him. He looked all around and was startled when he felt a small hand clutch his own and he looked to see Ruth standing beside him, healthy and smiling.

"You did it," she told him.

Before Markus could say anything, the sensors on his auto-limb felt someone else grasping his other hand. He looked to his left and saw Ashlyn standing beside him smiling proudly at him. Next to her was Esmerelda.

He felt a strong hand grip his shoulder causing him to stiffen but he felt the familiar warmth and believed it to be his father.

"Good job," he heard a voice say that was *not* Johnathon, and before he could turn around to see who it was, the entire feeling and image around him faded into black.

He opened his eyes to see himself hugging Daryl around the neck. The Werecat looked annoyed but when he saw Markus looking back at him he began to purr. Markus released the large feline back and turned to Abram who was smiling and nodding in approval.

"You did it," he said. "Good job."

Markus smiled deeply and said, "Thank you. I… I know you weren't trying to take over me, but it felt pretty real enough."

"I sure hope so," Abram said softly. "But you didn't give up, and that makes me proud of you. Remember, if you focus on what you are afraid of, you will be overcome. But if you focus on the good, and the people who make you strong, you can never fail."

Markus nodded to his teacher. "Thank you, Abram."

Abram smiled, creating more wrinkles to etch into his face. As quickly as they had come the wrinkles faded as Abram's smile slacked as he observed Markus who looked distracted now. "What is it?"

"Nothing," Markus said shaking his head. "I saw my sister, saw my friends, I just… I thought I would see my father there. I thought he was there in the end, but I don't think it was him…"

"Was it someone bad?"

"No, no. Just…" Markus shook his head again. "I'm sure it's nothing."

Abram raised and eyebrow and then shrugged. "All right, Markus, very well. We have plenty more to do as well, much more you need to train on." He stood up from his couch and stretched his back, releasing a ripple of pops that made Daryl's ears turn in his direction attentively. "Come on. Let's get back outside."

And so Markus followed his teacher back outside, ready to train some more and distract him from the thoughts of wonder that swirled about his head like a distilled beverage. Just who had that hand and that voice belonged to. Markus wanted to believe he knew exactly who it was.

And yet if it *was* Black, why hadn't he come as the memories of the others had? Why hadn't he made himself known- Or why hadn't Markus himself made Black's presence truly known?

Furthermore, where had his father been in the end?

At any rate, Abram was calling to him, and Markus hurried over across the clearing, ready to learn more.

<u>Ashlyn</u>

It had been the second day of Chuck's Coffee being in Xerxes and Ashlyn was getting more and more uneasy as the night of the dinner of parley was supposed to take place.

Twice, she accidently spilled some coffee on a customer while she was spacing out and thinking about all the many possibilities that something could go wrong. She apologized of course and made up for her mistake by serving them a free cup of coffee. This seemed to have surprised the customer who thanked her again and again after trying (and failing) to just buy a second cup.

One time Ashlyn noticed a young teenage boy who wouldn't stop staring at her. It wasn't uncommon for men considering the tight waitress outfit she was wearing, but it still made her incredibly uncomfortable. Still, she ignored the glances and kept her mind focused on her work as well as the mission rather than dwell on the bad things that could happen. Grim had gone over it with her the previous night, and she replayed it in her mind like a video recording.

The plan was to hack a drone and use it to listen in on the conversation between the two queens. Grim had found a spot on a rooftop where one of the Railcars stopped to restock, and Ashlyn was to stay there and provide a signal between the drone and Gabriel who would be in the streets below controlling the drone. Meanwhile, Grim would be in the castle and Silva would be on a different building covering the other side of the castle. If any other drones were to investigate, Ashlyn was to shoot them with a Pulse Rifle which would shoot out a concentrated microwave undetected by radar or human ears, which would cook anything from the inside out. Ashlyn, who had a lot of training on rifles in general was the perfect candidate alongside Silva while the men worked on their infiltration.

All she had to do was get up to the tower once more without being detected by cameras and drones, which was not going to be easy. She could travel under the streets through the sewers where the team had access to from beneath their shop. She had spent several hours already down there with the map made by Silva to have a general understanding of the layout before their mission began. At this point in time she was confident with her sense of direction in the deep, dank darkness, but as soon as she got out she would need to be careful. She could not risk getting caught, especially with a collapsible gun on her person.

But it would all work out. Everything seemed to be in order when Grim explained the plan earlier, but as closing time got closer and closer Ashlyn became even more worried than before. Tomorrow was going to be huge, and if they did not make sure it went off without a hitch then they and the whole city of Nineveh and Levitika would be in trouble.

She looked back up and saw that a couple were waiting on a refill and she ran over to the counter really quick to refill her canister before hurrying back to them and refilling their own cups. "Are you two doing alright?" she asked them with a large, unnatural smile on her face.

"Yes, we are, thank you," the man said politely his lips stretched into a wide grin.

"Tell your father we enjoy the coffee here," the woman said with a similar grin. "It's so peaceful here."

"I'll be sure to do that," said Ashlyn. She then left the table, her brooding look now disappeared completely from her face. She then took her place at her usual spot at the front counter, and while watching for more people to serve, her mind went back to the plan itself as well as Grim's latest speech from the night before.

And speaking of Grim, the mutant placed a hand on Ashlyn's shoulder, startling her.

"After these last few people leave, why don't you go and take a break. Gabe and I can handle it. But while you're at it, pretend that you're a newcomer and ask simple questions about the city. Don't give away anything that could compromise us. If they ask where you are from-"

"We came from south of Lakeshire and my father and I own a new coffee shop." Ashlyn nodded. "Alright."

In fact, she was glad for the break. It was her second day there and she hasn't even seen the rest of the city like Grim and the others had throughout their time here. Besides, she was interested in finding out what the people of Xerxes thought about their government and their city, and if possible, gather some information to see if possible to prevent unnecessary casualties should push come to shove in the end.

Grim smiled. "Good. Now please pour that gentleman over there some more coffee please. He's been eyeballing you for some time now."

Ashlyn looked to where Grim had nodded and saw the teenage boy quickly avert his eyes, a lewd smile curling upon his lips.

"Not funny," said Ashlyn to Grim.

Grim grinned. "Not even a little?"

"Not even then." Ashlyn said taking her pot and making her way over to the creep which she noticed as she got closer, through his smile that his two front teeth were crooked. She offered him a refill and he nodded vigorously without looking up at her and she poured him a cup and asked for the refill price. He dug out a few coppers and pushed them over to Ashlyn.

"Keep the change..." he said in a fast but hushed whisper.

"Thank you," said Ashlyn and she turned and started to go.

"Wait..."

Ashlyn groaned inwardly and turned about and tried for a small smile. "Yes? Did you want something else?"

"No," the boy said shaking his head. "I mean, yes, but..." He looked to be shaking, and Ashlyn wondered if the boy was that nervous or if the coffee was too strong for him.

"Yes?" Ashlyn repeated as patiently as she could muster. If only Markus could see this trainwreck happening before her.

"N… nothing, never mind," the boy said, and Ashlyn smiled again and saying nothing, left him alone. This of course did not stop him from catching a few glances in her direction whenever he could.

At last, Ashlyn left the shop out of uniform and in a pair of fresh clothes which consisted of a white shirt under a black jacket as well as fresh jeans and boots. They were Silva's jeans but the Angel was willing to share since she and Ashlyn were about the same size. She breathed in the fresh air free of coffee and then with her hands in her pockets began to walk down the streets that were almost vacant. She felt her pistol slapping against her leg inside her jeans which reassured her that if anything *were* to happen then she would be okay. She also kept a knife that Grim gave her tucked into the same pocket as her right hand. Best to have it and not need it than to need it and not have it.

It was nice to be outside, but the streets were almost completely deserted. In fact Ashlyn only saw like a handful of people walking around or talking outside besides the vendors who stood behind their counters looking as bored as ever. It was barely five o'clock and with spring in the air the sun was still out. The streets shouldn't be this deserted, it wasn't anywhere near the conditions Nineveh had been back during Baron Ovid's reign.

Feeling a sort of loneliness and uncomfortableness out on the street, Ashlyn went up to the next nearest vendor who's shop consisted of a legitimate hole in the wall of a building with a sign above the makeshift window that read 'Hole in the Wall Candy'. The owner looked to be fifty years old, but dressed nicely for a candy-man with a striped apron that was neither smudged nor grungy.

"Hello," Ashlyn said as she stepped up to the counter.

The old man eyed her coolly and his smile appeared strained. "Can I help you?" he asked bluntly.

Ashlyn shifted her foot thinking that this was probably a bad idea. "Got any caramel?"

The man ducked below and came back up with a jar full of caramelized candy on a stick. Ashlyn took one stick and laid out two coins on the counter which the man scooped up and shoved into his pocket without a word.

"So, what's the word on the street?" Ashlyn asked trying to sound as casual as possible before taking a small bite out of the candy which was hard and cold but otherwise sweet with the taste of molasses.

The man's eyes twitched somewhat, his smile still looking as forced as ever. "Oh, all's well. Everything is good here in Xerxes."

The way the man said it sounded rehearsed as if Ashlyn had asked a question of morality rather than how everything was going. It didn't make her feel comfortable in the slightest anymore than the old man appeared.

"How long have you lived here in Xerxes?" asked Ashlyn. "My father and I just moved in from the trade route, opened Chuck's Coffee down the road."

"I've heard," said the man still smiling. "I've lived here my whole life, and I'm glad to have done so."

"You like it here?"

"Oh, absolutely," the man said still grinning from ear to ear, the wrinkles on his cheeks appearing strained as if invisible fingers were forcing his lips to be stretched. "It is the safest place to be."

Ashlyn nodded feeling cautious as she did so. All at once the caramel in her mouth tasted of molten metal. The man was giving her the impression that his smile would open wide like a snake's and swallow her whole. "Is it really the safest place to be?"

"Yes," the man said his face now breaking out in sweat, his eyes seeming to dart every which way. "Will there be nothing else, miss?"

"No, I'm good," Ashlyn said waving her caramel stick. "Thank you for the candy. I'm sorry if I bothered you."

"That's quite al right," the man said, his expression one of pained as if he were saying, 'No please, leave me alone.'

"I'm just new to the area," said Ashlyn. "Just wanted to be sure that-"

"Nothing is wrong with Xerxes," the man said in almost a growl that startled Ashlyn. His face remained unchanged but his eyes were glaring as if he was saying 'Do you not understand me, you dumb bitch?' "Xerxes is the safest place in the world, and it will always be safe. So unless there is anything else you need from me..."

Ashlyn shook her head, too afraid to ask or talk about anything else. "Well, thank you for the candy ,sir."

"Any time ma'am," the man said waving like a robot.

Ashlyn quickly walked away from the hole in the wall, feeling the eyes of the man following her until she finally turned the corner. She sighed with relief and the next garbage bin she came across she tossed her candy straight into it and she walked on. She received some glances from whoever was still on the street which did not relieve her discomfort, and she decided to hasten her pace.

She eventually found herself at a bar with the sign above the doorway being that of a coffin and an arm sticking out of it holding a mug. The caption beneath it read, 'The Laughing Cadaver' which was about as welcoming as such a name could get. Ashlyn thought it sounded fitting however upon seeing the kind of patronage that was inside. Dead-eyed and gloomy, not quite as the people of Nineveh had been, but almost... worse in a way she couldn't quite describe.

Moving along, she saw that two boys about half her age drawing with charcoal against one of the walls. Intrigued she walked over to them. When they noticed her, they stopped what they were doing and bolted, running as fast as they could getting as far away from her as possible.

"What is with everyone here?" Ashlyn said to herself looking at what the boys were drawing, which to her discovery was not a picture at all, but a series of numbers all jumbled together. Not quite binary code which she only knew because Markus once told her so during their time in Levitika, but something else.

8-11-9-5-8-9-13-11-9-1-8-7-12-13-8-12-7-9-12

What is going on here? Out of some strange feeling that she was still being watched she looked behind her but saw nobody, but when she looked up she saw that a surveillance camera was pointing right at her and the wall full of numbers. Not wanting to draw attention to herself let alone associate herself with whatever those boys were doing, Ashlyn kept walking down the street.

Ashlyn soon found herself near one of the city walls, where many carts of fruits, vegetables and meats were scattered across the streets, and a few people picking the food of their choosing as if they were detectives trying to find the clues of a crime on each morsel. Unable to find anyone who looked even the slightest bit interested in talking, Ashlyn decided to take a seat near one of the walls. One of the ladies were kind enough to give her a stick of celery as a sample, but all Ashlyn could get out of her as well was that 'Xerxes is safe. We like it here' and all of which the man at the candy shop had said. Always sounding robotic, always sounding rehearsed.

She just didn't understand what was up with everyone here. Were they all just blind to the dangers outside the walls? Do they even know about Nineveh, and The Capitol? Ashlyn bit into her celery stick again deeply disturbed at the strange behavior of the citizens she met thus far.

"Well, well," said a voice to her left and she turned to see a guy about a few inches taller than her walking up to her. The guy had hair bright and more blonde than Markus' and his figure was slim beneath a brown jacket and black pants. His cheekbones were rounded and his eyes appeared completely circular and brown. He was smiling softly as he walked over to her, which was strange considering the freakish grins she was so used to having so far in this town. Still the fact that this random guy was coming over to her made Ashlyn go immediately on defense.

That, and she could have sworn he sounded familiar. "Hello," replied with a mouth full of the vegetable.

He stopped at her curt reply, his smile seemed to falter for a moment only to return just as soft as before. "You don't remember me, do you?"

"Uh, no, I just moved here into the city."

"No kidding?" said the boy. He looked older than her, and yet he acted so familiar with her. "Well, I doubt you recognize me anyway. I'm not in uniform, after all."

Uniform? Ashlyn thought in confusion. Already she felt antsy, ready to bolt at a moment's notice. "I'm sorry, I don't think you-"

"You and I met in Lakeshire," said the boy.

"We did?"

"Yeah, you and your brother and sister."

The answer struck her so hard in the chest that Ashlyn nearly gasped and dropped her celery stick. But she put on a big smile of recognition as she realized she did see this guy before. "Oh my god, Uzzah?"

The guy smiled broadly, greatly pleased. "The one and only last I checked. How the hell are you?"

"I'm... great!" Ashlyn said not sure of what else to say.

"Your siblings here as well?" asked Uzzah. "You three settling in okay?"

"More or less," said Ashlyn. "Our little sister didn't make it."

Uzzah's expression looked shocked. "No way… Damn, I'm sorry to hear that."

"Don't be, it wasn't your fault."

"I remember you three leaving, wishing I could have done more…"

Ashlyn shook her head. "Believe me, you did enough. We made it back to the caravan, and, well, most of us are here now. Not the mechanics, but most of the traders."

"Are you stationed here?"

"No we got a place in the city."

"Look at you," Uzzah said sounding impressed. "What's your business called?"

Before Ashlyn could think of an answer, a shrill voice called out, "Uzzah!" and he and Ashlyn turned to see an older woman with puffy white hair waving at him, that freakish grin on her face as well. "Come along dear, or we'll be late for dinner."

The guy groaned and for some reason Ashlyn felt a little sorry for the guy. "I gotta go," he said quickly. "Duty calls."

"Your mother?"

"Grandmother. It's just her and I, but my time in the army keeps her busy. What's the name of your business, I'll be sure to stop by and catch up."

Ashlyn was hesitant to tell Uzzah their place, but her and the rest of the group's story was convincing enough considering that they 'were' part of a trade route and set up shop here. She could make up everything else as she went and so decided to tell him about Chuck's Coffee.

"I heard there was a new joint on that part of town," Uzzah said nodding. "I'll be sure to check it out. Sorry, I gotta run, but what was your name again? I don't think you or the others told me."

Ashlyn said that her name was, "Anna."

"Anna, all right," Uzzah said starting to go. "I'll come by later, good to see you again, Anna. I hope you like it here in Xerxes!"

And with that he sprinted off towards his grandmother who immediately began badgering him with questions, causing him to smile as he nodded or shook his head. Ashlyn watched them go, feeling more empty than ever. Out of everyone she had ran into in the city, she had not expected to see the same soldier who struck a deal with Markus to get them some more supplies.

More so, she didn't expect him to be the most normal person she had come across.

Not feeling very hungry anymore, she tossed the celery stick into a nearby drain and began to make her way back to the coffee shop. She had to let Grim know about the story, and fast.

Back at the shop, Ashlyn got Grim up to date with what happened. What she had discovered while walking the streets of Xerxes, and who she had ran into and their history together. The mutant soldier listened intently and when she was done, he nodded thoughtfully.

"That is interesting," Grim said deeply. "But I'm not so surprised, given everything Gabriel and Silva had told me about beforehand. The people here… they aren't being very genuine."

"That's just it," Ashlyn said glad that Grim had finally put what she thought into legitimate words. "They all looked strained, except of course from the guy named Uzzah who had to run off."

"And they all said the same to at least a similar thing?"

"Yeah, saying they are happy, safe, etcetera."

Grim frowned. "Some of the customers I talked to today said similar things, made me uncomfortable that's for sure. In all honesty, I wonder if they even know what is going on outside the walls, or if they even cared. According to Silva, she thinks they are afraid of something."

"Like what?"

"Eavesdropping government agents," said Grim. "Like that candy man might have suspected you to be."

"That's ridiculous," Ashlyn said shaking her head. "I'm not-"

"I know," Grim said chuckling. "But how would he know that? He wouldn't, hence his caution."

"So weird," said Ashlyn shaking her head again. She thought of something else then, something she had not noticed before but realized now after thinking about Uzzah. "You know what else I have noticed?"

"What?"

"Not once did I see a single soldier. Only drones and a droid here and there, but not army-type. With the exception of Uzzah who was out of uniform, I saw no soldiers anywhere."

"Hmm... so what happens if there's a crime?" Grim pondered aloud. "I read you. I wondered that myself last night. All I saw were drones, but I think I know the reason why we haven't heard about much crime. I wasn't going to tell you this, but you've seen plenty and you deserve to know: Someone got killed last night."

"Who?" Ashlyn asked pausing in stance for a second.

"Some kid, got out after 'curfew' and got caught in the spotlight of one of the Tank-Drones. Thing didn't even stop, just fired a laser and killed the kid. Poor guy looked no older than ten."

Ashlyn felt her jaw drop. "That's awful."

"It gets worse. After the kid was laying cooked like a roast, the drone waited there with the spotlight still on it. Some people looked out of their windows to see what had happened but they all just returned inside. Minute or so later, an aerial drone flew in and took the body away. Today, no one talked about it."

"How can someone see something like that happen and not do anything about it?"

"The people are obviously scared, but of what? There's got to be more than just drones who kill people who are out at night. There are no soldiers in sight as far as we know, the whole city is as quiet as a ghost town, and worst of all: all the citizens seem to be hiding something and are only focused on how great their home is."

"But what could they have to hide?" asked Ashlyn. "What is going on here?"

"I don't know," Grim shook his head grimly. "None of us do just yet. All I know is the sooner we have an excuse to get out of here the better. Will you be ready for tomorrow?"

"Yes, I stopped by the tower you mentioned while I was in town. I can get up there."

"No one will be looking up, so I don't think you need to worry about people. But watch out for those drones up there. They see you and well… I don't want to have to explain to Markus that you got yourself shot."

Ashlyn paused and grinned at Grim. "Do you even know me? If I can sneak throughout Nineveh without the Guard spotting me, I think I can handle a couple of drones."

"Good. I want you to take my Pulse-Rifle along with the hacking device. I would rather you have it and not need it, then need it and not have it."

"I appreciate that."

Grim sighed and leaned back in his chair. "Boy, do I need a drink… Go get some sleep, Ashlyn, but don't bother Silva. She had a long day, and we all need to be ready to move out tomorrow."

"What about the coffee shop?" asked Ashlyn. "Do we still come back here when the job is complete?"

"Only if it all works out without alerting the whole city," said Grim. "Otherwise, I will let each of you know tomorrow where to go and where we will meet later. I have a few more things to check on before I finalize the last details should we get into trouble."

Satisfied, Ashlyn bade Grim goodnight and hurried upstairs. As she laid in her bed, she thought of Uzzah and how he had acted with her in comparison to many others in the city. Sure, one could argue it was because he recognized her.

But there was something else that was gnawing at Ashlyn's brain. Maybe he was the only normal one, because he knew what was going on outside because he was a soldier. Maybe, just maybe, it was because he wasn't a normal citizen at all.

Normal, of course, being the operative word here in Xerxes.

Esmerelda

As Markus was discovering the extensions of human capabilities and Ashlyn was preparing for the operation to take place in Xerxes, Esmerelda was leaving a recorded journal entry in her miniature Dragonfly bot, Q-Pid.

She hardly ever let Q-Pid out as much as she first did when Markus had built the little robot just for her, especially after the contraption nearly breaking during the attack of Nineveh and the Ice Witch. But Q-Pid often wandered the corridors of the castle and was always back at Esmerelda's corridors once it had received a full charge of it's solar-powered membranous wings. Q-Pid was of course a more sentient robot whose artificial intelligence was becoming greater as time went on. It had the entire castle mapped out and was capable of projecting that map against walls should Esmerelda ask, which she had done so from time to time and was delightfully impressed by how many secret passages and corridors were hidden.

It also made it much easier for her to keep an eye on the Council of Elders and Slagar as a whole, who for the most part spent a majority of time by themselves, doing their own projects or meeting with family members. Slagar in particular was always in his laboratory, constantly writing in his books or looking up history scrolls in the library. He never said anything remotely incriminating and so Esmerelda had no proof to present to her mother if the hypnotist had any ill will towards them.

As for Elder Kahun who would be joining her mother to Xerxes, the elder had only met with Slagar once after the initial meeting, complaining how he didn't want to go and to Esmerelda's surprise, Slagar had calmed the man and said there was no one else on the council that he saw more fit to accompany the queen than he. "Your job is to ensure that the queen is protected at all costs. Do not worry about your position here, the Council will not leave you out of any details. I can assure you that any action that must be taken here will be reported to the queen and you posthaste."

Kahun stroked his grizzled chin nervously. "But, Slagar, don't you think this is foolish? The queen could be wandering into a trap."

"That is a possibility," said Slagar. "That's why it is imperative that every single one of our guards are present with her at all times. I don't like it anymore than you do, but we can only follow our orders and do what is necessary first and foremost. So do your duty, and do not fret."

But Kahun was fretting very much so, and Esmerelda after listening to this recorded audio, had told Q-Pid to delete it and right after began her journal entry.

She had gotten the idea after Markus in particular had left. To her, leaving recordings of herself would make it easier for her to look back on this time, especially after Ashlyn had left, to preserve what she had learned both in her own studies and with the company of her best friends. She would be queen of Nineveh soon, and so would need to keep a record of her thoughts and decisions so that should they all be in question or prove faulty, she could listen to them all as she was older and either chuckle at a particular memory, or reflect on her hindsight.

At any rate, she was just rambling on about how lonely she had felt after her friends had left. "I've always felt particularly lonely here," she was saying. "But that just comes with the territory and how little children are in the castle. All I had were adults for company if that at all. Hence the books, which I'm glad, Ashlyn, if you ever hear this, I'm glad you found an appreciation for. I can't wait to talk about what I have been working on and get your thoughts on it. Rest assured I'll pick your brain about every single detail, and I swear I'm going to quiz you on spelling to see if you are doing your lessons while you're away."

She paused for a moment, and Q-Pid's wings fluttered metallically for a moment as if asking permission to stop. She shook her head and with a sigh said, "Now my mom is leaving too. First Markus, now Ashlyn, and now her. And I'm going to be ruling over Nineveh and Levitika until she returns. It feels so surreal. It doesn't feel..."

She paused, thinking about what the right word was. At last she decided on, "It feels too soon."

She snapped her fingers, indicating to Q-Pid that she was done and the little creature chirped as the audio was recorded in her memory banks. She then scuttled on her metallic legs across the table and up Esmerelda's extended arm like a spider. When the robot was perched on her shoulder as light as a feather, Esmerelda stood from her desk and started to leave her bedroom.

"It's about time," she told Q-Pid. "Time to say goodbye."

"Bye-bye," Q-Pid agreed, which made Esmerelda's heart ache but she gave no indication that it had.

Esmerelda went downstairs to the throne room and upon entering, saw that her mother was there talking to Slagar presently in hushed tones. None of the other Elders were present nor was Kahun at the moment. Her mother was out of her usual gowns and was instead sporting a pair of pants and a lovely fur coat that made her look like a noblewoman rather than a queen. Her crown was gone and her black hair was put up in a ponytail, something that Elizabetha never did and it was almost a cultural shock for her daughter.

When her mother noticed her, Slagar ceased speaking immediately looked up and after letting his eyes linger on Esmerelda for a time, he excused himself and left grumbling all the way to the door like the old man that he was. Esmerelda went up to her mother who smiled and hugged her daughter as she got closer.

"You look so different," Esmerelda said softly.

Her mother chuckled warmly and gave her daughter a squeeze. "It's bad luck to wear the crown during travel. Don't worry, I have my stuff already packed and will be presentable for dinner with Psyren."

"That isn't what I'm mostly worried about..."

Another squeeze, and Elizabetha said, "I know."

Q-Pid had crawled off of Esmerelda's shoulder and was now ascending Elizabetha's own. She buzzed up in a sort of hop right up to the queen's head where she perched upon it as if about to nest. Not failing to notice the queen let the robot remain where it was as it observed this tender connection.

"Please be safe," Esmerelda whispered. "And come right back, okay?" She knew that her mother would come back, she wouldn't just run off like whatever aristocrat who truly was her father, but the timid but very present adolescent fear of such a thing happening now had haunted Esmerelda throughout the night. Not because Elizabetha would just abandon her duties to the crown as well as her daughter, but because something terrible might happen.

As it was, her mother said, "I'll be back before you know it. I promise. Slagar and the others will be here for you, just remember that you are the rightful ruler of Nineveh and Levitika in my stead. Don't let them talk you out of it."

Her mother had paused and before Esmerelda could say anything in response to this, her mother held her out at arm's length and looking up at Elizabetha, she could see that the queen had been looking around almost cautiously.

She looked Esmerelda in the eyes more seriously than ever. "You will do good here as long as you remain strong and keep your wits about you. Should anything happen, anything at all, you must remain safe and keep your power in the crown."

Esmerelda swallowed a lump the size of a golf ball that had materialized in her throat. She fought back her tears as if to say, "Nothing is going to happen though, right?"

Elizabetha squeezed her daughter's shoulders and said, "Pray that nothing will. And remain prepared, always. Do you remember the codes to get to the Underground?"

The Underground had become their code for the inner sanctum of the whole island of Levitika, where the Eldest's Son remained connected at all times. Not everyone had access to it, save for only three people since the coronation of Queen Elizabetha. Now there were only two people with the codes to get down there, unless Markus and Ashlyn happened to memorize it all by some miracle.

Esmerelda nodded at her mother's question, and then smiling, Elizabetha added, "You won't be alone for long, hon. I'll return as soon as this whole thing is over."

"Do you think everything will work out?" Esmerelda asked her mother.

"I sure hope so," was the queen's response. She smiled and then touched her daughter's chin tenderly.

"Don't worry so much. Worrying never makes life easier. It only makes things more difficult before it is even over."

"I know, I just have a bad feeling...."

"What did we *all* promise?" Elizabetha asked, still smiling softly.

Esmerelda sniffed. "That you would return."

The queen nodded and lowering her head she kissed Esmerelda on the brow. "And I promise you the same. I'll be back soon, I promise."

Q-Pid made some sharp chirping noises and then her mother's voice spoke out through her speakers, "I promise."

Elizabetha couldn't help but laugh. Her laughter caused Esmerelda to smile. "Can't back out of it now, I see."

Esmerelda, still unhappy, nodded sullenly. "I'm going to miss you."

"I'll miss you too," said Elizabetha and she took Q-Pid off her head and presented the robot back to her daughter. When Esmerelda reached to take it,

Elizabetha took her hand and squeezed it tight, the robot now crossing their link like a bridge.

"Make me proud, okay?" she asked her daughter.

Scared, but determined, Esmerelda took a deep breath and nodded. "Okay."

About an hour later, Esmerelda watched as the Hellhound that was to take her mother and the Elder Kahun to Xerxes. The aircraft was not built for war but simple transportation, for it only had one pair of guns on it for defense purposes. There would be another Hellhound however, a militarized one, that would supply all the guards that would be joining them in Xerxes.

Esmerelda watched as the hovercraft leveled out beside the balcony and the Elder climbed aboard ready to get this whole thing over and done with, the servants taking both his and Elizabetha's luggage inside and then filing as solemnly out as they had many times before. The queen however turned to smile at Esmerelda.

'Make me proud,' that smile said again. Esmerelda nodded and then the queen blew a kiss to her daughter and hopped aboard the Hellhound. After the doors shut and some minimal adjustments for takeoff, the hovercraft pushed off the balcony and took off into the sky at the speed of a hawk. Esmerelda waved goodbye until the hovercraft faded from view beyond the walls of Levitika into the Wastelands beyond. One by one the servants and whatever members of the council came to see the queen off left the presence of the princess to continue their duties, leaving Esmerelda and the hypnotist Slagar alone on the balcony.

The old mage appeared to be watching the people down below sifting and moving about their business with both the look of pleasure for the people were not dismayed, and the look of amusement. Of what Esmerelda did not know, nor did she care for her eyes stayed on the horizon in the direction her mother had gone. Eventually Slagar bowed to Esmerelda and took his leave and began to walk away. Q-Pid who was on Esmerelda's shoulder still, seemed to be staring at the hypnotist menacingly as he walked away.

Esmerelda, however, turned to look at Slagar and called out his name. The wizard stopped with his back still turned to her, and she said, "What of our part here?" she asked. "What were my mother's orders to you?"

Slagar answered softly and simply, "My orders were to tell Vic to continue the production of battle droids. The more lives we can save if there happens to be a battle the easier it will be as we move further north."

Esmerelda nodded. "And you understand if you are to stray from your orders?"

"I am aware," Slagar said with a little bit of a tone that clearly asked Esmerelda 'Do you really think I do not know?' "And you have no need to fear, princess." He continued with a soft smile that was neither comforting nor reassuring. "I can guarantee, that my orders are for the good of Nineveh, and our own people."

"Very well," Esmerelda said looking back to the walls. "You may go about your business."

"And I shall." And with that Slagar departed with a posture that appeared as cunning as a serpent.

Esmerelda did not trust the mage, and she did so less since her mother had left. She would have to keep an eye of Slagar, and hope he doesn't exercise the length of the leash he was put on. Until then she would need more support of her own, and since she was in the good graces of the people as well as Vic now, she figured it would be a cinch to keep operations going as well as running the kingdom itself. How hard could it be, right?

She clicked her tongue and Q-Pid snapped at attention. "Fly out towards Vic's shop, I have a message for him. Make sure you return straight to my room and that no one sees you, all right?"

Q-Pid chirped loudly and began to hover. Before she took off however, Esmerelda gave the robot another order.

"Be safe, all tight?"

"Safe!" Q-Pid agreed and then took off like a bug in search for richer hunting grounds. Esmerelda watched the robot go and then looked back at the city still milling about. There was still so much to be done here both for recovery purposes as well as preparation should things turn sour between Elizabetha and Psyren.

At any rate, Esmerelda had work to do of her own, and some preparations to make for the future of both cities.

<u>Ashlyn</u>

Around three o'clock the coffee shop was closed down and Ashlyn was upstairs with Silva getting what they needed for the mission. Grim had already left to get inside the castle, and Ashlyn had voiced her concerns about Grim going inside.

"It's not like he's hard to miss in general..." she had said to Silva.

"Don't worry about that," said Silva using a makeshift tester in order to check the charges on the cartridges being used for their Photon-Rifles. "Grim has been doing undercover work for a long time. I doubt you'll even recognize him once the dinner begins."

"Okay," said Ashlyn and returned to getting her gear on. Underneath normal civilian wear was a jumpsuit that had multiple straps for her to conceal some knives and a 9-Banger pistol. There was also a stim in case she needed to recover from an injury quickly or give her a boost of adrenaline. She was still nervous about Grim but did not bring it up at all.

Gabriel, who had gone on to hack into the communications tower, eventually spoke into a single-way radio system connected to only the three ear pieces that were now in the other three's ears. They could speak to one another if they wanted to, but Gabriel was in the dark to avoid anybody tracking him. Should their signal become intercepted however, the Angel had a failsafe to direct all traffic to the tower and therefore give Silva and Ashlyn a chance to escape. Grim would have to figure it out on his own but that was none of their concern, only his.

He said into everyone's ear, "Just got confirmation from the walls. Two ships are coming in bearing the Angel Wings. They're coming."

Silva looked at Ashlyn with a serious but excited smile. "It's time."

Ashlyn released a great breath as if she had been holding it in for a long time. "Ready or not, right?"

Silva handed Ashlyn her rifle and told her to collapse it. As she did so the Angel asked her, "Are you sure you are okay going up there? I would think that it would be safer if you worked somewhere not as high."

"I can handle it," said Ashlyn, her weapon collapsed and now stuffed into a small sack that she looped over her head like a purse.

"All right," Silva said nodding. "And you know what to do once trouble begins or if Grim says so?"

"Shoot to kill," said Ashlyn shrugging as if it wasn't a big deal. "I got this." She remembered feeling scared in Nineveh, but that had been different. She would be shooting from a far distance, and worse yet, there might be the queen and whoever she had with her to consider.

"And?" Silva asked, waiting for the answer that she had driven into Ashlyn's head the past two days.

Ashlyn smiled and said, "Don't miss?"

Silva nodded approvingly. "Let's go."

Downstairs they opened the hatch in the floor leading to the sewers. Ashlyn went in first, and Silva followed shutting the hatch behind her, unaware of the figure looking inside the window up front.

They had split up after traveling underground for several minutes. Following her mental map, Ashlyn eventually came out of a manhole on the other side of the city. Ensuring that the coast was clear and sticking as close to the side as she could, she slipped down an alleyway that was in the blind spot of several surveillance cameras in the area. She followed her instructions up to the rooftops, proceeding higher and higher until she reached one of the Railcar support beams. She ascended one of the nearest maintenance ladders and eventually made it to the tracks, where she proceeded to lay prone on the platform alongside them with her body facing that of the Xerxes castle.

It was windy that afternoon and Ashlyn wished she had brought a face mask but then thought it would have been a bad idea, should someone had spotted her upon exiting the manhole. As usual, Xerxes was as quiet and as dead as ever, and taking her little sack, she unraveled the collapsed Photon-Rifle and pulled it into her arm. She put her eye near the scope and peered through, inspecting the castle as she did so.

She saw the many mobile towers on the castle turning about, and the landing pad off one of the high building's structures having the two Hellhounds bearing the mark of Levitika. She scanned all the nearby windows, finding little to nothing until Grim's voice came over the comms she and Silva were using.

"They're in," Grim's voice sounded in Ashlyn's earpiece. "East side of the building as predicted. Ashlyn, get your scopes on the windows on the east wing, seven stories up."

Ashlyn did as she was told and through painted glass windows, she could see shadows through her scope. Adjusting the dial on the scope itself, it shifted from various filters until at last she was able to see heat signatures through the painted glass. She saw two women and a man sitting together at the end of a large table, and all around them were multiple others all standing at attention. She reported what she saw using her finger to push a button on her earpiece, and then Silva came up on the comms.

"I'm going to move to a better position to the north, I think I can spot them through the opposite window. Gabriel, how are the drones around the castle?"

Ashlyn had not failed to notice the drones that hovered almost aimlessly about the towers. Gabriel said, "Blind as bats."

"Good," said Grim. "I'm just outside the dining hall. The other guy is taken care of. I got a listening device on the door, you should be able to hear what is going on momentarily. Ashlyn, keep your eyes on the queen. I know it's hard to see with infrared, but keep focused."

"Roger," Ashlyn responded and took hold of her rifle again. She could feel her pulse accelerating, and she wondered how long this would take and her body began to ache with how tense she was.

A moment later, she finally caught the words from an older woman, saying in mid-sentence, "-your side, before my final thread is cut."

"Of course," said another voice which was most definitely Elizabetha's. Ashlyn listened patiently, feeling anxious as to what would happen next and what she and the others would hear, and the left pocket of her jumpsuit all at once felt harder than ever. She needed to calm down, she needed to relax and remain focused.

And yet, the Buckweed she had meant to throw away…

She shook her head as if to scold herself. "No, no," she said to herself tightening her grip on her weapon. All at once her mouth became dry and she thought of reaching for her water, but instead she remained as still as a professional sniper, her reticle scanning over the heat signatures that were both Levitikan and Xerxan, the only defining difference being the massive cold Bronze-Alloy on the humped backs of the Angels that were nearest the table. As Elizabetha spoke to Psyren, she soon discovered which of the women were exactly her based on her movements as she spoke to the other.

Time passed, Ashlyn became more and more fidgety, and began to doubt her capability of shooting properly.

Her mind went back to her pocket, and the stress-reliever she had in her possession still.

Elizabetha

The landing on the pad beside the castle went very well, and as soon as Queen Elizabetha got out of the hovercraft she breathed in the musty air of oil and smoke. How long had it been since she had last been in Xerxes? She could not remember.

But as she got closer and closer to the entrance to the castle, the feeling of both déjà vu as well as if she was getting smaller and smaller seemed to enclose on her like a blanket. Around her, the guards positioned by Slagar to protect Elizabetha had formed a tight circle, their weapons clutched tightly and their Eagle's Wings all folded into the packs on their armored backs. They walked as she and Elder Kahun walked, who looked as pale as mayonnaise and had the eyes of a frightened rabbit.

"I don't like this, your highness," he said bluntly. He was looking at some of the guard towers, those who were sitting on them as if they were artillery guns turning the towers themselves and tracking their every move.

"Just relax and stay close to us," said Elizabetha. It was a wonder that such a man had been put into a position of power, considering he had never been in combat before, let alone take the chance to put his neck out on the line.

As she followed the servants which consisted of both androids and soldiers, Elder Kahun walked briskly beside her fidgeting with his fingers. "The stone walls feel like they will close on us at any moment..." he said.

On this, Elizabetha agreed but made no comment. She merely followed the servant to a room where she could change and her escorts followed her single-filed into the room where she was then offered a collapsable privacy wall where she changed from her travel attire into a beautiful teal dress. Without her servants here to assist her she applied her own makeup, admiring herself in the mirror and adjusting a few pins in her hair before finally putting on her crown. With a deep breath she left the room and Elder Kahum now in his own elegant suit joined in line with her and once again they were surrounded by their guards who followed the same servant further down to the dining hall.

It would be a bittersweet moment and Elizabetha was not mentally prepared for all that would require her in that room. She was glad to see the old queen once again, but would she be able to discuss the situation concerning both Xerxes and Nineveh without causing an uproar? She had to assume that Psyren's council would be present, if they were not it would be all and well; but if so Elizabetha would need to choose her words carefully as to not cause offence or accusations. They needed each other if they wanted to rise above The Capitol, who might even be planning to take back what was once theirs soon. There was so much to do still, and who knew how much time there was left?

She turned to Kahun finally and spoke to him sternly but not unkindly. "When we are in there you are not to speak unless I ask you out of counsel or your opinion. Do you understand me?"

"Yes," Kahun said too fast for comfort. He cleared his throat and added, "Of course, your majesty."

"I mean it, Kahun. If you are a nuisance of if you say anything that jeopardizes this mission, I can guarantee that it will not end well for you when we return to Nineveh. I do not trust your subconscious, but I require your wisdom. So please speak when spoken to and speak proud and true as you once did before you sought out selfishness."

Kahun's face twisted into a look of both insult and rage but it quickly subsided as fast as it appeared. "As you wish," he said.

"Good," Elizabetha said and before she knew it, they were before the double-doors leading to the main dining hall. Two soldiers that were huge in their black armor stood at attention, and stepped aside as the servant opened them and revealed the massive dining table within. He asked for everyone to come in side and as the group entered, Esmerelda caught eyes with a familiar set of eyes peering at her through the visor of the helmet.

It was a simple room beside a massive stained-glass window with many disfigured pictures of many colors. The table was covered with a long and white cloth, and candles were placed right down the middle that matched the style of the chandeliers in the ceiling above. The chairs were of polished wood with clean white upholstery, it matched perfectly with the table itself. Everything about the room was elegant enough to take Elizabetha's breath away. But what caught her attention most was the old woman sitting in a power chair sitting at the end of the table with her many tubes pumping oxygen and whatever medicine she needed into her lungs.

Elizabetha smiled at the queen, "Hello, Psyren."

The old woman whose head had been bowed looked up. Upon seeing the queen her wrinkled face spread into a large smile. "Elizabetha, you look as lovely as you did when you were just a child..."

Elizabetha raised her hand and her soldiers came around the entirety of the table, enclosing it within their elongated circle. Positioned around the room, the Xerxan soldiers who were assigned her stiffened and Queen Psyren raised her own hand and they relaxed but kept their eyes glued to the men now surrounding the table. None of the Angels however dared to get too close to Psyren for fear of invading her space as well as overstepping boundaries.

Elizabetha however told Kahun to remain standing for a moment and she came around the table towards Psyren who likewise turned her wheelchair away and rolled over to meet her halfway. Once they reached one another, Psyren reached out with frail and mummified hands and took both of Elizabetha's in them.

"My lord," she said fraily. "You've really grown so much..."

"It's been a long time," said Elizabetha. "Back when my mother was alive."

"And I've kept hers and your secrets my whole life," said Psyren. "Duka did as well."

"How did he pass?" asked Elizabetha.

"Peacefully," said Psyren somberly. "Twenty-two years ago. He would have loved to hear the rumors passing about the Wastelands about the rise of the City of

Angels again. When I heard that you had taken over Nineveh, it was no wonder that my troops had been pushed out."

Elizabetha nodded. She was caught off guard by that remark and had hoped to discuss it over food, but as it was there was little to be done. "I am hoping we can come to understanding as to what had happened and what needs to be done."

"I hope so as well," Psyren said now releasing Elizabetha's hands. "I'm not getting any younger, and I must do what I must for the good of my people. Sit beside me, let us talk before the food arrives."

Psyren turned her chair and returned to her initial spot. Elizabetha took the seat beside her and then waved for Kahun to join them on the opposite side. With her sitting to Psyren's left and Kahun her right, she now introduced Psyren to her council.

"What sort of name is Kahun?" Psyren asked him. "Is that from the Southern Sands?"

"Just off the border, your highness," said Elder Kahun. "Near Bronzeshire."

"Bronzeshire," Psyren repeated nodding her head. "Another village abandoned to the frontier."

Kahun looked at Elizabetha uncomfortably and so the queen of Levitika said, "Psyren, I would like to discuss with you what has happened so far, and where we are at now, both Levitika and Nineveh."

"Of course," said Psyren looking back to Elizabetha. "Tell me, please. I had not been told much since we began trying to break down that traitor, Ovid. All was the same, until my captains returned claiming that another army had come in and taken the city back when it was within our grasp. Don't look at me like that, Elizabetha. I am just speaking plainly. Please, tell me your side, before my final thread is cut."

And so, Elizabetha told Psyren the story of the crystals awakening. How The Keeper had arrived, and what had followed closely after. She explained that Ovid's elite fleet had been destroyed as well as Ovid himself, and what had transpired upon their arrival to Nineveh. When she got to the part where Xerxes had been run off, whatever was left after a battle ensued, that was when Psyren asked for her to pause for a moment, and the old queen drummed her fingers on the dining table thoughtfully.

At last, she said, "Yes, I was told you moved in. Killed many of my soldiers too by what I heard. You know, many in my castle rumor me insane to invite the queen whose kingdom stole the one we finally had a chance of taking. We needed the mine, and when we heard that Ovid was gone, we took the chance in hopes that it would be easy. And then you showed up. I must admit I am not really happy about that. I'm thin on soldiers as it is."

"I'm afraid," Elizabetha said choosing her words delicately, carefully. "That you are not being told the whole story."

"Whatever do you mean?"

"I mean your commanding officer sought to slaughter and enslave many people in search for a single item in Baron Ovid's possession."

Psyren looked at Elizabetha not with surprise but with acknowledgement. "Oh?"

Not liking that look, Elizabetha asked cautiously, "Do you still have *it* by chance?"

The Queen eyed Elizabetha coolly, almost as if she was trying to see her very thoughts. "If *it*, happens to be what I think it means then yes, in fact it is the only thing keeping me alive right now. Why?"

"Did you happen to come across another?" Elizabetha asked, ignoring the question.

"What does that got to do with anything?"

"Because your commanding officer was looking for another. And he was willing to sacrifice innocent lives to get it. He did not care about the mines you wanted so badly. In fact, a lot of the citizens were being loaded up on slave carts if they had not been killed outright.

The Queens eyes went wide only to shrink back as she peered at Elizabetha with a skeptical glance. "Now why would my officer do that?" she asked as a servant arrived announcing that dinner was to be served. Psyren told him to wait a moment, never once taking her eyes off of Elizabetha.

Kahun cleared his throat. "Your majesty, my queen speaks the truth."

"Was I talking to you?" Psyren demanded, her eyes still drilling holes into Elizabetha's otherwise passive face. "Some council for you, sir, never intervene when one leader demands answers from another. Especially, if both are in dire positions."

A warning of sort, both to Kahun, and Elizabetha both. Not out of unkindness, but genuine disbelief and demanding of answers.

She continued, saying, "My soldiers, all of them, does everything in order to benefit my people, and protect them from The Capitol. My commanding officer in charge of taking Nineveh was to preserve the city under a single banner, not to enslave. So what proof do you have of this?"

"My Angels had all been equipped with body cameras," said Elizabetha. "Many have witnessed cruel actions taken by some Xerxan forces against the defenseless citizens of Nineveh. I've no doubt that the best intentions were made in order to preserve, however, once you look into each and every single report presented to me, then you will see that your men either acted out of cruelty for cruelty's sake, or they were commanded to do so by whom your soldiers refer to as, the Hunter Ghost."

Psyren said nothing, her face remaining as impassive as a statue's.

"I accuse him of nothing as of yet, only reporting what I witnessed and what my Angels had witnessed, on top of other reports offered willingly by the Ninevite citizens. What I will accuse the Hunter Ghost of, is for the attempted murder of another crystal bearer."

Psyren reached for her side and took up her oxygen mask, the plastic all stained with mucus and other stains. She took a deep breath inside, the hissing of the machines keeping her alive sounding like a thousand snakes in the dining all. All awaited the queen's response with bated breath, especially that of the Xerxan soldiers who looked to one another nervously.

At last, Psyren removed her mask, saying, "If what you say is the truth, then it should very well be rectified. However, there had been many crystal-bearers since the fall of The Capitol, some of which had been members of the very same cult The Mad King had sought council from, most of which, my Hunter had been assigned to track down and kill. What makes this one that you claim so important, just as?"

"Because this crystal bearer," said Elizabetha patiently, although she had been waiting for this opportunity to come at last. "Happened to be the very person that brought Levitika out of the shadows at last. You know very well what our return to the world means, don't you remember, Psyren?"

Psyren's eyes narrowed, then widened as the recollection snapped into place at last. "You mean..."

"Yes," said Elizabetha. "Your Hunter had tried to murder The Keeper in order to take the crystals he had. The Prophecy has finally begun."

The queen of Xerxes made no movement in her wheelchair but merely stared at Elizabetha with unbelief, joy, and concern all at once. During this time food had been permitted to be brought, However, neither queen made a move to go for the food which consisted of some fish fillets and potatoes and soup, save for Kuhan who ladled and unladled his soup over and over as if attempting to paddle to some far away place. The Angels nearby only watched for Psyren's reaction, and the Xerxan soldiers looked to one another with greater vigor and disbelief.

Soon, after minutes of uncomfortable silence Psyren backed up in her chair, and then turned to face the window overlooking the city. She remained silent for a moment more before she spoke her voice cracked and weary.

"So it is true..."the queen said never turning to look at Elizabetha. "The dreams, they told me *something* was happening. But I would have never thought of this."

"Yes," Elizabetha said feeling compassion for this woman whose entire world and what she thought it consisted of being challenged once again.

Psyren shook her head still looking outside. "I don't know what to say."

"Say that you will join us as you once promised," Elizabetha implored Psyren. "This whole thing is much bigger than you and I, and greater still than all three kingdoms combined. I don't know what your Hunter had been thinking, but this needs to be rectified immediately, and any crystals in your possession must be given to The Keeper so that we can ensure that the terrors will end and The Capitol cannot resurrect their monstrosities ever again."

"The Mad King," said Psyren to Elizabetha's surprise. "I hear him sometimes in my sleep. He is always laughing. Always vowing to come back from the grave. Tell me, Elizabetha, will he do so?"

"Not if we can stop him first," said Elizabetha.

Psyren shook her head. "I just can't believe-"

All of a sudden, the metallic sound of a trap being sprung and the spurting of rendering flesh filled the air, and horrible choking sounds followed. Turning about, both Elizabetha and Kuhan watched in horror as the Xerxan soldiers began to clutch at their throats, blood seeping through the metal armor and down their front. They had dropped their weapons in this sudden pain and surprise and were now falling to the floor thrashing and gurgling as blood filled their mouths.

"What the hell?!" Kuhan said standing straight up and knocking his chair back. All the Angels had turned about now, watching in mute horror but keeping their weapons drawn as all the Xerxans convulsed on the floor. Psyren who had turned her wheelchair to see the commotion had enlarged eyes and was breathing hysterically into her oxygen mask.

"What is this?" she demanded. She looked towards the door, mouth opening as if to call out to some other guards when the entrance to the dining hall burst open, and someone came charging in stepping over the corpses of the two soldiers out front, one of their helmets removed and a gray and ashen face revealed speckled in blood and Elizabetha recognized who it was immediately and stood to give her command.

"Seize him!" she bellowed pointing at the intruder who waltzed right over the body of Grim. He was a tall man, garbed in thick black rags that covered what looked like leather armor and wore a mask of black metal in the shape of a skull, the teeth elongated pipes that hissed out steam as if it were a tank engine. The eye sockets of the skull were deep red, and clutched in both hands were a pair of serrated knives.

The Angels sprung into action, and that was when the *true* chaos began.

Ashlyn

Ashlyn was horror-stricken.

She had taken her eye off the scope momentarily, just a brief moment, to reach into her pocket and remove the tin-foil wrap that was inside. From it, she removed a stocky piece of wrapping that looked like a stogie and had just stared at it for a moment. She then placed the thick blunt into her mouth and her mouth immediately salivated at the taste of the paper used to wrap the Buckweed.

She wanted to light it, but she had no lighter. Even if she had, the smell would linger and she wouldn't have enough tine after without risking being spotted after this was over. She was trembling, but the mere taste of the Buckweed had calmed her, and she had pulled her head close to the scope again and resettled it on the dining windows.

Suddenly through the infrared glass of her scope, she witnessed a scene that caused her jaw to drop, the Buckweed dropping from her mouth and plopping onto the platform before her. Those who were along the walls of the dining hall had dropped their weapons, clutching at their throats and then collapsing to the ground, the Angels reacting startled.

"Uh, did you see that?" Silva's voice came over the comms.

"See what?" Gabriel's voice then asked. "Grim, what–"

Ashlyn didn't hear whatever was said next. All at once the attention of the entire dining room was focused to her right, and before she could say or ask anything, something moved in too fast that it caused the infrared to blur. One by one the Angels fell to the ground, like a pencil connecting dots and each man did not get up until at last the blur faded like dissipating mist and then someone was standing right behind the figure that was Elizabetha who had stood up in the sudden confusion.

The man who had been sitting right in front of the queen was standing too, and the figure behind Elizabetha made a sudden move and the man before her head snapped back before likewise collapsing to the ground.

Not wasting any time, Ashlyn settled her sights on the figure right behind Elizabetha who had taken the queen hostage, an arm hooking around her throat. The reticle bobbed and weaved over the head. Ashlyn tried to calm herself, to settle her breathing so that she could properly shoot. She tried to squeeze the trigger, and her finger only trembled, almost defiantly.

Elizabetha

What had happened was too fast for Elizabetha to process. The Angels all raised their guns at the masked intruder, but before any of them could fire off a shot by her orders, the man suddenly disappeared as black smoke suddenly burst from several places in his armor, casting the entire place into sulfuric darkness.

She heard cries of surprise followed by gurgling, and some of the Angels were firing blindly into the smoke. Then one by one something struck one of the Angels with enough force to rip his throat completely open and as he was collapsing to the ground, the next one collapsed as well. Kahun screamed as the two Angels closest to him suddenly collapsed, their throats likewise ripped open until those directly behind Elizabetha were falling to the ground and she whirled to and fro blindly in the shadows until the shouts and cries of the remaining men ceased abruptly.

Then she felt a rush of wind directly behind her and before she could turn around, a thin but strong arm hooked around her neck and pulled her in tight, and a serrated blade coated red with blood appeared right in front of her face. Kahun's eyes widened as he looked at her and then suddenly the gloved hand holding the knife reeled back and came forward again, letting loose the flailing dagger which plunged into Elder Kahun's left eye, causing his head to snap back and he collapsed to the ground, his body cushioned by the dead Angels who had fallen before him.

Psyren had rolled closer to the table, her eyes squinting in the smokey shadows with her face covered by her oxygen mask. She was coughing badly but her eyes widened when she saw that Elizabetha had been captured.

"Shadow!" her voice cried out muffled by the hissing oxygen mask. "What are you-"

"Calm down, your highness," said the man in the mask, his voice very deep and each word causing steam to break free of the pipping in the mask and almost singing the skin on Elizabetha's face. "Have orders from Ghost to take care of these terrorists before they destroy our city."

"What?" Psyren demanded, her brows knit furiously. "Release her at once!"

"Can't do that, even now we are being watched as spies. This woman lies, she is trying to win your trust and then take over your city."

"He's lying, Psyren." Elizabetha said as calm as she could before the second knife which had been used to slaughter her entire guardship came around again, nearly poking her in the cheek.

"Shut yer trap," the man said.

"I am queen here," Psyren said now attempting to stand from her chair. Her blanket fell from her waist and she nearly collapsed as the oxygen tubes from her mask wriggled and wavered like live wires. "I command you to let her go!"

"Command denied," the man said and pointed his knife at the queen who stared in disbelief. "Sit your wrinkly ass down, *now*."

"Guards!" Psyren attempted to scream out. "Guards!"

"No one's coming, your highness," said the one called Shadow. "Either sit down or I'll pop your kneecaps once I'm done here."

Looking scared and lost at the same time, Psyren collapsed in her chair as she realized what was going on. "If Ghost has commanded you to do this, then I will make sure you are forgiven. But unless you release her right now-"

"And why would I do that?" Shadows demanded. "Ghost had made it pretty clear he wants this bitch dead. Even paid and everything, how can I deny a paying customer?"

Elizabetha locked eyes with Queen Psyren. While the old queen was trembling with such fright, she tried to swallow her own fear and keep her composure as she told Psyren, "This is what you have been dealing with."

The hooked arm came loose and grabbed the back of Elizabetha's head. She was forcibly shoved down her face smacking into the table and then dragged back up again by her hair before the arm hooked around her neck again. Her crown had fallen in the process as well as some pins that let her curls fall loosely about her head like a wig.

"Stop!" Psyren commanded as blood trickled from Elizabetha's nose.

"Under the command of the Hunter Ghost, whom you have put in charge during your sickly absence," Shadow said almost mockingly. "I have been required to restrain you until his return, and an explanation will be given for all of this. Apologies, your highness. But I have me orders."

Psyren was saying something else but Elizabetha didn't hear. Her right ear became tickled as Shadow breathed upon it through his ventilated mask and he said in a voice that was almost moist with the steam, "As for you, scream for me."

"Go to hell," Elizabetha said defiantly.

Shadow chuckled. "You first."

Suddenly the glass window before Elizabetha made a popping sound, a hole having been melted through one of the painted glass pieces. Shadow grunted and his arm came loose from Elizabetha's throat. She lunged forward, her hands catching the table so that she wouldn't fall. She whirled about as she grabbed the table knife and lunged for the man in the mask.

But he was already upon her, his mask hardly dented but merely scorched by the concentrated laser that had punched into the dining hall. He seized her wrist and twisted it, causing her to bow over and as he threw her weight into her, he pinned her to the table and taking his own knife, he laughed as he drove it into her heart.

Elizabetha gasped out once, the wind being knocked out of her as Shadow pushed her ever more onto the table, seeming to push the very life out of her as black spots clouded her vision. The last thing she truly saw before she died was the impractical black skull that stared back with crimson eyes.

Her last conscious thought, was of how sorry she was for Esmerelda, and wishing that she had never become queen, and had been a better mother.

<u>Ashlyn</u>

Ashlyn couldn't believe it. She had successfully managed to finally fire off a shot despite the screaming and clamor in her ear between Gabriel and Silva demanding what was happening. She had shot the man who had grabbed Elizabetha and he nearly fell, but then he was on the queen again and before she knew it...

Ashlyn's mouth twisted and trembled in horror and realizing what had just happened, she covered her mouth and screamed into it, her tears now streaking down her face. She tore her hand away and almost shoved the earpiece all the way into her ear as she practically screamed, "Grim! Elizabetha! The queen is-"

"Oh..." Gabriel's voice came out in almost a moan over the comms. All around the castle the drones were pausing and now hovering near the windows. "Oh my god, no..."

"Gabe, what's going on!?" Silva demanded. "Gabriel! Answer me!"

"The queen is... Oh, god, she's dead. They're all dead!"

"What!? Ashlyn, what the hell-"

"He killed her," Ashlyn said her body now jerking with sobs. "Silva, she's dead!"

"Grim is too," Gabriel said hoarsely. "Oh god, it's a freaking massacre..."

"Ashlyn," Silva's voice came out more commanding than ever before. "Listen to me, abort now. Get your ass out of there."

"But-"

"Guys," Gabriel said almost startling. "I think they found me..."

"What do you mean?" Silva demanded. "Gabriel, can you-"

"Gabriel out," said Gabriel abruptly and immediately the comms went silent.

"Silva?" Ashlyn tried to speak. "Gabriel? What-"

A muffled explosion sounded across the city and Ashlyn looked to see a mushroom cloud of smoke rising from the buildings. Immediately the drones that had been hovering around the castle suddenly began to plumet towards the city below, their power source no doubt lost wherever that explosion was. She tried again and again to reach someone but the comms were dead silent, and with a curse she pulled the earpiece out and hurled it into empty space. She stood up and hurried towards the ladder and began to slide down it. She had forgotten the Photon-Rifle but she didn't care. She felt as if her entire body had gone numb, her mind a lump of matter that could only think of a single thing: get out.

That, and the plagued images of Elizabetha being stabbed followed by the news of Grim's death and the sudden and abrupt explosion which seemed to end Gabriel. She slipped down another building and down a pipe but before she could escape the alleyway, saw that a Behemoth had been hiding nearby and immediately roared to life as it stood up and faced in her direction. She back peddled and hurried down the alleyway just as she heard a shot fire and brick and mortar from the nearby building suddenly erupted like a pipe bomb.

With her original escape route compromised, Ashlyn threw her shoulder into a back door and tore inside. The building looked condemned but if there was anyone inside no one bothered to stop her as she hurried through it and came out another door a block down. She looked down the street seeing that the Behemoth had disappeared down the same alleyway she had gone in and she hurried across the street towards a storm drain on the curb and grabbing hold of it she pulled it open and slipped inside, falling for a moment before crashing down onto the walkway and then spilling over the edge and into the rushing sewage underneath. She managed to get her head back out and she crawled out of the muck and onto the walkway before hurrying down the corridor and upon finding a maintenance hatch, remembered where she was and she took a left and kept going.

She kept going through the rank and disgusting darkness, her body dripping with sewage but not making her feel as miserable as the very idea of what had just happened. Everything had gone wrong so fast, and now she was on her own unless she could meet up with Silva and Gabriel if he was still alive.

For now, she had to return to the coffee shop. That had been their deal should anything happen, and she prayed that it wasn't going to be a mistake, and that she wouldn't arrive alone.

"I... I couldn't..." her voice said sounding hollow in the perpetual darkness, but she couldn't bring words to what she couldn't have done.

The only word resonating in her mind was that she had failed, that she could have saved Elizabetha, but didn't. And the guilt of that simple fact weighed down on her greater than anything she had ever felt in her life.

Somewhere overhead at some point in her return, she thought she heard a single gunshot muffled by the stone walls of Xerxes' sewer system. She thought nothing of it, and kept moving.

Ashlyn

Ashlyn climbed up the sewer ladder that led to the hatch door of their coffee shop. She pulled the knob and pushed the hatch opened and screeched as her head passed the floor, for the barrel of a gun was aimed right at her.

Relief washed over her as she saw Silva holding the weapon, and the woman's whose face was set and ready for a fight, brightened with relief as well and she pulled Ashlyn up the rest of the way and embraced her, wincing at the pain in her right arm for she had been shot in the shoulder.

"Oh, thank god," Silva was saying as she held Ashlyn close. Feeling herself being hugged Ashlyn lost all grip on herself and started to cry. Immediately, Silva pushed Ashlyn away and held her at arm's length. "Ashlyn. Ashlyn!" she barked with a quick shake. "Calm down."

"The... the queen," Ashlyn managed. "I-"

"Don't talk about that right now," said Silva holding a finger up for silence. "That doesn't matter presently. We're in a lot of trouble, and I need you to-"

An explosion blew open one side of the building and eyes widening, Silva then shoved Ashlyn, sending her sprawling back into the hatch and down into the sewers below. "Run!" she screamed as she shut the door and Ashlyn stared up at the blackened ceiling as gunshots sounded. As quickly as they had come they were gone, and a gruff voice began shouting up above.

"Who else is here?" the voice demanded. "Where's the rest of ya, woman?"

"Screw you!" Silva shrieked.

"No thanks," said the voice and another shot sounded. Ashlyn clapped a hand over her mouth in horror as she understood what had happened.

The hatch immediately opened, revealing a face peering in with thick goggles covering his eyes. He smiled broadly, his teeth as thick as tombstones. "'Ello, poppet."

Turning her body about, Ashlyn made a break away from the hatch. She sprinted down the corridor, her shoes nearly causing her to slip and fall back into the sewage and then the deafening roar of a gunshot filled the sewers, momentarily blinding her with a flashing light from behind and Ashlyn cried out as she felt something bite her in the left forearm. She hooked it and cradled it in front of her as she turned the corner and kept running.

She heard the man cursing and then shouting, "Get down there and find her!"

"No way, it stinks in there."

Bang!

"Anyone *else* wanna take a piss on me? 'Ey, you, toss a napalm grenade down there."

"Crap," Ashlyn gasped and grabbed the nearest ladder she was at and climbed up it. To her dismay however the hatch door above her was locked. She cried out and whipped out her knife and began to stab a hole into the rotten wood. She had to hurry before the grenade went off, for she heard the faint clink of a metal striking stone. She stabbed and stabbed until a hole was made big enough to fit her fist through. She reached in and felt around until her fingers caught a latch and after removing it she kicked the hatch open and climbed out just as a deep sound like air blowing against the hollow of a mountain reached her, followed by an intense heat that seemed to flash through the hatch door, catching the door itself on fire. She stared at the flames emitting from the sewer entrance until they soon died down and she was able to see where she was. It looked like an old warehouse, and finding the door between two crates of apples she stepped outside back onto the streets.

Overhead she watched as drones flew towards the direction of the coffee shop. Ashlyn went the opposite direction, sticking to the alleyways to get as far away from the shop as possible.

However, when she finally arrived at the alleyway she had left them in, the alley was empty. But what caught Ashlyn's eye more than the desolated area itself a large isolated tank sat in the roadway surrounded by a few Xerxan soldiers. They all suddenly jumped and Ashlyn stared in disbelief at the person who just appeared out of nowhere. But... that wasn't quite right for the black rags that covered his body wavered about him like flags as if he had been running and came to a complete halt.

Then she saw the boots the man was wearing and the strange light that was coming from the soles. The man was huge, bore a black skull mask and was talking to the soldiers who stood at attention afraid and unsure. What was happening at the castle was anyone's guess, and before Ashlyn could turn the other way and keep going, she saw the same man with goggles turn the corner, wielding a large rifle in his arms and he approached the large black-masked man almost as if they were acquaintances.

She heard the one in the goggles say, "Had one more rat trying to escape. Burned the tunnels, Sid."

"Don't call me that," the man in the mask said in a growl, steam hissing from the tubes that were the skull's teeth.

"Oh, what's wrong?" the one in the goggles said in a mocking tone. "Sad I got the others before you?"

The one in the mask growled. "Enough. What of the body?"

"Don't get your panties in a twist," said the one in the goggles who hefted his rifle and held it over his shoulder like a soldier. "We found it. Burned to a crisp."

"Good, that makes for all spies." The one in the mask turned to the other soldiers. "Good work men, the city is safe now. Those of you who are with Ghost, return to the castle. We need to get it on lockdown immediately. Quickshot, want to join me in checking on the queen?"

"Ooo, royalty!" said the one in the goggles. "Sounds fun."

I wonder who the corpse was they found... Ashlyn thought feeling bile rise into her throat once again. The man in the mask continued to speak to the nearby soldiers. "Clear the area, anyone come outside today, shoot them. No one is relieved from curfew until dawn."

"Yes sir," the men said in unison and the two men who had to be Hunters climbed abord the tank which began to tread down the road causing a minor quake in the ground. Waiting for them all to go and being careful not to be seen, Ashlyn then took off and ran as far away from the scene as she could.

Ashlyn soon decided to stop in an alleyway not far from The Hole in The Wall. On her way to her current position, she had enough time to think and come up with a plan. Grim was dead. The others were dead, and she was all alone. She came to a halt near the wall rested her head back against it and sighed as a single tear trickled down her cheek. The fear of being alone now being mingled with the guilt of allowing Queen Elizabetha to die.

"No… no…"

"Hey! You!"

Ashlyn whirled around and saw a soldier at the end of the alleyway. He was raising his gun and Ashlyn dove behind a dumpster a shot was fired off. A second was fired, and she saw the laser beam shoot right above her head and into the back wall.

Remembering her sidearm, Ashlyn reached for one of the straps underneath her jumpsuit and pulled out the laser pistol inside. She took a peek around the corner and pulled her head back just in time before she got shot. After a second of collecting herself, she popped up and took aim clutching the gun in both hands and once the sights were trained on the soldier now startled by the weapon in her hand, she squeezed the trigger three times, the recoil on the weapon next to nothing.

"Anna, wait!" the solider suddenly said, holding out one hand as if to catch the shots the moment she had fired at him.

Two of her shots had gone too high, passing by the man's head and nearly striking his helmet as well as his left shoulder. The third however struck him in the belly and he doubled over as a splotch of black bloomed in his midsection. He collapsed to his knees and at this point the voice registered in Ashlyn's brain.

"Oh my god," Ashlyn said now rushing for the soldier. "Uzzah?"

Uzzah was cursing, clutching at his belly and heaving. Having been struck by concentrated energy, the radiated heat from the laser beam was no doubt poisoning him as well as burning him. As she neared he held up a hand and said, "Get back…"

She paused, now hearing the sound of whistles shrilling not so far away. Uzzah heard it too, and he turned his helmeted head in the direction of the nearest blasts. He turned back to stare at her.

"You're… you're…"

He collapsed to into a fetal position onto the alleyway ground. Ashlyn started for him but he was waving his free hand at her not looking back. "Just go, get out of here…"

"But-"

"Go!" he nearly begged in a cry of anguish from the pain in his belly. This time, Ashlyn didn't argue and she turned on her heel and ran. She ran past the dumpster as the whistles grew closer and closer, and then the clamoring of men finding Uzzah in the alley, and someone demanding for a medic drone to come in.

Ashlyn ran on. But the more she ran, the more she heard the presence of soldiers running down the streets as well as the hum of drones overhead. Unable to stay out in the open much longer, Ashlyn turned to find another

Ashlyn kicked the manhole cover open and jumped inside. To afraid to say anything she took off running down the main pipeline water and sludge splashing around her feet as she sprinted away. She had to get as far away from the soldiers as possible. As she was on the move, she heard the sound of boots sloshing through waters up ahead and she immediately took a corner near an exit piped and jumped into it. She held a hand over her mouth listening to the sound of the splashes getting closer and closer. She then saw the beam of a flashlight and soon a soldier with a gas mask passed the pipe she was hiding in. He did not look back however, but kept running on panting heavily as he searched the tunnels. When it seemed safe enough and the guy was gone a distance, Ashlyn crept back out of the pipe and kicking off her wet shoes she took off running down the line of the pipe on the little walkway now moving as silently as the rats that were scampering about. She did not look back as she grabbed ahold of the ladder which led up to another drainage silt in the street. She squeezed her body through the drain and ended up back on the streets of Xerxes, she then got back up and took off running. How long she ran or how far she did not know. But she wanted to put as much distance between her and the search party as possible.

When she finally decided to stop Ashlyn was near the southern wall panting heavily. This was it. She was stuck here. Was the man lying about the gates? Probably. But she could not risk trying to leave through the main entrance, she would need to find another way out. But first she would have to find a way- somehow to communicate to Nineveh about the queen.

At the thought of the deceased Elizabetha, Ashlyn began to sob. All because she took her eyes away for a brief moment, and in the time the carnage was happening, she was too scared to do anything.

You let her die, a voice seemed to say in Ashlyn's head almost mockingly. *You got them all killed.*

She angrily wiped her tears away and sat down between a pair of crates as thunder began to rumble overhead. The rain would wash the slime off of her, which was a good thing but she would be stuck outside in the cold. She could not risk putting someone else in danger by sneaking into a house. She didn't want anything to do with the people here. She had been reduced almost comically fast once again down to a street rat. The streets would be her home until she either found a way out of the city without getting caught or radioing someone from the outside to help her. She had to let the others know, but right now the only thing on her mind was to survive.

She took out her knife and opened it up. She cut off the straps of her jumpsuit and peeled it off, discarding it in the corner and although the suit had protected her from the sewage, her clothes were damp and becoming more so in the rain. Then taking her ponytail, she cut her hair right above the rubber band she kept it up with. Seeing her long auburn hair now disconnected in one hand now made her sad, but she tossed it into the nearest trash can and let her new hair length tumble onto her face. It didn't alter her appearance too dramatically, but it would be enough for her to remain unnoticed at a distance. She then shoved the knife and her pistol into her belt and began to walk the line of the alleyway. She soon found an old poncho that was brown and stained with black stuff. She placed it over her shoulders to keep the rain from giving her hypothermia. The sludge was washed away at this point so that was a plus. But the sense of horrid cleanliness was not enough to purge the pain in her heart. Grim and the queen were gone, and she was all alone in the Industrial City.

She soon found a small dumpster that appeared empty and she hopped inside ignoring the rancid smell within. She propped herself against the inner wall and sighed. She was safe for now, but the familiar sense of being a street rat once more began to seep into her consciousness. *Back at square one*, she thought bemusedly.

She wished Markus was here. In fact, Ashlyn would have given anything if Markus was only here with her, not to share her suffering, but to give her a sense of confidence- a sense of hope. Because when he was around, no matter the circumstances, Ashlyn always knew that with him everything was going to turn out alright. Until she saw him again, Ashlyn would have to remain strong on her own. All she could do now was wait until morning, and pray that Markus, as well as the people of Nineveh and Levitika both were okay, and some way, somehow, knew what was happening and would come for her.

"Help me…" Ashlyn then whispered to no one in particular as she closed her eyes and fell asleep inside the dumpster, the only sound being the rain drumming off the top being her only company in the city where she was truly alone.

A street rat, once more.

"Help me…" she whispered once more as the rain continued to pour overhead over the city, as well as the Wastelands beyond, as well as her own rain rolling depressingly down her cold cheeks.

Everything had been taken away from her seemingly out of nowhere. She had managed to escape Nineveh with the help of Markus and Ruth, end up becoming good friends with them and becoming stronger with Markus through their time in Levitika together, only to be reduced to nothing. All her training, all the plans made with Grim and the others, and all of it had been reduced to nothing; a full revolution of her chance at a new life and a new beginning, all lost because of fate, bad luck, or perhaps her own carelessness in delving back into the very drug that made her numb to the every day life back in Nineveh. She seemed to have escaped, just to come back and lose her chance at revenge against the person who had done it to her in the first place, only to end up as nothing once again by another sinister force.

Tears of despair mingled with tears of outrage. The injustice of it all was so great that Ashlyn couldn't help but tremble with a force far greater than the cold rain could ever provide. This proved to her as ironic because deep down she blamed herself for what happened to her team. She hadn't been paying attention the entire time, and had gotten Queen Elizabetha and perhaps the others all killed. This full circle she found herself in having only been complete the moment she had decided to sneak in that damned Buck Weed with her into Xerxes.

Those bastards…

Yes, perhaps this whole situation was in part her fault. What happened to her and her team now may partly be her fault, but it was those Hunters who had executed their chance. Those who had given chase to Ashlyn and would no doubt be looking for her, maybe even Uzzah himself. She was alone now, and no one was going to come to her rescue just yet. Unless word managed to get sent out what had happened to Elizabetha, Levitika wouldn't come to her rescue just yet.

Yes, she was a street rat again, lost in a city she had no business being in. But perhaps that was in itself a good thing, because at least now, Ashlyn had a chance to make things right. She might have played a part in causing all this to happen, but she could at least try and do something about it.

Wiping her tears away, Ashlyn went out into the city and as she had done so in Nineveh, she stuck to the shadows, the small places where someone like her could hide. She would do her part here in Xerxes, because to accept defeat was not an option for her. Once more she was back in a position of being prey for a great horde of predators. Now she would have to prove to herself at the very least, that she could at least fight back. Somehow, in someway, if Levitika still comes for Xerxes or even just to avenge the death of the queen, Ashlyn could at least do her part here, on the inside. What part that would be, she hadn't a clue still. But she refused to go back to how it had been back in Nineveh. She refused to wait for someone to come along again. She refused to go back to the damned drug that helped in getting herself in this mess in the first place.

She owed it to the team, to Elizabetha and her daughter who would no doubt be devastated. More importantly, she owed it to Markus as well as herself.

"Please," she found herself saying despite going out with no destination in sight, at least not yet. "Help me."

She was going to need all the help she could get.

Esmerelda

Esmerelda awoke from a terrible, terrible nightmare.

She sat bolt upright in her bed, her raven hair heavy with sweat and more coating her back causing her nightgown to stick to it like a second layer of skin. Her eyes were wide, taking in every minute detail in her darkened room, and in the corner of her eye she saw a faint glow begin to appear on her nightstand as Q-Pid began to boot up, and she realized she had cried out loud for the robot never powered on unless she heard Esmerelda's voice.

She looked around the room as if to convince herself that this was real and that the nightmare had truly ended. She had seen Markus laying in a pool of blood on some beach far away, a skull and crossbones brand on the back of his neck. Ashlyn was locked up in some prison somewhere, her wrists and ankles in shackles her face beaten and bloodied. Her mother…

Her mother was dead. But she had come to Esmerelda in her sleep as if she had come all this way back only to tell her so. The front of her favorite teal dressed was stained black with blood, her eyes as silver and dead as ball bearings. She was reaching out for Esmerelda with arms that stretched all the way from the foot of her bed to her pillow where they began to grasp at her neck and shake her. Esmerelda, paralyzed with terror could only sit there gasping for breath while in reality her body merely ceased breathing, the dream far too real to convince her brain otherwise.

"My daughter," Elizabetha said in a raspy voice. "There isn't much time- Wake up!"

Elizabetha had tried to scream but nothing had come out of her mouth. It was as if her own vocal chords had been cut off and she was left wheezing as her mother proceeded to shake her. Seeing something just past Elizabetha, Esmerelda glanced and saw a young boy standing almost directly behind the corpse of a queen. He was very small, thin, with gray and wrinkly skin looking no better than a mummified corpse himself. That is, except for his eyes, which were a bright and luminescent green like neon. Esmerelda knew this child well. He had come to her in her dreams ever so often.

"Esmerelda," he said in his shrill whisper of a voice. "There isn't much time. Get up. Get up."

"WAKE UP!" Elizabetha screamed in Esmerelda's face, her face turning as gray as the child's only to peel away to a screaming skull.

That was when Esmerelda had finally woken up, taking a deep breath and crying out loud in terror in the dark of her room. Now Q-Pid was hovering towards her, landing softly into her lap like a cat and looking up at her curiously. Recalling the most gruesome of details from the dream, Esmerelda began to shiver, her arms hugging herself as if to restrain whatever warmth she still possessed.

"Just a nightmare," she said to the curious Q-Pid who chirped as if to ask what was wrong. "Just a nightmare…" But she was said this as if she were merely trying to convince herself.

And what a nightmare it had been. Esmerelda couldn't remember having one so horrible, so lifelike. And why had the Eldest's Son been there? He hardly ever came to her anymore, not the way he had when she was a child. The last time she had even heard from him was when she introduced Markus and Ashlyn to him, and even then there was hardly anything to truly be said.

So what could this mean?

Bang-bang-bang! a sudden and brisk knocking sound came and Esmerelda jumped, having to clap both her hands over her mouth to hold back the terrified scream that nearly escaped her. Q-Pid who had been launched into the air because of her knee began to hover back down turning it's little metallic head back and forth as if to shake itself back into reality.

"Princess Esmerelda?" the guard on the other side sounded out of breath and hysteric. "Your highness?"

"What is it?" Esmerelda demanded. She slipped out of bed and put on her slippers. She slipped into a fluffy robe and demanded with greater vigor, "Has something happened?" as she approached her bedroom door and opened it.

It was a new guard, not the one who had been on duty outside her room earlier. The guy had removed the helmet of his power armor and looked paler than cheese. As if he had seen a ghost.

"It is Slagar, princess," the guard said with lack of breath. "He needs to see you, immediately."

"Tell him it can wait until morning." Esmerelda said pulling back on the door but then the guard stuck his foot in and reached in, grabbing her by the wrist. Esmerelda tried to recoil, but the man had the iron grip of a shackle.

"What are you doing!?" she demanded.

"He said to take you there one way or another," the guard said as he dragged her out of the room leaving her door hanging ajar. He started pulling her down the hall seeming completely complacent as Esmerelda dug in her heels and tried to pull her hand away.

"What is the meaning of this?" Esmerelda demanded as she fought the guard. "Let me go! I can walk! Why is this so important?"

The guard ignored her question and her demands. "Hey!" She stopped pulling and leapt up, punching the guy in the back of the head and making him stagger forward but he still didn't let her go.

Something brushed by her and a metallic dragonfly had clung to the side of the man's head and she watched as the robot shoved it's metallic abdomen into his ear. This got the man's attention and he released Esmerelda and began to swat at the robot who buzzed about his head distracting him. Esmerelda took several steps back and when the soldier looked back towards her, in the dim lighting of the gas-fed torches, she saw that the man's eyes were slightly tinged with red, something that she had not been able to see while she was in the darkness of her room.

The guard had mentioned Slagar...

The guard lunged for Esmerelda, grabbing her arm again and when Q-Pid tried to intervene again, Esmerelda told the robot to stop.

"Get out of here!" she commanded the dragonfly. "Fly away from here, find someone, anyone who can help."

Q-Pid ignored this and went to attack the soldier again. He cursed and tried to grab at the robot again and then he grabbed hold of his laser pistol and raised it.

"No!" Esmerelda pulled all her weight down, dragging the soldier down with her and sending his gun aiming towards the ceiling before he fired and it left a burning hole in it. Q-Pid was still buzzing about frantically and chirping shrilly.

"Just go!" Esmerelda commanded the robot. "Get out of here, get help!"

Q-Pid buzzed angrily but then she shot down the hall back in the direction they had come from. The soldier was glaring down after the dragonfly, raised his pistol as if to shoot again, but then holstered it, cursing the robotic bug and hauling Esmerelda to her feet. She still fought, cursing the man and threatening his very life once this was all over. She even tried to say the few words that often broke the hypnotic trance of Slagar, should he go out of his way to do such a thing to anyone in the castle. As her mother once predicted, the words were meaningless, as Slagar had learned the words and changed them.

She was then shoved into the main throne room where all the elders were as well as Slagar who was looking out the main window with his back turned to them. They all watched as Esmerelda was shoved to the floor and they all backed away as Slagar turned about. Glaring at each and every single one of them, Esmerelda saw none of the red tint in their eyes meaning that these Elders knew exactly what was happening. Judging by their passive expressions as well, they were all very much afraid.

Esmerelda stood up angrily, padding through the throne room as she had lost her slippers in the struggle with the guard who had shut the door as he left. She marched straight over to Slagar who smiled as she approached, as if he was enjoying the sight of the princess being here now.

"Slagar, what is the meaning of this? I demand an explanation." Esmerelda crossed her arms as the wizard turned around with a grim expression on his face.

"Princess Esmerelda," he said just above a whisper. He motioned to the throne nearby. "Why don't you have a seat?"

"I'll stand," Esmerelda said curtly. "What the hell did you drag me out of bed for and with a hypnotized guard no less? You better have a good reason for this." She began to drum her fingers against her forearm as she awaited an answer from the old man.

"Men," he said to the Elders looking over Esmerelda's head as he often had many, many times before. "As I have predicted, the princess is obviously under duress and needs a rest. I propose we proceed with Act four-point-two as signed by Queen Elizabetha.

The Elders nodded murmuring approval. Glaring at them and then returning her eyes back to Slagar, Esmerelda demanded, "What are you talking about?"

Slagar shook his head in mock sympathy for the child. "Oh, come now princess, you are obviously greatly upset, considering you have just found out that your dear mother is dead."

Esmerelda's heart stopped dead in her chest as she scowled at Slagar, her arms slipping from one another to hang at her sides. She was clenching her fists angrily.

"You're lying."

"Oh no, I am afraid I'm not. Your mother was killed by Queen Psyren's own men, gunned her down in her own castle."

"That's impossible, how could that be!?" Tears were threatening to spill from Esmerelda's eyes, but her outrage and sudden fear of what this Act 4.2 has kept them at bay, at least for the time being.

"It is possible, and it has happened," Slagar confirmed. "I have just received confirmation from poor old Elder Kahun's life monitor. He has been killed as well. The deal has been botched, and the fate of Nineveh and Xerxes has been sealed, sadly by your mother's blood."

"No..." Esmerelda shook her head as she fell to her knees. "No, no, no, no!" She looked up at Slagar with fierce tears in her eyes. "You did this! You knew it was going to happen, did you!?"

She shot up and clawed at the wizard who shoved her back onto the ground as if she was a little child trying to play. She laid there unable to stop the tears and she was now crying helplessly trying desperately to not believe the words that have entered her ears.

"You bastard..." she sobbed.

"See men?" Slagar said pointing to the princess. "She is very unstable and needs rest. I will be taking over operations here in Nineveh now, and will take role of leader of both cities."

"You can't do that!" Esmerelda shouted, her rage causing her tears to fly as her head snapped back up to yell at Slagar. "I am the princess, I am ruler here!"

"Not anymore," said Slagar shaking his head. "You are in too much distress, you are too unstable to rule. As part of Act four-point-two, as signed by your mother, should you be under great duress and unable to rule, I will take over in your stead."

Not believing this, Esmeralda looked at the Elders for help. None of them met her gaze, all eyes looking down at their polished boots.

"You can't let him get away with this! I am the one in charge here!"

The Elders offered no help once so ever, and Esmerelda jumped at the sound of the doors slamming behind her. She turned to see Vic lugging towards them. Relief washed through Esmerelda at the sight of a potential friend in need. Q-Pid had come through after all.

"Ye summoned me?" Vic said to Slagar and then saw who it was on the floor. His three eyes turned wide as he turned back to the Mage. "What is going on here?" He demanded as he started for the princess.

"Stay where you are," Slagar said holding up a hand, his eyes turning crimson momentarily. He had grown stern, not as cocky as he was with Esmerelda.

Vic paused, his three mutant eyes turning a shade of crimson as he came to a complete stop, standing upright with a look of complacency on his face just mere feet away from Esmerelda.

"What is... happening...?" Vic asked in a monotone.

"Nothing that concerns you," said Slagar pointing past the large man. "Leave us."

Vic started to go, albeit very slowly.

"Vic!" Esmerelda cried out as he was turning. "My mother's been killed!"

Vic had paused a second after this news came. He slowly turned back as if reversing in slow motion. Slagar's eyes narrowed at the large man and he commanded Vic to leave again. The mutant paused again but he didn't resume to look back at the princess nor did he turn back to leave.

"The queen…" he said. "Is…"

The Elders were all looking at Slagar nervously. At their gazes Slagar swept a free hand before him as if to clear the air. "He's under my control, don't fret. This might turn out better than I had hoped. Vic, look at me."

This time, Vic turned completely like a robot, staring over Esmerelda and directly at Slagar.

"I've heard you've found a batch of Pluton-Oil north of the city, correct?"

Vics brow furrowed but then relaxed with the flexibility of a relaxing rubber band. "Yes…"

"And what was it you were making with such an element?" Slagar asked his eyes piercing through Vics.

Vic seemed to be struggling, his mouth shifting and moving. When Slagar repeated the question, Vic answered, "I was making a new oil for the queen's battle-droids. We have plenty but she wanted an oil that could keep them going forever."

Esmerelda's eyes widened at this. So Vic had been lying about the weapon he was making? He was working for her mother this whole time?

"Slagar," one of the Elders said. "Does this mean the queen has another plan for the droids? Nothing batter-operated as before?"

"Appears so," said Slagar shaking his head. "Elizabetha had been scheming it seems. Can't say that I blame her."

"Vic!" Esmerelda called out to Vic again, breaking free of her paralysis thanks to the news of her mother's plans. "They're doing this, I know you can hear me, you have to-"

"Vic!" Slagar bellowed, seizing whatever will the mutant had left. "Take the princess to my quarters. She needs much more than rest I believe." He said this with a cruel smile on his lips as he stared down at Esmerelda.   "No wait!" Esmerelda said trying to stand as Vic lunged for her and his massive arms hooked around her body. He lifted her straight off the ground and she tried to fight without hurting the man. She glared at Slagar and pointed at him. "You can't do this, Slagar!"

"Oh, but I can." Slagar said. "And these men before you, they have no choice. They must follow the leader of Levitika for the good of their city."

"You're no leader!" Esmerelda shouted and then to the Elders all in turn even as Vic started to pull her away slowly and yet deliberately. "I am your princess! I am the rightful heir of Elizabetha! If you honor my mother at all, then seize that bastard!"

She had pointed at Slagar who smiled as the men did nothing. None of the Elders dared to meet Esmerelda's gaze. None looked to Slagar either. No one was speaking for her benefit.

She couldn't believe it. "You cowards... you can't do this! I'm the princess, dammit!"

"And you obviously are too distraught right now to make any decisions for the good of the city," Slagar said addressing those around him. "Isn't that right, gentlemen?"

They all nodded somberly. Even Vic.

"Vic!" Esmerelda said turning to look into the tranquil face of the mutant. "You can't let him get away with this!"

"What... choice do I have?" he asked her helplessly as he continued to drag her towards the door.

"You're insane, Slagar!" Esmerelda shouted back at the hypnotist. "You monster, a goddamned traitor! I'll see to it that you pay for this!"

Slagar sneered at the princess. "And you are in no position to address me in such a way." He turned to the Elders. "Gentlemen, one of you call for one of our generals to head to Vic's shop with a squad and raid it. Remove any illegal weaponry and problematic matter. But bring the Pluton-Oil here. We'll put it to good use."

They all murmured in compliance to their new leader.

"And, Vic?" Slagar said as soon as the mutant reached the door. The mutant turned and the hypnotist gave one final command to him. "Make sure that the princess is well restrained. She will need much more to remedy her ailments..."

He said this whilst licking his lips at the princess which sent a shiver down her spine. As Esmerelda was then taken through the doors, she heard Slagar say to the Elders, "Well men, let us toast, to a new era and a new time for Levitika. A new ruler, and a new future." He paused for a moment and then spoke just as the doors closed blocking him from Esmerelda's sight as she screamed. "It is all mine now."

Esmerelda screamed as she was dragged down the hall, desperate for someone- anyone to save her and put an end to the nightmare she had been awaken to. Vic shut the door and started down the hall. She fought more vigorously than ever before, and still the mutant kept walking, and no one heeded her screams.

"Mom..." she whispered as she went limp in the mutant's arms too tired and broken to fight any longer. "Mom... no... please..." and she wept bitterly.

<u>Markus</u>

Markus was balancing on a piece of rope that was stretched between two stumps as he balanced some rocks in the air, levitating them with the energy between them and his hand as the crystals glowed dimly in the dark area around him.

The clouds were coming in fast, and the salty air smelled like rain was coming, and fast. Some of the villagers were restocking their firewood before the storm came by, and the women were taking their clothes inside. Markus who had been constantly training his body in tests of strength, endurance, and most recently balance, decided to stop for the night and help in any way he could. By the looks of Abram who was smoking a pipe in front of his house, he had permission to do so.

Markus jogged over to a lady who was carrying some wood over to her house. Markus stopped her and offered to take the wood for her.

"That is so sweet of you, thank you," the woman said with a toothy grin.

"Happy to," Markus said picking up the bundle of logs as if they weighed no more than a small stack of clothing. He followed her to her cabin, keeping his eye out on the others as he did so. He caught the eyes of the same girl who had been watching him the first time he arrived on the island and she looked away in a real hurry.

The woman began to chuckle. "Looks like you have an admirer."

"Oh, I doubt that," Markus said modestly.

"Doubt all you want," said the woman. "I can tell when a girl likes a boy. Chloe there is a sweetheart, comes from a good family."

"I'm sure," said Markus as they reached the cabin. He asked where the woman wanted her logs and she directed him to a miniature shed to pile them into.

"That will be enough," the woman said. She looked at Markus and said, "I know you have been busy with training and don't have time for the likes of us, but I wanted to take the opportunity to thank you."

"It's no problem," said Markus. "I was happy to help."

"I'm not talking about the firewood," said the woman. "Although I am grateful and appreciate it. It's about Abram."

"What about him?" asked Markus curiously.

"You lifted a great burden off his shoulders." The woman looked in the direction of Abram's cabin and continued, "That man came here back when we were considered in Ronin's territory. He was a broken man, and when he spoke to our chieftain, he spoke of wonders that we never would have thought possible off the mainland. We thought him crazy, until he displayed his true power. That crystal he carried, he used it to protect us from Ronin's pirates, make our food grow, make life easier. But he always did it as a way to cope with something, we could all tell despite how grateful we were for him."

The woman looked back at Markus and sitting down on her front porch, said directly to him, "I don't know much about these crystals and what true significance they have. I and others don't put a lot of stock in this Dreaming you and he talk about, but I know that for all the good it does, it leaves a heavy burden on whoever wields it. Ever since you destroyed his crystal, he seems much livelier than before."

This was true. Ever since the destruction of Essau's Crystal, Abram was participating in more of Markus' training with little to no rest. He wasn't as powerful in magic as he had been before, but the old man still contained some trickle of power which surprised Markus from time to time. Along with that he wondered about the protection this place had, and had thought to ask the old man on it but hadn't gotten to it yet.

"I really don't blame him," said Markus. "The way I see it, he's been trying to make things right ever since."

"And he's done well with those who had come seeking his guidance," said the woman. "But like all things, he deserves rest. So from the bottom of my heart and behalf of the rest of us, thank you, Markus."

Markus nodded. "Of course. I'm grateful to him for all he's shown me so far. And to you guys, of course, considering where all the food's coming from."

The woman chuckled. "Before you go, Abram has been discussing something with some of us older folk. Discussions concerning a possible 'welcome to the family' party either tomorrow or later down the week."

"I'm honored," Markus said smiling. After all this training, a celebration would be great. He only wished now that Ashlyn had stuck through with coming with him. Thinking about that only made him wonder how much longer he would be in the Kaiken Isles.

The woman bowed slightly. "We are glad you are here Markus, and taking on a path that many would never dare too. Not many are able to withstand their own demons, least of all someone else's."

"Well, one can only hope and push on," Markus said.

In truth, ever since coming here, he had been worried that he would lose control like before. But he was determined to keep training and preparing himself for the future. If he could do that, maybe he would never have to worry about losing control again.

"Besides," Markus added. "The spirits have been more than helpful." His eyes lingered to the crystals that glowed dimly, and beyond his hand on the porch Markus saw a flash of a green snake that winked at him, and in a flash it was gone once again.

He smiled but it felt out of exhaustion. Nokama appeared to be growing comfortable with him just as Abner did, but regardless of what they felt, what he experienced when severing Essau's link to the real world and The Dreaming had been terrible. Abram had done good in comforting Markus and making him feel capable of wielding magic again, but to do that for every single crystal still out there, it made him question his own sanity and dread what would happen in the future.

"Just remember that they were once like us, Markus," the woman said both in following up with Markus' statement, but also in some way, feeling as if she knew exactly what he was thinking. "They have their own agendas as well. However, I am glad they chose you, and are fighting for the best cause."

"Me too. Thank you miss…?"

"*Mrs*. Campell," the woman smiled. "My husband may have died a while back, but I haven't given up on him yet."

Markus laughed. "That's good." He turned to see Mylo helping his mother take laundry inside. He waved at Markus who waved back. He turned back to Mrs. Campell. "I better go help the others before the rain comes."

"No problem, thank you for talking to me."

"Anytime." He stood and started to go when Mrs. Campell said one more thing.

"You should say hi to Chloe," she suggested with a smile. "I really think you'd like her!"

Markus laughed and waved at the woman. "I'll think on that." With that Markus took off not noticing that the old woman was looking up at the skies that were growing darker, a look of sorrow etched on her face.

Some time later, Markus was helping a man tighten the tethers of one of his cows when Markus felt something that made him stop. He looked up on a whim to see a golden owl perched on the roof of a nearby cabin. The bird hooted and then flew off into the night sky. That troubled Markus. Abner usually never materialized unless something was important. He looked over to Abram who was helping another villager get some water out of a nearby well, and noticed that the old man seemed troubled as well, for he was always looking off into the distance. Markus frowned and turned to the man he was helping.

"Is that good enough?" he asked.

The man nodded and tipped his black hat to Markus. "Yes sir, thank you very much. They don't mind the rain, but the lightning might frighten them don't want them winding up lost or bothered by boars."

"Glad to help." Markus immediately took his leave and jogged over to Abram who sent the other villager home. When Markus reached Abram, he asked, "What is it?"

The old man groaned. "I don't know. Difficult to see without my crystal..."

Markus frowned. Even with his own, he couldn't tell what it was either. "Come on, we should get back to the house. It's gonna rain soon."

The old man lingered for a bit and then finally gave in slowly following Markus. "Yeah. Let's. You should look at the entire island once we are inside."

Markus agreed that was a good idea.

That was when the wind began to pick up, and at that moment Markus didn't only feel anything, he *smelt* it. He spun around facing the forest across the field and peered at the darkness. And sure enough he saw it, whispers of many figures lined up behind the tree line. They were massive, human-shaped but by the smell Markus knew better and he reached over his shoulder for his sheathed sword as he said it. "Lacertas."

Abrams eyes went wide as he pulled out his own weapon. "Kris! Jack! Get your asses out here! We got company!"

That was when a deafening roar filled the air and looking up, Markus saw a Hellhound coming in fast overhead. He ground his teeth at the sigil of Xerxes emblazoned in red on the sides and as the Hellhound passed over the villages, many figures began to drop from the ship which was just barely twenty feet off the ground, kicking up dirt and grass and casting a great wind all throughout.

Except, who were coming out of the ship to land on the rooftops or the grass of the clearing were not human. They were more Lacertas, all wearing minute clothing over their torsos if any at all, wielding various spear-like weapons and roaring their challenges as they plunged into the village whose men had already taken up arms while the women and children were running for the trees.

"Get to the boats!" one man was yelling at the women. "To the boats!"

That was when a Lacerta landed beside him having dropped from the passing Hellhound and when he turned around, the Lacerta which was much larger than Slitzar ever was grabbed him by the shoulders and lifted him up. The man screamed and had dropped his sword in the process and the Lacerta opened it's massive jaws only to close them in a snap upon the man's head.

Shouting, Markus left Abram who was accompanied by the Werecat known as Daryl, who was growling at the intruders and was already bounding off towards the village and rushing past Markus in a blur of movement and fur.

Markus didn't have his sword but he didn't care. He rushed headlong into the village which was now locked in combat with the large lizard people. The Lacerta who had eaten the head of the man shouting at the women and children to flee turned when it saw the Werecat coming and Daryl tackled it to the ground, his teeth biting the back of the creature's neck but unable to paralyze it through the thick scales. That didn't matter however as Daryl's hind claws went wild at the soft underbelly of the Lacerta, ripping it open and bringing it down little by little as he proceeded to rip it apart in a flurry of purple blood.

Markus passed them and taking up the fallen man's sword, rushed for another Lacerta that was smaller than Slitzar and was trying to jab it's spear at another villager who swung his sword wildly in an attempt to dissuade the chuckling creature.

"Hey!" Markus shouted as he accumulated energy into his legs from the crystals and leapt in a nearly twenty foot arch towards the Lacerta. It turned it's head just enough to see Markus coming who swung the sword with all his might and it sank into the back of the creature's neck. It didn't cut all the way through and Markus winced as he heard the squeal of bone against metal but his momentum had brought the creature down and the other villager rushed in and drove his sword into the Lacerta's midsection, bringing it down for good.

They nodded to one another and Markus turned to see Abram rushing for him. He had with him the scabbard which contained Black's shocksword and he hurled it at Markus who abandoned the sword still stuck in the Lacerta's neck and he caught the scabbard and stripped the sword naked before tossing the piece of leather aside.

His weapon in hand, Markus gathered more energy into the crystals, and returned once more into the fray.

It was absolute chaos. There was simply not enough men from the village to hold against the onslaught of Lacertas who were here for blood. Overhead, the Hellhound proceeded to fly overhead as if merely spectating, but Markus didn't bother with it for it was not attacking and instead focused on the battle at hand as some houses began to burn around them.

Markus fought madly, madder than he had back in Nineveh. There he was fighting men who were threatening to take his home, and he had lost his father's staff and his Eagle's Wings in the process. Here, he was fighting what he considered to be nothing more than monsters, and that alone made him fight like a monster himself. He would cut a Lacerta down only to finish it off when it collapsed to the ground and then whirling about he would swing his shock sword again, snapping spears apart or cutting through scales and flesh sending great torrents of violet sailing into the air.

Some of the Lacertas had abandoned their weapons and dropping to all fours, began to gallop towards the villagers and especially Markus and Abram like charging horses. When this group joined their brothers in the clash, it was like nothing he had ever experienced before.

Leaping at an incoming Lacerta, Markus drove feet-first towards it, passing it's grasping claws and the soles of his boots connected to the monster's face, breaking it's jaw and sending it skidding across the field before crashing into another house. Markus got up quickly as another Lacerta went for him, stabbing at the ground with it's rusty sword and hissing indignantly at the boy. It rushed and swung at him but Markus ducked and got deep within it's reach before stabbing it in the chest. Another came at him and after cutting its fighting hand off Markus grabbed the beast's head with his auto-limb hand and pulsed. There had been a flash of light and Markus felt hot dew splatter his cheeks and the monster collapsed to the ground without a head.

Another Lacerta came swinging what looked like a logging saw welded to a large piece of wood like a makeshift sword. Markus had just blocked it with his auto-limb as if it were a shield and before he did anything else, he saw a blade stick out of the creature's neck covered in purple slime and when it fell Markus saw Abram panting heavily behind the fallen corpse. Before Markus could thank the old man, another monster appeared behind Abram, ready to cut him down, but before he could do so a laser shot it in the chest sending the monster falling back it's insides cooked from the concentrated beam.

Markus looked to the man firing a Laser Rifle only to cry out as he saw the man blown apart by a Lacerta that had ran to the cabin and after pushing a trigger exploded in a massive fireball that managed obliterate all who were around it including the men. Before Markus' very eyes one of the men fell off the cabin roof and began thrashing around as flames licked the meat off his bones. Two more monsters then took out some bottles and tossed them against the homes, and they exploded into flames as they struck the wood, adding to the ever-growing fires. Everything that had been the village, the cabins, the gardens, even the livestock which were all screaming in terror and in pain, were all going up in flames.

"Markus," said Abram and the boy looked to the old man with a mixture of outrage and adrenaline. The old man was panting but appeared as calm as ever. "Don't worry, they are just wood. We need to protect the people. Stay focused."

"O... okay," Markus said looking past the old man and seeing the Hellhound had disappeared from the sky. He had not seen where it had gone.

"Come on," said Abram as the yowl of a Werecat pierced the air. "We gotta get to Daryl."

Markus looked at the men locked in combat and Abram said, "They'll be fine, come with me."

Markus nodded and they hurried towards the rest of the clearing together.

They arrived in the midst of the battle against the Lacerta's coming in from the tree line. The villagers fired their weapons, dropping many of the lizards but many had already fallen upon them, including Daryl who was snapping his jaws and snarling at two Lacertas who were trying to jab at him from both ends with their spears.

Abram broke for the Werecat while Markus rushed for another Lacerta that was chewing on one man's arm while the man was screaming, very much still alive but unable to stop the monster no matter how hard he punched it's head with his only remaining hand.

Lunging forward like a swordfish, Markus sailed through the air and ran the monster through his sword. The Lacerta's jaws opened wide in a pained roar, dropping the villager to the ground who scampered away clutching at his bleeding and half-eaten arm. When Markus backed away as he pulled the sword out he thumbed the trigger on the hilt and an electric current passed from the sword to the Lacerta, who convulsed even after the sword was freed and it collapsed to the ground in a heap, smoke drifting from the stab wound and from the corners of it's reptilian mouth.

A deafening roar pierced the air and Markus turned to see the biggest Lacerta he had ever laid eyes on. The monster was ginormous, nearly twenty feet whilst standing with great spikes protruding from it's arms and shoulders, and with thicker spikes running down the length of it's spine all the way down to it's tail. The teeth were so large that they jutted past both lips, the bottoms nearly puncturing the creature's nose. As it dropped to all fours and laid it's baleful yellow eyes upon Markus, the ground shook with it's very weight. Such a thing of massive proportions should have caused the whole village to quake, and yet it had come seemingly out of nowhere.

But that wasn't the case, for Markus felt something in the creature's life essence. Something that was both familiar and not. It felt almost as if the witch Lameika had come back reincarnated as this monster, or that warrior from Xerxes he had encountered. Then he realized as he saw something arc across the sky right above the Lacerta's head that it was Abner's spirit form, and in a flash of lightning that cracked open the sky, the spirit disappeared as well.

This creature had been changed with magic somehow, and now the Lacerta was galloping towards Markus, it's great claws breaking up the earth and sending it sailing through the air as it went for him.

"Man-witch!" the thing roared as it lunged for Markus.

Markus dropped straight to the ground and upon his auto-limb hand touching it, he pulsed and in the spot right where the Lacerta was about to pounce, the earth cracked open and bedrock from deep within the island's struck out like a protruding spike. The rock itself having been angled so that the Lacerta fell upon it like a lance, piercing it's abdomen and spearing out the back in a flurry of purple blood.

The weight and momentum of the beast was too great however and the spike Markus had conjured from the depths snapped and he was forced to roll away as the

Lacerta collapsed and skidded, smearing the very ground Markus was on mere seconds ago.

But the Lacerta was getting back up, it's torso pierced by the rock still, it's eyes burning with pain and hatred as it turned towards Markus. "I'll smash you, eat your bones!"

It reached for Markus, it's mighty arms nearly closing the distance the moment the boy began to stand. Swinging his sword before him, Markus lopped off the extending fingers and slicing open the other hand as it went to grab him as well. The Lacerta was now upon him and bowing over him with it's massive jaws gaping. Markus was able to see the creature's rotten molars and the uvula in the very back behind the reptilian tongue.

He struck at the side of the creature's head, creating a great gash in the Lacerta's cheek and jaw. It turned away growling and whirling about, Markus sliced open the right forearm of the creature which had clutched to the earth to stabilize itself. As it's weight dropped bringing the head of the beast closer, Markus reached out with his auto-limb arm and upon touching the beast's lower jaw with his palm, he pulsed.

In the brief moments he had before the Lacerta's head exploded, Markus received numerous flashes of the Lacerta's memory.

It's name was Ripjaw to it's people. It had protected them and led them within the depths of the Bubbling Bog far north near the northern mountains right off the edge of The Capitol. It had lived for almost two-hundred years, and in that time had barely managed to survive these past ten. Then a warrior clad in black armor came, and offered them a better place in exchange for their service. When Ripjaw had challenged this man, he was presented with horrible images of his family being put in cages, the cages doused in oil, and then someone, a Metalhead or a pirate, dropping a lit match. All the while as their spirits departed the inferno, blaming him for his cowardice.

Markus's eyes napped open, he had not realized he had closed them. Laying before him in a heap was the bulk of the enchanted Ripjaw, his head completely gone and the ruins of his neck belching black smoke. He backed away, looking at his auto-limb hand which had purple ichor that had been cooked against the metal.

Markus looked in the direction of where Abram was, knowing what he knew now, he rushed to find the old man. He had to hurry, before it was too late.

Abram

When Abram finally reached Daryl he sliced at the calf of the nearest Lacerta, bringing it down and allowing him to behead the beast in one additional secondary swipe. Taking this opportune distraction, he lunged for the second who backtracked, leaving an opening for Daryl to lunge and tackle him to the ground, his strong head thrashing to and fro until an audible snapped broke through the thunder and the lightning and Daryl roared his victory over the broken corpse.

He approached the Werecat, his free hand extending in order to comfort the giant feline and inspect his wounds. Daryl's head snapped in his direction, his ears flattened against his skull and he let loose a warning hiss. Not out of malice but because he was in pain, and the message was simply to warn Abram away from touching him.

Abram pulled his hand back cautiously, his eyes scanning the Werecat. He had been nicked and cut in multiple areas, and his left ear was trickling blood and in the light of the lightning flashing overhead, Abram could see that the tip was now missing. The cat's white and black fur was on edge, making him appear even bigger than before. The wounds themselves were of no dire consequence, but if this kept up, Abram wouldn't be able to do anything. Without his crystal, he could only do so much.

"If you won't let me help you," he told Daryl softly and yet at the same time sternly. "Then you need to get out of here."

The curled lips of the cat softened, the large eyes taking Abram in questioningly. Despite having no crystal, there was enough magic still lingering in Abram's body and his bond with Daryl just strong enough for the old man to know what the Werecat was thinking. Stay, fight, protect the dowt.

"Then let me near you or flee," Abram told Daryl. "I won't let you waste your life here on my account."

He was looking towards the village, sensing little to none of it's former residents remaining save for the few brave men who were fighting off the remaining Lacertas. Markus in particular was locked in combat with a very strong Lacerta both in might and magic.

He returned his gaze to Daryl who had slackened his haunches lowering himself to the ground. He placed his chin on his paws as if telling the old man to do what he had to. Nodding gratefully, Abram went to do just that. He extended his hand and placed it upon the nearest wound the Werecat had on his shoulder and as soon as his frail palm touched the bloodied wound, that was when the Werecat's ears pricked upright and then suddenly Daryl turned on him with a snarl.

But it wasn't an attack, and as Abram felt the weight of Daryl's bulk strike his chest and knocking him to the ground, that was when the sharp whine of a laser beam cut through the air and he watched in agony the bolt of red struck Daryl in the side of the head and when the weight of the Werecat fell upon Abram it was slackened and immobile. Daryl's feline face which was tinged almost humanoid as his race had become was in a state of frozen desperation, as if his last moment on earth was simply to protect his dowt, his brother, at all costs.

"Daryl?" Abram asked as he saw the Werecat's life essence suddenly go out like a snuffed candle. He tried to push the cat off of him but the weight was too heavy for him, and he had no crystal to bring the energy forth necessary to complete the task. As he struggled, he fought back tears as his companion who had traveled with him from the mainland to the island was now lost forever in the void. The Werecat whom he had found injured in the Wastelands his legs haven been broken by a Leaper Dragon during a scuffle for a carcass. He had stayed with the cat despite it's murderous intent and had hunted for it and after feeding it for some time getting it to trust him, he was finally able to get close enough to put him to sleep and then heal the broken bones using the power of his crystal. Daryl, whom he had named after the Werecat began to follow him towards the coast, never left his side since.

This loss... it was just as great as the loss of Abram's own wife back when he lived in The Capitol under The Eldest's reign, long ago. Such a loss, he never expected to feel it again.

"Damned cat."

Abram's eyes widened as he heard the electronically changed voice and he looked in the direction the laser bolt had come from. A man in black Xerxan armor was walking towards him and Daryl, his beetle-like helmet crackling with images from within the glass dome. He carried with him a laser rifle and had two sword handles visible above his shoulder line. The identity of this warrior would have been lost to anyone, but to Abram who could still see the life essence of any creature still as well as sense when a crystal was near, recognized this man instantaneously and his heart ached at this realization.

"You..." he whispered as he pushed Daryl's head up just enough to begin squirming out from under the cat.

The Hunter Ghost paused his advance less than ten feet away from them and took aim with his rifle at Abram's head, the interior of the barrel beginning to glow a dull crimson as a charge began to accumulate.

"Long time no see, old man," said Ghost and he squeezed the trigger.

Having already planned this, Abram whose hand was digging into the earth pulsed, and the dirt suddenly rose like a tidal wave creating a wall which caught the laser but still gave off immense heat on the side he was on as he finally freed himself from Daryl. The wall suddenly broke towards him and the Hunter Ghost was lunging for him, the rifle's bayonet having been extended and sailing towards his heart.

Abram got his sword up and struck down at the bayonet, driving the rifle into the ground. He then stepped onto the rifle itself, applying just enough force to crack the barrel and he threw his shoulder into the chest of the Hunter who staggered back having lost his grip on the sword. Despite his lack of strength, Abram had managed this feat easily enough, but he had heard something snap in his arm and he winced in pain as he leapt back just as Ghost unsheathed his two katanas and made for the assault against him.

Keeping both hands on his sword, Abram deflected one blow after the other. With Ghost being so fast and nimble even with both swords, Abram felt himself tiring out and he cried out loud as one of the katanas slid against his left bicep, creating a great, red gash.

"You've gotten slow, old man," Ghost said as he advanced again, and again.

The two danced taking and deflecting each others attacks in a flurry of sparks. While in the midst of this fight Abram looked back and sent an urgent cry to Markus who had finally killed the giant Lacerta, hoping his mind was open to the communication, but fearing that without his crystal his cry for help wouldn't be enough to get The Keeper's attention.

To Ghost when they locked swords a second time Abram said, "Never thought you would use Lacertas as a distraction to get to me, sacrificing all these innocent people."

"They were no longer innocent the moment they took in a coward," Ghost hissed as he kicked Abram back and attacked once again. Abram successfully blocked the attack and kept Ghost bust despite his flurry of attacks and berserk swings.

"You have gotten sloppy also," Abram said trying to goad the Hunter into making a mistake. "Still can't stand against this old man, even without his crystal."

"Shut up," Ghost exclaimed as he struck at Abram with enough force to knock the old man clear across the fields that were now catching fire. Abram had managed to catch the blade in time before it hacked him apart, but the force nearly broke his wrist and he was panting heavier now even as Ghost shot towards him with a boost of his rocket boots.

"Where is it?" Ghost demanded as he struck at Abram with both swords as a single horizontal slash. Abram caught the blade but it nearly knocked him off balance.

"Gone," Abram said struggling to keep up with the attacks. "Gone, forever."

Ghost's glass helmet began to blink rapidly and with a growl he struck at Abram again and again, no longer seeming to care how he was going to bring Abram down but simply meaning to cause as much pain and damage as possible.

"Damn you!" Ghost shouted angrily as he proceeded to strike again and again and again. "*Damn* you, Abram! Do you have any idea what you've done!?"

"I'm doing my part to make things right," Abram said saving his breath and not shouting. "And what about you? What have you done since they lost you?" When they locked blades again, Abram twisted his sword so that he could get in close and he tried to peer through the glass helmet, seeing only his reflection among the flickering lights. "This is *not* worth it! What happened to you, my pupil?"

Ghost planted a sharp kick to Abram's knee, causing him to buckle and with a second kick, sent the old man crashing against a tree. Abram then dove to the side as Ghost's blades stabbed through the trunk.

"Don't call me that!" Ghost shouted ripping his blades free in time to catch Abram's attack now. "Any pupil of yours ends up dead or worse. I'm still alive because I refuse to be a pawn in your games anymore."

"I'm not the one at fault!" Abram cried out. "I've only done what I could to help Levitika."

"Yeah?" Ghost said striking at him again. He was chuckling maliciously now. "Look where that got me."

A sudden image of a dungeon cell. Voices in his head. Then Abram felt a consciousness that he knew personally, unfortunately very well, and hot tears began to spill from his wrinkled eyes.

"That isn't my fault!" Abram shouted while defending himself, his voice hoarse from the effort and the fighting. "It wasn't anyone's fault!"

"You have been lied to as well!" Ghost insisted.

"Please, fight it!" Abram begged the Hunter. "Don't let The Eldest control you!"

"No one is being controlled! We simply share a common wish: Your destruction!" Ghost swung yet again, scoring a hit by stabbing Abram in the left shoulder. It hurt but Abram was able to open his free palm towards Ghost, there was a sharp snap and a flash of light and Ghost backed off holding a forearm against his face. What he saw only Abram knew, a flash of his worst fears.

The forearm came down and Ghost was breathing heavily. "Your magic tricks won't work on me, Abram!" Ghost shouted and came at him again. "I am too powerful now! And when I'm done with you, that brat's next!"

Abram's defenses were getting weaker as he felt blood drip from his arm. His vision became spotted with black spots and he felt very dizzy. At last, Ghost's latest strike brought Abram down, the swords having collapsed his arms and sending him sprawling to the ground. Ghost approached Abram and stomped down on the old man's chest, knocking the wind right out of him.

The katana in the Hunter Ghost's hand was lifted up, and lightning struck the sky again and droplets of rain began to fall. "Give your other pupils my regards..." said Ghost, and he brought the sword down.

But not, just before, a great boulder came out of nowhere, striking Ghost in the back and sending both him and it sailing over Abram's head. Abram glanced upwards towards where Ghost was flopping across the terrain before he managed to get back up on his feet with a snarl. Abram looked up past his chest to see someone coming, running towards him his body wrapped in rags that were now dripping wet and he was shedding them off, wearing only pants and as his bare chest was exposed, Abram saw the purple crystal glowing bright and blue within, and Abram began to convulse as his heart began to hitch in his chest.

"No..." he choked as the boy approached him, his own lavender eyes full of concern. "The second death..."

The boy was now upon him, looking Abram over, his words lost to Abram's ears as he felt his heart cease beating, the entire left side of his body growing numb and then pained, and Abram's last vision of this world was what The Eldest had attempted to do long, long ago.

And he was gone.

<u>Zachariah</u>

"Hey? Hey, old man. Hey!"

But it was no use. The man he had saved from the soldier was dead. The life essence having been snuffed out the moment the old man whom Akuta had called Abram had laid eyes on him.

Before he could process this, Zachariah raised his head towards the warrior who was now standing all the way up, holding but one katana in his hand for the other had been lost when the boulder had been thrown at him. Seeing him again, Zachariah bared his teeth. He had come all the way here for Abram only to find him dead. But now that Ghost was here...

Ghost was laughing now, a breathless sound of awe and excitement. "At last..."

With a growl, Zachariah lunged for the soldier who sidestepped with a boost from his rocketboots. He had been trying to punch at the warrior but having landed close to a nearby tree, Zachariah went for it and seizing it, felt the crystal pump more energy into his muscles and with a mighty heave he pulled the tree out by it's very roots and whirling about, struck the incoming Hunter with it as if it were a baseball bat. The trunk cracked against the force of the strike and as Ghost struck the ground, Zachariah leapt for him and attempted to smash his knee into the warrior, and yet Ghost had rolled out of the way just in time and had struck at Zachariah with his sword, rendering flesh across his chest but Zachariah reeled back his fist and punched the Hunter, sending him sprawling back several feet and in that instant, the gash in his chest closed as if he were made of clay, bloodless and inconsequential.

"You," Zachariah said as he went for Ghost again. "My whole village was massacred, because of *you*."

"Was it?" Ghost demanded, sidestepping as Zachariah grabbed and punched at him, trying to get a strike in with his own sword. "*Good!*"

With a rageful howl, Zachariah went for Ghost with the intent to kill.

<u>Markus</u>

Markus saw the warrior and some kid fighting up ahead, which was odd since the kid had no sword and yet was going after the warrior and matching his speed. But he didn't care about that. All he cared about was whom he saw lying in the grass, and as he passed by the corpse of Daryl, a mournful moan escaped his throat and Markus collapsed to his knees next to the lifeless body of Abram.

He began to shake it, unwilling to believe that he felt no life essence in the old man.

"Abram? Abram? No..." He pulled his hands away which trembled with loss and rage. The old man was frozen in a death throw of what looked like fear, and Markus turned his eyes towards the two beings fighting with a rage that was unparalleled. He took up his sword and rushed for the confusion just as Ghost got behind the kid and sliced open his back. The boy had cried out and collapsed face-first into the ground and now Ghost was on top of him, reaching for the back of his head with his hand.

"Hey! Asshole!" Markus shouted.

The Hunter turned just as Markus leapt into the air and struck him down with his sword that managed to drive deep into the warrior's shoulder. He had used the crystals in his auto-limb to provide the force behind it and Ghost crumbled for a moment with a grunt before his rocket boots blazed to life, scorching the back of the kid who cried out in surprised pain and before he took off, Markus swung his sword and sliced off the rocket on the left heel.

Spinning almost comically through the air, the warrior tumbled back onto the ground several meters away and Markus left the kid who was groaning and lunged for him again. He struck at the warrior who got his sword up just in time to block the attack and then Markus reeled his auto-limb fist back and struck the warrior in the chest, sending him flying across the clearing only to smash into more trees.

"How do you like my new arm, you bastard!?" Markus bellowed as he charged in again. Ghost had gotten up however, the gash in his shoulder and his loss of one rocket boot seeming a minor inconvenience as the two clashed blade to blade again, sending sparks flying only to be snuffed out by the rainfall.

Ghost growled behind his face shield and pushed back against Markus whose strength had intensified with the surge of energy from the crystals in his auto-limb. "No one here to save you now, kid."

"Shut up!" Markus shouted. He sidestepped, his sword sliding along the length of the warrior's sword. The Hunter, as Markus realized what this warrior was for his movement and fluidity upon twisting his body about to avoid getting sliced along the arms reminded him of how Black would fight, backed away but then came in fast, striking at Markus and forcing his guard up before spinning about and nearly cleaving his legs off. Markus however had leapt high into the air, kicking out as he made his ascent and would have kicked the Hunter in the head if the man hadn't leaned far back only to flip over and back onto his feet again. When Markus landed, he lunged for the Hunter again, his rage for Abram's death and all this man had done to him fueling the crystals and through them his energy; all for the sake of one thing and one thing only: Killing this man.

They locked swords again, both of them trembling against each other's strength. He felt outrage and frustration emanating from the man's life essence. Good.

"You're a freakin' annoyance!" Ghost shouted as purple lightning coursed up his arms and through his sword. Markus felt his body tense as the tendrils coursed over him and nearly left him lightheaded. "I'll be sure to put you out of your misery once and for all!"

"Ghost!"

Both Markus and the Hunter whose name had to be Ghost turned and saw the kid lunging towards them both. Markus' first thought was What's that in his chest? before he slackened his resolve and fell back, causing Ghost to fall forward and at that moment, the other guy seized the man by the head and his momentum carried him over to another tree which he slammed the Hunter against, smashing his helmet against it again and again and causing sparks to flare from the cracked glass.

"I'll kill you!" the guy vowed, his eyes glowing bright and purple as the crystal in his chest, and seeing this from where he laid on the ground, Markus' eyes widened.

The Second Death...

Ghost cried out and an invisible force pushed both the guy and the tree he was up against away. The kid would have landed on Markus had he not moved out of the way fast enough. He bounced off the ground and continued to tumble across the ground before coming to a stop again. He did not get back up again.

Markus turned back to the Hunter Ghost who had lunged for him and he got his sword up just in time. Through the crack in the man's helmet, sparks of purple and yellow snapped and crackled.

"This time I'm going to make sure you never get up again," Ghost vowed.

"I ain't going down easy this time," Markus roared back, his rage resurfacing like a pot boiling over, and he shoved Ghost back and swung at the warrior's feet. Ghost leapt into the air and stabbed downward, missing Markus who sidestepped and attacked again. The two exchanged blows in a flurry of sparks. Markus was able to extend his palm towards the warrior, and try to break into his mind but Ghost would fight back, knocking Markus' hand back and tackling him to the ground in an attempt to stab him. But Markus would toss Ghost off of him as if he weighed no more than a child and came after him again, all the while the rain poured upon the two warriors as if the heavens above were crying for their savagery.

But the rain didn't matter. Everything around him didn't matter. The more this Hunter fought back against him, the more Markus wished more than anything that the man would slip up, or that the spirit in the crystal he had in his possession would betray him and allow Markus the killing blow. To break open that armor and make him suffer for what he's done, and Markus felt the surging energy making him go faster and faster, all the while the world around him became darker and darker, leaving only the man before him, and nothing more.

This... this isn't right, Markus thought to himself. Something was very wrong, and he couldn't tell why.

"Enough!" Ghost shouted and extending his palm towards Markus the moment the two disengaged, the air between them seemed to spread outward like an explosion and Markus staggered back, surprised that such a thing was possible. Manipulating the ground and animals and even plants was one thing, but the very air itself? Also, it felt as if the air was filled with nothing, for Markus gasped for oxygen that was completely pushed out of the space they had.

That was when Ghost moved in, his free hand slipping past Markus' defenses and grabbing hold of his forehead. "You're mine!"

Markus then felt a sharp pain in his head, and he cried out as his vision blurred into a bright light and then he was no longer there.

He had blinked when the light came to be, and when his eyes opened, the Hunter was no longer there. He was in The Dreaming, and found that he was back on a rocky island with the millions of stars and planets around him. He stood up as he saw many creatures flying towards him, circling overhead like vultures waiting to see if he would keel over.

They were monstrous creatures unlike anything he had seen here during his training, all varying in size and appearance. He saw eels with black wings and teeth as sharp as many swords, he saw Ahools that spewed smoke behind it as it flapped its terrible wings, and even a humanoid creature with a crow's head and snakes lower torso. All three circled overhead with such hunger and hate that Markus could feel the Nightmares effects on his body as his rage became nothing more than terror, and perhaps sensing this, they all swooped in as one.

As they drew near, Markus could feel their presence- and they were not at all pleasant. It was as if the closer they got the more negative his feelings became, gnawing at his spirit and eating away all hope. Before his eyes as they Nightmares landed and advanced on him, Markus saw the faces of all who he had killed and who had died because of him. The villagers he had failed to protect, Veegar, even Ruth... All whose faces were covered in blood or reduced to skulls screaming at him for help. The sense of failure and regret was overpowering and as the Nightmares finally lunged at Markus all at once, he had no hope or will to fight and allowed himself to be taken down and pinned to the ground. The crow and Ahool held his arms down, screaming at his face while the eel seemed to caress him, as if it enjoyed seeing Markus in his misery.

A cold chuckle reverberated throughout the dimension, not the Eldest for his presence was not what Markus felt here. High above him and the Nightmares in the eternal sky, Markus saw the face of someone he didn't recognize materialize into the air, and he realized he was looking up at the face of Ghost. His face was pale and covered in many scars, his eyes were blackened like his soul, and his grin was terrible and cruel. This was what lied beneath the beetle-like helmet. This was the face of the monster who had tried to kill him.

"Poor fool," Ghost said, and his eyes sparked like lightning and flashes of Markus' dead family flashed in his mind like a slideshow. "No mother, no father, no sister. You are all alone."

Amongst the horror before him, Markus then began to see flashes of something different. His father and sister were still there, but they were smiling. They were happy. He saw his sister riding a bike, his father helping him build his first battle-bot, and the three of them eating dinner together for that last time before his father was killed. He also saw Black jumping off the ledge of Levitika and showing Markus how to fly across the sky- the joy he felt then seemed to pour into Markus now. He even saw Ashlyn's smiling face full of beauty and life waving at him, as well as Esmerelda who was throwing him a book. He saw Elizabetha showing him the spot where she had in mind to bury Ruth, Vic building his new arm, Jim and Kaltrina pouring him a drink with Aventis smiling behind them; all of these memories, they brought a sense unlike anything Markus had ever felt; as if he was being washed through with clean holy water. The sight made him tear up seeing those images, and amongst the images, he saw Abner and Nokama smiling down at him. *You are not alone.* He heard them say, the words echoing through his head since the time Ruth had died.

"I'm not done yet," Markus said wrenching his auto-limb arm free and grabbing ahold of the crow Nightmares' head, it squawked once and its head suddenly exploded in a flash of black smoke as Markus pulsed and released his energy into it. It fell back and Markus reached for his sword and brought it around and hacked the head of the Ahool off its shoulders; it too fell back in a flash of smoke. The eel hissed and wings extended lunged at Markus who was getting up. Markus then sidestepped and holding his blade a certain away, it slide right through the jaws of the eel and as it zipped past him the blade cut through the body until the eel was split in half in a flash of black smoke. It wriggled and hissed until it soon dissolved into smoke and thick black ooze that pooled on the ground. Markus then turned his attention to a very surprised Ghost-apparition. "I'm not alone," Markus said. "And I'm not afraid of you."

Ghost's face shook with rage, he suddenly cried out and the apparition disappeared, and as if he materialized out of thin air the true form of Ghost in full armor came flying out of nowhere and lunging at Markus with all of his might, his blade ready to slice him in half. Markus got his sword up-

But someone else was there, stepping between him and the incoming Ghost and with a loud clang! this stranger's sword and Ghost's own sent sparks flying every which way, Ghost himself seeming suspended in the very air as if his sword was all that held him up against his opponent.

Markus stared in awe at the back of the man who had stepped in front of him, shoving Ghost back in a flurry of wind and sending him back before landing nimbly several meters away.

"You..." Ghost grumbled as Markus' defender turned to look back at him, his face impassive as it had always been before, but his blue eyes shining bright and alert.

"B... Black?" Markus asked in amazement and disbelief.

Black turned his attention back to Ghost who was already leaping through the air, his sword upraised as if to cleave the memory of the Hunter in half. "Bastard!"

Be ready, Markus heard Black's voice clearly inside his head. Black himself was ready, a memory of the very sword that was in Markus' hands technically gripped tight in his own as he prepared to defend himself. Realizing what was to happen, Markus grasped his sword tightly with both hands, feeling the strange sensation of several others seeming to grasp it with him. Glancing back just for a brief moment, Markus could have sworn he saw Ashlyn, Esmerelda, Ruth, and several others including Abram himself. All seeming to back him up as he looked forward and the moment the figure of Damion Black dissipated into a plume of black smoke, Ghost was already too far in his sword too deep in it's strike, and he fell upon Markus' blade as he thrust forward, the sword breaking through the armor and coming out the back.

Ghost gasped as Markus did not budge from his spot, holding the warrior on his sword even as the Hunter's feet finally touched the ground. When Markus reached out with his auto-limb hand, Ghost seized it by the wrist and his strength refused to allow the boy to move anymore.

Trembling on Markus' blade, the voice of Ghost behind his helmet was seething with murderous intent. Raising his opposite hand wielding his other blade, Ghost swung at Markus, attempting to behead him.

Markus ducked however, and surging energy into his auto-limb, he pulsed and with Ghost's contact, the Hunter was jolted and was forced to let go. Markus seized the Hunter's head-

Only to find that he couldn't break through. The Hunter Ghost's mind, it was like a steel cage around a dangerous machine. An impenetrable force that had shocked Markus, leaving him open for Ghost to kick him in the chest, sending both him and his sword away from him. Blood spurted from the wound in Ghost's midsection, but he stood upright as if not bothered by the injury at all.

"You're out of your league, kid," Ghost said now approaching the downed Markus. "Doesn't matter what you throw at me, I will always recover faster than you ever would. And your illusions of Black won't help you again."

Markus sat up, his sword clutched tightly in his hand, his auto-limb lifting him up from the ground.

"Go ahead," Ghost told him. "Try to cast a spell. I've already won."

"Not yet you haven't," Markus said and he pulsed again.

This time, the rocky floor of the island they were on opened up directly under Ghost's feet. However, instead of falling into the black abyss within as he should have, the Hunter was remaining levitated above the hole as if there were invisible glass covering the entrance. Ghost laughed at Markus' expression.

Behind Ghost, an enormous black cloud was forming on the horizon. A great bulbous thing of liking smoke, and Markus could see Nightmares flocking about this thundercloud like nightbirds, and Ghost laughed as he saw what Markus saw.

"Guess our time's up," said Ghost. "Been nice knowing you kid. I'll take good care of your crystals for you. Goodbye, and good riddance."

Then he was gone in a poof of black smoke. Markus stared in disbelief where Ghost once stood, and above his head he noticed that the Nightmares were flying away- as if they were trying to get away from something and in the far distance Markus heard a distinct growling sound as if an avalanche was coming right for him. He peered in the distance and saw the cloud of black smoke had a tinge of red as dark as blood. Markus felt a presence within the smoke, and before the smoke fell upon him, Markus knew who it was. The Eldest had found him in The Dreaming.

Hello, Markus, a deep and melodious voice said inside his head as he was soon engulfed into the darkness of the cloud which seemed to be alit with many fires but he felt no heat; only coldness within the darkness of the cloud.

I've been waiting for you.

Ghost

Ghost's vision flashed as he returned to the real world. The boy had been standing in the exact same spot as they had been upon entering The Dreaming, and now The Keeper was swaying, collapsing flat on his back with his arms splayed, his expression laxed and his eyes silver orbs.

It had been only mere seconds in real time since they had entered The Dreaming together, but to Ghost's body it felt like hours had passed. He was panting, exhausted from the effort as well as the wound in his midsection. He was surprised at this as he had never been injured in The Dreaming, even from something crucial. This kid was shifting the balance between The Dreaming and reality, and Ghost was both impressed as well as annoyed.

Damned kid just didn't know when to quit. The more Ghost looked upon that laxed face especially through the crack in his helmet, he couldn't help but marvel just how much Markus looked like his father as much as had his stubbornness.

And the Hunter Black… How did the boy conjure such a likely image of him, and *why*? Furthermore, why had it felt so real, so… so…

Ghost shook his head. It didn't matter. At this rate, The Keeper was trapped in The Dreaming, and was no doubt having a personal conversation with The Eldest. The evil spirit no doubt had his eyes on this boy since the very beginning, and now it would see that the prophecy The Great Owl had spoken of will end here. Ghost almost left the boy there, went to fetch 464 and allow The Eldest to take the boy's soul and become stronger if that was what he deemed necessary. In the end however, Ghost had been waiting a long time for this. He had lost his chance in Nineveh, but he was not going to lose him this time.

First, he placed his hand on the entry wound in his body. He pulsed, and felt the magic coursing through the hole all the way out to his back which he felt the flesh searing together, cauterizing it as if he had shoved gunpowder into it and lit a match. In a matter of seconds, the wound was healed and it became easier for Ghost to breathe. He took up his sword, and stepped aside so that his feet were perpendicular to the boy's prone body. He then took the sword in both hands and raised it, his eyes resting on the developing Adam's apple of The Keeper's throat.

The Eldest was going to have to do without Markus of Nineveh. Because now, Ghost had a debt to pay, and he was not about to-

A surge of energy pulsated through the air like lightning and Ghost looked up but not before 464 came barreling out of the darkness in a flash of purple lightning that coursed over his body and seeming to be emanating from his eyes and his crystal heart. The boy had lunged at Ghost, his fist a torpedo bulleting through the air only to make contact with the side of Ghost's face. The helmet completely shattered, the metal and glass pieces sailing everywhere and when Ghost's pale face was finally met with Zachariah's knuckles, he was thrown nearly twenty feet away his body tumbling before he finally managed to steady himself.

He looked up, his face a mummified husk of leathery white flesh as it had appeared to Markus in The Dreaming. Thick ropey scars covered his bald head and face, and he was missing most of his ears as well as his nose, looking as if he had been exposed to radiation for a hundred years. The temple of which had been struck was bleeding, and with a pulsation against his head, the wound closed up automatically.

464 stood between him and Markus, and placing his palm on the ground, 464's body pulsated indigo light and then the earth seemed to clam around The Keeper's body like a shell, shielding him from the rain and no doubt meant to protect him.

Exposed to the rain, the lightning flashing overhead causing Ghost's face to appear as spectral as his namesake, he bared his teeth in both outrage, and excitement.

Zachariah

Zachariah took a quick glance to the motionless kid unconscious in the grass. *That's him,* he heard Akuta speak but Zachariah ignored the spirit and placing his palm on the ground, he imagined a capsule of some sort and The Keeper was swallowed up by the earth, his body noticed only by a the earthy cairn he had created.

He turned his blazing purple eyes back to the Hunter Ghost who was standing, his sword still gripped in his hand, his helmet destroyed and his ugly mummy-like face in a grimace. This man had been the first one Zachariah had seen upon waking up. It was because of this man he had gone through so much torture. It was this man, who had taken everything from him.

"You took everything from me," Zachariah said coldly as he advanced upon the Hunter.

Ghost's grimace turned more into a mocking smile. "I'm not the one who massacred your entire village."

"Maybe not," Zachariah agreed, feeling his crystal accumulate in his chest like a charging blast. "But you sure as hell can pay for it, as well as what you've done to me."

He launched himself at Ghost, who sidestepped too fast to be human and Zachariah barely got his arms up to protect his face as the Hunter struck near his face. He felt the sting of the sword slicing open his forearms but the moment he struck out at Ghost again, hitting him hard and fast in the chest and causing him to stagger back, the magic had already closed his arms up instantaneously. He then took his chance and his hands clasped to either side of Ghost's head and Zachariah pulsed, digging as deep as he possibly can.

"Why did you do this to me?" Zachariah demanded when they appeared in The Dreaming. Where exactly was anybody's guess. All was sandy, all was barren, all except for the constellations above which were endless.

Ghost drove his sword deep into Zachariah's belly, causing him to bow over and Ghost released it, letting it stick and he brought both hands on Zachariah's head as well, the two looking like they were trying to crush each other's skulls. Overhead, shadows were circling the two, curious as to what had entered their domain.

To one another, they were wrestling. Both trying to break down the barricades of their minds but neither succeeding. Ghost's strength was not as mighty as

Zachariah's, but his experience was far greater, and the two were locked in what felt like an iron cage together, forced to endure and never escape.

"You are meant to be the ~~monster~~ powerful weapon in my army," Ghost was saying, and whether Zachariah was breaking through the barricades or Ghost was allowing him entrance to see the laboratory and all they were attempting to do, was a complete and utter mystery. "You were the first, and you won't be the last. You have proved to us that it is possible to create the perfect soldier. I don't want to kill you, Four-Sixty-Four. But I don't need you if you keep fighting me. Stand down, let us talk, and we can take the boy's-"

In his anger, Zachariah punched Ghost in the head and threw him aside, making him skid across the sandy landscape. "Leave him out of this," Zachariah growled as he marched towards Ghost who was trying to get back up. "This is between you and me, you bastard."

Before Ghost could do or say anything, Zachariah punched him once more, making him spin. All of a sudden Ghost was no longer Ghost, but a man garbed in a tan tunic with long white hair. He looked familiar but Zachariah could not place a face. "You failed your family!" the man shouted at Zachariah accusatorily. In his panic, Zachariah struck again, this time the form of a young girl once again looking familiar took his place. "Why did you leave us to die?"

Zachariah shook his head, unable to believe what he was seeing. The girl suddenly lunged for him, calling him a murderer, and in his panic, he kicked her and sent her sprawling into the dirt. The figure got back up and it was then Alma appeared wearing a thin white nightgown that revealed all of her curves and edges, causing Zachariah to pause in his tracks, his heart aching.

"You left us without warning!" she screamed. "You left me, how could you!?"

Angry now, Zachariah grabbed Alma's throat and upon lifting her off the ground Alma was gone, and who took her place was-

Mother?

Looking into his mother's eyes Zachariah felt weakened, and broken. He gasped and he felt tears brimming his eyes. His mother gave him a sneer of a smile and then her faced morphed back into a mummified face.

"Poor child," Ghost said as he placed his hand over the crystal in Zachariah's chest and immediately Zachariah felt all pain and sorrow. He felt as if the ghosts of his past were flying around him, filling his head and threatening to burst back out. He released Ghost and they then returned back to the real world. Zachariah still holding his head fell to his knees in anguish, and between his fingers he saw Ghost still standing before him.

"You do not need to suffer what you have forgotten any longer," said Ghost. He turned and started walking towards the mound of earth that was covering The Keeper once again. "Just trust in me, and I promise you, you will never feel pain again. Never-"

"No!" Zachariah cried out and reaching his hand out and pulsing her saw Ghost go rigid in place. He then began to look around as if something was flying around him.

What he saw Zachariah knew not, but watched as the fears that he had collected from Ghost's conscious materialize in front of their prey, and frighten him dearly. He then backed away from the mound of earth as if something malicious was crawling out of the depths and he gasped aloud with fright.

"No, no, no!" Ghost said wheeling to and fro and swiping at whatever he was seeing. Zachariah managed to stand and when Ghost turned to him, he screamed. "No!" He clicked his ankles and his one rocket boot went off, sending him up into the air only to crash down to the ground. He began to crawl backwards away from Zachariah who appeared to be walking towards him, but in truth was going for Markus.

Ghost removed a switch from his belt and clicked it, and immediately the very Hellhound he had brought in flew overhead and levitated over their heads. Zachariah held up an arm to shield his eyes from the hover plates beneath it. Ghost then shot a grapple-hook up the open cargo doors and zipped up the hovercraft. He clung to the undercarriage as if his life depended on it, and even from this distance, Zachariah could see the terror and pure hatred in the Hunter's baleful eyes.

"This isn't over, freak!" Ghost shouted. "If ever see you again, I'll carve that crystal out of your damned chest and the boy shall have it instead!"

With this vow of anger tinged with a desperation that was uncanny, Ghost climbed along the side of the ship and as the doors closed the Hellhound turned and took off in a flash of light back to where it came from. Zachariah swore and punched at the ground creating a small crater and kicking up mud. He panted loudly as his head roared with thought.

"Dammit! He got away!"

We will catch him later., Akuta claimed.

"Yeah, when?" Zachariah demanded wiping the mud off his arms.

Soon, but right now, he needs your help. Zachariah turned to see the kid still lying unconscious, and noticing the two crystals in the robotic arm. *He is The Keeper, and he is in grave danger. I can feel my brethren with him, and they need help.*

Zachariah crawled over to the mound and using his bare hands dug out the unconscious child. He looked no older than Zachariah despite his alteration with the experiments. Ignoring this thought and upon placing the boy's head in his lap, Zachariah placed his hand over his forehead and breathed in. He then crossed the bridge made between his mind and the child's, and upon entering The Dreaming he uttered but one word that he had never heard before until he first made contact with this boy who was The Keeper, the key to him understanding what he had become and who to turn to when it came to his connection to The Dreaming.

"Markus..."

<u>Markus</u>

Markus was still lost in the cloud of misery as flames rose and darkness crept in, giving him a sense of claustrophobia and a fear unlike anything he had ever felt in his life.

It was as if all the bad memories were increased tenfold, snuffing out any opportunity Markus tried to conjure a good memory, the vision being swept away like sand in the wind. His head was pounding from the unrelenting pressure, and he felt like he would pass out at any moment the negative energy was so melodious in a terrible way. His sword was out but as he spun every which way Markus saw nothing to strike, and every time he turned to the sound of a whispering voice he saw nothing but glowing darkness. It seemed like there were many people inside the vortex with him, men, women, children, he heard all kinds of voices whispering to him. It was all mostly nonsense, but in this place of shadow overridden by voices speaking in tongues, he was very afraid.

"So," a voice both cold and somewhat soothing spoke somewhere in the dark cloud. "This is The Keeper, the Child of Prophecy, and The Savior of Levitika. The whispers appear to be true… I never would have thought it would be you, Markus."

"Who are you?" Markus shouted in every direction. "Who are you and how do you know my name?"

"As to how I know you is quite simple, I knew your father, after all he *was* someone who could bond with the spirits of *my* crystals. I got to know him very, very well when you were born, before he fled and took you from me."

The Eldest, Markus thought with his heart full of dread. *The Eldest…*

"Indeed," said the voice. "One voice among many, to describe the god I've become."

"What do you want?" Markus cried out desperately searching telepathically for Abner or Nokama, but received no word from either spirits. It was as if they had left him too along with his good memories. He looked down at his arm and saw that the crystals were dim as if no light was shining in them anymore and they were mere gems.

"They cannot help you, child, not when I am around. And what I want, Markus, is what they want. Freedom. However, I do not wish to die as they do. I wish to be free of this realm, I want out of The Dreaming, and return to my home, where I shall take what was rightfully mine long ago. It has been so long I forget what it is like to smell the fields again, to feel the wind on my face but alas: I will never sense these things again, for I am no longer the man I once was. My time trapped in here for many years, under constant attack of Nightmares and visions, have allowed me to learn even more about just how powerful The Dreaming really is, and as a result, I am eternal.

"All I need now, is you. Surrender the crystals to me, and surrender yourself to me, completely."

"Never!" Markus shouted. "I won't let you!"

"You don't have a choice, Markus," said The Eldest, and suddenly the sword in Markus' hand was wrenched out, and it hovered before him the point aiming directly at Markus' chest. "You shall become my Second Death."

Markus tried to wake up. He tried to break free of this hold, but it felt as if invisible hands held him in place, his terror too great for any chance to escape. The Eldest perhaps sensed this, and he laughed all around him.

"You, are a joke to me," said The Eldest, and suddenly the pressure in Markus' head intensified, all of his fears began to flood his brain and drown his heart. He cried out grasping for some explanation, as he felt himself dragged to the ground choking for his life.

"You are in my world Markus, and you shall be the first to see the true glory of Ulroc, The Eldest, The Dark King of Nightmares!"

Before Markus he saw a shadow that appeared to be humanoid materialize in front of him- it was as if Darkness himself was strangling him. The Eldest was about to reveal his true self, and when he did so, Markus would be gone for all of his strength, his energy, his hope, would be drained away and consumed by the monster that dwelled among the Nightmares of man. Markus' last thoughts reached out for something wonderful, and saw his family. He saw his father, Ruth, Ashlyn, and Esmerelda, all reaching out for him as if begging for him to grab ahold and let them save him, even as the point of Damion Black's sword touched his chest.

"I'm sorry," he whispered as he felt the shadow pass over his eyes like a veil.

But it wasn't the end, for he felt a tremor crash through the whirlwind of shadow, the materialization of The Eldest backtracked with an outraged cry and someone else materialized before him, seizing the sword and cutting through the darkness as if it were black cloth.

Someone placed a pair of hands on Markus' shoulders and he heard Abram's voice, "Get up," sound behind him.

Markus looked back, unable to believe that Abram was here. The old man was smiling sadly and he nodded, saying, "My work here is done. Do not give in to fear, protect your mind, Markus, as if it were the most precious of treasures."

He then dissipated into white smoke, seeming to rise straight into the constellations only to disappear as the shadows closed in.

"He's right, Markus," said the one who took the sword and Markus looked to see Damion Black standing there as well, his sword in hand and his calm demeanor seeming to act like water against the oil of the shadows that churned around them.

"Black?" Markus asked. He shook his head and despite the situation asked, "Are you a memory? Really?"

Black shook his head. "There is no time. Focus!" He tossed his sword back to Markus who caught it nimbly before he could drop it. "There is a lot to be done, Markus. A lot of people are hurt, some have died. You cannot stay here. Your family needs you."

Markus tried to say, "Wha-" Then the shadows turned into a vortex all around them, the anger of The Eldest whipping them all about.

"YOU!" The Eldest roared. "HOW ARE YOU HERE!?"

Damion Black looked to Markus and as he winked he said, "Fight."

He disappeared, and where he once stood a blast of purple lightning pierced through the darkness and struck the ground, causing the shadows which were attempting to rush in with Black's absence to shy away like frightened wolves. A deafening and chilling cry seemed the echo throughout The Dreaming as the figure who had come like a deity from the stars stood before him.

"Who are you?" Markus demanded of the guy who stood between him and the darkness. The man was pale and ragged, bald, and wore no shirt. But what caught Markus off guard, was the guy's purple eyes, and the crystal that seemed to be embedded into the guy's chest- where the heart was supposed to be. Again, Markus was reminded of The Second Death

"A friend," said the guy turning his attention back to the shadow. "So this is *him* huh?" He seemed to be asking Markus. "We gotta get out of here."

"YOU SHALL NOT ESCAPE!" the shadows cried out growing in size and rushing in like a collapsing hurricane, the shadows tinged with red lightning the black fabric of The Eldest's being sewn with the howling souls of all whom he had murdered for his power.

"Not tonight," the stranger said and upon grabbing ahold of Markus' head he cried out. "Hold on!"

There was a flash of light as both Markus and the man shined as bright as suns and the shadow began to crumble away as light touched it, and as Markus felt himself leaving The Dreaming he heard The Eldest roar throughout the heavens.

"NOOOOOOOOOOOOOOOooooooooooo....!"

When Markus came to he was cold and wet, and in a fury he sat up fast and backed up gasping as if out of breath. He turned his head from side to side like a wild animal still feeling the cols strain of those shadowy hands on his neck and creeping into his very being. He felt sick- as if millions of worms were eating at his insides and threatening to crawl out of his skin. He reached for his neck expecting to feel bruises but his skin felt as smooth as ever despite the ugly feeling crawling up his neck like bile. He suddenly went alert and flicked his sword up and touching the point of his blade against the neck of the guy who sat squatted before him. He raised his hands as if to show that he meant no harm but his essence was wrong- very wrong and it made Markus uncomfortable especially considering the experience he had just had.

"Who are you, and what are you doing here?" he demanded in a soft and dangerously low voice.

"Hey now, relax," said the stranger. "I'm not gonna hurt you."

"Shut up," Markus said. "Just tell me who you are, and what you are doing here?"

"Can't you tell who I am?"

"I didn't have the pleasure to find out when you pulled me out of that place."

"You're welcome by the way," said the stranger.

"Will you just-"

Markus, said the voice of Abner in his head.

"About damn time," Markus snarled at the spirit.

Calm yourself, said Nokama and to Markus' surprise, a third spirit called out. *I am Akuta. And this is my friend.*

Markus looked at the guy who was nodding vehemently. He appeared to be just a little older than Markus but his eyes did not belong to a man reaching his adult age- but those of an old man, ancient yet powerful. "My name is Zachariah. I came here, looking for Abram."

The reality of Abram's death made Markus nearly choke and he demanded, "What for?"

"To see if he could explain this." the man called Zachariah said pointing at his chest where the crystal glowed all the brighter. Markus felt a brush against his conscience and thought that was either Abner or Nokama returning to him, which of course they did but this presence was different- familiar yet totally different.

Zachariah then reached into his pocket slowly as if to show Markus that a single hand wouldn't hurt him. From his pocket he removed another crystal of blood red color. This one Markus recognized immediately, and he had to fight the urge to recoil.

"And this is Tabitha, at least that is what I hear."

Markus' eyes grew in size as he felt the essence of that crystal as well, and he got up onto his knees driving the point of is sword closer to Zachariah who froze in place at the increase in pressure. "Where did you get that?"

"Buddy, you need to relax," Zachariah said in a low voice.

"Don't play with me! Where did you get that?"

Zachariah looked at him irritated but said, "I picked it up after a Hunter dropped it out in the Wasteland."

"Did he wear power armor?" Markus asked quickly. "Black with yellow striping? Missing a foot maybe?"

Zachariah's eyes narrowed. "You know him then?"

Markus sat back down lowering his weapon. His head was still pounding from being in The Dreaming but he had to think. So the cyborg was alive? And he got away- he still has The Eldest!

Markus shook his head. "Well great," he said mostly to himself rather than Zachariah. He turned his head and looked at the broken figure of Abram lying in the grass not too far away. He frowned, feeling tears well up in his eyes. First Black, and now Abram...

"I'm sorry," Zachariah said as if he felt Markus' sorrow.

Ask him how that happened. Markus did not need to ask Abner what he meant as he looked back up to Zachariah and pointed to his chest. "So what happened here?" he asked. "Where's that Hunter?"

Zachariah looked down at his chest and frowned. "It's a long story."

Markus looked at him but nodded. "I'm too shaken up right now to ask anyway." He then got up and started to walk away.

"Wait- where you going?" Zachariah stood suddenly.

"I'm going to bury the dead," Markus said ruefully. "Does me no good to just stand around. Later I'm going to look for the others."

"Others?"

"The other villagers," Markus stopped to explain.

"I saw no one when I came in." Zachariah said. "I didn't see anyone leave other than Ghost."

Markus nodded with sorrowful realization on what that could mean. He just only hoped that most of them got out. He looked down sadly, the rain making him look like he was in tears. His fists were clenched and were shaking with rage as he grimaced at the impossibilities of anyone making it out alive.

"This is my fault." He finally said.

Zachariah walked over to him. "You can't blame yourself for this."

"I led them here."

"You don't know that. You can't blame yourself like that."

The words of Ashlyn echoed through Markus' head when Zachariah said that. But Markus also remembered what Abram said about the crystal helping him hide everyone here. He wanted to bring it up, but in the end, Ashlyn's words spoken as Zachariah's, won.

He nodded. "All right…"

"So," Zachariah said awkwardly. "The Keeper…"

"Apparently…" said Markus.

Zachariah looked like he was going to say something else, to place a hand on Markus' shoulder, but thankfully he did not. In fact, he actually froze, turning his head as if he saw something in the woods. Markus looked in the same direction his new acquaintance looked.

"What? Where?" he asked.

"There's someone in those trees," Zachariah said his eyes glowing all the brighter. Markus thought it was creepy how they glowed in that color but gave no comment. "He's got somthin-"

He suddenly stopped mid-sentence and dropped to the ground. Markus bent over the man and saw that there was a dart in Zachariah's shoulder sparking with electricity- It was a stun dart. Markus whipped up his sword but too late as he felt a sharp sting in his chest and he fell to the ground gasping as he felt his muscles lock up and he suddenly felt all the more tired than he did upon exiting The Dreaming. In the haze of his vision clouded with rain he saw someone walking up to him and Zachariah- who it was he could not see for it was too dark and for some reason Markus was unable to read the mans essence- it was as if he lost all his power in that one single dart.

He heard laughing and realized there was more than one- and they were surrounding him and Zachariah. Who were these guys, and what was going on? "Who…" he managed in a weak whisper.

"Looks like we found some live ones," he heard one voice say and felt a toe nudge his side. "Barely."

"This one's got a crystal in his hand- and in his chest!"

"Lemme see that!"

"Give it over,"

"Shut up." the first voice said sharply and paused. "Interesting, and very pretty. I like that one in the man's chest though, but I don't know what we are going to do about this." A sharp snap sounded in the air, followed by a cry and numerous curses.

"It's electrical!" someone said.

"Let's dig it out!" a high voice shouted.

"Shut up, we'll take them with us and figure it out back at camp."

"What about this one?" Markus felt a foot plant on top of his chest making it difficult to breathe. "He's got fancy sword, an auto-limb and there's two more gems in it."

"See if you can pick them out. *Carefully*." Markus then felt hands grab his arm followed by a sharp *snap* as soon as he felt hands touch the crystals. How he was able to sense the sensation of the crystals but not speak to Abner or Nokama, let alone use his powers was beyond him. He heard someone crash to the ground twitching after the auto-defense system in his arm went off and shocked him.

"Booby-trap!"

"Heh, booby."

"Shut up, you morons," the first voice snarled again. "Cut it off."

Markus then felt something strike his arm only to bounce right off. "Damn," A gruff voice said. "This stuff is strong- that was my best swing."

"Maybe you just getting weaker."

"Shut up."

The first voice spoke up again. "Enough, we'll take them with us."

"Just cut it at the shoulder." Markus then felt a finger jab him in his flesh right where the auto-limb met the shoulder bone.

"No, if the auto-limb is that strong then the nerves are reinforced as well, otherwise he wouldn't be able to use it correctly. No, that won't do, it won't do at all." The first voice paused for a moment. And then, "No, we take them to Ronin. We need our slaves alive."

"You're no fun sometimes, Jinx."

"Do I look like I care?" When there was no reply the voice that had to be Jinx spoke again. "Ronin wants slaves, and he prefers them *alive*. These two are obviously valuable, so we'll show them off as soon as we get back. I'd rather not mess with the gems we can't remove yet until we know more. So hop to it! Get 'em on board, the rest of you loot the bodies."

Markus in desperation reached out and caught an ankle with his real hand.

"This one's still kicking!" he heard someone said and the foot pulled away from him only to come right down on his face. "Nighty-night." And everything faded to black.

Markus would slip in and out of conciseness every so often, seeing that he was being carried away, only to close his eyes and opened them to see a massive ship at the shores of the island. When he closed them again he was being thrown on board and rolling over to his side against a wall in secluded darkness. He then felt a mass smack into him and realized it was Zachariah still unconscious. Markus attempted to sit up and saw someone in the doorway of the cage he realized he was in. The man's figure was hazy due to the lack of light but Markus was able to see the man raise his gun and shoot him. When another paralyzing dart struck his chest Markus fell back down on his face and he knew no more as the darkness closed in when the man closed the cage door. Markus' body went limp and his mind put him to a heavy sleep and he knew no more besides the recalling laughter full of chilling terror he had witnessed in The Dreaming.

<u>Lee</u>

When Lee finally reached the base of the dormant Mt. Nudushi in the far reaches of the north just east of The Capitol, it was past nightfall and the chilling rain bounced off his armor as he climbed the carved steps up the mountain.

It was arduous making the climb because of his missing foot and damaged legs, but he climbed the carved steps with a purpose. This place had been discovered centuries after the Great War had reduced this place to ashes and lakes of radiation, only to become preserved as a sort of holy place, as it was maintained for centuries more. What had transpired here was obviously well beyond when Lee had been born, he and his sister's mother having been meant as a sacrifice in order to maintain the bloodline of those who had discovered this place. As fate would have it, they had returned. As fate would have so now, he climbed these steps now all alone.

Every so often The Hunter would pass a torch that flickered and hissed as rain struck the flame, or he would pass a guardian who stood at attention underneath a crevice that served as a shield from the rain. The guardians wore robes of black and masks of black veil as to hide their identities, but the threat that seemed to seep from their cloaked bodies were imminent; for Photon-Rifles stayed at their side at all times, and the blades that were equipped along the barrel of the weapon shined menacingly in the brief flashes of lightning. This did not concern Lee however, for he was expected inside The Well of Souls to meet with his master. It would be difficult to explain his sister's absence, but Lee was convinced that he would be able to explain what happened without the master getting too angry.

After all, he had what they needed right in his hand. In fact, at the mere sight of The Eldest, the guardians appeared taken aback and shrunk into the shadows where they belonged as if the darkness provided them the comfort they sought as they felt the presence of The Dark Master. Some even fell to their faces in reverence, and some had their veils slip away from their faces, and Lee saw the molting disfigured masses of their faces from the constant exposure to this inhospitable place.

The staircase seemed to spiral around the volcano, occasionally passing beneath bridges or crossing chasms that had broken into the mountains side. Vultures flew overhead in search for the dead or dying, and the rain continued its relentless downpour on the blackened rocks. The mouth of the volcano was eroded to the point where it looked like the maw of a giant beast breaking free of the earth and roaring to the heavens above, and from the maw a green glow shined through it.

Eventually Lee found the doorway that was carved into the side of the volcano and entered. He passed through a circular room with many candles on the floor and stacked onto the rocks, all flickering their dim lights against a massive statue of a man wielding a sword and wearing a helm that had curved horns on the side. Lee passed this statue without a second thought as he marched through another set of corridors on his way to the center of the volcano, ignoring the few cultists who were scattered around the feet of this statue, hands raised in prayer.

He soon entered a vast room with an open ceiling being the mouth of the volcano. The room was circular and the floor was manmade, carved many years ago to build upon it and commit the sacrifices needed to create The Eldest as well as the other gateways into The Dreaming. Here there was little shift in the balance between realms, and here, Lee could hear what his sister could see with the power of the crystals. The low moans and shrieks of the demons which they called, Nightmares.

A hole about ten feet in diameter sat in the center of the floor and appeared to have once been bigger before being altered in some way that had been long forgotten. From within emitted a pale green light, the heat intense and sulfurous and as Lee passed this hole, he looked down to see the green lava bubbling miles below. There, brewed from the very core of the earth and shattered by the nuclear bombs from millenniums past, was where reality had been torn as delicate as a thin piece of fabric. Here, revealed and kept secret by the Nudushi People, was possibly one of the only true pieces of evidence that the whole world and perhaps the universe itself, was but a small plane of existence woven into the fabric that extended on eternally. Here, what was reality had been punctured, and deep in there, should one survive the fall or the intense radiated heat, one could enter The Dreaming, which in itself had become the spectral space where minds wander unconscious and unchecked.

This volcano, this Gateway, was the Well of Souls.

Lee continued to walk until he reached the old man reading an old book before an alter that had many equipment on it both ancient and new. The altar itself seemed carved from the very igneous rock that constructed this volcano, and upon it were carved the many languages once spoken all over the world, including a few that had been lost to history. Above the old man's head was a monitor that had long been shut off, and various other switches and computers perhaps built as security measures for the volcano, including a seismograph and a Geiger-Müller tube. On either side of the alter reflecting indigo light upon the old man, were two braziers lit with purple fire, the coals within mixed with pulverized bone burning brightly and casting sinister shadows upon the man.

"I have returned, Cath," Lee said upon approaching the alter.

The old man grunted and closed his book with fragile fingers. He turned to Lee, revealing himself. He was an older man with a hunchback so prominent, that his chest was perpendicular to the floor. His face, like many of the guardians were a bulbous and fleshy mass, with leathery skin and two eyes as pale as the moon. A golden tooth glistened in his otherwise toothless smile, and like the guardians he was garbed in robes of black. His grotesque smile gave Lee a sense of uneasiness.

"I see you have," Cath said in a deep and gruff voice. He walked over to Lee, his heavy footsteps thundering throughout the volcano. "But I count only one of you. Tell me, is your sister dead, for I have been unable to reach her since the two of you departed for Nineveh."

"It is as you said, she is dead. She sacrificed herself in order for us to obtain this." With that he revealed The Eldest that glowed all the brighter in this familiar place. Cath's eyes went wide and greedy as he reached for the crystal and gingerly pried it from Lee's hands.

"Master…" Cath said to the crystal with a tremor throughout his body. The very word itself echoed from the walls of the volcano. "You have returned, and soon you will be home wholly again. This, the Nudushi swear…"

He looked up to Lee. "I am sorry for your sister; we shall make sure her death does not go unavenged. We have The Eldest here now, all we need are three of the crystals and a sufficient sacrifice and I believe we will be ready to proceed in the return of The Eldest."

Is that all you have to say, Father? Lee thought.

The old man looked at Lee sharply, whose thoughts were no better than spoken within these unholy halls. "Do not mistaken my callousness for carelessness, boy. She knew the risks. You did too, and yet here you are. Now then, you come back with The Master. This is good. But where is Lameika's crystal, my son?"

"I am afraid Lameika lost hers," Lee answered stiffly. "So we will need to find the others. However, I know of someone who has two, and would be a perfect sacrifice for our king."

"He has told me," Cath said. "In fact, he met the boy if that is who you were going to suggest. The Keeper, the child of prophecy. Yes, he would be good. In fact, The Master almost had him, but there was a hiccup, a disturbance as you might call it." Cath then peered at Lee with unwavering eyes. "I want that child, Lee. We cannot allow him to shut the gates. We need to stop him before he destroys them."

"He can do that?"

"He already has done one in. There are six left, he has two, and he is with someone who has one *in* him."

"A host?"

"Not quite, he is still very much in control of his body, but he shares it with one of The Seven."

"How despicable." Lee said simply, not sharing that he had already met such a person, nor did he dare to think this. "And I gather you want me to bring them both then?"

"The sooner the better, my son." Cath nodded. "The Master has spoken to me, and I know where they are. The pirates have found them. It will not be hard to apprehend them. The war in the east is taking all of the attention of the other districts, this is the perfect time to try and get them."

"What if they join the fight?" Lee asked.

"Then they fight. Nothing much else can happen other than that. But the Nudushi cannot interfere at that point, for fear that we are discovered here and bring everyone here. And you know how the new queen of The Capitol is, she would jump at the chance to gain power from here."

"She's going after the city of Xerxes who are in possession of the other crystals," Lee informed the old man. "Should we not just take them from there?"

"Have you not listened? If anyone knows what we are doing here, we'll be drawing the attention of a thousand flies before a dead carcass. And we do not want flies buzzing around, do we?"

"No," Lee agreed, but not appreciating the condescending tone of the old man. It sounded way too much like his sister's. "We smash them."

"Good." Cath looked Lee up and down as his son removed his helmet revealing his torn face. "You are tired and are in need of repair. We will get you ready to make for The Great Sea."

"Thank you," said Lee. A rest was definitely long overdue.

Cath then said, "But you shall be leaving very soon. I want those crystals, and I would like the boy as well. But if he will not come willingly, or forcibly, kill him. We will use someone else; we cannot risk him staying alive and destroying the rest of the gateways to The Master's realm."

"Yes, Cath. I will not fail you."

"Do not do it for me, Lee," Cath said taking The Eldest and setting it upon the alter, right on top of the book he had been reading earlier. At its touch of home The Eldest began to glow all the brighter. Those who were in the other room with the statue had begun to file in as if being drawn to the pulsating gem. They gathered around the alter, around Lee and Cath, and all bowed their heads and chanted the tongues of the Ancient One. As one, the Nudushi chanted in prayer, and Cath looked back to his son, the color of his eyes returning as if by magic, back to a baleful, stormy gray.

"Do it, for *him*."

The Legend continues in,

The Legend of Levitika:
Anthem of Angels

www.ingramcontent.com/pod-product-compliance
Lightning Source LLC
Chambersburg PA
CBHW070507310726
48976CB00002BA/374